Rise of a Queen

book 1

The Vampire Realm

J.S. Riddle

ISBN-13: 978-1482649628

DEDICATION

Without the Muse the Queen would never have lived

CONTENTS

PART I

CHAPTER ONE

I used to love the night. I craved all the things that came with it; the gathering of people that you would otherwise not give a second glance to if you walked past them on a busy sidewalk, three dollar Kamikaze's that kept you warmly happy on the inside, and the deep pounding of your heart that unmistakably matches rhythm with the loud trance of techno music. I longed for the dark clubs that had too many bodies pressing up against one another; feeling the music, the flashing lights, without a single care in the world. The drug of their choice coursing through their liquid moving bodies. There was always that last bite to eat, around three in the morning, at a run-down diner with a waitress named April or Sally who would disappear to the back, making you wonder if she was with the cook getting that late-night screw.

Now all I can think about is how much I miss the day. I want the breaking light through the crack of my curtains, that first sip of over-sweetened coffee, and the herding of all the eight to fivers as they hold their purses or briefcases too close to themselves in paranoia; rushing around always ten minutes behind.

Yes, I do miss all of that. I miss those things people take advantage of until they no longer fit into their life. Life...I contemplate that very thing as I look out from my overly indulgent penthouse window. I scan the city for signs of my old life. Is this my kingdom? Are all the subjects below truly mine to control? Of course they're not. They don't even know I exist. They continue on with their pleasure-seeking ways; ignoring the shadows I slum through. How close I live with all these people and yet they are so far away from their true comprehension of who, or what, I am. Would they understand my need for companionship, my constant searching for meaning, or my want for knowledge? I think they would cast me aside for lack of understanding. The only thing they would see is my darkened soul, my unholy manner, and my thirst for warm, salty blood. They would hunt me down to get rid of the abomination that doesn't fit in with their God-fearing ways. These are the same people that have pushed the tiger into near-extinction. Their reasoning? The tiger, like me, has a thirst for blood - just packaged differently in the likes of wild game and sometimes the unsuspecting child that has wandered too far from his village. That is how the tiger was made, and for that, it is punished and sold off into pieces for all sorts of exotic cures and concoctions. How funny it is, that the people created from a God that they worship deeply, would mutilate and murder another of their father's blessed creatures, and not even think about any sort of repentance. They would think of me the same, I know. Am I no different from the enchanting tiger?

I am the Goddess of my own urban jungle. Little do these people know how important I am to the natural cycle of life. Our race is on this earth to hunt down the weak and keep the world from overpopulating. So here I am, looking out of my window just as the tiger lurks in the brush, seeking, always searching out for that next feast.

Seven years. Has it really been that long? If I weren't in a business where I had to mark off the days on my calendar, the days would bleed together. Bleed. Such an apropos word. That is what all creatures do;

Bleed. From the prick of the enchanted rose to the gash of the knife. Of course nothing beats the puncturing of the flesh of mankind with the gushing of warm liquid gold. The intake, so full of explosive orgasmic drinks. Nothing can beat that feeling of pure satisfaction coursing through these replenished veins.

I turned from my window and glanced at the pale wanderer lying limp on the couch. *I might have taken too much this time. I got caught up in the oneness of our joined souls.*

"She will survive," said a deep dark voice from the shadowy corner of the room, "Barely, but she will live." It was Bryon, one of my most loyal of human servants.

"I took too much." I said with a low sigh. I bent down and touched the powdery cheek of my helpless victim. I stood up and walked away. "She will be frightened when she wakes up," I stopped briefly in the front hallway, "Move her to the guest quarters and keep an eye on her. I am going to The Black Raven." Without a second thought I slipped out the door.

The Black Raven was one of the businesses that I happened to have owned. It had its fill of Nuvo-Goth humans, who cried out their pitiful souls to each another while the silent competition of who was in the most turmoil played out. The music was deep and dark like the mood I was in as I went through the back entrance. I made my way down the stairs to the other level of the club, cleverly called the Dungeon. That was where my kindred went to partake in the orgy of sexual madness and intensified blood taking. The victims thought it was all just role-play until the first bite and then one of two things happened: they either let out a terrifying scream and tried unsuccessfully to fight off their poacher, or they delved into the feeling; having let go of their fear and inhibitions, so much that they experienced multiple orgasms until they passed out from the blood loss. The one rule in my club that existed, and offered severe punishment to any blood drinker who broke it, under no circumstances were they allowed to drain their playthings completely of blood. They had to leave enough in the body so that it replenished itself so as to not have caused the stirring of the police.

I pushed through the pits of flesh that lined the halls of the Dungeon until I reach my haven. I moved aside the dark netting and sat down on the pile of violet velvet pillows that were carefully placed on the floor. The nearby scantily clad slave boy rushed towards me and knelt down. I found it amusing that people dressed so strange just to be part of my darkened world.

"What can I get for you my immortal enchantress?" He kept his head bowed as he knew never to look into my eyes.

"The House Special, and to not be disturbed." The House Special was our word for bottled blood; we always kept some in stock to avoid as much accidental deaths as possible.

"Yes mistress." He nodded and rose to attend to my asking.

As I lounged in my private thoughts, my slave returned and handed me my glass. "Now leave me and cause no more interruptions." I waved him on. I touched the glass to my lips, slowly tipped it, and allowed the nectar to flow through to my rough tongue on down my throat and into my chest. I closed my eyes and savored that first sip. It was sweet and refreshing.

I heard the curtain as it was pushed aside, "I said no more interruptions."

"I didn't get that memo." A calm brooding voice spoke.

I opened my eyes and looked at my maker as he

stood over me. I stood up quickly. “Greco, I...” I was at a loss for words; I had always been that way around him. I could be calm and collected until the moment a thought of him entered my mind and then my body completely gave into the weakness under his control.

“No worries. Sit, Tessa, let’s chat.” His smooth words flowed out as he motioned for me to resume my comfortable position. Seated, his hand glided over to mine, and brushed it gently as he took the glass away from me and set it on the floor. “I am beginning to get worried about you. I have been hearing some burdensome things.” His dark eyes looked at me with much care and thought.

I turned slightly from his glance; embarrassment and shame filled me. “Greco, I don’t know what you mean. As you see, I am doing fine.”

“On the outside, yes,” he moved closer towards me, his cold lifeless breath brushed up against my neck, “But I fear that you are not enjoying fully all that I have given you. Do you not love your gift? Do you not enjoy all the luxuries that have come with your immortality?” He pressed his body up against mine and embraced me like he always did. “Do you not wish to be with me any longer?”

I sat quietly and gathered my thoughts. I did love Greco, he was my master and he had cared for me as his trusted consort. *How had I thought that my unhappy thoughts would escape him? Had my regrets been so strong that my body showed every last feeling?* “Greco, I don’t understand. You know, since that night you offered me your gift, I have lived in acceptance. I have enjoyed being by your side, ruling as the Queen of our children that are bound to us by blood and loyalty. Why would you think otherwise?” I turned and decided to look at him, but quickly learned it may have been a mistake.

"Isabel is worried. She sees you feed like a raging beast. She watches as you toss your prey aside, practically draining them of every last drop of blood without care. Then you either stand for hours looking out the window or sitting in moonlight holding tight to your journal."

Damn Isabel. She had always been the first to tell of any inconsistency in my actions. She wanted to be Greco's chosen one. She had detested being the lowly human handmaiden of mine. "Isabel exaggerates too much. I am fine. I just get lonely for my old life every now and then. That isn't anything to be concerned of is it?"

"Not in itself, but you need to be careful my child, because you need to appear strong now that the Krones are striking up a treaty that will join our two clans together again after all these centuries at war. If they sense that you have any doubts about being a true Levé, and my vampire queen, they will take that as a sign of weakness of our whole clan. They will cancel the treaty and try to wipe us out once and for all."

Greco was right. Things had already gone on for seven years; I should be over these feelings for now, shouldn't I? I shouldn't live in my past for I have an eternal future ahead of me, waiting for me to uncover all of those hidden and ancient secrets. I touched Greco's cheek, "I am sorry, my love. I didn't realize that this hurt you so much. I'll be fine; you have nothing to worry about. I will be strong, especially for our gathering tomorrow. No more living in the past." I forced a smile on my lips; I needed to feel and sound as sincere as possible. I hadn't wanted to have those feelings.

Greco nodded and kept his somber expression.

"Thank you." He stood up, and pulled me up with him. "Now, my dear, I want you to drink up and then head home. Daybreak will be in a little over an hour and I want you to be refreshed for the next evening."

"Yes, Greco, I will." He pressed his lips against my hand then walked away through the curtain.

* * * * *

"My Queen, it's time to rise," Tessa heard Bryon's voice in the back of her mind. She didn't open her eyes; instead she rolled over to revel in her soft linens for a moment or two longer. "Isabel is waiting to dress you for the meeting with the Krones." Bryon continued, not giving up on waking his majesty.

Tessa opened one eye, then the other as she attempted to wake up; she noticed her caretaker hovered over her. "What time is it?" She stretched her arms like a kitten that had been curled up in a ball.

"Nine. The meeting will take place in two hours."

Tessa popped up out of bed, and rushed around her room. "Why didn't you wake me earlier?" She searched for the clothes she were to wear to the treaty signing, not even a shoe in sight.

"There was no need, you have plenty of time." Bryon stood in her path, "Isabel has everything ready for you in your dressing chambers."

Tessa moved on to her dressing chambers to get ready. Isabel sat on the plush stool and looked slightly agitated. Tessa had known that Isabel had always been jealous of her. Isabel probably played a role reversal in her mind over and over; made herself the lovely bride of Greco while Tessa was the handmaid who watched helplessly at the love that unfolded before her eyes.

Isabel helped to lower the extravagantly handmade

necklace, which was passed down from each Queen of the Levé's to the next. The heaviness of the gold and jewels weighed too much for most humans, even for the human royalty who were used to the decadent massive amount of jewelry, but Tessa wore it as if it weighed as light as a feather. What was coming was supposed to have been a momentous occasion; history in the making between the two clans. Tessa only felt nervous and full of uncertainty.

She stared into the mirror and noticed the jealousy in Isabel's eyes. "I am getting tired of your ill feelings of me."

"I don't know what you mean." Isabel lied and avoided Tessa's eyes, as it was apparent she knew that she was being watched.

"You dare lie to your mistress?" Tessa's voice grew colder.

"I 'm sorry." Isabel stopped short.

"It has been years Isabel, I was chosen as his Queen, and this will never change." Tessa reminded her.

"You won't be Queen once we become allies with the Krones." She snapped back.

Tessa turned around. "This alliance has nothing to do with my royalty."

"Don't be so naive. The Krones do nothing but dominate. They will make you kneel to them or make you perish." Isabel venomously snapped in pure bitterness.

"You need to stay out of our affairs and tend to your humanly duties, which at this moment, is serving me!!!" Tessa's voice boomed as she pushed past Isabel. "I do want you to know that this treaty is only the beginning for the Levé's. We will be taking over the human race very soon, beginning with this city. You can stand by my side as my slave or be part of the bloodbath that awaits them. It is your choice." Her fangs protruded. She quickly moved to Isabel and pressed her cold lips to her ear, "And if I find you are against us I will personally enjoy hanging you and let every drop of your blood drip to the floor so that I can bathe in it, cursing you to walk in purgatory for all eternity."

Isabel backed up slowly and tried to escape from the room. "You're mad." her voice trembled. *What did she think that she gained by speaking to her mistress in this manner*, Tessa thought.

Her eyes burned like fire; her fangs bore completely, "Do not mess with me human. Stay away from Greco and for fucks sake just go wait in the foyer." She had enough of Isabel's disobedience for the evening.

Isabel turned and ran out as quickly as she could.

The rage filled Tessa so fully that the black blood began to boil beneath her skin. She picked up a vase and threw it at the door just after Isabel barely escaped.

Tessa headed down to where Greco had been waiting in the limousine. Once inside the limo she sat quietly beside him.

"I am certain that there is a logical explanation for your tardiness," Greco spoke in a calm, under toned voice.

"Isabel was becoming nervous and paranoid about the joining of the Krones and Levé's." She had known it was in her best interest not to bother him with too many unnecessary details.

"How so?" He questioned.

"She feels as though once the alliance is done that you and I will be cast aside." Tessa gave as short of an answer as possible without going into the rough details.

"Did you settle her fears?" His tone rose slightly out of only minor curiosity.

"I did the best I could," She said then peered out

into nothingness. The rest of the ride went silent as she only had thoughts about how nervous she was.

*****

"Are we ready my queen?" Greco held out his hand; his head was down in a courteous bow.

Tessa took a long breath, placed her hand gently on top of his, and lifted her chin, as the colossal doors were pulled open. The two walked slowly behind the procession of their underlings until they reached the throne room, which was purely for decorative purposes; they were the original thrones for the King and Queen of the Levé's. They proceeded through the antechamber and into the boardroom. The chairs they sat in were almost as extravagant as the thrones themselves, which sat slightly higher than the rest of the chairs. The six members of the Levé council were seated to their right. Once Greco and Tessa were settled, the boardroom doors opened up and in came the Krones council. The King and Queen of the Krones then made a procession of their own to their designated seats, slightly more decorated than the council's, but still wasn't as glamorous as Greco and Tessa's. It had been imperative to gain a mental upper hand on one's own turf. They sat straight across from each other, the Krones and the Levé's.

Tessa had only heard tales of these ancient rulers, until this very evening. King Renos was a very fierce and savvy businessman. He had fingers in everything that you could imagine, although the technology that his companies came up with had been completely astounding. He had ruled his people for over a thousand years. Aside from his business demeanor, he was more of a quiet King. The ruthlessness of his rule came from the support of his Queen, Desdemona. She was the one to be afraid of. She was not shy about what she wanted, how she wanted it done, or how many lives were taken to get to that point. She cared for no one but herself and sometimes her King when it best suited her. She was out for power; she craved it more than she craved blood. Being a vampire had suited her completely. She was everything people had imagined. She had been by Renos' side throughout his rule of their people, although she was much older than he was; she knew just how to take advantage of a situation when the moment arose.

As the two clans sat across from each other they only glared. The tension could have been cut with a knife. They both knew the reason they were there. It was to make peace and sign a treaty for the greater good of the vampire species. If they did not do this, they would be left in the dark of the massive plan to take over the human race that would be soon in working order.

There was something greater out there than just vampire clans with their Kings and Queens and their councils. There was The Vampire Nation. It was the vampire equivalent of the United Nations. Members from each clan gathered to speak, make plans, and derive ideas on better ways for vampires to co-exist with the human race. Politics at its finest. In the previous four years there had been a different plan though. One that was keen on turning the tables and becoming the dominant species on the planet. Each clan had their specialty, their own thoughts on how to run things. They had in mind the territories they would take over in order to ultimately rule the world and make the humans into their slaves. Of course, the initial taking over would no doubt result in massive bloodshed and near genocide of the humans. Once that had settled down, conditions would be more on The Nation's terms. Businesses had to be run, life needed to continue in the same fashion as before the takeover. Trade needed to exist as did the population in general or they, the vampires, would die of starvation without their blood supply. The humans would have all rights stripped from them so they wouldn't get any ideas of equality. They would live and breathe only as workers and cattle for the vampires. If they refused, they would perish. It was quite simple.

The Levé's already had their buildings ready to go for their human and vampire workers alike. There were plans for underground quarters further than a mile down beneath the surface. The first step was to wipe out all communications around and outside of Chicago (where Greco and Tessa resided) and all other major cities around the world. Then a mass bloodbath was to begin where humans were offered up and tore to pieces. The next wave was to capture, then kill, those who resisted. Once in captivity, they were to be classified into different groups depending on their previous experience and worth. The humans were, of course, nourishment for the vampires. There were plans in place for a special shield technology. Greco had been working secretly with technological engineers to make a grander version of the one he had already in place at the main headquarters in Europe. Once it was up, nobody could enter except for specified designated areas and they were not to leave without special permission. The shield also controlled the day and night settings with a virtual "shade" on the shield, which made it safe for the vampires to walk around whenever they wished. This is where the Levé's came into play, Greco especially. They held the secret to the shield technology; none of it was to go into effect until a treaty was signed. The Krones' business and technological advances alone were important, but to get The Shade (as it were to be called) up and around the world, they needed the Levé's. The Krones offered military technology as well which was quite imperative to The Nation. The precise moment of this meeting was very important to more than just those present in the boardroom. It was critical to the entire Vampire Nation.

"I will not proceed with any talks until that *child* leaves this room." Desdemona stared at Tessa, with eyes as violet as the flower itself but were much colder than ice.

"She is my Queen; she is my equal in this," Greco said in his usual calming tone.

"How can you call *that* you're equal? She not only is a vampire made by your hands, but she has not even been amongst our race for longer than a blink of an eye. How can we sit here knowing that she still lacks the knowledge and experience that it takes to truly be a vampire, let alone a queen of an ancient clan."

Tessa retorted in anger, "How *dare* you say that to me. You know nothing about me or what I have accomplished in conjunction with the Levé's. It is true that I was just a human seven years ago, but when Greco held me and turned me into this magnificent being, I embraced everything that became Vampire. If you do not understand how much I have done for my people and how hard I work, then that is your loss. But don't sit there accusing me of being a child just because I am young in age. My soul is as old as yours and I understand more than you ever will."

Desdemona stood up, and pointed toward Greco, and seethed, "You will be the one held accountable and you will be the one The Nation comes to eradicate when this treaty is rejected. All because you could not keep that tongue of your young lover in her head." She turned and stormed out of the boardroom.

Greco stood up, grabbed Tessa's arm, and drug her into the back office behind the boardroom. "Do I not provide well for you?" The door slammed shut and left an echo through the marbled chambers.

"Yes, my love, you do." Tessa looked into his eyes quickly aware she may have overstepped her bounds when she spoke out of turn in the boardroom.

"Do I not treat you like my equal partner and as my Queen?" He asked her, more as a reminder than as an actual question.

"Yes, you do." Tessa nodded.

"Then why do you stab me in the heart so?" He seemed genuinely hurt.

"It is not meant for you my love. Desdemona, she does not respect me as a true Queen, as *your* Queen." Tessa tried to justify her words, uncertain if they were getting through to him.

"She merely stated a truth that we have to come to terms with. I did a bold, brash thing in taking a human and making her my Queen. This is usually done with someone who understands a lot better, who has been a vampire for at least a hundred years."

"She had no right to offend me so!" fumed Tessa, as she behaved very much like the child she was accused of being not moments earlier.

Greco roared, "She had *every* right. She is over two thousand years old; she is wise and does not want our dominance to wait any longer because of someone who still holds ties to the human race."

"But I hold no such ties." She stared at him blankly as a response mechanism. She knew better, deep down, but she also knew this was not the time or place to announce those feelings.

"So you tell me." Greco sighed. "I fear I was foolish in my judgment, not realizing the massive repercussions that could take place."

Tessa walked up behind him. "Do you no longer love me?" She quivered with anxiousness of the answer.

Greco lifted his head, looked at her from the corner of his eye, and then turned a cold face once again. “Love is not what matters at this point and time.”

Almost heartbroken, yet determined, Tessa walked in front of him and tried to catch his eye. “I became your partner because I loved you and wanted to be with you for all eternity. You have taught me well in these years and I have yet to make a mistake. I rule well, my love, because you and I rule together. It isn’t about just you or me; it is about us together. The King and Queen of the Levé's.”

Greco looked at her. “Yes, you are right. Times have been changing, that is what this alliance is all about in the first place. We are vampires and we shall rule accordingly.” He stood straighter, less worried and more confident.

“This is the Greco I know and love.” Tessa looked into his eyes and the two kissed passionately, which put an abrupt end to the conversation.

The meeting reconvened in the boardroom, Desdemona sat in her chair, very poised, as she eyed Tessa.

“I want to apologize on behalf of my Queen.” Renos spoke first, to everyone’s surprise. “She is just anxious to get everything signed and moving forward for our two clans. We have agreed to continue with this meeting, both Queens by our side.” Renos looked at Desdemona and then at Tessa in a silent form of reminding them to behave.

Greco nodded, “And I apologize for my Queen, she sometimes has a habit of speaking before she thinks.” He looked at Tessa and she glared back at him with a not-so-happy expression. “So let this meeting proceed in that we will soon join forces and become the true power that we deserve to be.”

*****

It is on its way, the end of the human race as they know it. No longer will they walk about freely or make the simplest of decisions. No, it is coming and they won't even know what hit them. They tell me three months time, that's all it will take. This may be what I need to shake all these mourning thoughts of the life I once had. It never did me any good anyway. Greco truly saved me from everything that was consuming my human life bit by bit. So why do I miss it so? I have everything that I could ever want and more.

Look at them down there, poor souls. Poor, poor, defenseless souls. We're coming for you. Are you going to give in? Are you going to be my slave? You don't want to die do you?

"It is time for us to sleep, my love." I heard Greco in the background as he summoned me to our sleeping chamber.

"Soon." I waved it off gently. *He is watching me I can feel it. I can tell of his uncertainty of my loyalty. Yes, I do stand here and I do think over many things. From time to time I like to go over old memories and think of alternative endings to them. I wish that I could tell him that I will stand by his side through everything, even the slaughter of these poor souls. Maybe Desdemona was right; I am too young to fully understand and I am just a child. I suppose I will have to try harder with each passing day, starting with getting rid of my journal. No, I suppose that will be one of the last things that I destroy of my old life. I am still writing in it to this day, but Greco will no longer know it; no one shall. Sometimes I feel as if it is my only sanity and that it holds the key to my true purpose in this world of the undead.*

Three months is so soon. I have much to prepare for if I am to be the Queen of so many more subjects. Three months; goodnight human souls, enjoy the life that you have now, for soon it will be forever changed with nothing but darkness to guide your paths.

CHAPTER TWO

The night sky was darker than usual; it seemed to look back at me as it gave me the evil eye from up above. Maybe it was just my paranoia. Either way it seemed completely uninviting and even sent chills down my spine. *How does one of my kind get chills anyway*? Tonight was the night that we had all been waiting for. I spoke of my brethren for I doubted that any of humankind would truly wait for something this horrific.

I had done better, I suppose. In the previous three months I had done nothing but school myself on every bit of vampire knowledge that I was able get my hands on. One would think that I was in college for I was in the midst of all the books I had retrieved from our sacred archives. I had learned much; yet not grasped anything. With all the knowledge of the vampire race in my mind and in my blood, I still could not block out those human emotions, the longings, the regrets. What a good part I did play though; Greco seemed ever so proud of me. He truly wanted The Vampire Nation to know that I was completely devoted to our cause and the only things that drove me were hunger, passion, and power.

In just a few minutes Bryon would walk through the door and tell me it was time to go. Greco wanted us on our throne for all to see. He had it set up so that when all the outside communications ceased and the shields went up, we would broadcast our intentions. Chicago was only the beginning for the Levé's; each royal in place was to do the same thing. Once all the major cities were taken over by other clans we would proceed to push outwards until the entire world was ruled by the vampires; each town, each human captured and tortured until their very last breath spoke loyalty or death.

"Your majesty," Bryon came through the doors like clockwork. "We must be leaving."

"Yes Bryon." I only responded with acknowledgment. I couldn't help but look through the window and out into the streets to watch the world below. This would be the last time that I saw the world as it was. Everything was about to change.

I walked over to Bryon and looked into his eyes, "How do you feel about all this?"

"My feelings have not changed my Queen. I have pledged my loyalty to you and Greco and I stand behind all that you do and say."

"And your family?" she asked.

"They are safe. There is no chance for them being harmed. They are thankful for this chance to be spared." His tone hinted at fear, but that was to be expected.

"Bryon, I assure you, your family will be treated no less than you have been treated all these years. You should be able to watch your children grow up and know that they are going to flourish amongst this new world that is being created. Because of you they are going to be royalty amongst the human race, having more advantages than was ever placed in front of them before."

"I do understand that and I thank you." He held a reinforced smile and kissed my hand. His lips were so warm against my skin.

"Let us proceed." I said said, trying not to feel so sentimental.

* * * * *

Greco looked at me from his throne. "Are you ready my Queen?" He could tell of the nervousness I still held; *such a human trait.* I took a deep breath and smiled with a smug look on my face. *This should please him.*

"I am ready to begin the bloodbath." My natural vampire instinct took over; nothing could have been better at that moment. That small insignificant part in me that was scared for those lowly humans was nowhere to be seen. I was the Queen of the Levé's and soon would be a true royal of a glorious kingdom that all would see, worship, or die at the hands of my brethren.

Everything fell silent. The television cameras in front of us waited for their cue to broadcast across the entire city and the surrounding area. The lights cut on in front of us and Greco squeezed my hand.

Someone from behind a camera pointed to Greco, and he raised his chin in a proper fashion and began to speak. "Good evening," he paused for a few seconds to add a little drama to his speech, "As of right now you may be wondering what has happened with your telephones, your computers, and your televisions. All your communications have been cut off from the outside world and we are all that is being broadcast. Do not attempt to leave this city; it will do you no good. There are barriers in place that you cannot penetrate." His grin unfolded brilliantly over the big screens that were displayed all over the broadcasting cities. "I am here to greet you. "I want to welcome you as my new loyal subjects for this is now my kingdom. No longer is this the Land of the Free or the Home of the Brave. A higher power has taken over and it is not just here, my people. It is all over. We are taking over and there is nothing you can do about it except bow down before your new King and Queen. This race that I am talking about is the vampire race. We have been waiting for thousands of years to rise above the secrecy of our existence. We are tired of lurking in the shadows forced to feed on the homeless and sick. From this moment on we will forever be above you as your masters. I suggest you do not resist, for then your death will be certain." He stood up and tugged on my hand; I joined him. "So bow down before your new King and Queen to let my people know that you peacefully offer your indentured servitude to us once and for all."

The cameras were turned off and I searched my lover's face. Satisfaction was prominent amongst every feature that he possessed and I was happy for him. This was what he deserved; this was what he lived for. "I would like to see what is going on. It is only natural to have curiosity. It is not everyday that a huge feast is just waiting outside ones door." I attempted enthusiasm and was actually a little excited to get down in the trenches.

"We must stay here. It is not safe out there, not for us. I am certain the few hunters that are in the city, inside The Shade, saw our broadcast and would love nothing more than to be rid of us firsthand." His concern was endearing, but still bothersome.

"Then may I go to the rooftop? That is a much safer place to be." I begged, I did not want to miss any moment of all things I prepared for.

"You may go, but take the guards with you."

"Fine." *I can't believe it. He is treating me like a child.* Of course I probably was acting like one, but it didn't hurt my pride any less.

Once on the rooftop I seated myself on the ledge and spoke to the guards over my shoulder. "He said for you to watch me, protect me, not to hover over me. Stay your distance." They still had to listen to me: I was their Queen and of course I loved to remind people of that.

I watched with mixed emotions at the scenes that

played out below me; massive crowds that ran in every direction as they screamed with fear and uncertainty. The vampires rushed around enjoying all the panic and free-range feasting. The population was going to be down by two-thirds. The remaining humans would live out the rest of their lives being our blood banks and servants. Deep down inside of me, that hard to kill feeling of disgust boiled up through my veins. Tears burned my eyes as I did nothing but sit there on the ledge of the building. There was nothing I could do, this I knew. It didn't change how I felt, though. It was something the equivalent of sympathy I suppose. I kept thinking *what if I was out there? What if I was a human, would I choose to fight and die, or survive and serve? What would I do if I went as I was, not a queen but a vampire? Could I truly tear through people throwing the judgment of whatever angel was the destroyer*? I became quite confused with the inconsistencies of the religious texts, taking each one with a grain of salt. I do believe if we're going on the fun one, I would have to choose Samael in Christianity. He seemed kind of fun and not as boring as Michael or Gabriel, depending on who is speaking. Yama seemed pretty cool, more like the god of judgment I would think. But what I believe I see the most makes me think of The Morrigan. As the goddess of battle, strife, and sovereignty I could imagine her flying above my people assisting in their bloodshed. All of this followed by the Valkyries. What a vision that began to swell in my head and a reminder of how much time I had spent in the archives, because humanity's history was just as important as our vampire history and the stories are so much fun. Death, Violence, Judgment....good stuff.

Hours upon hours went by as I sat there not speaking a word. The streets started to grow desolate, a few stragglers running about. Maybe they will get past the guards, past The Shade. I doubt it, but there was always hope for them. I kind of rooted for them in the back of my mind.

I had to look past all of that; I knew it was going to happen. It was their fate, was it not? As it was my fate to fall for Greco and become his eternal partner in what is now The Vampire Realm.

I stood up and looked at the guards that still surrounded the rooftop. “We shall leave now, the damage is done and I am now safe to walk amongst my new followers.” That was the persona that I needed take on; there was nothing more that I could do and the empathy that I felt for those menial human beings would have to subside if I was to truly be by the side of my King as his equal ruler of our new powerful dominion.

* * * * *

Tessa stretched out her arms as she awakened to the sound of Greco’s voice. “My dear, we have lots of work to do. We must meet our new followers.” He had a pleased look on his face at the thought of the impending night. Night was a bit of a stretched word from that point. It would mostly be night. For Greco, it would take a lot of getting used to the concept being that it had been such a long time since he had been to the original compound in Europe.

“My love, I must first prepare myself so that I can stand beside you just as tall and as powerful as you appear.” Tessa sat up in her bed. She had felt that the previous night’s massacre was just that of a dream and when she saw Greco standing in front of her with his happy grin she knew those events did in fact take place.

“Of course.” He nodded. “Isabel is waiting outside

the door to help you with your preparations." Greco gently took her hand and helped her get out of bed.

"Thank you, my King." Tessa stood there completely bare to her husband. Instead of behaving as the sensual being and Queen that she was, she bowed her head to him.

Greco proceeded to the door. "I am very proud of you Tessa and I know I can count on you to help me. Am I right?" He heavily suggested.

"With utmost certainty." She forced a smile on her face. She knew that her tasks were going to be much heavier, but she also had a feeling that there was a possibility that the Greco she fell in love with would sweep her up in his arms and treat her more than that of his child queen.

He walked out of the room as Isabel entered. Tessa sported a harsh and cold look so as to intimidate her, since she had been walking around sulking about her last run-in with Tessa.

Isabel zipped up the back of Tessa's gown and finished brushing her hair long chestnut hair then waited for the waves to spring lively once again. Tessa watched her for quite some time and then spoke, "Have the Krones come to murder us yet, Isabel?"

She looked shocked and just lowered her head in shame. "No, my lady, they have not." The shell of the woman stood in front of her. It was the first time, and the last, that Tessa would see her that resigned.

"And why is that, do you suppose?" Another question that really needed no answer. Tessa was in just the right mood to pour salt in someone's wounds first thing, and why not start with the woman who hated her the most?

"There has been a treaty signed, they will not do such an irrational thing. You and Greco are too powerful." Even though Tessa knew Isabel was only telling her things that she had wanted to hear, she liked to hear the words spoken from her own vassal's lips.

"That is right. I hope that the recent events have put you in a new place and perspective."

"Yes, my Queen, it has. I am thankful to be your servant and for being given the opportunity to be a key member of my new community." Everything she said sounded almost rehearsed.

"That is very fortunate to hear." Tessa turned to her. "Tell me, my dear, when does your service end?"

"I have two more years." She smiled cautiously as she spoke.

"What are your plans after that?" Tessa asked, sounding almost sincere with her curiosity of her slave's life.

"I am hoping that The Nation will grant me eternal life as a vampire, as I have been wishing about this for quite some time." Isabel said with a slight upbeat tone.

"I see." Tessa contemplated. "You do know that I am a very important member of The Vampire Nation, correct?"

"Of course you are. You are the Levé Queen." Isabel could not deny the remark.

"I just want you to remember that as you stand there and despise everything about me. As long as we no longer have any more outbursts like that night a few months back, everything should go in your favor. Are we clear?"

"Yes, ma'am." She bowed in obedience.

"That is what I like to hear." Tessa stood up and kissed Isabel coldly on the cheek, as she sensed the fear in her and fed off of it. Tessa walked away in an imperious fashion, full of arrogance and royal aire.

* * * * *

Time passed slowly for Tessa in the daily dealings with the humans. Each day was the same. Long lines of newly enslaved humans were brought up to the King and Queen to be "judged" and placed. Luckily they had the help of other high ranking officers or the job would be endless in itself.

Tessa quickly grew bored of all the judging and hoped that it would come to an end soon. She despised having to sit on the throne waving her hands and marking the person for the rest of their life. Marking wasn't an understatement, either. Each human, soon after being "judged", was branded with a laser making the mark similar to that of a tattoo. On the back of their necks appeared two symbols; the primary one was that of the Levé clan and the secondary was the symbol of the vampire house of the one that captured that human. They had full possession of the human from that point forward, only taking orders from the royals themselves. Tessa rubbed her wrist at the thought of possession. She bore the mark of the Levé's herself, but on the inside of her wrist. It looked more like a scar, something that each carried on them in one form or another. Hers just happened to be bigger and more prominent due to her master.

In Vampire Order, things could get quite complicated in a sense. Vampires, as ancient scripts often tell tale of, derived from The Mother. She had many names but the most common and well-known one is that of the name Amara. Legend told that she had been around since the early years of time, some figuring as early as 3200 BCE. She was a Priestess amongst her people who worshiped the god of night, Khros. Being that she was a woman, her wishes of becoming the leader of her people would never become true. She constantly obsessed over her looks and became paranoid about her body as it aged. Her prayers to Khros stayed unanswered and her faith faltered for he was all that she knew and worshipped. Her hunger for youth, immortality, and power finally drove her to the breaking point and she came to the conclusion that if blood is what kept a body alive, then drinking the blood of others could possibly give her immortality.

She went throughout the village in the middle of the night and murdered all the men(if it weren't for men she would have been able to rise to her much deserved position), sliced open their throats, tasted the blood of each kill, and left them to bleed until every last drop of blood had dripped from their body. She slowly climbed the temple stairs in her deranged state, her garments stripped and her naked body covered in blood, and was met by a bright glowing light. The Moon God, Khros, stood there with his Scepter of Judgment in his hand. He spoke to the priestess. He told her that she was to be punished for her ill deeds. He did not answer her prayers because he felt she was unworthy and had much to learn. Amara was cast out of the land, cursed to walk the land of darkness forever. The land she wandered in had no beginning or end; just darkness. She had received everything that she wanted, just not in the way she had hoped and prayed for. She was the only survivor in that land so she became its ruler. She also became an immortal being with beauty beyond all comparison, but nobody to revel in her greatness.

Many moons passed by and Khros watched her from above. He took pity on her as he watched her cry endlessly out to him, and asked for forgiveness. In a weakened state he sent her a companion, a young orphaned man who Khros had raised on his own in the mountains. This man, never named, kept Amara happy and they loved one another.

Amara, not long after joining in union with her newfound lover, became pregnant. It wasn't long before she started to crave something that she had remembered tasting many years before. It was the blood; the blood of man. There was only one man she was capable of fulfilling her need so she had come up with a plan. Each night she lulled her companion to sleep and sipped from a tiny wound she had created on his neck. She took only enough to stop the cravings. One evening he awoke and found her on top of him, that time her need for it was so bad that she was attempting to drain him dry. Her feral state shocked her lover. Amara was so crazed that she could not stop feeding. She felt something inside had taken control of her. He threw her off of him and bound her hands with hand-woven rope. Once secure, he carried her off to a deep, darker place, a cavern. He kept her there until she gave birth to their twins; a girl, Keaira and a boy, Kern. As much as it pained him, he had to leave Amara tied up in hope that eventually she would die of starvation. The fear that drove him to the conclusion was that she would still have blood-lust and kill their children.

He raised his two children as best he could with what was offered in the Land of Darkness and the luck that they had a goat that blessed them with its milk, since they had no breast to suckle. When the twins came of age an all too familiar thing happened. Something came over them and a strong rage grew inside. It was the same rage that consumed their mother during the time she was pregnant with them. As silently as he watched the children grow, Khros had not forgotten about the curse put upon Amara. Unbeknownst to any of them he had vowed to curse her entire bloodline as he did her. They started to hunger for blood. One night, after they had drained every animal that was in their vicinity dry of all their blood, they still hungered for more and were not at all satisfied. The did not know what else to do to satiate their appetite. They found their father asleep in his tent and an almost primal instinct fell on them; they fed on him ravenously until he lay deathly still. It didn't faze them what had happened until it was too late and the grieving only lasted until their next craving. That craving set them to wander the Land of Darkness for anything they could get a hold of. From that point on Keaira and Kern, having found no other living soul, fed off one another. Their bond grew strong and natural instinct took over and they mated multiple times. The twins knew nothing of an outside world, for they still roamed the Land of Darkness. Tale tells that they had seven children, who had become the beginning of the seven vampire clans. Those children wandered throughout the Land of Darkness until they mysteriously found the entrance into the human world. It had been centuries and Khros had been losing followers. His power was not strong enough to keep them contained any longer and he grew tired. Once beyond the barrier their children adapted to their lifestyle and became the vampires that are recognized to the very day. Always craving the blood and were always sticking to the shadows.

Throughout history the clans kept their numbers to a minimum, trying to stay below the radar of the human race. Over the years, though, they had felt there needed to be an order to the vampires in their clan so houses were brought up, each lead vampire had control over every subject that they had turned into vampires and their servants. The Levé's had seven houses, six of which sat on the Levé council and the seventh being Greco, the leader of them all. Their governmental system was well oiled like a fine machine, even with as many intricate parts.

That was amongst the first of many ancient stories Tessa had read in the archives, a place she would rather be than where she was. The monotony of the judging of those people grew tiring and she felt that she was better than that. She had more important things that she could be doing that would greatly benefit their new world, but Greco wouldn't hear of it. He was old-fashioned in many ways. He liked the history of old with all the Kings and Queens and all their subjects. His appearance seemed to take a step backward to reflect his vision of what a King should be. He relished in the fact that he was the one thing that stood between them and their death. Tessa hardly felt anything during that except total and utter boredom, especially when she realized that she was not made to be royalty in nature.

On the brink of dusk on the fourteenth night Tessa went to Greco after the last human had been judged for that day. "I want to ask something of you, my love," she said nervously.

"What is it?" He turned to her, his head cocked to one side.

"I do not mean any disrespect to you or our people, but I grow tired of sitting on my throne from waking to slumber condemning people to their fates." Tessa touched his shoulder with tenderness.

"But you are my Queen, what else do you feel you need to do?" He took her hand from his shoulder and held it.

"I am of no use in those kind of matters. You are very wise in your decisions and you needn't me to hinder those with my opinions." She said with her utmost sincerity.

"Have you any thoughts on what your opinions might be good for?" He seemed uncertain of the direction the conversation was going. It was apparent to him that she was not happy in the current situation she was in.

"I was thinking about the archives." She looked off to the side as she lowered her voice.

"What do you mean the archives?" Greco asked for clarification.

"I have been spending many months in there reading as much as I can about anything that is written. It is in a complete chaotic mess. Nothing is where it should be and the time line is sporadic to say the least. If we are truly going to keep our brethren knowledgeable about everything it means to be a vampire, don't you think that the archive is the place to do it? I know that is has helped me understand my journey as a vampire." She informally asked for his permission.

Greco thought for a minute and then touched Tessa's cheek. A small smile grew on his usually solemn lips. "Then you may do that, my Queen. It is very honorable to tell me the truth on your feelings and very ambitious of you to suggest such a modification to our archives. I am truly proud of you. I knew you were destined for greatness." He watched Tessa smile with excitement. He had not seen her that happy for a while and it pleased him to see her like that.

CHAPTER THREE

The trees swayed in the night and blended all too well with each passing light that followed the train tracks throughout the entire journey. Tessa sat in their private car of the train as they make their way to Montreal. She would normally be enjoying the break away from the endless days she has been putting in organizing the archives, but this particular trip was not for pleasure. She and Greco were called to visit by Renos and Desdemona. Tessa didn't want to do it, leave Chicago, not at that moment. There was a feeling in the pit of her stomach that just overflowed with fear and uncertainty. Everything about the trip seemed completely wrong to her.

"Tell me why we have to go to Montreal?" She turned to Greco who just sat there winding his pocket watch.

"Renos needed me to take a look at the progress that was going on with the new building."

"And I had to come because...?" she whined like a small child in her grievance.

"Because I wanted you by my side. I feel like you need to stop obsessing over the archives for a little while just to take a break." He said, never looking up at her.

"First of all," She began, with a burst of confidence "I have been overseeing all the literature that is seen and distributed amongst humans and vampires alike. That is a very important job, more than just doing what I started a year ago when I reorganized the archives. I have done something revolutionary. The vampire literature is now reproduced for each major city to hold onto. I call that an accomplishment; not an obsession." She felt the need to legitimize the task he had given her permission to do in the first place.

"I am very happy that you have found something that you have an interest in and I am especially proud that you chose to embrace your vampire heritage." He turned to her and smiled. It was a true smile. "But I still wanted you to come with me, if only for the reason of your companionship. I may not show it very often, but I do enjoy having you around. We don't get to spend much time with each other anymore and I felt this would give us a chance to do exactly that."

"Could we not have chosen a better place to go? I really don't feel all that comfortable being in the Krones territory, especially knowing that I will be in Desdemona's house." She frowned.

"The treaty has taken off well. We have shared all sorts of technology; offered many skills and trades. I think you may be blowing this out of proportion." He scoffed.

"Oh really, so I am overreacting knowing that I will have to sleep under her roof with that she-devil not too far away? I plan to sleep with one eye open as it is." Her temper flared at the thought of their long-known disdain for each other and she knew what Desdemona was capable of.

Greco laughed at her out of sheer amusement. "My love, I can't tell you how you can sleep, but I would feel better knowing that you were sound asleep beside me." His sincerity was lost to her.

"So this is funny to you?" Tessa crinkled up her nose and crossed her arms.

"I think that you have taken up a feud with Desdemona and are trying to bring me in the middle of it." Greco behaved as if there hadn't been a past between the two queens. He even pushed aside the past that he had between him and Desdemona, the whole feud; everything.

"I wouldn't be discussing this if you had left me in Chicago." She quickly reminded him as if they hadn't been in the same discussion.

"Back to that again I see." Greco shook his head. He knew he was not going to get through to her, her fears and disdain would stay as they were.

Isabel opened up the car door, cutting the tension quickly. "I apologize for my interruption. I just wanted to inform you that we will be pulling into the station in just a few minutes."

"Thank you Isabel. Will you gather my things?" She asked her now very obedient servant. Isabel had not tried to even speak a word against her for fear of everything that she knew Tessa would enjoy doing to her.

"Yes, my lady." She bowed and left the car. An internal pleasure took hold of her every time she did that. Tessa turned to Greco and gave a satirically pleading look. "Is it too late to talk you out of this trip?" She had admitted defeat without having to say so.

Greco laughed as he walked out of the car.

Tessa shook her head knowing that deep down Greco didn't take her seriously and really considered her a child in many aspects. Sometimes she felt that he was growing tired of her as his queen and was treating her more on the lines of his vampire offspring. Those were only feelings that crawled underneath her skin, but they wormed their way up each day. She knew he loved her. They were nothing but perfect for one another and she couldn't even think about loving anybody else.

As Tessa entered through the main door of the Krone's modern day castle, a chill ran up her spine. So many things of elegance filled that place. The wallpaper was gold-leaf tipped, the stairs of a deep mahogany, and a chandelier the size of a small car hung above the entrance filled with golden arms and dangling crystal. A marble fountain greeted them in the foyer, a tiny human looking cherub sitting in the middle pouring a pot of what looked like red water into the pool. They called that their place, yet it felt so empty. There was no love in that place. Greco stopped to speak to the butler about their arrival.

In only a moment's time the smell of blood began to fill Tessa's nostrils seductively. That smell, that feast, beckoned to her; drew her up the rotund stairs and down the long hall hall sending her into a hypnotic state. When the aroma had brought out the primal beast in her she knew that she had reached her destination. She gazed into the room where she came face to face with an elderly human gentleman. The hand that was holding a razor began to shake uncontrollably. He was frightened of her, as he should very well be. She was there to feed and he recognized the look of hunger in her eyes. She walked as if floating gracefully towards the man whose face was still covered with shaving cream. She touched him on the chin with her finger and immersed the tip of it onto the one lone droplet of blood that clung to him. That was what called her there, almost out of her control; that was what had brought out her true nature. One single drop of blood was all that was needed to remind her of what she truly was.

"Have we gotten lost?" Tessa was broken out of her trance and looked toward the doorway where Desdemona was standing, in all her evil and grandeur. "I do not know what your customs are on Levé territory, but we do not feed off our help." Her voice was shrill yet overly enunciated.

Tessa looked at Desdemona with a feeling equivalent to that of getting her hand caught in the cookie jar. “I don’t know what had overcome me. I apologize.” She lowered her eyes shamefully then turned to the old man who was still too afraid to move. She smiled wickedly and said to the human, out of pure spite she said, “You need to be more careful with yourself, we wouldn’t want any more unnecessary incidents to occur.” Tessa pushed past him and joined Desdemona in the hall.

Desdemona touched Tessa’s arm in a threatening manner. “From now on I would advise for you not to wander around my house unless you are specifically invited. Do you understand?” She barked orders.

Tessa kept silent as she yanked her arm away from her. She proceeded to walk ahead of her hostess.

“My sincerity is to not be construed as a suggestion. I am strongly advising that you adhere to my wishes. This is my house and I am in charge.”

Tessa stopped quickly and turned around, took in a deep breath and said, “Tell me where my room is and I will happily be out of your way.” She was trying to be as good as possible for the sake of Greco and the treaty. How much she despised Desdemona could be settled at another place and another time; which she was certain would happen more sooner than later.

“Good, I’m glad that you understand my intention.” Desdemona smiled with a fiendish grin that brought to life the evil that she harbored inside. “Let me show you to your room then, *child.*” The emphasis on that one single word dug deep into Tessa's soul, it brought forth more hatred than ever before. She knew that feeling was going to fester as their trip continued. Desdemona led Tessa down a longer and darker corridor than the one she had already been down, to where she and Greco were to slumber.

* * * * *

They had been in Montreal for just a few days and Tessa could do nothing but pace back and forth in her quarters. After the first night of them being there, Greco felt that he could not just let her go outside of their designated wing alone while he oversaw the project he was brought there to look at. He showed her as much sympathy as possible to attempt to calm her frustrations, but it was to no avail.

Tessa still wasn't sure what she had done that was so terribly wrong. She was only being what she really was; she figured that Desdemona would be happy that she was behaving as one of them. It was obviously Desdemona's twisted version of what had happened that had landed her in that room, about to go mad.

It was late in the night and Tessa had begged Greco if she could go out on the town. He advised her against it. He said it really was not the place for a Levé to wander around in Krone territory, but she had convinced him otherwise. She promised him that all she was going to do was look around town and maybe go to one the clubs, one still exclusively for their kind. To make it sound even more innocent she told him how much she had missed being able to just dance, no royal duties to attend to. She reminded him that Montreal had always been know as quite a hotspot, even in the depths of the vampire world. Greco had finally given into her begging and pleading. Tessa wasn't certain whether he really wished for her to be happy or wanted her to just leave him alone for a little while to think and stop pestering him. The reason didn't matter, she took full advantage of it.

It didn't take long for her to find a suitable place for her needs. She did what she had promised Greco and enjoyed herself. All the pent up anger that she had felt toward Desdemona for keeping her locked up in the house just melted away into the depths of the pulsing beat of the club. For once she just fell into the trance of the beat; she closed her eyes and moved her body in perfect syndicate with the music. She looked ravishing on the dance floor; long flowing hair caught the illumination of the lights as they flashed about. She had the look of pure seduction from head to toe. That was probably what caused the problem. Many a vampire in the club took notice of her and her intoxicating aroma. She waved aside most of them in a bid to keep to herself, but a group of three young vampires did not take that as a sufficient answer.

“Come on now, why do you have to be like that?” One of them said after he moved in on her a bit closer than she would have liked for him to be. He had to have been no more than a teenager when he was turned. His mannerisms showed her that he was quite fresh from his make; the cockiness that he had possessed overshadowed what he truly was. His apparel was proof of his mentality that went along with the whole 'thug for life' vibe.

Tessa didn’t stop dancing, she found no need. “I prefer to be alone. Find another fool to seduce.” As if they had disappeared she closed her eyes again as she unsuccessfully waved them on.

“Now don’t be like that.” The second said. He looked as young as the first but was definitely a lot older. He was dressed more in the manner of a GQ gentleman and his actions proved to be a different approach. His attempt was to sweep her off her feet with his smooth pick-up lines, which Tessa was certain had been used and abused for decades. He went behind Tessa and pushed her hair to one side, ran his arms up her shoulders to her neck. "I am certain you will like what I have to offer." He sounded over-confident.

"You offer me no more than what I can get out there on the streets." Tessa paused only for a moment, thinking *is that all he can say to me? Is that all he has to do to get a girl to go home with him?*

"Why the attitude? You must not know who we are, which can only mean you are not from around here." The third man said. He was the embodiment of what a vampire should be. He emitted a pheromone pulse of pure seduction, which led Tessa to believe he had been around for quite some time.

Tessa pulled away from the second guy and slinked towards the mature one. She traced her finger from the side of his face down to his overly muscular chest. She was going to play their game after all; she was definitely good at it. "Yes, you are right; I am not from around here. Are you somebody that I need to add to my numbers? Are you that important?" Her lashes were batting like an old movie siren, one of those that was not full on smarts.

A grin came over his face in pure conceit. As far as he was concerned he won this round over his buddies. "I'm the owner of this place and I would have to say that I am a really good person to know if you want to have a good time."

"Oh really?" She continued to rub his body with her long red nails. "What do you have to offer me?" She purred.

"I've got an unlimited feeding pass." He said flatly.

"Those are hard to come upon." Tessa played dumb knowing better that someone had an unlimited feeding pass unless he was doing something completely unorthodox, even for Krones. Not saying that he didn't, but the likeliness of that happening was slim to none. He definitely played by a different set of rules, though. The unlimited feeding pass was a simple no-rules allowance. 'Drain and drop' as the clean-up crew liked to call them.

"Not if you know people, and that I do." He flashed his fangs and an orange glow intensely shimmered in his eyes. "So what do you say?"

"About what?" Once again she played dumb.

"About you and me going back to my place, feeding on however many humans you can possibly take and then sharing a little of ourselves with one another." He licked his fangs at the thought and pressed himself closer to her. To most vampires nothing was better than sharing in a feeding frenzy, biting the partner (or partners which wasn't so uncommon for them) and then sharing themselves to the most vulnerable extent.

Tessa had no intention of sharing herself with anyone except Greco. "As much fun as this sounds, I am going to have to decline. I am spoken for." She backed away from him slowly.

"You are such a tease." He snidely remarked. *Of all words to choose it had to be tease?*

The other two quickly surrounded her with a complete menacing presence. The first one she had spoken to said, "We don't like teases." *Again with that word.*

The second vampire said, "It makes us want to teach a tease like you a well-deserved lesson."

"I don't think so." Tessa pushed past the three men, eager to get out of the club and back into Greco's safe arms. All the thoughts of sharing herself with someone brought about her libido and thought about her lover. He was the only one she could think of.

The club owner grabbed her by the arm tightly and pulled her back. “Where do you think you’re going?”

Tessa looked at him with a hateful glare. He had his hand on her wrist, which she had covered by a leather wristband; something she felt was a necessity in the Krone territory. To most it looked no more than an accessory. She nervously glanced at her wrist and hoped that what was underneath would not be shown; nothing good would come out of it during an unveiling. He was probably the only brain of the three so he could possibly string two thoughts together without getting a headache.

The owner watched her as she glanced back and forth between the wrist and his face. “Are you hiding something, my vamp?” He pulled off the leather strap and was astonished by what he saw. In perfect script was the letter L. It was a mark that had been made soon after Greco had made her into a vampire. He had used a special instrument made of pure silver that had burned deep into her skin, scarring her for all eternity. Silver was something that vampires could never recover from. The tale that it was only for werewolves were complete nonsense. The pain was brutal if left unattended. *Who am I kidding? It's just a fancy cattle brander* she often thought to herself when doubt overtook her mind at the scar. It was the mark of the Levé’s and to some of the Krones it was as bad as the mark of the beast himself, the one that was written in the Book of Revelations in the Christian Bible. “You bitch!” He slapped her hard across the face; her lip was bleeding the dark blood that was harbored inside of her. Her fangs grew to their full length quickly and her eyes were bright crimson with rage. It was a sight hardly seen from her, that much hate that she turned red.

“She’s a Levé!” The first one became just as angry as the owner, almost transforming into his creature self.

"We don't take too well of your kind venturing into a well respected place like this." The owner spoke bitterly. "We are definitely going to have to teach you that well sought after lesson that we had been promising."

The second man grabbed her by the waist and tried to carry her off the dance floor. At that exact moment the music had stopped and the crowd passively watched the event unfold. Tessa grew even more enraged as she pulled away with as much tugging and wiggling as she could but it was of no use. Instead she lifted her legs around the first man, who was across from her. She took her thighs, clamped down, and twisted his neck until it snapped. If he were a human being he would have been dead, but that move only rendered him motionless for a while. Tessa pulled away from the one who was holding her finally and threw multiple punches in his direction. He only wiped his mouth as she stood there in battle ready position.

"Oh, so we're playing are we?" The owner said as he loosened his tie. Tessa fought with both of them with the skills she had learned from training with Greco's trainers and obviously some perks of being a vampire. She was quick, almost as if she were floating on air. She was much quicker than many of the vampires she had trained with. She figured that up to all the hours she spent honing her fighting skills, ready to do battle at any given point.

Tessa jumped, twisted, punched, and kicked her way around the fight, looking like one of those old kung-fu movies. She had decided to finish off the one that had been holding her by using her custom made shoes for the occasion of going outside of her heavily guarded facility. She slammed silver tipped heel through his groin, a message sent loud and clear. She was not to be messed with. She then jumped on top of the club owner. "How about sharing with me now?" She pulled his loose hair, shoving his head to the side so she could sink her teeth into his neck. She didn't just use her fangs and feed; she mutilated his neck by ripping and tearing his flesh piece by piece as he screamed for her to stop. When she had gotten tired of ripping apart his flesh she stood up and looked down on the screaming vampire. "You were such a disappointment." She spat on him and walked past the crowd of petrified and cowardly vampires. They stood completely silent.

She had made it halfway down the block to make sure nobody was going to come for her after what they had been a part of, when two vampires that she had recognized as Desdemona's guards went in her direction. She realized it was better not to fight them; she needed to get away from the situation that she had created and even though she didn't want to go back to the house of evil, she didn't want to stand out in the streets any longer than needed.

They brought her face to face with Desdemona, who used it as a wonderful excuse to keep her locked in her room throughout their stay; indefinitely. Greco had yelled at her yet once again and she felt like a mere child; he had not even listened to her explanation. It wouldn't have done any good to have kept up with the argument. Her intention was valid, but with her being royalty it was not something that she needed to have been doing.

All she could do throughout their visit was pace. She had wandered a little in the wing they were assigned but it was completely desolate, even of furniture so it didn't take long for her to get bored. It was getting late and she had nothing better to do but wait for Greco to come back from his duties. She felt as though she were a caged animal, because she was a beast destined to wander the world. Feast on whatever came her way and not worry about the constraints of the modern world; especially the vampire ones. It was worse than a cage to her, it was a sentence in a well decorated cell for something that she could not help, and added to it was the fact that she was not a true elder so there was no respect for her position. Desdemona saw her as a parasite sucking on the dregs of what her kind had molded for the vampire race. She would never see her as anything more. It became truly clear to her at that moment.

Greco came through the door of their sitting room, Tessa stood still, waiting for him to acknowledge her. She felt more like a loyal puppy than his queen. "Hello, my love. How have you been getting along?"

"You should know," She lamented, "I'm not the kind to be cooped up, especially in a place like this; *her* place." She couldn't hide her anger even if she had tried. Each thought infuriated her more.

Greco came over to her and started rubbing her shoulders to calm her down. "We're leaving tomorrow; you can handle it until then can't you?" He attempted to comfort her.

"I'd much rather leave tonight. I don't like this place, I don't trust her; she's got something up her sleeve." She had thoughts of the endless possibilities of the torture Desdemona could put her through with just a snap of the fingers.

"Paranoia will drive you crazy." Greco was never very good at making jokes but Tessa smiled in amusement. "Besides, we have been invited to a formal dinner on our behalf with Renos and Desdemona. It gives me a chance to tell them how things are going with the construction."

Tessa sighed. "Tomorrow then? We're out of here

as soon as we can go, right?" She turned around and looked at him deeply.

"Yes, tomorrow. As soon as we wake up our bags will all be packed and we take the train back to Chicago." He assured her.

"Thank you." She hugged his neck.

Greco accepted the hug but pulled her away to tell her one more thing. "We are expected to be down for dinner within a half hour. You're going to have to have Isabel help you get ready." Those were more like orders than words of endearment as Tessa had hoped would flow from his lips, the disappointment proved more common that she would like to have admitted.

"Yes, my King. I will begin to prepare immediately." She said, as she watched him leave the room.

* * * * *

"I am getting a little weary of your inconsistencies." Queen Desdemona spoke from across the long mahogany table. Renos sat quietly beside her; he situated the long sleeves of his formal robe, and then stroked the grey beard that was perfectly groomed.

Greco sighed and sat back in his chair. "Desdemona, there is nothing to fret about. Vampires have had control over this city for a year now and things are going as planned. Renos is more than capable of taking care of things from here and you have plenty of workers to do the job that were trained quite well."

"Not soon enough!" She slammed her fist on the table in outrage. Nothing was done quite right until she added drama.

"There is nothing we can do while we wait for the human slaves to truly succumb to us being their masters.

The ones that we brought to help out should have you taken care of until yours do. It is all I can spare because we have a lot of humans rebelling on our end."

"Nonsense." She stood up and turned her back to him as she looked outside the dining room window. "You only use your stall tactics so that I cannot rise to the full power that my people need. Montreal is my kingdom, I urge you to remember that." She looked at him annoyed with his neutral assessment.

"Forgive me, Queen Desdemona." Tessa swallowed her pride and spoke up after she sat quietly by Greco's side, watching his dignity get torn to shreds by that woman. She could sense that he was beginning to be irritated.

"Oh, the child speaks." Desdemona said dryly as she rolled her eyes. There was still no respect for Tessa, something that she had come to accept begrudgingly.

Tessa ignored her snide remark. "What is it that you are so impatiently awaiting? Is it the fortress that our human workers are building for you? Is that what you are truly upset about?" She stood up; Greco grabbed her wrist only to be tossed aside in her bid to flush the truth from the Krone Queen. "Actually I think that you are overly eager to get rid of us for good, Greco and I, so that once again you are full reigning. Our people, humans and Levé's alike, disregard your power as Queen, don't they?"

"Foolishness." She motioned her hand in disregard.

"No, I don't think so. I think you crave the power that you had when you had millions of people worshiping you. It's not the same is it? For some reason the fear you bring to them is not enough to make them your loyal subjects as long as we are in equal commands of our cities." Tessa let out a scornful laugh "They find us more tolerable than they do you and Renos."

Tessa gazed in Renos' direction to only see him stare away. He was afraid and it was not being covered up all too well. "I am sorry; I was meaning no disrespect for you. You are a wonderful and intelligent King. But your Queen," Tessa looked back at the shadowy figure at the window. "Your Queen has no true thoughts except the ones that have her put as true ruler of the human race and vampires alike. It doesn't matter how much blood is shed as long as she reigns Supreme Being. Am I correct?"

Desdemona turned around. "Your words are shallow. Nothing is feasible in your ranting." She looked to Greco, the anger and dismay flashed in her violet eyes. "I fear your child Queen has yet to know her place, I suggest you remind her."

Greco stood up and took Tessa's hand. "Her place is beside me, as my companion and equal ruler, the same as you and Renos." Greco left the table, tugging his companion with him. "I suggest that you remember that as long as the two of us live that our treaty is solid so as we can focus on taking over the human race and dominate once and for all." He led Tessa towards their chambers.

* * * * *

Isabel took the red velvet robe off of Tessa's shoulders gently. "Isabel, once you have hung up our robes, I want you to bring us a carafe of blood wine." Tessa commanded. Greco and her had settled in and decided to relax by the light of the moon. It was a lovely ritual that they had grown accustomed to while they were there in Montreal. It was a perfect spot for gazing into the night. True night, with stars shining and the moon above.

"Yes my lady." Isabel bowed dutifully.

Tessa leaned back in the chaise lounge as Greco unbuttoned a few buttons of his high collared shirt. "We are still going back to Chicago tomorrow right?"

"I fear that we will have to postpone the trip back home for now." Greco smiled at her apologetically. He seemed to show deep regret.

Tessa whined in frustration, "What is the point of us staying here? There is no real purpose."

"I have been trusted in overseeing the building of their fortress. I did not know that they needed me as bad as they did until our dinner this evening. You forget that my expertise date back to the grand architecture of Rome."

"Don't remind me." Tessa sighed. "That just recalls in my mind of how young I truly am." She sat at the edge of the chair while Isabel came in with the carafe and began to pour the blood wine into their crystal glasses. "Do you ever have any doubts of taking such a young queen?"

Greco walked up to her and took her hand. "My love, much of my day is spent reminding myself of how great of a queen that I have and how lucky I am to have you rule by my side. You have come far, and ever since you let your human life drift away, I have felt even more confident and closer to you."

She smiled at him not daring to mention how those shreds of humanity wouldn't let go of her no matter how hard she tried. "You are such a fair and just king and I thank you for that." She grabbed the stem of her elaborately decorated crystal and gold glass and stood up in front of him. He picked up his glass, preparing for a toast. "I want us to drink to our happiness and our eternal love."

"That is the best thing that I have heard all day."

She said to him with a grand smile. He raised his glass and slowly brought it to his lips. Tessa followed suit.

"My Lady!" Shouted Bryon from the doorway. He had startled her enough to cause her to drop the glass quickly soaking the blood deep into the light carpet. "Stop!" Fear emanated from his entire body.

"What is the meaning of this?" She yelled violently at him, and then realized he was holding Isabel by the wrist forcefully.

"Your drink." Bryon stuttered. His voice was chilled and his face pale in fear.

Tessa realized what he had been warning her about and as she twirled back around she saw Greco grab at his throat with one hand and the other grasping the corner of the table. He dropped down to his knees.

"Greco!" She cried out as she fell to the ground with him.

"Burns." One single world that said so much. The pain and fear was heavy in his voice, metallic droplets poured from his eyes, ears, and mouth.

"What is happening?" She screamed with fright, looking at Greco then Bryon, not knowing how to stop Greco's pain. Red tears flowed from her smokey eyes.

"He is dying and there is nothing you can do about it." Isabel sneered, her lip curled up on one side. Hatred filled the room. "There is no remedy, no cure, absolutely nothing!" She cackled then pointed at her nemesis, "As you should be if it weren't for this idiot." She stared at Bryon, her eyes burned deep into him.

"Tessa!" Greco bellowed from the floor in sheer and utter pain. She felt his body begin to get hot.

She held his head in her bosom and shushed him. "I am here, Greco." Her tears flowed as she was stuck knowing that all she could do was hold him. "Tessa, I am truly sorry." He started to apologize, despite all the pain he was going through. As his body temperature rose it began to glow like hot embers on a blazing fire.

"Hush, my King." She whispered gently, as she stroked his chocolate hair; she touched his face and hands as she felt the heat that radiated from him become almost too much to touch.

"I am sorry that I brought you into this world promising eternal life and love; something that I know now I had no right to promise." His apology was sincere, which made her cry even more.

"I did this willingly. I did it to be with you." She was overcome with sadness.

"Tessa, I..." He touched her cheek softly and the life drained from him completely. Tessa cried over his lifeless body for just a short moment. When she bent down to give him one last kiss, his body began to turn bright orange with metallic bits flowing from cracks, bits and pieces of him turned to ash a little at a time, and left only enough time for her to say farewell to Greco. He had fully disintegrated in front of her and left nothing but gray ash. There was nothing to show of his existence. She wiped her tears and stood up.

"What did you do?" Her voice boomed as she turned to face Isabel, her eyes lit up in bloody flames.

"You two do not deserve to be King and Queen. You can't lead the people where they need to go. We must conquer, become one with the vampires." Her words sounded all too familiar, and like that of a traitor. "The Krones promised us this world and we are tired of waiting." Isabel answered like she had been waiting to spout that speech for some time.

Tessa looked at Bryon in confusion. "What is she talking about? Who is this 'we' she speaks of?"

"Your eminence, I am not in agreement with Isabel. I have always been a loyal subject to you and Greco." He pled his case to her satisfaction.

Tessa moved in closer to Isabel. "I need an explanation! What you just pulled cannot go without one."

"Colloidal, or liquid silver." Isabel laughed as if she were part of some little joke only she understood. "In your drink that is. She knew you would drink the blood wine. She sees the two of you sitting together drinking your wine like royals of old; apathetic to the human race. She knew as long as you were around there would never be true vampire rule."

"Fool!" Tessa knew she was speaking about Desdemona; she would be the only one to fill someone's head with the nonsense she just pulled. She stared at the petty excuse for a person down coldly. Her hot yet sweet breath left its mark in Isabel's nostrils, the last fragrance she was to ever sense. "You are human yourself, not fit to be Vampire!" More fury built up like a champagne bottle about to be uncorked. "She used you and to do what? Murder the one man your heart wouldn't let you stop loving?" Her rage grew inside of her, a beast demanding to be let free. "I will *not* be defeated and his death will not be in vain!" Tessa roared viciously and bore her teeth. She pulled the woman from Bryon's grasp as he backed away from them. She gripped the front of Isabel's throat with her hand firmly and started to tear huge chunks of skin from it with her mouth, just to spit the flesh to the side. Isabel was tossed down to the ground. Tessa then proceeded to rip her clothes to expose her victims flesh, taking bites from her waist, a breast, her thigh, and various parts buffet style. She looked like only half of a skinless cadaver, blood squirted around the room.

Isabel tried to stand up to hold her neck as the blood poured out like the fountain in the foyer, as if it were her only wound. She attempted to speak but could not say a word. Her gray eyes spoke for her. She fell to the floor, on her knees almost in prayer, possibly asking for forgiveness from her God.

Tessa stood above her. “I want you to suffer and remember me when you are in the depths of hell for all that you have done. I *am* your Queen!” She snarled and Bryon took that moment and grabbed her arm tightly to take her out of the room.

“Hurry, before Desdemona realizes that you are not dead right alongside Greco.” The two ran as fast as they could out of the room. They left everything behind; there was no time to pack. All she had on was a sheath of a nightgown that was stained with blood. Her feet were bare.

“Where are we going?” They fled out the kitchen back door of the house and into the field.

“I know a passage out of here; if we go swiftly we can be out of Montreal before she starts a hunt for you.” The urgency in his voice was dominant and she knew it was best to listen to him. He seemed to have her well-being at heart.

Tessa stopped for a moment. “How am I an outlaw when I have done nothing wrong? I shouldn’t be fleeing; I should take Desdemona down while I can, give her the element of surprise that I am still alive.”

“To her you are an outlaw and my guess is that she would have an arsenal ready for any attacks headed her way. You are the only thing standing in her way of being the ultimate Queen now. As twisted as that sounds, it is the way she thinks, and from what I understand she has always been that self centered. Now come, let us get back to our kingdom where you will be better protected.” They got inside a very small automobile that had apparently been waiting for them, should any certain circumstance arise. She had no time to ponder about what that was all about, only happy that it was there for their escape.

Bryon drove to the train station and they quickly boarded. "I must advise the captain to go as swiftly as possible, for your safety." He said as he seemed to keep his wits about him.

Tessa hugged him tightly. "Thank you Bryon, you have saved my life and I don't know how I will ever repay you."

"We are not out of danger quite yet." He sighed, "And if I were such a hero as you insist, Greco would be standing right beside you at this very moment." Silently he took off toward the front of the train as Tessa went to the car that she and Greco not too long previous had shared.

Things had started to change and Tessa knew that. She also knew that Desdemona was not going to stop until she was a supreme ruler, having pushed aside the fact that the Levé's were not her only competition. As the thoughts of Greco's death burned deep in her mind, as he literally burned in front of her, the angrier she became. She knew that Desdemona would have to pay. The Vampire Nation would not stand for something of the very nature. Tessa knew that she would have to wait until she got back to Chicago, but she would seek the revenge she wanted; to make Desdemona pay for everything she had done to Greco, everything that she had ever done to the Levé people, and especially for her treatment of Tessa herself. Revenge would be the sweetest of all tastes to her, sweeter than the fresh drop of blood on the tip of her tongue.

CHAPTER FOUR

Tessa sat nervously at the massive hunk of metal that seemed to be a decorator's idea of a conference table. The glass doors were the only thing that separated her and Desdemona, whenever she were to arrive. She didn't know who it protected more, her because of the failed attempt on her life or Desdemona for the sheer reason that Tessa heavily wanted to mutilate and torture her as many ways as possible.

Her escape back to the Levé territory had been quick and quiet. By the time Desdemona had realized Tessa had survived and escaped she had already been too far to do too much damage. There was one moment when it seemed she would have been caught. The train had been stopped close to the border of the Krone territory but Tessa had eluded the train search by climbing on top of it, then in clandestine movement she hid under the train until they had cleared it for travel.

As soon as she got back to the safe haven that she called home, Tessa contacted key members of The Vampire Nation for an immediate seizure of Desdemona for the charge of murder. It did not take long for them to assemble to begin the trial that was meant to get to the bottom of what had really happened to Greco. They wanted to know both sides of the story.

Back in the coldness of the dark room filled with artsy metal objects, Tessa sat impatiently. Her fingernails made an annoying clicking sound as she tapped them in anticipation. The anticipation of being able to see the wretched she-beast once again. *What was taking so long?* The rest of the members of the council were there, they spoke amongst themselves about how terrible it was that Greco had perished. *Had Desdemona changed her mind and ran away instead of facing her accuser?* Tessa started to become enraged and spoke loud enough for the whole council to hear her. "Enough! Let's get this over with. I don't want to have to cater to a murderer any longer than I have to." She slammed her fist down and pushed herself away from the table.

"Do not worry yourself, everything will be settled quite soon." Tyr of the Vordan clan spoke in his deep Scandinavian voice. He was the embodiment of everything anyone ever knew of a Norse God. He was worshiped as such throughout his people's history. His red scruffy beard and massive body left nothing to the imagination when it came to what he was powerful enough to do. His Queen, Brynia, sat there by his side quietly. She was one to still be figured out and her quaint appearance confused Tessa, since she knew vanity was a major flaw in all of the vampires she had ever run into.

She was about to scream out one more time when Desdemona and Renos walked through the doors. Everything seemed to go in slow-motion to her as they took their place at the table. "It's about time." She huffed terribly displeased, a small pang of anxiety thumped in the back of her mind.

"I do not go by your schedule." Desdemona quipped back without even looking in her direction.

"Let's get this meeting started." Viktor of the Strega clan raised his heavily Russian voice as well as he could above the bitterness of the two women. "Tessa, I want you to tell me why we are here. You were the one that called for this meeting to take place."

Tessa stood up and looked out at the members. Each clan was there to hear the terror that Desdemona has caused them by her actions. “I have asked each one of you here to make sure that Desdemona never gets a chance to murder any of you. She started with Greco, she poisoned him, and she tried to do the same to me but was unsuccessful. She wants to rule the world and we’re just simply in her way.” She condensed the entire purpose of the meeting in those few sentences, leaving for a great opening remark.

“If what she is speaking is the truth, this is an *outrage*!” King Braeden of the Falor clan spoke up. He was never one to hide his feelings. He ruled all of the European region. “One of our council members, one of our brethren, murdered by his own kind. I thought we had passed all this!”

“That was what the treaty was for wasn’t it?” Kali, Viktor’s Queen, spoke up. She sat there calm and collected in her traditional sari. Tessa always thought how amusing they were playing dress up; not out of fun but because it was tradition to them. *They want to change the world, one tradition at a time* she would always giggle to herself.

“I assure you, the treaty was not broken,” Desdemona spoke up as she calmly attempted to brush aside the accusation that had been bestowed upon her. “What this Queen, this half-ling, has spoken are simple words of bitterness. She never wanted the treaty signed.”

“What does that have to do with you murdering my husband, Greco?” Tessa bowed at the mention of his name, as did the rest of the clans. It was a simple gesture in respect for the dead. *Once again, tradition.*

“Lies; fabrication.” She avoided the stare from Tessa’s cold hateful eyes.

"You murdered my husband, and tried to kill me in the process." Tessa stated factually, once again.

"It is not my fault you could not control your human slave. She probably just got tired of the two of you." Desdemona laughed lowly under her breath in sarcasm.

"You know that is not the truth. You had been whispering in her ear for quite some time; You had been speaking with her even before we came to your home, which was regarding a peaceful matter might I remind you."

"Nonsense." Desdemona rolled her eyes.

"You gave her colloidal silver." Tessa accused and the council gasped at the sound of those awful deadly words. "She poured it into our blood-wine. If it were not for Greco and my dutiful servant Bryon, I too would have been dead and you would have had the benefit of taking over all the territories that we have under our control."

Whispers circulated amongst the vampires. Finally, the Tempore King spoke up. Guayarokun was the eldest looking out of all who were in that room. He had a long beard and wrinkly skin that made Tessa always think of Confucius. For all she knew he really was who people thought was the founder of a peaceful religion, although that would make no sense from a vampire perspective. "Is any of this the truth?" He looked straight at Desdemona.

"Of course it is not the truth. We had signed a treaty, all is fair," was her response.

Tessa looked at Desdemona, so full of hatred and wished to murder her right there and then. The Nation's slow methods were not doing Greco any justice. King Renos looked at Tessa and then at his Queen. His burden seemed heavy.

"Tell them the truth Desdemona." Renos spoke up. He had been silent in too many affairs for way too long.

That moment was likely his breaking point; the last straw.

"Whatever do you mean, my love?" It was obvious that she was going to try to look innocent through all that Renos was about to confess.

"I saw you. I saw you give the silver to that human slave. You told her to pour it in the blood-wine; you knew they drank before they retired for the morning. Your jealousy over Tessa as a Queen of a more powerful clan than yours took over; you just wanted to have it all for yourself, no matter what the Nation had decided as fair rulings."

"My King!" The look of betrayal on her face was truly amazing to Tessa's eyes. She felt like she could feed off the horror of it and she tried to conceal the smile that was growing inside.

"I am sorry. I have to do what is best for my people and you were leading us down a dark and winding path of self-destruction." Renos apologized, with complete sincerity.

The council talked amongst themselves. Layla, the Queen the Algoran tribe, was chosen as the speaker of the judgment. With a thick Bantu accent she spoke heavily, yet clearly. "Take her away. There will be a conviction in three days time. That is when we will decide what we mean to do with Desdemona. We cannot stand by and let this happen between our own people, for this shows weakness amongst our race."

The guards took Desdemona away as she put up little fight and Renos walked up to Tessa, who was internally celebrating her small victory. When she noticed his approach, she made sure that there was nothing but a solemn look on her face.

"I am truly sorry for what my wife has done. Greco was a wonderful man, and you are a magnificent Queen,"

Renos said with complete respect and honesty. It took her by surprise to be considered magnificent, not a child.

"Thank you." It meant a lot to Tessa for Renos to say those things, but she still hadn't felt satisfied. She knew that she wouldn't be until justice had truly been served, or that she had a few moments alone with Desdemona to subject her to excruciating pain by opening wounds and pouring the liquid silver in them; whichever came first.

"I hope my wife's ill-doings will not affect our trade agreement and peace treaty," Renos said, which brought Tessa out of her happy thoughts.

"As long as justice is served and she is no longer harmful, then yes, the treaty will still stand," She said then they bowed to each other in respect.

After the trial was complete Tessa became quite tired physically and mentally. She was tired from having confronted Desdemona and then going through all the painful memories of Greco's death once more. She decided to excuse herself to retire to her home.

* * * * *

It was no more than a couple of hours when Bryon came rushing into Tessa's quarters, wind at his back. She had been lying in bed but not asleep because she had been tossing and turning from nightmares with all the bad memories surfacing instead. She had to think she was a fool to even contemplate sleeping.

"My lady?" He hated intruding on her in any manner, but he would not have done so unless it was something of urgency.

"What is it, Bryon? You know it is time for me to sleep." She rolled over onto her side.

"No disrespect, but I knew you haven't been

sleeping at all since Greco's passing."

"Fair enough. Now what is it?" She stood, completely bare, and moved toward the chair that her robe draped from. Clothes were a hindrance to her as she slept.

"It is Desdemona. She's escaped." His words were silent yet deafening to Tessa's ears.

"*What*?" Her reaction was frightening, especially for Bryon who could have at any moment taken the brunt of her anger.

"Some of her loyal subjects broke her out of her prison, killing fifteen of the council's most trusted guards. It seems like she fled directly to where Renos was staying." He paused to let his queen process the words before he continued.

"He had probably helped her. No matter what she had done, he loved her I am sure." Tessa went into speculation. *Would this not be what Greco would do?*

"No, he didn't. That's what is most shocking of all. She killed him." He let his words sink in for a moment.

"This is ludicrous!" She screamed. "This is an act of war!" She went to her closet and began to throw clothes on. "I want you to go to The Nation and tell them I am treating this as a hostile situation. I am going to hunt her down myself and they either are behind me or against me, but be warned that all people against me will be prisoners set for execution in my land!" She laced up her long black boots then looked up.

"And what are you going to do?" Bryon asked.

"I'm gathering up as many of my skilled trackers and hunters to find her. I will not rest until I have found her and make her pay for everything that she has done." Tessa's rage seemed to cloud her judgment. She was out for revenge and nothing was going to stand in the way.

She looked over at Greco's dresser. Everything was

still in its place from where he last left it. She looked at a wooden box that lay on the corner. She ran her fingers over the engraved letter L and snatched it up before she headed out the door. The last time she had seen the instrument that lay inside was the night she was made into a vampire. Its chosen path was going to be used as a tool for a much different purpose, against a woman whose time was coming to a draw.

*****

The night winds continued to blow the autumn leaves around in a whirlwind as Tessa stepped out of her chauffeured car. Her brown locks swirled endlessly around her like a halo of hatred. It had been two weeks since Desdemona's escape and she has finally been found, not a moment too soon as far as Tessa was concerned. *Now comes the time of reckoning* Tessa thought as she took one step closer to where Desdemona was being held captive. They had found her in a small village in a remote part of Ontario. Tessa's human soldiers had kept her prisoner in the small house until the sun began to set and she was free to roam about the unshielded countryside.

She pushed open the door to the Cape Cod style house, one that had been lived in by humans up until that recent moment. There was a lifeless body laid out on the table, it was of a young woman apparently in her twenties. She had been completely drained of her blood. Desdemona had been reckless and it was quite apparent that she had been starving for every drop of blood that she could get. Tessa walked past the body and up the blue paint-chipped stairs.

As she turned the corner she heard voices, from the far room, at the end of the hall. Tessa proceeded slowly;

her hatred growing deeper with every step. The door was open and she caught sight of a pathetic mess that was kneeling on the floor. Desdemona's hands were bound behind her back and she was shackled heavily around her neck. Her clothes were torn and terribly stained with the blood of her last meal; the poor victim downstairs. Her black curls filled with sticks and leaves; she had been running on foot for some time, shoes gone with nothing but dirty feet.

"When did your loyal servants decide to abandon you?" Tessa asked as she leaned against the doorway, her arms crossed her chest. She noticed the four hunters who surrounded her foe. There was extreme caution when having to deal with her foe, considering her lineage and all that she was capable of. Desdemona was more of a true vampire than all of them combined.

"They didn't desert me, your hunters murdered them." The helpless beast said in a gruff low tone. She looked up at Tessa through the strands of hair that covered her face, her violet eyes burning mental holes into Tessa's mind. "That is what you are going to do to me, isn't it?"

Tessa uncrosses her arms and took a few steps towards her; the heels on her black boots clicked on the wooden floor. She stopped short of standing directly above the Queen of the Krones. "How ironic do you suppose this is? Here you are on your knees, shackled like a slave in front of me, the made child bride of your sworn enemy." She bent down and touched Desdemona's chin, tilting it so that she had her complete attention. "Does this make your skin crawl, me touching you? Breathing on you? *Owning* you?"

"You will *never* own me; no one has ever owned me." Desdemona spat at her.

Tessa moved her arm and wiped the hate-filled

spatter of the once high Krone Queen. "That is where you are wrong." She pulled thick leather gloves out of her pocket and slid them onto her hands, making sure they were nice and snug. She turned to one of the hunters, who was holding the wooden box. "I'd been dreaming of the best ways to exact my revenge on you. I'd had thoughts of murdering you many different ways. Some were quick and some excruciatingly slow. I have also thought of a multitude of ways that I could profoundly torture you, but then I came to a decision. I kept coming back to the same idea over and over again. The best way to give you unbearable pain while I exacted Greco's revenge on your worthless body," she said with a suspenseful tone.

Desdemona did her best to show a façade of calm and said, "You can do what you want, it's not going to change anything about me. I am strong; I can take any torture you can hand down to me."

Tessa shook her head, "Des, tell me something. What is the very thing that you hate the most?"

Desdemona's face grew solemn except for a slight grin that snuck from the corner of her lips. "I hate you, everything you are, and are what you are afraid to be."

"Exactly." Tessa smiled with the most unnerving of grins. She tapped her fingers on the wooden box. Click, click, click like the sound of hundreds of marching ants. "Do you happen to know what this is?"

She stared at the box, trying not to show how nervous she had quickly become. "I have no clue."

Tessa opened the lid of the very old box that was only the size of a dagger. What was inside was something more valuable than any dagger would be in the situation she was in. She pulled out a silver branding iron with the Levé symbol on it, the same symbol that was on Tessa's wrist. "Let's try this again. Do you know what it is now?"

Desdemona began to stutter. "You're mad. What is the purpose of this?" She showed fear of Tessa's intentions.

"You admitted the one thing that you hated most was me, what I represent; my age and my power. What better way than have you live out the rest of your life than in my service?" She motioned toward two of the hunters. "Hold her."

They ran quickly to Tessa's aid as they gripped Desdemona tight. She thrashed and jerked about. "What are you doing? You can't do this! The counsel will not tolerate anything of this sort." She screamed louder than a banshee as she tried to unsuccessfully fight off the hunters.

Tessa pulled at her raven hair with one hand and pressed the branding iron into her forehead. Her screams were of excruciating pain and Tessa fed off every bit of it, she even let out a little laugh. Desdemona's porcelain skin sizzled from the pure silver that was slowly burning through her skin. The smell of burnt flesh filled the air.

When it seemed like it had been pressed into her skin long enough, she took the branding iron away and put it back in the box, then handed it over to the one who had the privilege of keeping it before.

They let go of Desdemona and Tessa stared at the lump laid out on the floor, her bound hands attempted to touch her singed skin. Cries of mixed emotions escaped her lips. Blood dropped from her eyes in what seemed like tears. Until that moment Tessa wasn't even sure she knew how to make a tear. She watched her as she wriggled on the floor in complete agony. The more she moved and cried the more Tessa drew power from each moment.

She bent down once again and whispered in Desdemona's ear, "Now you will know what true pain will be. From this point on you will bow down before me. Everyone you see will know whom you serve; there will be no mistaking that. Every day I will rejoice in knowing that I am better than you in every way possible." She looked at Desdemona's destroyed face; the embers of the burn still glowed faintly. When Desdemona looked up at her, Tessa spat on her as she had been done earlier.

Tessa turned and walked out of the room saying, "Bring her to my car and put her in the trunk. I don't want to have to look at that face the whole ride back to Chicago."

"Tessa!" Desdemona screamed from the floor. "Tessa! Don't you walk away!" Old habits died hard for some royalty when their demands were not met.

Tessa stopped, almost out the door, to listen to what she so desperately wanted to say.

"Why didn't you just kill me?" She sounded so frail at that moment.

She laughed, still facing away from Desdemona. "I would much rather watch you die a little inside every single day instead of giving you the quick death you so now beg for." Tessa continued her walk out the door.

The ride back to Chicago was a very quiet one. Tessa watched the passing trees and shadows. She felt as though she had done a great justice in a manner Greco would have been very proud of. As much of a ruthless killer Greco was, he always believed in true justice. She did all that for him as a way to show, in spirit, that she had learned well. That is what he would have wanted her to do.

With each thought that went through her mind about the revenge she swore to, thoughts of Greco followed. She couldn't help but miss him; she never even got a chance to mourn him. He was her love and the reason she gave up her human life, to be by his side for all eternity. Red tears rolled silently down her cheek. She felt ready to be able to mourn him properly. With nothing to stop her and nobody to watch, she broke down into a chaotic mess.

Once in Chicago Tessa woke up from the sleep her misery drew her into. She was in the safety of her people and in her protected land. She got out of the sunlight-protected vehicle and went to the trunk where Desdemona had been resting during their trek back to Levé territory. Once the trunk was open she looked down at her enemy. "Take her to solitary and let her sit there for a few days. I want her weak enough to appreciate what little blood we give her." She ordered her subjects. She talked to Desdemona. "When you're down to the level of nobody, that is when you will be allowed to feed on the dregs of rats and vermin that happen to be thrown your way. You will have no honor. You will sit in the cage to be stared at, poked at, enjoyed."

Desdemona was pulled out of the car. "What about The Nation? What will the say about you doing this to me?" She asked unsuccessfully appealing to Tessa's compassion.

"They value everything about what our Levé's clan can bring them. They would not try to break our pact just to protect a murderous she-beast such as yourself."

"You do not know these people. They will save me." She began muttering plea's of a madwoman.

"My stipulations for keeping with The Nation Treaty are of more importance. They weigh the odds, which are in my favor, that's all. You just happened to be on the losing end of it." She waved her hand in dismissal, "You can take her away now."

* * * * *

Into the depths of my cold dark soul flickers a flame of the tiny remainder that is my humanity. No matter how I try to snuff it out, it remains untouched. How is this possible? I have done everything imaginable, yet I cling to that last piece of myself without even trying.

It creeps into my thoughts when I feed; I mean truly feed. I cannot help myself really; I am what I am. I relish in the embrace I have with my human subjects as I feel the beating of their heart against my chest; the warm crimson life flowing into my mouth. Oh yes do I love that. It takes me to ecstatic heights that I do not wish to repel from. Then my wanton lust gets greedy and pines for every last drop that I can take, only to be cut off by the logical part of my mind. Most of the time I stop before things go too far where I leave the human to live, but other times are not so lucky. Sure they survive the feeding, clinging to that last breath that they are taking as they wonder if that was truly how they were going to make it, only to hang on for another twenty-four hours before finally dying a painfully drawn-out death. This is when that minuscule piece of humanity puffs out its chest and screams guilty thoughts into my ear. I didn't care how wreckless I was. I wasn't the same as when I was first turned.

I am in constant conflict with my very soul. I cannot help but wonder if there is something different about me, something special, which holds me apart from the rest of my vampire brethren. I am sure it is only my vanity that links those eccentric thoughts, but they come to me none-the-less.

My certainty as the one true leader of the Levé's falters more on the scale near uncertainty. There is so much I have yet to learn about being a true queen. If only I had listened, really paid attention to Greco when he was trying to school me in leadership and what it is like to be one of our kind. Instead I felt it was important to delve into books and learn history and teach it to all that would listen. Our history, the vampire history, is not what is going to help me now.

What is going to help me now is a clear head and a sound council. I must discuss with the Levé' council about the future of our kind, what will become of the Krones, and the whispers of a human rebellion taking foot on my very soil.

I must stand tall, be smart, think clearly, and weigh all the odds that come before me. This would be the only way for me to truly shine as the Queen of the Levé's. I will show The Vampire Nation that I am just as great as they are no matter how I became Greco's lover, partner, and ultimately his equal.

PART II

CHAPTER FIVE

Emma Stewart turned the rusty faucet and watched the brown sludge turn to water in the dingy sink. She splashed cold water on her face and stared into the cracked and smudged mirror. The girl that looked back at her had only a slight resemblance of who she was. She had a look of sorrow and despair, an empty shell with vomit permeated hair, sunken dark eyes, and hollow cheekbones. She knew it couldn't have been her; she would never let that happen to herself.

Then she flashed for a moment to an earlier time; a time where her reflection may have begun. She saw herself curled up on the floor of her old room with her knees pressed against her chest as she rocked back and forth; makeup stained tears running down her face.

“There you are!” Emma accused her reflection in a somewhat sarcastic tone. She turned the water off and stumbled out of the bathroom into the mildew covered motel room. She spotted on the table by the bed a half empty bottle of vodka and a little white pill alone beside it.

Emma picked up the pill and looked at it. “So you're the one that's going to give me my life back.” She popped it in her mouth and chased it down with a few gulps of vodka.

She sat down on the bed while still holding the bottle, and slowly whittled away its contents. It wasn't long before she was passed out on the bed, vivid dreams danced around in her head.

Emma now felt the familiarity of her bedroom. She

saw herself, as if she were an invisible bystander, sitting at a desk in the corner of the room. The book lay open to her world literature studies and a highlighter in her left hand. She had just started a week prior at the local community college and was already inches deep into studying.

"Hey girl." Slurred a voice from the doorway. Emma sighed then turned around to see her uncle standing there. The only thing that kept him falling over was probably the wall he was leaning on.

"Hey Ron." She sat there in frustration as her father's baby brother struggled to walk a few steps forward. "I'm busy studying. Why don't you go to your room and lay down? I'm sure you're exhausted." She walked towards him and wrapped her hand around his arm, beginning to escort him out of the room.

"No, no. Not yet." He pulled away then looked at her, unable to stop his head from slightly swaying. "You know, I always told your dad how beautiful you were, and that one of these days you were going to break his heart."

Emma rolled her eyes and said, "That's good to know."

"If I were just a little bit younger I'd have to tap that ass. Yes sir, you're too yummy to resist." The vulgar words seeped into Emma's ears.

She grew disgusted and raised her voice. "Enough. You're drunk and I don't have time for your bullshit. Get out already." She reached for his arm again.

"Get off of me!" He yelled and swung around. He punched Emma in the face and sent her falling to the floor. "I'm not done with you." He said with anger as he looked at the young girl on the ground. He reached for the door, shut it tight and locked it behind him.

The ethereal Emma watched in horror at the

memory that replayed itself, reminding her of why she was there. She continued to watch. Her uncle moved slowly towards the innocent Emma, her eyes wide in fear. She scrambled to get off the floor. Before she could push herself up, Ron threw another punch. Her eye felt the blow and before she could reach to feel the damage, her uncle stood towering over her.

"I'm going to have to teach you about respect." He reached down and grabbed her up like a rag doll. "While your parents are away, I'm the man of the house and you need to treat me as such."

"Uncle Ron." She cried following a slap to the face, blood trickled from her quivering lip.

He ignored her sobs and threw her onto the bed that lay in the center of the room. Each time she tried to get up he pushed her back down. He was much bigger and stronger than she was.

"Stop! No!" Her pleas fell on deaf ears.

"Shut the fuck up you dirty little whore!" He yelled, wild-eyed. "If you weren't such a slut then I wouldn't be here right now." He grabbed her legs and yanked off her shorts.

Emma's panic quickened and she fought even harder to get up but he grabbed both of her hands firmly with one of his massive hands while he tore off her underwear with the other. He gazed at them and inhaled the aroma for a moment before he looked at his niece and stuffed her mouth with them.

Still holding her hands, he used his free one to unbuckle his belt and let his pants fall to his ankles. He wrapped the brown leather belt around her wrists tightly, leaving her bound and helpless. "I'll be your teacher; you're not going to disrespect me anymore, you teasing little cunt."

Emma's eyes glazed over as he lay on top of her.

Tears flooded down her cheek, her self-awareness faded away with each movement, hardly hearing the constant profanity escaping his lips.

Once he was done, he let the girl go, pulled up his pants and untied her hands. He stared down at her with hatred as he pulled the panties from her mouth and put them in his pocket.

Emma tried to get up, but the pain between her legs and the weakness of her knees proved far too difficult for her and she collapsed onto the floor.

Ron grabbed her by the hair and met face to face, his sour breath filled her nostrils. "You're not going to tell anyone about this, do you understand?" He didn't wait for a response before he said, "If you do, then you will really pay for it. I won't be so nice next time." He let go of her hair when she nodded.

She drew her legs close to her and rocked back and forth as he opened the door and walked out. That was the image that faced her in the mirror.

The broken down Emma gasped as she woke up suddenly from her nightmare, followed by a cough. She rolled on her side in an attempt to sit up on the stained sheets. Once up she reached for the liquor bottle beside her. In an attempt to take another drink, she realized that it was empty and threw it down.

Still in her haze, more memories filled her thoughts. It was of her parent's screaming and yelling at her.

"You need to take responsibility for your own actions!" Her father yelled with disappointment in his voice. "And stop trying to point fingers for others you want to blame."

"Jim, calm down." Said her mother before looking at Emma, "See what you've done? You've upset him. All because you can't admit that you are lying about your Uncle Ron. I don't understand why you would even bring such tales of him like this. He is a good Christian man. He was only doing what he thought was right, in the eyes of the Lord."

"But it's true. He raped me! He beat me, and then he raped me. Are you so naïve that you never noticed the bruises on my body?" Emma cried, sitting on the couch. "Why won't you believe me? Is it that hard to understand just how messed up your brother is? He would say anything to cover his tracks." She looked at her father, then noticed her slightly younger sister, Melinda, peering from the top of the stairs; eyes wide with fear. She looked back at her parents, "It's not something I would fabricate. I don't understand how you could choose to believe him over your own daughter."

"What's true is that you took advantage of our trust and got caught sinning." Her mom continued.

Her father added, "What the truth happens to be is that you were stupid enough to have sex with a young man in our own home. You disregarded all of our rules and are now paying the price for your actions. I will *not* be responsible for the consequences you have brought against yourself."

"That's not what happened. I'm telling the truth." She said unable to convince her family.

"Ron told us about all of it. You were lucky he didn't tell us right away. He thought he was protecting you," said her dad. "But when you decided to get knocked up, he felt he needed to come forward. It was then you came up with such an extravagant story, just to blame him for catching you. I'm completely appalled at your total disregard toward your uncle, me, and the man upstairs."

Her mother sat down still stunned. "You've ruined your future and now your uncle's reputation." She cried into her husband's shirt.

"I'm not going to stand for this. We didn't raise you to be such a harlot and a liar!" Her dad roared. "We're through with you; this was the last straw. You're not going to party on our dime." He straightened his tie and cleared his throat. "I want you gone by the morning. Only God can help you now." His face was cold and stern.

She watched her mother bawl heavier into her dad's shirt as she ran up the stairs, shoving past her sister and into her room.

The drunken Emma stumbled in her hotel room, trying to hold onto anything that she could. Her stomach began to cramp and her nausea got heavy. The room swayed back and forth. She opened up the door in a panic from the pain she felt in her abdomen. Emma knew something wasn't right, it wasn't supposed to be that complicated. She had to get help.

"Take this second pill with a full glass of water, nothing else. You will be able to pass the fetus much easier and you will only feel minor cramps." The doctor's words echoed in her brain. She realized that maybe drinking vodka wasn't the brightest idea she ever had. She just knew she wanted the whole situation to be numb.

As she staggered through the parking lot she saw a figure a little way down the side of the building and shouted at it that she needed help. There was no answer. Before she could say anything else she looked down and saw her pants soaked in blood just moments before she collapsed unconscious onto the ground.

* * * * *

As her eyes slowly fluttered open, Emma became

aware of her surroundings. The steady beeps of machinery, a dank yet sterile smell, and tubes flowing in various directions. Emma looked around what seemed like a hospital room and was very confused. The table near the window held a vase of brightly colored flowers. She thought to herself, *how did I get here?* Moments before, she came to the conclusion that she had to get out of there quickly.

She sat up, swung her legs over the side of the bed and shook herself a little more clearly. A moment later she began ripping out the IV that was in her hand. She pulled the little wires attached to square nodes on her chest, along with the heart monitor attached to her finger. The beeping changed sounds like the monitors were telling on her. She couldn't find her clothes so she felt her best bet was to walk slowly out of the room before bolting for an exit.

Before she could leave the room a team of three nurses came running in her direction, obviously aware of her change in status. Just as a deer stands staring at the headlights that were going to send it to its doom, as did Emma in the doorway to her room. She resisted slightly when they touched her but she didn't have the strength or energy to fight them; it didn't help that she grew quickly tired the moment she felt a quick pinch on her arm from the needle one of them was armed with.

Emma was facing deja vu when she woke up for the second time. The second time awake she watched a short plump black woman in dark purple scrubs and bright white shoes tending to what looked like a fresh cut of flowers on the table.

As if on cue the woman turned toward her and smiled. “I hope you don't plan on running again because I'm not wearing my running shoes today, but apparently I should have.”

Emma sat up and attempted to speak but all that came out were scratchy crackling sounds. The woman noticed and quickly poured her some water from a pitcher that closely resembled the color of that pink nausea medicine they sell over the counter. Her next attempt at speech was slightly more successful than the last with actual words coming out of her mouth. "What's going on?" A simple question with not a simple answer.

"Well," the middle aged woman said then smiled almost like it was her job to put a big smile on her face. "You were brought in a few nights ago. Do you not remember?"

Emma shook her head, "I, uh..." the memories came flooding back. The dark of night, the nausea, the drunkenness, and the bleeding. As if a light-bulb had just turned on, she remembered the terrible bleeding. By instinct she lifted her blanket and looked below her waist half expecting to see a pool of dark red liquid.

The nurse took her hand, gently lowered the blanket, and shook her head. "You'll be okay. They fixed you up quite well. I'm sure you'll be able to have plenty of other babies."

Emma thought it was an awkward thing to say, but then it was probably the kindest way to tell someone who just lost a baby. A sort of relief fell over her. *It Worked.* Changing gears, Emma pointed to the flowers. "Who are they from?"

The nurse shrugged. "No card. I only know I am supposed to bring fresh ones every day."

"What for?"

"I was hoping you'd have the answer to that one. You've been a big question mark at the nurse's station."

Emma was confused. "I don't understand."

"When you were brought in you had no ID and apparently no fingerprints in the system, which I should have to say your parents were dumber than a sack of rocks to not fingerprint their baby girl. What if you'd been kidnapped?" The woman looked at Emma, then after realizing she had been rambling, she cleared her throat. "Anyway all we know is whoever brought you in must have big connections in this hospital. They've set up the best care for you and we're under strict orders to make sure everything is taken care of, no matter the cost."

Emma glanced away for only a moment while she processed the information. "This must be a mistake. It makes no sense."

"No mistake ma'am. They've got you color coded and everything since they didn't have your name." She nodded to the green band around her wrist. "What is your name anyway?"

"No, no name." The last thing she wanted was her family being called. She preferred to stay as anonymous as possible.

"If you're worried about getting a bill in the mail, relax. Your mysterious friend made sure of that."

"This 'mysterious' friend, have they come to visit at all? Have you seen them?" Emma grew more perplexed at each mention of her savior.

Another head shake. "Not a soul. Makes it more of a conversation piece. Some of the nurses are thinking its some romantic thing and your stranger will come in and whisk you off your feet. Others are a bit too bitter and say that it's a waste of time and resources with the extra attention."

"And you?"

The nurse shrugged. "I'm just curious, that's all. Oh and there's the fact that I stopped smoking just a few days ago so it makes it an easy distraction coming in here with the extra rounds. I may become addicted to fresh flowers though." She laughed lowly. "Terrible things they are."

Emma raised a questioning brow. "Flowers?"

Another laugh, "No, no, no. Cigarettes. You would think as a nurse I wouldn't even think about it, but over half of us spend our time out in the back alley puffing away like chimneys. I'd trade them in for flowers though." She seemed to come to an epiphany. "I think it may be cheaper in the long run." She stopped talking for a moment and looked at Emma with a gentle expression. "Well, I'm Maggie so if you need anything feel free to ask for me," she paused, "You know it'd be nice to have something to call you by, even if it's just a loaner."

Emma shook her head in regret and stayed silent.

"Well," Maggie said. "The doc will be in here in a little bit. He was called during your not-so-great escape."

"Thank you, Maggie." Emma said cordially as her nurse left the room.

Many thoughts swirled around in her head, and always settled back to her stranger. Nobody she knew would just leave her at the hospital. They'd end up calling her parents so they could tell her how God was punishing her. She deducted that even though it wasn't the most logical, and quite possibly unbelievable, that it really was someone who was being genuinely good for the sake of it and not for reputation or reward. Of course the realist in her screamed it was someone doing something they weren't supposed to be doing and her being at that time and place made it impossible for them to not be The Good Samaritan. A *really* Good Samaritan to pay for all her bills.

* * * * *

Emma sat at the counter of the rundown diner and stared into her dark, burnt coffee. *Drink up*. She thought to herself. *Beggars can't be choosers*. She hated coffee, didn't understand the appeal from a taste point of view. The benefits were only fleeting with a burst of energy. The moment she drank the last dregs the waitress came to fill the cup up again. Emma shook her head and covered the cup with her hand. She reached behind her into her backpack and pulled out a red leather journal and an envelope tucked into it as a bookmark. She pulled out the envelope, opened it, and stared at the single twenty dollar bill that sat inside. It was hard for her to imagine that it held a grand just a few months before. When the last of that disappeared so did the identity of Emma completely.

When Emma checked out of the hospital she was given a key to what ended up being a locker at the bus station. There were clothes that she was brought to the hospital in, which she immediately dumped because they were completely blood stained. In the locker was her backpack. It contained her wallet, a few changes of clothes and the items she had been using from the hotel room, which wasn't much because her funds were depleted. The first thing she looked for was her journal. She felt a sigh of relief when it was sitting there in one piece. One thing that wasn't in her backpack before was an envelope. She opened it up cautiously and noticed the money inside along with a typed unsigned note. “I hope this helps you start your new life's journey.” *How odd* she thought to herself. Her mysterious stranger obviously had wanted to finalize his good deeds and she was okay with that.

The money lasted quite a while. She did the best she could; spending it on cheap food, cheap places to stay, and a decent set of clothes to wear on interviews.

To her dismay the interviews never got to anything concrete. She was lucky she had a few on the spot. Who wanted to hire someone with no official address or telephone number? Sure, she left the number to the motel she had been staying at and its address, but the moment they caught wind of her living arrangements she was certain they were throwing her application in the garbage. As the envelope got thinner so did her food consumption and sleeping arrangements. That changed to the shelter down the street from the diner she sat in. If she missed the food it didn't bother her as much. It was the pillow at night. She preferred a cot, but instead was stuck at the diner all hours of the night and drank coffee in order to keep herself up in hopes to grab a bed the next night.

Twenty dollars. That had to last her. She knew she was running into hopeless territory and quite close to the label “bum”. The waitress afforded her some leeway, Emma was certain that it was somewhat a pity thing and another for security that she wasn't alone through the middle of the night.

Emma set the envelope into the back of her journal as she took out her pen to write. She had so many thoughts she wished to convey, all for nobody to read, because it was self-fulfilling. It relaxed her, helped her feel that it was okay to disconnect from the world for a while. As she jotted away, the bell over the diner door chimed and boisterous laughter filled the empty diner. Glanced out of the corner of her eye, she saw a group of young adults. Three young men almost towered over the short girl that was smashed up against their obvious drunkenness.

One of the men seemed to be around Emma's age. He walked his group over to a booth then went up to the counter, slapping it with too much energy mixed in with a tad of pompous foolishness. “A couple of menu's sweetie and I think my dumplin’ over there's in need of some water.” He thumbed back toward the one female of the group he was laying claim to. He winked at the waitress who sighed through her false smile and nodded. That man, that fool, looked over at Emma. “Watcha got there?”

Without looking up Emma responded with, “Nothing of interest to you, so if you could kindly leave me to it I would be grateful.” Her attempt at being cordial didn't really fit in with her counter-mate.

“I don't know, it seems kind of interesting.” He snatched the book from her hands and started to flip pages. “Oh how boring. You've got your life written in here. Anything I might like? Some juicy details?”

“It's not yours! Give it back.” Emma was swinging to only miss the book that was being tossed back and forth between his hands.

“Ah don't be like that. You should be happy someone like me is showing any interest in you.” *Someone like him,* she thought to herself. He was nothing but what looked to be the son of a rich daddy and never really had anything else to do in life but treat women like shit. She was almost certain that he probably couldn't even remember the names of all his step-mothers. His hair blonde, his eyes blue, the perfect poster boy of handsome arrogance. He looks over to his group of misfits. “Hey David, take a look at this. You like to read, tell me if it's any good.” He tossed the book to his friend, who sat up from the booth just in time to grab the journal.

“Seriously, stop.” She grew frustrated but stuck on what to do. She looked at the ones at the table. The other male there with them looked quite younger but very similar to her tormenter. She was certain that was his brother. The girl, she just sat there watching everything unfold, a nervousness about her.

"It's in a bunch of scribbles dude. I'm too drunk to read this." David stated. He tossed it on the table. "You read it yourself, Bret, if you want to." The journal lay on the table long enough to be grabbed up by the girl.

"Let me hold onto this for you." She said, coldness in her tone. It appeared she didn't like the situation, but really not much could be done.

Bret walked over to the table, a few menus in hand as the waitress eased over with the waters. "Don't worry your pretty little head, Alicia. We know you hate to read." He attempted to grab the book out of her hand, and as she reacted by pulling it away from him, one of the glasses of water spilled on the table and splashed onto her and the journal.

"Dammit Bret!" She squealed in anger and pushed David, who was beside her, out of the booth. Throwing water off of her she noticed the book was a bit wet.

That was the first thing Emma noticed and she began to fill with panic. She watched as Alicia ran off to the restroom, book in hand. She figured it was the perfect time to get it back. Emma grabbed her backpack and rushed off behind Alicia into the restroom. When she walked in, there stood the young woman, paper towels in hand, wiping herself off.

In the dark lighting of the bathroom she noticed how worn Alicia looked, covered by her average beauty. Nothing screamed special about her. She didn't have long flowing hair, she didn't have sparkling eyes, hell she didn't even had much going on in the chest department. Nothing but plain. Dirty blonde hair pulled up in a clip, freckles spreading across her face and down her neck, and nothing more to tell. She looked past all that when the two locked eyes for only a moment.

"Shit!" Emma said when she noticed the wet book sitting on the edge of the sink. After she rushed for it she realized how bad it was. In a panic she pushed for the automatic hand dryer to turn on and then took notice of the sign on it that said "Out of Order". *Great,* she thought to herself.

"I'm so sorry." Alicia spoke after drying herself the best she could. "I tried to get it back for you but my boyfriend is such an ass. He seems like he's doing the world a favor by picking on people less fortunate than him."

Less fortunate? Emma thought, then realized it was the complete truth. No matter what she felt inside, on the outside she looked nothing more than a run down homeless person with the self esteem of a rat. "I'm sorry. I should go. Thank you," she said as she broke eye contact.

"I'm the one that should really be up on the sorry's. Let me make it up to you. Buy you something to eat? Drink?" She extended sincerity.

"No, I've done enough of that. Thank you though." she responded politely.

"Then can I drive you home? I have no problem in leaving those jerks behind here in the diner."

"Um..." she glanced around and sighed. "That's not necessary. Thank you enough for what you've done."

Alicia gave a perplexed expression which changed to one of understanding. "How 'bout this. Need a place to crash? I'd hate to see you walk out of here without me helping you at least a little."

"I'm not charity." Emma scoffed. Then thought that she just might be. Twenty dollars. She wasn't penniless but damn near it.

"It's not what I meant." Alicia said then sighed. "Look, not to be rude or blatantly honest, but it looks like you could use a nice bed to sleep in, maybe a hot shower. I have an extra bed. It couldn't hurt for the night." She tried to be convincing then glanced at the journal. "You know, I've got a pretty good hairdryer that might be able to rescue the pages in that book for you."

Emma smiled, just a little, and nodded. "Just for the night. I shove off in the morning."

Alicia nodded. "Just for the night." She then stuck out her hand and said, "Obviously you know my name is Alicia, so how about I learn your name?"

Emma nodded and thought for a moment. The moment to start completely new. "Tessa." They shook hands, as if she were making a deal with the devil inside herself.

*****

The room for the night turned Emma, or from that point on Tessa, into a roommate. It wasn't until the next morning that she realized how much in need she really was. They talked for hours over breakfast that eventually morphed into lunch. Tessa explained how hard she had been looking for a job with the living conditions she was dealing with and the lack of funds, but refused to go back home due to a big family issue. The problem she had with them was going to stay a secret, she made quite certain of that.

"How about you rent my room?" Alicia offered after she took away the small chipped plate that had held the crumbs of a gobbled down ham sandwich.

"I have no money for that. Remember, I don't have a job."

"Well, I can help you with that I think. My manager at the club owes me a huge favor and I can bet I can get you a job there."

"Really?" Tessa attempted to not look so enthusiastic but it wasn't pulled off quite well. She did get serious quickly, though. "It still doesn't negate the fact that I have no cash flow."

Alicia brushed it off and said, "Trust me. You'll get the job. Now the best thing for you to do right now is take a nice hot shower and we'll head to my closet to see what I can do to liven you up a bit."

"Thanks." Tessa said with sincerity mixed with sarcasm. She could only imagine coming out looking like a clown in a run down circus after being made over by her obviously new roommate. She set her empty glass on the counter and took off towards the shower.

* * * * *

I can't believe it's already been a year since I started my work at Kraze. I honestly wouldn't have thought about it but Dick was pretty insistent on having a little after-hours get together to commemorate the occasion, although I understand that it is quite an accomplishment given Kraze's turnover rate. Of course there was only so much celebrating I could do, but things will change next week. 21!!!! Why is it I feel so excited about that number? I've already been through more than the average 21 year old has, yet I'm elated none-the-less. I am quite lucky to have Alicia around, she really treats me right. I can't say the same for her asshole of a boyfriend, Bret. I couldn't count the times they had broken up only to get back together, quite loudly I might add, and continue running around in circles. My head hurts just thinking about it. I've grown quite accustomed to my room to put it nicely. There's nothing that could make me go out into the next room to make nice with the same group of guys who treated me like a homeless bum the first day they met me. Stuck up pricks. Funny though, the way they looked sub-human the moment they decided to "party". They liked to do that here. Why they can't do it at their own place is beyond me. Maybe it just didn't seem right shoving things up ones nose, smoking some nasty herb, or sticking a bunch of dirty needles into the arms. Not in their neighborhood at least. This was more their style. Slummin' as they would call it. Yay for us for being in a shitty ass part of town and living in a shitty ass apartment.

I actually kind of like it in here, in my room. I spent a little bit of money and got me something for music and headphones, so I don't have to hear all of their unnecessary activities going on in the other room. I've done my best to save up the money that I have. I'm thankful that rent here is cheap and I really have a tough time parting with my money. Of course I have an even tougher time parting with it to a bank, call it paranoia. So I guess old school is the way to go. Nothing wrong with sticking my money in a mattress. It will make it easier to leave the moment I get a chance. As much as I love Alicia, I really can't handle it here anymore. Not as long as Bret keeps causing drama and bringing in half his drug-addicted friends. Funny how I call them his friends. I am quite certain the proper term would be clients. Mr. Rich boy obviously has too much time on his hands, or not enough brains (I opt for the 2nd) to be dealing some strong meds. It kind of freaks me out in a way. It doesn't happen often, most of the time it's with Alicia and a few other people.

Poor Alicia. I'm quite certain she has her own problem, although she scoffs at the idea. I don't mind the weed, which seems to be standard fare nowadays. I'm more worried about the scripts she carries. You know she has it tough with the job as a bartender till all hours of the night then having to sleep through the day. One pill before work and she's the liveliest person pouring drinks, another when she gets home having her pass out ten minutes after she takes it. I only know that much because I have been the unfortunate one to see her lying on the floor on the way to her bedroom and I will tell you right now, she's not a light person. Took me quite a bit, with no cooperation on her part, to get her into bed. I do not look forward to doing that again.

All in all, things are standard. I could go on and on and on about it all, but I have to save more for tomorrow because I'm certain my days drama's will turn into quite a few pages of ink.

* * * * *

The excitement was in the air. Finally of a legal drinking age. Kraze was filled with coworkers and anybody willing to be a friend for the night, any reason to drink and have a good time was the way they rolled. Tessa was slightly sad that Alicia wasn't able to make it, but Bret had taken over the apartment and that was more of a party her friend enjoyed. It all went in the back of Tessa's mind after hearing the first toast from the bartender, Dane. After a push up onto the bar top, Tessa stood staring at the crowd. The colorful lights moved throughout at a quick pace as bodies stacked like sardines attempted to move to the pulsating sound of the bass. Kraze was always filled to capacity and today she felt like everyone was there just for her, and she felt more loved than she had in a long time. Tessa looked down as the super sexy Dane, who earned quite a bit in tips off his looks alone. What more could a person want than a man in skin tight shirts that showed every definition of every muscle, seducing blue eyes, mocha hair placed perfectly, and a smile so bright that his dimples were prominent. Many a dream did she had that involved him in it, but she knew she wasn't quite the gender he preferred. It never changed the dreams though.

The music lowered a bit as she heard the resident DJ Red announce on the mic "This is our birthday bitch Tessa. I want you to give it up to her and her 21st!" He waited as the crowd cheered and whooped. "She needs to be loaded up on alcohol and I'm looking to you all to take care of that tonight!" More yelling from the crowd in cheers. "We're willing to give you a special for the next hour only. Drinks are half off *if* we get our birthday bitch a minimum of 5 of her choice!"

Talk about spoiling. She stood there smiling at the crowd and mimicking their enthusiasm. She sat on top of the bar after being crowned the official Birthday Bitch with a plastic tiara and a sash. She knew the night was going to be long and memorable and she wouldn't want to change those moments. Those were what memories were supposed to be; instead they were only a glimpse of what possibility normal may look like.

The escort Dane gave her from the club to her apartment topped off Tessa's grand night. She kept it together; well maybe the word should have been vertical, long enough to get past closing time. After she gave Dane a big bear hug, she giggled to him about how hot his butt was; she fumbled for her keys, and entered her building. She slowly walked up the three flights of steps which worked to take what was left of her buzz away.

When she got to her floor she heard a loud crash and screams from her apartment. After rushing in Tessa took notice of the room around her. Bret's "friends" were sitting on the couch, one on the floor, all looking completely dazed without a care in the world. She hoped that the one curled up on the chair was asleep, but there were never any guarantees. She looked at the glass coffee table and a plethora of narcotics seemed to flood it. Long lines of white powder sat next to a razor blade and some sort of metal straw; a clear tube burned around the end laid on top of a nice Zippo lighter; a bag of opened pot, and what could easily have been confused for a bowl filled with candy was, instead, a variety of colored pills. It was choose your own drug night.

Her distaste for the type of partying that was going on in the room was suddenly broken from her mind as she heard loud bangs coming from her room. Tessa made a beeline in that direction to only be stopped by Alicia.

"Hi." Alicia said like nothing else was going on around her. Tessa took one look at her and realized that she was playing in LaLa land; one of Alicia's favorite things to do was to drink all night while washing down Xanax. Her eyes were glazed over and her body was swaying, which she probably didn't even realize she was doing.

"What is going on?" Tessa asked her friend, but not waiting for a response she ran to her room and pulled Alicia along by her wrist hearing mumbles coming from behind her. She burst into her room and watched in horror as Bret threw what little furniture she had all over the place. On the ground already broken was her lamp, the dresser turned over, curtains pulled down, and closet rifled through. "Bret!" She screamed to get his attention. His hands were on her mattress, pulling it up off the box springs.

Bret looked in her direction, eyes wild and bloodshot with a look of psycho for that extra special touch. "Alicia says you owe her money for rent."

"What?" Tessa looked back at Alicia then focused back on Bret. "I owe her rent on the next paycheck, but what business is it of yours and what the fuck are you doing?"

"I'm getting the money! I know you have it here, she told me you stash some green away."

She tried to see eye to eye with Alicia, to get her full attention. "Why is he doing this?"

Alicia shrugged as if it weren't a big deal. "I told him I didn't have the money for him yet, you know, for the meds he gave me. I said it was all good, I was coming into some rent from you quick enough." She stopped with her explanation and propped herself on the door.

Tessa heard a loud rip sound and turned back around. Bret had taken a pocket knife and tore all the way down her mattress looking for some money. If he was smart all he had to do was look at the corner that had been sewn shut. It was evident at that point that stashing cash in her mattress was not the best thing to do.

Bret pulled out a roll of money and smiled. "I think this will cover your tab my dear dumb sweetheart." Bret winked at Alicia.

"That's not yours!" Before even thinking, Tessa darted towards Bret and attempted to grab the money from his hands. She couldn't just let him steal from her like that. It was all she had; all her savings that was going to get her out of that shithole called an apartment. She successfully grabbed the money and pulled away, only to be knocked down by Bret. Lying on her stomach she tried to crawl a bit further, but he had her by the legs.

"That's mine you bitch! You're not going to take it from me that easy." The next thing Tessa felt was a sharp pain in her shoulder blade as Bret had thrust the knife into it. It was enough pain to cause her to lose grip of her money and he grabbed it once again.

Alicia stood up from her slouched position in the doorway and spoke with every word slurred, “I don't think you should do that. Maybe it wasn't a good idea baby. She's my friend and now you've gone and hurt her.”

“Get out of my way.” He said as he walked over to to Tessa, who was trying to pull herself up and ignore the pain that ran through her back.

Alicia stood in the doorway and blocked him from leaving. “I don't think so.”

“Well I do.” After he said that all Tessa could see was Alicia doubling over and joining her on the ground and hearing Bret yell to his friends that they had to get out of there fast.

She knew there was no way she was going to be able to go after him. She observed the pool of blood that quickly surrounded Alicia. She rolled her over and realized that he had stabbed her in the abdomen. “Alicia.” She spoke as she tapped her friend on the cheek. “Hey,” she repeated until she saw Alicia’s eyes barely open and her mouth pursed as if to speak. Instead her mouth widened and her head rolled to the side, leaving a blank milky stare in her eyes.

Tessa, in a panic, screamed her name a few more times as she listened for a heartbeat and felt for a breath. When it was apparent that neither existed, she made her way towards the telephone leaving a mixed blood trail behind her. Her call to 911 was short since she really didn't have to say too much except robbery, knife, and dead. She hung up after that figuring they'd get the details when the got there.

When the emergency crew appeared alongside the police, Tessa was sitting beside the lifeless body of her friend; the only person that took her for who she was, never asked questions, and was always there when she needed her. The blood that was everywhere had not fazed her, and neither did the fact that she was pulled out of the way while they attempted to revive her. She stared blankly at the paramedic working on her, she barely heard the voice. She was too busy watching curiously in Alicia's direction.

The paramedic patched Tessa up enough to get her into the ambulance, she was told that she was losing a lot of blood somehow and they needed to stitch her up. Tessa thought to herself that may have taken into account why she felt so lightheaded or tired. *I'm probably still drunk.* She didn't dare say that out loud but it still didn't make it any less true.

Tessa sat on the tall hospital bed surrounded by curtains. The attending had just finished cleaning her wound and cleared her for discharge while the police sat surprisingly patient waiting for that to get done. The hospital was the last place she wanted to be; the police were the last people she wanted to see. Yet there she was.

Begrudgingly she met them in a small corner of a waiting room and talked as they took notes. She could only tell from her point of view what was going on, although they probably filled in the gaps. The big question was about Bret. *Damn, why did I never learn his last name? Oh yeah because he was an asshole and I didn't care.* She knew that it was not going to end well with him. All the information she had, about him dealing out of their house, using drugs himself, all those things were going to add up and probably not be good for Tessa in the long run. She had to tell the cops though. The tests on her came back negative of certain controlled systems in the body, except for alcohol of course. She was pretty high on the chart but she wasn't driving or doing anything damaging so it didn't seem to matter to them too much. What mattered was that she was cleared to go for that time being.

Tessa paced outside the hospital, the situation finally took a hold of her psyche. She was given a ride home by one of the officers. She knew she wasn't safe going back to her apartment but she had nowhere else to go. She was certain that they would find Bret so maybe he wouldn't be a threat right away.

Tessa didn't get any sleep that night, and had a really hard time sleeping at all as the week went on. She picked up extra shifts at the club just as an excuse not to go home. She really wasn't sure when the breaking point was but she had just stopped going back home. Everything of hers was stolen or destroyed. The only thing she could salvage was the journal, and how it survived without a scratch was a complete mystery to her.

Her boss, Mr. Dick Preston, didn't make too much of a fuss with her sleeping on the couch of his office. He was hardly there when she was sleeping anyway and Tessa figured he was a bit shocked and quite possibly afraid to ask her to leave. She joked with him at one point that he at least knew she would be on time for work. That was probably the only joke she had made since the incident.

* * * * *

Tessa sat on the couch after folding the blankets and pillows she used to become a tenant at Kraze. It was part of her morning ritual. After brushing her teeth, showering (she didn't even want to ask why the office had more of a loft vibe to it), and right before coffee and the paper. She took a sip of the crappy coffee that she'd gotten so used to when she had no real place to call home, and for just a moment realized that she was practically in the same situation. The only difference was that she knew where her head was going to lay down.

She perused the articles on the main cover; it didn't seem to really make a difference to her. Not in her world that was. She thumbed to the local section. Bret had yet to be caught and she assumed the only way to find out was through the paper, like calling the police station wouldn't give her any information if she just had asked. She did set her coffee down, though. Instead of seeing the face of Bret in nice tight handcuffs and a few missing teeth (she constantly imagined the cops roughing him up quite a bit before taking him in), she saw faces of her past. Beside those faces was a crumpled up car and under that the headline *Car Accident kills 2, injures 1.* She got up, puts the paper down on the coffee table. She saw Mr. Preston walk up the steps in perfect timing. "I need to borrow your car."

"You need to what?" He shook his head questionably.

"I don't have time to explain. But I need to borrow your car. I'll bring it back, I promise."

Dick sighed and threw her the keys. He still was treating Tessa with extreme caution and was certain there had to be a reason for her to want to rush out of the club, a place she hadn't even walked outside of since she set up residence there.

She gave him a sweet kiss on the cheek followed by "Thanks" before she ran out the door and into the seemingly spotless hybrid car. She laughed to herself thinking how funny he would own anything earth conscious considering how he was more worried about image than anything. *Gotta be the wife's.*

For once, Tessa had parked in the actual parking lot of a hospital, albeit it was one a few towns over so it probably didn't count towards her record as a patient of St. Josephs. Once inside, she fled to the desk to find out where she could find the one victim that was injured, in hopes it wasn't too late. She didn't wait even a second after being given the room number to hear the clerk say "but there are no visitors." None of that mattered to her.

Standing at the elevators and pushing the button repeatedly, was just making her even more frustrated and impatient so she glanced over to a sign that pointed to the stairs. She realized that was the best method to get to her destination, as if it were a race. If it was a race, the checkered flags ended at room 308. It was closed, but she didn't really care. She took one big breath as she pushed open the metal door.

A man stood there, coffee in hand, in a bit of surprise at the visit. "Ma'am, you can't be in here. There aren't any visitors." He towered above her, wore hospital standard scrubs, and an ID clipped onto his pocket that read "Dr. Michael Baldwin."

"I'm not a visitor, I'm family." Tessa said then looked at the figure sitting up in the hospital bed. Right there with bandages wrapped around her left arm and around her head, bruises covering every exposed part of her body, sat her sister. The look of shock on both their faces could have been considered priceless.

"Melinda?" Michael glanced over at the patient, a look of worry on his face.

"Its okay, honey. She can stay. Why don't you get something for you to eat?" Her sister said quietly and waited for the doctor, obviously her love interest, to leave the room.

Tears welled up in both their eyes as they still

couldn't take their eyes off each other. “Mel...” was all that came out of Tessa's mouth. She was Emma; Tessa had left the room for the time being.

Melinda started to cry more and just shook her head silently telling her something she already knew. Their parents were dead. “I tried to save them, I did.” She cried heavily. “But it was too late. I couldn't get out of my seat in time. I'm so sorry Emma. I'm so sorry.”

She rushed to her sister's side and wrapped her arms gently around her, cautious of the small delicate frame, to avoid hurting her any more than she possibly could. “It's okay. There's no need to be sorry. I read the paper; I don't think you were at fault. You didn’t cause that big truck that hit you guys.”

They stayed there just a few minutes, she consoled her younger sister, Melinda, who was two years her junior. The two looked nothing alike, but yet people always figured they were sisters. Finally, after getting a lot of the tears out of the way they started talking about each other and what they had been doing since she was kicked out of their house.

“Well, I have a job and I pay bills. No boyfriend, nothing special.” She had not felt like telling her everything that had happened, although she was waiting for the one question that was unavoidable. Where's the baby? That was an answer for Tessa, the thick-skinned persona and not the vulnerable young lady she used to be.

Melinda didn't bring it up, though. Instead she gushed about how much she and Michael were in love and that they were going to get married the moment he finished up his residency at the hospital. She, herself, had been going to school for business management and that everything that had been going on in her life was just close to perfect.

She knew there had to be more. There was no way her sister got to live the perfect life, have the perfect job, with a perfect soon to be husband who looked more handsome than the television doctor all the ladies crooned over. She thought about all the misery she had gone through and none of it added up and she began to get jealous. “Congratulations.” She offered up with all the effort that she could muster.

“Emma....” Mel said with a change of tone setting them out of the comfort zone once again. “I just want to say I'm sorry.” Her eyes darted away, avoiding contact with her sister.

“About what? I already said this accident wasn't your fault.”

“No.” She quietly mouthed. “I'm sorry I didn't tell Mom and Dad about Uncle Ron.”

Silence fell across the room. All the background noise ceased to exist in her mind and the feeling of being in a vast amount of nothingness had overtaken her, but finally brought her back to reality. “What do you mean about Uncle Ron? What didn't you tell them? What do you know?” Those words didn't even sound like her. They sounded like the hissing of a snake in alert mode, ready to strike at any sudden move. Tessa was awake once again.

“I...I saw Ron walk out your room. I saw you crying on the floor.” It probably took every bit of courage to say it and she instantly began to justify her actions and said, “But I didn't want him to see me and I didn't know what happened. I thought maybe you just mouthed off to him or something. I didn't know what he had done. Not really. Not until it was too late and you were already pregnant and they were throwing you out of the house.”

“*You!*” She boomed with anger. “You could have backed me up. You could have told them there was no way Ron was telling the truth because you were there. You could have kept me away from all the shit that's happened to me since I was forced to leave."

"I'm sorry." Tears flooded her puffy bruised eyes. "I was scared. I didn't know what to do and I panicked."

Emma/Tessa moved in uncomfortably close to her sister. "Well let me tell you something little sis. Because of your fear and panic, my life became nothing but a royal shit-fest." Nothing but anger had filled her lungs at that point. "You know he beat me. He tortured me and forced my legs open. The baby that I carried, that was from our dear lovable Uncle Ron? Well that baby's dead. I killed it. Yep. Two little pills and away it went." She started speaking as if she were drunk on the anger. "But of course it couldn't have happened easily. Noooooo. I bled out, got stuck in the hospital. And then, just to spice things up I ran the streets looking for work and a place to stay."

"...." Melinda couldn't say anything, she was in shock.

"Oh no, it didn't end there." She spewed hatred in every word. "When I finally found a place to live, had friends and a real life again, my roommate's boyfriend steals my money, stabs me and kills his girlfriend having me live in fear till the day he finally gets caught."

"I don't know what to say." Melinda began to tear even more, but that time they were tears of pity.

"Nothing you can say. It's obviously something you're good at; staying silent." She shook her head in disgrace. "There was a time I thought we were close, that nothing could come between us. Never would I *ever* think you were capable of letting something like that happen to me." She started to back away from the bed; one step, two steps. "But now I know I was wrong. And I was wrong for coming here. So don't worry your pretty little perfect head about anything. It's all forgotten, at least to me because I no longer have a sister."

Tessa rushed out of the hospital as quick as she could and into the safety of the borrowed car. Once inside she started slamming her fists on the steering wheel repeatedly and wailed in emotional pain and agony, the entire conversation with her sister on auto-repeat through her head. Then the incident with her uncle. Everything that had ever happened to her overtook her mind and took residence there as some automatic guide took control of her body and drove her back to Chicago.

It was roughly past two in the morning by the time she got the car back to Kraze. She decided it was probably smart to park the car nowhere near the club, since people were starting to file out of there slowly and the last thing that she wanted to tell her boss was that she let one of his drunken patrons hit his precious little hybrid. Three blocks down the way, she found a safe parking garage where she had no problem in paying a parking attendant to keep watch over it.

Having grabbed most of her composure during the long drive, her tears had been dry and her hands stuffed into the pockets of her old worn-out jeans, she started her brisk walk back to Kraze. Each step she took, the more confident she had come to the right decision when she left her sister. With her confidence, she felt something different. She looked around, saw nothing, and then continued her walk. A few more times she felt uneasy, as if she were being watched, and each time she stopped to look around she saw nothing but groups of people stumbling down the walkway. She shook off the feeling by the time she got to the front door. The doorman was trying his best to get the last of the patrons out the door since the bar closed at two.

"Hi Luther." Tessa mumbled as she brushed past him quickly into the fully lit club. Trash was on the floor, in piles mere inches from the garbage can that was neon green and easy to see. She avoided what looked to be a wet mark on the concrete floor, slightly afraid of what body fluid it might be. She took one look at Dane, who was cleaning up his area of the bar and said, "Two shots of whatever the hell you want to give me. I need it. Bring beer too; I'm probably going to be in my booth for a bit."

Dane looked up at her, smiled, and nodded. It was almost ritualistic of Tessa, not necessarily the getting drunk part. After the club shut down, she felt it was best to decompress while nursing a drink and writing in her journal. Old habits die hard. She flung her ratty backpack into the booth, flopped in beside it and pulled out the stained notebook. Pen to paper she scribbled the horrendous tale of her unhappy reunion with her sister. She didn't even notice the tall, dark man approach her table.

CHAPTER SIX

"Is anybody sitting here?"

She didn't even look up. "If you haven't noticed, the club is closed down so you might want to think about heading out of here." Tessa said.

"Ah, but I am here waiting to speak to the owner." His presence felt familiar, yet unnerving at the same time to her.

"Then how about I try to be as nice as possible and let you know that I do not need company and that I am quite busy." She didn't sound the least bit nice, her tone spoke volumes.

"Yes, that's right, your journal." He said, as if he knew what she were doing.

Tessa gazed up at him at this point. "What did you say?"

"I have noticed you sitting here before, always in the corner and always in deep thought as you pour out what seems to be every thought and feeling through that pen of yours." The stranger remarked.

"Do I know you?" She cocked her head as she tried to place his face.

"No, not formally." He said lightly.

"So you just take up stalking to bide your time then, huh?" Tessa smirked slightly. Sarcasm was something that she had an overabundance of.

He laughed a condescending laugh. "Something like that." He acted as if he knew a part of a joke that she did not.

"There's my new business partner." Mr. Preston

said in a loud boisterous tone.

He said he'd see Tessa around and went to talk with the manager. She couldn't help but feel as if she knew him from somewhere. Not just as a passing stranger, but someone she really knew.

The next morning Tessa awoke to a lot of yelling. The manager was on the telephone screaming and pleading. "Well fine then. Just don't even bother coming back." He then proceeded to throw the cordless phone and it shattered against the wall.

"What's going on?" Tessa stretched out her arms.

"Oh nothing, except that Donnie just called in sick, again. So we're out yet another bartender. I don't know what I'm going to do at this short of notice. It's Saturday and this place is going to be hopping tonight."

She edged in closer to her boss. "Um, I think I can help you."

"What does a coat check girl know about pouring drinks?" He looked at her with severe scrutiny.

"Alicia had been showing me what to do over the past few months."

"Oh really?" He scratched his head and thought for a minute. "Show me what you got."

"Excuse me?"

"Show me." He nodded, and then led her to the main club. "Get behind that bar and prove to me what you're made of."

"What do you want me to do?"

The manager looked around the club. He spotted two inventory people, the accountant, and a vendor that was stocking up their supplies. He called them all over and told them they were testing her, so a couple of rounds were on him.

They were thinking up some hard ones, and she aced every single one, her charismatic nature made it a nice adventure. The whole experience showed what she would be worth to her boss.

"All right then." Dick smiled. "Looks like everyone's happy and I'm happy." He leaned against the bar. "We'll see how you do tonight." He got a serious look on his face. "You'll have to settle for just a few bucks more an hour plus your tips." Tessa knew it was still a low number but it was better than her minimum wage position. Most bartenders brought in good tips, on the weekends anyway.

"Deal." She squealed with delight.

"Just a few things though," he pointed out to her. "I'll advance you some money to buy you some new clothes. To be one of my bartenders you need to dress hipper, sexier, I've got an image to maintain. And second, I need you to find a place to live; all that cleaning you've been doing in my office is driving me nuts. I'd go home to my wife more often if I wanted to deal with that." He said with a dry laugh.

She agreed and took the advance. She went shopping at a couple of Alicia's favorite stores. Tessa got back around dark, showered and got ready for work.

She already had a few dollars in tips before midnight. By the end of the night she was tired, but thrilled, at her financial haul. She knew she at least had three hundred bucks in cold hard cash. It made her wonder how Alicia lived in such a slum. Of course that just made her realize how much Alicia was really abusing her body.

Tessa sat at her usual table, but she was busy counting her money instead of plugging things down in her journal. She set aside the money to pay her boss back.

"I hear that you got a promotion." A dark and familiar voice spoke.

Tessa looked up to see the man that she had met the night before. "By default and pure luck, but I'm not complaining."

"May I sit?" He asked politely.

"Sure. I'm feeling pretty good tonight, so why the hell not." She offered up the booth.

"I don't believe we have been formally introduced. I'm Greco." He stuck out his hand.

"Tessa." She shook his hand then he turned it over and kissed it. "What was that for?"

"I suppose I feel that I need to be respectful in the presence of a lady. I am sorry if I offended you."

"No offense taken, just a little bit surprised, that's all." She folded her money and tucked it inside her shirt for safekeeping. "So tell me, Greco, you said you knew me informally, explain."

"Just through your boss, he had been telling me a little of your misfortunes as of late."

"Oh really? And what exactly do you know of my 'misfortunes'?" She got on the defensive.

Greco jumped back to try to restate himself. "Oh, he hasn't said too much other than the fact that you came to him troubled and bad luck has tried to keep you down."

"Are you sure that is all he said?" She asked him, feeling as though her life may have been run on the six o'clock news.

"I am most certain."

"Then how come you seem to know so much about me?"

"Well, you see, I am sort of empathetic to people's feelings, so sometimes it seems as though I know the person deep down more than I actually do."

She sighed. "That doesn't help me in understanding why I feel like I know you, I mean really know you."

Greco leaned in and spoke softly with a smile. "Maybe it is just fated for us." His voice was so gentle and completely drew Tessa in.

She gazed up at him and into his eyes. Maybe it was true, maybe there was such an unexplainable connection between the two of them. Tessa took a shot in the dark. "I know this may sound a little bit forward, but how would you feel if we got out of here and got something to eat. Maybe continue this conversation."

"Well, I'm not that hungry right now, but I would love to go out just for your company." He smiled, almost a deep smile as if his soul was doing it for him.

"Good, then let's go. I'm starving. I know this great place that serves the best pie at this time of the night." She grabbed her coat and the two of them headed out the door of the club.

They spent the next hour talking at the diner until it got close to sun up. When day was getting close to breaking Greco excused himself after he grabbed the tab for her, even though he didn't eat a single bite.

They spoke of their lives. Tessa told him some of her recent misfortunes and Greco told her of his numerous trades. He used to be a great structural engineer, but then he felt as though dabbling in many businesses made him much happier. The club was just his newest venture.

The two spent the next couple of evenings just talking. She continually looked for a place to live but had no such luck. The places were either in a bad neighborhood or it was out of her price range. Tessa was telling Greco of her issue and he surprisingly offered up a suggestion.

He just happened to own an apartment the he used when a client from out of town came in. She was more than welcome to stay there, he had told her.

Tessa said she didn't want charity that she could go at it alone. Greco spoke of how hardheaded she was. She questioned the comment but Greco gave a suggestion. They settled on a rent price and he gave her the keys. He told her he would have his driver take them there.

They arrived at the building that was in a very nice neighborhood. They went up the elevator to the twelfth floor. Tessa was giddy. The apartment had two bedrooms and was designed with modern minimalist qualities. Lots of high tech stuff and a kitchen big enough to cook in. She got excited, squealed and jumped in his arms; she repeated the words "Thank you" to him as she gave him a huge hug.

His blood started to pump as he felt her warm body against his. The smell of her passion fruit shampoo mingled with the blood that pulsed right under her soft delicate skin. She looked at him, eyes locked on one another, staring into each others souls. Tessa leaned in and kissed him tenderly at first, but as soon as Greco responded, the kissing became heavier and more full of passion. He started kissing her on the ear and on the neck; she held him as she lost herself in the moment. Greco felt hot and started to smell the blood beneath her skin. He felt the throbbing of her pulse beneath her throat. His eyes turned golden and his fangs grew long. He was about to take a bite, ever so wanting to feed as the passion was heightened, but quickly pulled away and turned around in fear and shame. He enjoyed Tessa's company far too much to just turn her into what probably would have been the most delicious meal he had ever had.

"I'm sorry, I can't do this." He lowered his head and shook it.

"Oh my God, I'm sorry." She gasped. "I thought

maybe you had the same feelings I do."

"It's not that. It's just far too complicated to explain."

"Are you married? Is that what it is?" Her eyes looked at him trying to find a reasonable explanation.

Greco sighed and shook his head no. "I've got to go." He grabbed his coat and walked out the door leaving Tessa baffled and confused.

A month went by and Tessa saw no sign of Greco. He didn't even come into the club like he had been doing in the past. She finally got fed up and and the frustration festered inside of her and she couldn't stand it any longer. She went to her manager, who was in his office looking down into the crowd.

"Where is Greco?" She asked, as she started a long conversation.

"Now why would I give you any information on him?"

"Well, I'm in one of his apartments and I need to get him this month's rent check. I just haven't seen him around to give it to him."

"Greco is a very busy man." He brushed her concern aside.

"Yeah, I figured." Tessa rolled her eyes.

"How about I tell him that you're looking for him will that do?"

"Come on, do you take me for stupid?" She asked.

"I was about to ask you the same question." Mr. Preston raised one eyebrow.

"What do you mean?"

He sighed and sat down in his oversized chair. "Don't think I hadn't noticed that you and he had been getting quite cozy? It didn't bother me since you seemed to be on the top of your game. So last month when he came to me saying that he wanted me to look out for you,

I had to ask him why. All he told me was that he needed to distance himself from you for a while. If you were to come asking I was to tell you he went out of town on business, something that he does quite often anyway."

"So why didn't you just feed me that line?"

"Look, I don't know what's gone on between you two and I don't want to know. I just don't want to see you get hurt, kiddo. You've been through enough, so if I can make it a little easier on you then that's what I will do."

Tessa threw up her hands in near defeat and frustration. "What the hell am I supposed to do then?"

"Best bet is to give up and get on with your life." He leaned back in his chair. This was coming from a man who had to deal with plenty of women in his life, being on his third marriage.

She shook her head and pulled out her checkbook in a fiery rage. "This is a check for you to give Greco. If he doesn't want to see me, then fine. But no way am I going to be a charity case." She finished writing it and signed it. She handed the check over to Dick. "But you deliver this message right along with it. I deserve nothing less than an explanation." She turned heel and darted out of the office in an angry mess. She pushed past the crowd and went out the door.

"Hey, what's you're hurry?" Said a young clean-cut guy who just happened to be waiting in line to get into the club.

She looked over at him and before she broke down in tears she thought for a minute. He was a pretty good-looking guy. She had waited long enough for Greco to come back and she was going to take her boss' advice and get on with her life. "Nothing now." She went up to the man and smiled. "How about you take me inside and help me forget all my troubles?"

"I would be up for that if you don't mind keeping me company out here in the cold."

"I can do you one better." Tessa touched his hand lightly. "I'll get you inside in a matter of seconds. I just don't want to have to wait."

"That sounds like my kind of girl." He smiled an arrogant grin and winked at the friends that were around him in line. She ignored all that and got them into the club.

She spent the next couple of hours drinking and dancing with the young man, Russ, like she had never done before. Two o'clock came around and a very drunk Tessa invited Russ back to her place. Of course he was not a man to decline on such a scrumptious offer. They took a taxi uptown and she stumbled trying to get into her apartment. Once inside she threw the keys and misses the table completely. She motioned for Russ to come to her. They started kissing like heated animals and began to rip their clothes off. They gradually moved to the living room.

Russ stopped quickly and screamed, "What the fuck?" Tessa turned toward the direction Russ was looking. Greco was sitting in the tall wing-back chair in the shadows; his eyes glowed in the shadows.

"Greco!" She said, startled.

Russ turned towards her. "You know him?" As he looked at Tessa, she was staring at Greco, all her thoughts pounded in her head at once.

"This is his place." She said to the young man then spoke to Greco. "Why didn't you say something to stop us as soon as we came through the door?"

Greco looked over at Russ who was quickly picking up the clothes that were thrown on the floor. "I was enjoying the show. Bravo." He applauded the young man.

"Naaah." Russ shook his head. 'This isn't right." Russ turned towards her. "I don't know what you're into but I don't do with weird voyeur shit. I'm outta here. And don't bother looking me up." He took his stuff and slammed the door on the way out.

"What are you doing here?" Tessa walked toward Greco.

"Your manager told me that you wanted to see me."

"Is that all he said?"

"He said a few choice words and that I owed you an explanation."

"Is that why you're here?"

Greco sighed then stood up. "Actually I'm not sure why I'm really here."

"Then leave. I gave Dick the rent check so I'm paid up for this month." She crossed her arms.

"It's not about the money."

"Then what is it? You've already ruined what could have been a spectacular night."

Greco shook his head. "It was only a façade. You had no feelings for him whatsoever. You would have been just going through the motions."

"What do feelings have to do with it? For some unnamed reason I have been worked up lately with no outlet to disperse it upon. It was only a matter of time I would try to find someone to hook up with." She looked at him questionably. "Besides, what do you care? It's not like you wanted the heavy task."

"Its more complicated than you can ever imagine."

"Try me." She was not going to take the short answer.

"It's not that easy." He walked toward her.

"Did I imagine the connection we were having?"

"You tell me." He seemed have been trying a bit of psychology on her, which wasn't working.

"What kind of answer is that?" She shook her head in frustration. She took a step toward him. "Do you, or at least did you, have some sort of feelings for me?"

"There have been strong unexplainable feelings for you since I first saw you."

She took another step toward him, looked into his eyes, and felt his hot breath. "Did you want me to kiss you?" She pressed herself even closer to him.

'Yes, I did." He answered, not quite disheveled, yet seemed uneasy. There she was taunting him with her life once again, and yet another battle with him had begun.

She leaned into his ear and seductively asked, "Did you enjoy it?" She left such a hot steamy message on his ear. It left for a very exotic adrenaline rush.

"Very much so." He breathes in and out calming himself while the vampire part of him screamed from inside demanding to feed the hunger raging within.

Tessa rubbed her cheek against his, her moist lips traced the hair of his skin. "Do you want me to do it again?"

Greco closed his eyes for a moment, and almost touched her lips once again. As soon as her lips touched his, he did not resist and gave into the indulgence. But as soon as he realized that his monster was about to be unleashed, he pushed her away.

"We can't do this." He turned from her.

She screamed in frustration. "You're doing it again!" She threw her arms up in the air.

"Its not that I mean to or don't want to." Greco looked at her almost pleading. He touched her cheek. "I want to give into you so much it is tearing me up inside. I care for you deeply."

"Then why?" She pushed his hand away. "Why are you playing these games? You bring me in only to push me away."

"I'm afraid."

"Of what?"

"Of what really might happen if I do give in." He admitted.

"Oh so you're worried about a love affair is it? Trying to protect your own ass?" Tessa had gotten quite tired of him dancing around such a simple thing.

"No, I'm afraid of what might happen to you if I fully give in; let all inhibitions to the wind."

"You make no sense to me. I mean if you're worried that you'll hurt my feelings, then too late, the damage has been done." She exploded with anger.

"It's more than that."

"I don't understand." She shook her head.

Greco looked at her semi-nude body. "Get dressed."

"So now you're giving me orders?"

"No, I'm about to give you answers."

She got her clothes on and they went downstairs and into his car.

The ride was silent as they drove further and further downtown. He finally stopped the car and turned the engine off. "You are right, Tessa, I have feelings for you. Deep ones. I can't explain the bond that we have between us and why it is so strong. Trust me; I have been pondering this endlessly." He was speaking of all the days that had gone by that she filled his thoughts, no matter how he tried to push her out of his mind. "See, you really don't know the extent of things. Why I fight it the way I do. I hope that I can show you how I really feel and for you to truly understand."

She gazed out the window and saw a shady hotel. "Um, Greco, you didn't have to bring me all the way out to this kind of place to show me that. We were in a nice warm apartment not too long ago, you know." Tessa's dry humor didn't make any of the situation easier on him.

Greco signed. “It's not that.” Then he looked at her with a questionable glance. “Do you not recognize this place?”

She looked at it quickly and then shrugs. “I’ve been here before, but that was a long time ago. Nothing really that important.” She had put those memories behind her, or attempted to no matter how often they creeped up.

“Get out of the car.” He gently ordered.

“What’s this about?” She stepped out of the car and Greco joined her at her side.

“You’re much deserved explanation. Come,” He extended his hand. “Follow me.” She took his hand as he led her down the dark alleyway beside the hotel. Tessa held his arm for more comfort. He turned the corner to the shadowy rear entrance to the run-down hotel.

“Now do you remember this place?”

She looked at it for a little while; she had wondered why all the strange sounds and eerie shadows seemed all too familiar. “I...I just don’t know.” Then she turned towards Greco. “I still don’t understand. How is this an explanation?”

“This is where it all started, my connection to you. This is where we first met and where I first went against everything that I knew.”

“What? But I don’t remember you. How can this be?”

“But I remember you. Ever since that day I have not been able to get you out of my mind no matter how hard I tried.” Greco pointed toward the green dumpsters. “I was over there. It was not long after midnight. I hear the back door slam open and someone babbling endlessly to themselves between tears of pain.

I thought nothing of it until I heard a hard thud. I came running out of the shadows and there you were, lying motionless on the ground."

She turned towards the spot he pointed out. Her memory was coming back and she was frightened. She didn't want to remember any of that part of her past.

"I went over to you and noticed that you were lying in a pool of blood. At first I thought very selfish thoughts as the possibility came to take full advantage of the situation, but something stopped me. It was as if a little voice was whispering that you were meant to stay alive. I also sensed that you had just lost a life that was inside of you; your hold on your own life was fading. I touched your face and your eyes opened."

He continued, "You told me to let you die. You could barely speak. You said, 'I don't want to live anymore, I can't live, and it hurts too much.' The pain that came from you voice, it hurt me to hear it."

Tears began to flow down Tessa's cheeks. She fell to her knees as she envisioned everything.

"I pulled you close to me and held you in my arms. There you were begging to have your life end and I could easily have taken you up on that offer. But I couldn't. It was as if everything I had known had frozen and a consciousness I hadn't known for a long time took control. Our eyes met and I could sense all the screaming and pain inside behind them. It was almost if I had known you and loved you since the beginning of time. I pushed your hair out of your face and forced a strong smile on my lips as I told you that it wasn't your day to die, I wasn't going to allow it. If you were going to give up, I was going to have to fight for you. I tried to be as strong as I could, for you."

"You then told me that I didn't understand and that you didn't deserve to live and didn't want to. You told me I couldn't just come up to you and try to play hero."

"I then told you, 'I'm taking responsibility for you until you can get back on your feet. I'll be the voice of reason until you are clearly thinking.' which you obviously were not. It was understandable because of all the pain I could sense you harbored inside."

"You looked at me with confusion and then finally acceptance as you passed out in my arms. I then brought you to my car."

She said with enlightenment, "You're the one who took me to the hospital. You paid all my bills, yet I didn't even know who you were. I thought it was all a part of my imagination; too good to be true." She stood up.

"Yes, I was that person." Greco nodded.

"Why did you not stay around? You could have at least checked up on me, but you disappeared instead."

"I'm not sure. I think it was because I was struggling with who I was and I didn't want to make anything more complicated than it already was. But I watched you; I followed your life. Every triumph I cheered, every ordeal I cried. I had decided it was best not to interfere, but then I couldn't help it. I wanted to touch you, talk to you again."

She turned towards Greco, a question burned in her thoughts. "What was a person like you doing in a place like this?"

"To answer that would be to reveal my most sacred secret and I'm not sure you're ready to know all of that."

"You wouldn't have brought me here and dig up these dirty horrid old memories if you weren't going to tell me everything. You still haven't given me your real explanation. No matter how it was when you first met me, there's something deeper that has stopped you from really being with me."

Greco grabbed her hand and held onto it for a

second and then dropped it again. He was in conflict once more.

"I'm a monster, Tessa. A terrible evil, selfish monster. I'm afraid you will be frightened of me, not understanding me, or worse, I will try to hurt you." He caressed her cheek tenderly. "The last thing I want to do is hurt you, Tessa."

She thought for a minute. "When you first saw me what were those thoughts running through your head? What terrible things were you planning to do to me?"

"Tessa, don't make me do this. Once you know, it cannot be undone."

"I want to know. I *need* to know. You owe that to me. You saved me from death only to have me die a thousand deaths inside each and every day since that moment."

Greco's eyes watered as he squeezed her hand tightly. He lowered his head to avoid her seeing him cry. Why did she have such a pull on him? Why did he even care? "I was finishing up my meal and when I saw you, the first thing I thought about was that I wanted to feed off of you."

She took a step backwards. "Like cannibalism?"

Greco shook his head. "No, like feeding off of your blood."

"But..." She didn't know what to say.

"The aroma of all the blood that you had spilled enticed me. I wanted to taste it on my lips and feel it run down my throat."

She started to back up more quickly. "I didn't know you were this kind of person. You couldn't be." She shook her head. Images of serial killers flashed through her mind and stopped on the likes of Dahmer.

"I told you that I am a monster. I didn't stop short on the truth."

"No, Greco, I don't believe that. You just need help, that's all." She said to him, who took a step toward her every time she took one back.

"You don't understand. I'm not a murderer; not in the way you think. I'm the hell in the shadows, the demon of the night, a child of darkness." She turned heel and ran quickly, only to bump into Greco who had moved to block her path. She gazed up at him, his eyes glowing dark golden embers and his pearl fangs showed. "I'm a vampire."

She looked at him and screamed. Greco covered her mouth and talked gently into her ear. "Now you know why I was so afraid. I was afraid for you to find out because I care for you so much. I was scared that if we get too passionate together that the demon inside would ravage you to death and I didn't want that to happen."

She calmed her struggles and listened to his words as she tried to understand.

"I think I love you, Tessa, something I had forgotten how to do over all these centuries. I want to cherish you; oh do I want to feel your body pressed against mine. I really do." He closed his eyes for a moment and began to whisper. "I don't know what I would do if anything ever happened to you."

She stopped and listened. He let her go and backed away. "That is why we must never be together, intimate ever. I must say goodbye." He backed further into the shadows and disappeared.

She began to cry and looked around. She realized that she didn't want to be left alone; at that moment, or for the rest of her life. Some switch inside her turned on the idea of fate and how each moment led up to them being together. "Greco, no. Don't leave me. Don't leave me out here alone in this cruel world. I need you." She began to weep furiously. "I don't think I can live without you."

He didn't answer her. He just looked at her from above.

"You saved me from death itself, now let me live my life with you in it. You couldn't hurt me that day and I know deep down inside you won't hurt me now or ever."

Greco pondered those words from the rooftop of the hotel. He wanted to know that she had spoken the truth, but past history had proven that it couldn't be done. Not in the ultimate end.

"You need me!" She screamed. "And I need you. Just please don't leave me." She cried endlessly as she repeated the words over and over again until she became a big ball on the ground crying and rocking herself.

Greco's tormented soul couldn't help but go to her. He had to give it a try. He gave in and quietly went to her. He wrapped his arms around her and gently spoke, "Shh, I'm here. I do need you. We'll figure this out...somehow." He stroked her long brown hair to comfort her. They stood there and embraced for what seemed like an eternity. He sensed that the sun was soon to come so he broke their tender silence. "I need to get back soon. Would you mind if I rested at your apartment?"

"I'd like that." She smiled and the two proceeded back to her place. The ride back was quiet, but their embrace was tight and comforted to each other.

"I will be resting in the guest room." Greco said as they walked through the door. He turned to a painting at the entrance to the apartment and pulled on one side to reveal what looked to be a breaker box. He used a small key and opened the box. Inside there were a couple of switches. He used one of them and there was a loud electronic whirring sound. Greco walked to the guest room and opened the door. Tessa watched as steel reinforced shutters covered the windows and locked the place too tight for sunlight. Greco turned to her and touched her cheek gently. “I will see you in the evening.” He smiled, proceeded into the room, and shut the door behind him.

She took a deep breath. She was tired but had way too much to think about just to go to sleep. She decided that she was going to make something to eat, the night’s events made her quite hungry, and take a long hot bath. She felt completely relaxed and thought about doing one more thing before she went to bed. She pulled out a book, her journal, from the bookshelf and decided that she was going to write down all that had happened that evening. She knew she couldn’t tell anybody else, like they would believe her anyway. Her journal was always there for her, though. It documented all the good and the bad things since before puberty. It was almost like it was an actual part of her being. Without it she might have gotten lost amongst everything that seemed overwhelming.

As she tried to fight sleep as hard as she could the last words about her evening barely made it onto the page before she fell fast asleep. She awoke to banging on the door. She jumped. “I’m coming.” She said as she wrapped her robe around her tightly. The loud booming sound of the knocking was insistent and Tessa got frustrated. "What part of ‘I’m coming’ do you not understand?” She looked through the monitor and there stood a man and a woman. The woman looked quite impatient.

She pushed the button to talk. “May I help you?”

“Where is he?” The woman said with disrespectful hatred. Her hateful words masked the beauty she possessed, which was easily seen past her unkempt blonde hair.

"Where is who?"

"Don't play games with me. I know he's in there." She pounded on the door one more time.

The man stepped up to the camera and cleared his throat. "What she means is that we are looking for Greco. He wouldn't have happened to stop by your place at any time during the night would he?"

"Maybe. Who's asking?"

"I'm his assistant Bryon." Tessa looked at the two of them for a moment and decided to open the door. As soon as the clicking sound of the lock disengaged, the door was pushed open.

"He's in the guest room sleeping." She looked back and forth between the two intruders.

The woman went straight to the box behind the painting, used another key, and shut the blinds in the whole apartment. She turned toward Bryon and spoke sternly, "It will be safe to wake him now." The man walked back to the guest room.

Tessa looked at the woman, who seemed to be in her mid-twenties. "He told me who he was, but I have no clue who you are or why you are even here in my apartment." She began to wonder if letting them in was the right choice, given everything that had happened that night.

The woman looked at her as if she were a fly buzzing around aimlessly. "I'm Isabel. I am also Greco's assistant. And we are here to make sure Greco is doing okay. He never contacted us last night so we thought the worst. It figures that he had disappeared, only to be with you."

"What is that supposed to mean?" She cocked her head and felt the iciness in Isabel's tone.

Isabel sighed and rolled her eyes. "I just fear that he has lost sight of his main objective by becoming too involved in your menial life."

"I don't know what his main objective may be, but I do know that until recently I was unaware of any involvement he has had with me in the past." Tessa stared into Isabel's eyes. "So whatever you feel is at fault on my part, you might want to double think that."

Isabel walked up to her and looked eye to eye. "You do not know the extent of what he is or what is going on with him. Only someone like me can even grasp that concept. Sometimes Greco doesn't always know what is best for him, and I think separating himself from all of this would be the wisest." She pointed towards Tessa, moving her arms in presentation.

"I'm more than just the person that you give me credit for."

"I would advise you to leave this to rest and forget about any involvement with him. You would just wind up getting hurt one way or another."

She smirked, "I don't back down so easily, so I would have to say that whatever happens in my life with Greco, past or present, is only between him and I."

Isabel's expression grew from cold to bitter as she was about to say something Tessa was certain would start the next battle stage.

"Ladies." That was all Greco had to say as he walked into the living room. Tessa stepped away from Isabel and Isabel turned towards him, as if she was expecting a command to be ordered. "Is there a problem?" Greco looked straight at her.

"No sir, I was only informing her of a few things."

Greco walked over to her and ignored Isabel's too positive spin. "Is everything okay?"

She looked at Isabel and she spoke to Greco, "Do you mean aside from these two strangers barging into my home and telling me how unimportant I am? I'm doing just fine." Her sarcasm was strong.

"Good." He took a hold of her hand, not sensing the bitterness in her voice or maybe just chose to ignore it. "Although I do not answer to my assistants I fear that they are correct in searching me out. There are a few delicate matters that I must attend to."

She nodded and smiled. "I need to get ready for work anyway; I've got a long night ahead of me and big tips to make."

Greco walked over to Isabel who was starting to look like a puppy that was about to be scolded. "Whether you like it or not, I have brought Tessa into my world. I want you to make her time amongst us as comfortable as possible and not start any problems, do you understand?"

She nodded, "yes sir."

Greco headed to the front door, "I'm going to take care of our little problem," He looked in Bryon's direction, "I want the two of you to go back to the office. You are no longer needed here." He glanced over to Isabel. "I do not want to hear of any indecencies."

Isabel nodded one more time as Greco left. Bryon stood next to Isabel and ushered her out the door. Tessa just stood in the middle of the living room, uncertain of what exactly had just happened. It was obvious that Isabel felt protective of Greco, *but why?* She thought to herself. *Was it because she was loyal to him or did it stem from something much deeper?* She felt as if it was something that she had to ponder at a later time. For now she had to make sure that she was not running late for work.

CHAPTER SEVEN

There was something in the air tonight. I could sense the tension building up between Greco and me. You would think that I would be used to it by now, and to some point I am. There are still those parts of me that want to be completely involved in his life, and I know that cannot happen. As time has gone by I have come to the realization that I will always be a small part of a bigger whole; a speck of light in the never-ending abyss of darkness that is his world. The moments that we share together are wonderful and often. When we are together I feel that nothing can pass between us or interrupt that deep connection that we have for each other. It is the moments surrounding those times I have a hard time dealing with. I completely understand his role as a vampire. He is a leader of a very strong clan of vampires; many people rely on him, which makes it easy for him to get distracted. If only those distractions would vanish, if only for a day. I am always looking from the outside, and I am certain that I am a burden; of course Greco would never tell me that. He lets me continue on, day in and day out, living what is left of my hollow existence. Each day that passes I feel more and more withdrawn from the community and wanting more and more to be a part of Greco's life.

Greco has come to me once again. He holds me in his arms; he caresses me; he kisses me. He has come quite close to being intimate with me physically. I say physically because every time we are together, our moments are intimate. I take them for what they are; moments. Greco seems to be getting better at restraining his most primal urges as a vampire. The more time we spend together throughout the days, the longer these moments are.

But, like I said, I feel something in the air tonight. From the time Greco arrived at my apartment he was lost in another world. His eyes hollow and empty of the one I love. He came over with good intentions, I am sure. Of course that was before he was so inconveniently interrupted by his minions. I wasn't sure what to do when they all showed up. There were four of them, all deep in seriousness. All I could do was disappear like a wallflower. Bryon tried to make me feel as comfortable as possible, but Isabel was as she always was; cold and bitter towards me. Sure, she puts up a great front, but deep down inside she has nothing but jealousy towards me. It is easy to see how she gazes upon Greco. Every time the two of us ladies are in the same room with him, she constantly tries to step in front of me to get as much attention as humanly possible. And that is what she is; human. She is just like me in every sense of the word. I am uncertain as to what her role truly is, except that she only has the wish to serve Greco fully to her capabilities. I suppose she would be equal to being an assistant. She does any task he asks of her, no matter how menial. Sometimes those tasks involve helping me out one way or another. Nothing frustrates her more than that, and I do know it isn't easy. Maybe I should be more cautious of her. Somehow, though, I feel that Greco would never let any harm come to me; or at least I hope.

The only thing I could tell from the moment his vampire friends came in was that there was a dark seriousness in their actions. The words they spoke were faint, although I doubt it would have made any difference. I could swear they were speaking in Latin or some other old language. Of course, how was I to know what Latin sounded like; there was never a need for me to learn it. All I know is that the moment I tried to head outside and leave them to their business, Bryon insisted that it would only be a moment and to sit tight.

I 'sat tight' for more than a couple of hours. The only solace I had was this journal, although it seems this made the guests uneasy, but they never acted on it. I hardly got any acknowledgment from them at all to tell you the truth. I suppose, I preferred it this way. More than anything it seemed as though I was just a simple fly in the room; nothing for them to worry about.

* * * * *

"I do apologize for the interruption." Greco said as he wrapped his arms around Tessa and gazed into her sad eyes. "Tessa, you do know I do not plan on these interruptions."

She pulled back a little. "I know, I know."

"Then why do you seem so sad?"

She sighed. "It's not as much sad as it is frustrating."

"What do you mean?" He figured what was about to be said, but he was going to let her lead the way. He actually had been expecting the conversation for a while.

"I do love being with you, I do. But..." She turned away to avoid the look on his face; one that seemed to be making it much harder to tell him how she truly felt. "There always seems to be one interruption after another. Granted they are all probably warranted, but of course I wouldn't know." She figured that she just needed to lay the cards all out on the table before she changed her mind. “You are always keeping me in the dark. I never get to know you or anything that you do.”

“You know that is all part of my responsibility.”

“Yes, yes I do know. But I want to take on part of that responsibility. I want to be someone that you can lean on or come to for comfort. I want to share that burden with you and help you realize that you are not alone; I am by your side. Right now, I am afraid I am nothing more than an amusement.”

“You know better than that. I am just dealing with a lot of things at the moment. Big things are happening and you just wouldn’t understand.”

“I don’t understand because you don’t even try. It goes back to secrets that were kept from me in the beginning before you revealed to me what you were.”

“That is not true.”

“Oh really; so tell me something. What were all those people doing here? Who were they?”

“They were my soldiers.” He hesitated. He really shouldn’t have used that word, soldier, but it was the first word that popped into his head.

“Soldiers? Why would you need soldiers?” The look on her face grew even more confused and frustrated. "More secrets."

“There is more going on than you can understand.” Once again, he brought up her lack of knowledge.

She threw her arms up in the air. “See! That is what I am talking about. Every time something comes up I get thrown aside or made to feel less important somehow.” She said, “I’m just tired of it.”

“Tessa, you are overreacting.” Greco tried to calm her down.

“I may be overreacting, but you have to realize that I have given up a lot of things to be with you. I have taken the fact that you are a vampire and I am okay with that. I am willing to be with you through thick and thin, no matter the cost. But you have to trust me. You have to let me in your life completely if you want me in your heart. It is a complete package. I give you all of me and you give me all of you. I want to know that you love me."

"You do know that I love you." Greco tried to pull her close to him. "But for security measures, I cannot just divulge things that are in regard to the vampire world."

"Is that because I am not one of you?"

He nodded. "I am afraid so." He tried to spin things in a positive light. "But it is not something that I alone have decided. We have an entire council that sets those rules and watches every decision I make. It is in your best interest not to be involved. You would only be a liability to them and possibly even sentenced to death if you leaked anything to anyone."

"God, it sounds as though you are in the middle of a war." Her frustration started to grab hold once again.

Greco was silent for a minute. "We are."

Her eyes grew big. "So you are telling me that you are in the middle of some huge war that I haven't even heard of? Who is it with? Can you even tell me that?"

"It is with a rival. We haven't seen eye to eye for quite some time." He stopped himself short. "But this is all that I can tell you. Since you are not a vampire everything is at risk. I seriously do not want to get you more involved than you need to be." He pulled her close and cupped her face in his hand, and looked intensely into her eyes. "I love you far too much for that."

A tear trickled down her right cheek, a look of despondence in her eyes. "I don't doubt that you love me. I know that you have shown your love unconditionally. I also know that each day we grow closer and closer. I even understand that you have been trying really hard to keep me protected, even if that means we cannot make love, as much as that pains me in itself." She touched his hand that was placed on her cheek ever so subtly. "I just don't know how much more I can take of this. I love you so much it hurts every time I am put in the dark. Every single day I have to live with that fact. I am not sure that I can do it anymore." Tears moved from a slight trickle to a smooth flow as she uttered those words. She had been thinking those things for a while, she just wasn't sure that she was ready to say them out loud.

Soft red tears began well up in Greco's eyes, a reminder how emotional he was when it came to Tessa. "Don't you think you are overreacting a bit?"

"It may seem like I am, and maybe that is the case. But no matter what, the fact that I am not even half involved in your life really hurts. I just don't see any of that changing anytime soon."

"I wish you would understand."

"Me too." She said as she removed his hand from her face and grabbed her keys from the table. After taking a deep breath Tessa said, "I'm going to the James and get a room. I will send for my things once I find a new place to stay."

"Tessa." Greco cried softly.

She shook her head and kept herself from crying even harder. "You have plenty of time to find someone else. I'm not really that important in the grand scope of things. I just know that I only have one lifetime to live and I want to share a life with someone as a whole entity, not just a piece." Tessa opened the door and took a step into the hallway.

Before Tessa could shut the door Greco muttered, "What if you had an eternity?"

Tessa stopped short and kept quiet. She waited to see if Greco had really said what she thought he did.

"Would you choose to be like me?"

She turned around. "You mean a vampire?"

Greco nodded. "Would you want to be like me forever? Could you?"

"Would it change our relationship? Would you still keep me in the dark?" Tessa asked. "If that were never to change then I don't want it. I would feel like I would be spending an eternity miserable and alone if none of that were to change."

"You wouldn't be alone." Greco answered.

"All I have ever asked for was to be with you as a loving companion, not just a guilty pleasure. I dealt with it for quite a while, but how could I not feel alienated, as my love for you has grown? It seems the more I love you, the more I realize our predicament; I just chose to ignore it until now. I'm tired of being hidden like a dirty little secret. I exist in your life and that is it. Forgive me for wanting more."

"If things did change, would you then take consideration?" He gently touched her.

"Does it even matter? All this is talk; the woulda, coulda, shoulda's. None of it matters because it could never happen." She moved his hand from her arm. She was afraid to even have him touch her because she knew that she would just fall right back into his arms. She was always drawn to him. "One thing that Isabel has made clear to me is that you are forbidden by The Nation to just turn every human you happen to want to turn, on a whim. I know it would be chaotic. That is one thing she won't stop talking about and that when her faithful servitude to you is completed she will be able to be with you forever."

Greco smirked as if imagining Isabel happily

becoming a vampire. "Isabel is correct with some of it. Normally the rules make it near to impossible to just go and create vampires whenever I felt like it. Everything has to be strategic and planned. It is a complicated process and one simple slip up could be disastrous in many different ways. Isabel has been with us for a few years. We have made it clear that if she stays as one of our familiars there will be a time when she will be considered to partake in the ritual of becoming a vampire." Greco paused. "But she has never been promised to continue to be a part of my life, specifically. She is quite imaginative in that part." He tried to reassure her.

"So if it is that complicated than why are you even bringing this up to me? I have never pledged my allegiance to you or your people."

"But you have done that, at least to me."

"How is that?"

"You have given me your love; in that sense you have pledged to me your heart. I find that loyalty." He shook his head. "I would hate to see that love disappear. I have not loved anybody this much in a long time. I want to make things okay with us. I don't want to see you walk out that door. The only thing that I feel will keep you from doing that is bringing you into my world fully, even if that means giving you eternal life." He lowered his head and muttered, "Even if that means going against The Nation's wishes."

"That could cause a lot of damage. I don't think that is something that you need to be dealing with, not if you have a war going on."

"It is much more complicated than just a war. But I think that The Nation views me as a strong leader, and will not risk losing me. I have been loyal to them for far too long for that and they do understand I am not one to just quickly jump into something before I think."

"I wouldn't want you to get into that kind of predicament."

"If I can be with you, it will be worth it." He looked at her with the most innocent of eyes. Tessa felt as if he was trying to give her a glimpse of his soul that lay deep down inside of him.

She stopped and thought for a few minutes. When she finally spoke, Greco perched on every possible word that would come out. "I just don't see how this would work out like that. There is so much more than the fact that we want to be together."

Greco's ears perked up. "Does this mean that you would want to be with me?"

"That is not what I was saying." She tried to backpedal just a little bit. It seemed as thought Greco was not hearing everything that was coming out of her mouth.

"That is all that matters to me." Greco came face to face with her. "Don't you see that as long as you want to be with me and I want to be with you? I will do whatever it takes to make that happen."

"Turning me into a vampire is what it will resort to?" Tessa struggled with herself to grasp the situation.

"I want to make you my eternal lover, to be my queen."

Tessa stopped short. "You want me to be your queen?" She sighed. It seemed like everything was just coming at her from different corners of her mind and it was beginning to weigh heavily on her.

Greco nodded. "In my world I am the equivalent of a king. We live as though we had long ago. I am the leader of the Levé's and for me to take on a life-partner; she must be willing to my queen, to help in my reign."

Tessa sat down on the couch. "This is just so much

for me to process. I don't think that I would be someone that would be a good leader. That is the last thing that I would want. All I know is that I want to be with you." She started to cry again.

Greco stroked her hair trying to comfort her some more. "Let's not focus on any of that. I shouldn't have even brought it up to you."

"How could you not? You have a very important role and you need to have a very important person by your side. I am most definitely not that person."

Greco got eye to eye with her. "I don't want you to worry about that. I just want you to think of you and me. Think of the connection that we have had since the moment we met. I love you with every last bit of my heart and will do anything to make sure you understand that. I can only hope that you feel the same way about me. I want us to get past this and move on." He smiled at her sincerely. "Will you be my eternal love?"

Tessa couldn't help but smile just for a second. "Is this a proposal?" She knew that in some way it was and maybe that is how she needed to view it as such.

"If you look at it like that then I suppose it is." *How could he not have realized that was exactly what he was doing? He was pledging his forever love and that constituted a proposal.*

Tessa felt that was something she could understand better. "Greco," she took a deep breath "I am going to have to think about this." She chimed in quickly, "But this does not mean I will say no. I just have to give myself a little bit of time to think things through."

Greco accepted her answer and shook his head. "Of course. I understand. It is a very tough decision to just make in the matter of minutes." He clasped his fingers with hers. "I just want to make things right between us."

Tessa nodded. "I know, Greco." She smiled faintly.

"But I do think that for the time being I need to be alone with my thoughts, so I will go ahead and go over to the hotel."

"How much time do you need?"

She shrugged, "I don't know. But I can tell you one thing. I am not walking out this door and out of your life. No matter what decision I make I will come to you with it. I promise you that." It was her way to reassure him she would not just placate to him so she can leave without any more argument. She kissed him tenderly on the lips and made her way out the door.

* * * * *

Tessa stood outside the penthouse door. It was the moment that would stay in her mind through till the end of time. Once she walked through those doors, the girl she was, the life she had, would forever cease to exist. She could never go back. Tessa knew, though, she had nothing left to go back to. Her parents were dead, her sister was no longer a part of her life, and she really had no close friends. She only had Greco. He loved her unconditionally and she did not want to be without him.

She knew that she was ready for the next chapter of her life, her awakening. From that point forward, she would never look at things the same. The Tessa she knew and once was, died in that back alleyway where she should have hemorrhaged to death, if it weren't for Greco.

She breathed in heavily and exhaled a second breathe until there was none left. She knocked softly. Greco answered with a smile. A smile so sweet and loving. Greco had spared no expense or sentiment. He knew he loved her and wanted her to know that. What was about to take place was a one-time thing; the most special of occasions, for both of them. There was no turning back, and hopefully no remorse.

Tessa continued into the penthouse. The room was filled with candlelight that danced seductively on the walls; the aroma of flowers and incense filled the room with intoxication, and the sound of soothing harmony mixed with deep rhythm filled the air with songs of a time long past.

Before Tessa took a step further, Greco reached around her waist and pulled her into his arms. "I am glad you are here."

She gazed up into his deep dark eyes. "I couldn't think of a better place to be."

"Are you sure of this?"

"I've never been so sure of anything in my life." She thought for a moment. "No pun intended."

A smiled formed on Greco's face for only a moment before disappearing once again. "I want you to be serious. I want you to know the full extent of what will happen."

"I do understand, Greco. I really do. I just want to think about us being together. I want to make love to you with nothing holding us back. I want to endure whatever it takes to be with you completely."

"You know it is much more than that. It will be painful, it will be terrifying, and it will be sad, but also glorious, wonderful, and complete all at the same time."

"Yes, I do know."

Greco handed her a glass of wine. She showed no interest in it.

"I would suggest you have a few glasses. It will make things a little easier for you." He handed it to her one more time.

She took a few sips to appease Greco then set it down.

"Keep drinking. I added a little something extra to help relax you just a little more."

Tessa nodded and finished her wine. She placed it on the table beside the bed. As she braced herself on the bed, Greco leaned into her. She closed her eyes as his hand gently held her head in a sweet embrace, while their lips and tongues move in synchronicity. His other hand moved slowly up her side then he pulled her towards him, now kissing her even deeper with more passion. Her breasts pushed tight up against his chest, practically heaving from the seductive top she had been wearing for her very special occasion. It did not take long before the two of them were pressed flesh against flesh. Tessa and Greco had gotten this far before. He had gotten better at controlling himself, which was true. Sometimes it almost seemed like she dealt with a teenager, always seeing how far one can get without backing out. It always was so hard for Greco when her heart started pumping faster and harder, followed with an abundance of pheromones. It was peak feeding time for him. Senses were at their highest point and the blood tasted the sweetest. That time it was different. He was truly showing Tessa the love that she deserved and wanted. They threw off their clothes in between the passionate kisses and touches.

His desire became more intense as they began making love. They were truly making magic. Greco felt his primal instincts awaken the closer and closer they climbed towards ecstasy. He started rapidly breathing and almost lost control. He gazed down at Tessa as she locked eyes with him. She saw his pupils fill out and start to be circled with a golden color. Everything was perfect for her. She reached her hands around Greco's back as she felt completely lost in the moment. She pressed her fingernails into his back, slowly dragging them down as she let out a few loud moans. That was the breaking point that lead to the next level. She signaled her satisfaction. His mouth watered in anticipation as his fangs grew dripping wet. A low growl came out as he looked hard at her. His animal nature came out as he bore his teeth. This did not frighten her. She sat up and said, "I'm ready, Greco."

Greco took that cue and situated himself behind her and smelt the sweetness of strawberries in her hair as she moved it out of the way. He traced his fingers at the pulse point on her neck and felt her heartbeat begin to escalate. She was nervous, which she had every right to be.

"Are you absolutely sure you want to do this?"

"Yes, Greco I am."

That was his final cue. He brought his right arm around her front and braced her as he bared his fangs and punctured her neck. It hurt Tessa for just a moment, but then it felt as though she was in some kind of dream. She felt more tired as the feeding continued. Tiredness turned into fear and she began to panic. Immediately she attempted to pull away, an automatic reaction. Greco held her even more firmly. He knew all too well of the fear that comes along with a humans life force being drained from them. Tessa's fight began to get weaker as she ultimately gave up. Greco felt her breath slow almost to a complete stop. That was where it became tricky and had to be precise. He slashed his wrist with his fingernail and pressed it to Tessa's lips. "You must drink."

She shook her head in protest, but he forced her to drink his blood. "I am not going to let you die! You wanted to go down this path and I will not give up now." He held his wrist right against her lips forcefully until she began taking the blood from it on her own. After a while, it seemed quite easy for her to drink from his wound. When it seemed as though enough of his blood was in her system, he went back to emptying her body of her own blood. He was replacing hers with his, which would make her as eternal as he was. He felt the last bit of worth from her veins and pulled away, almost scared to make any mistake that would take her from him forever. He knew that if he had taken too much too soon, she would never awaken. If he was to not take all of her blood at the most intricate of times, she could turn into something much worse than a vampire; more like a zombie. Greco paid no attention to the few droplets of blood that dropped toward her. The drops trickled down the side of her neck; all but one continuing down the collarbone. A few drops made their way into an open wound just in time to be absorbed back into her body before she started to heal herself. Greco took notice of the excess blood, but only happened to wipe off what remained; not knowing of the most simple of events would change the course of history forever. He turned back to Tessa who was beginning to get engulfed in his offering. He knew she would have to stop soon or he would succumb to a deep sickness. Turning a human took a lot out a vampire, especially when done the more traditional way, even for an elder vampire.

Greco pulled his wrist away from Tessa and wiped the blood from her lips. Only moments later his wound sealed up completely. She looked at him, mostly dazed. He moved her up onto the pillows to try to make it more comfortable before her body started changing. At that very moment she looked so innocent and peaceful, a part that she will hardly remember after what would happen soon after. He knew the next few days would be the most terrible pain that she probably ever had gone through, or ever would. He had prepared well for this, knowing that he would have to stay by her bedside throughout the entire transformation assuring her safe transition. He had locked both of them up as if they were sealed into a vault, under strict orders to not be disturbed no matter what. None of his actions were condoned by The Vampire Nation; he was going to take his chances after the fact.

It wasn't but a few hours later, Tessa began to show signs that the changing was taking effect. Her body began to break in sweats and with fever, as it was trying to cope with the idea of non-human blood. That battle was never won, which then came the first of many terrible stages. She couldn't stop herself from vomiting every free breath she had, once again a slow reaction to her body realizing it was dying. More hours passed by, in which she rested. Sharp pains shot through her body as if she were being severely beaten. This went on for almost half a day. Her entire body was doing nothing but screaming out in agony and there was nothing anybody could do about it. Again she rested. On the second day she awoke to even more terrible pains than the ones she had before. Those pains were uncontrollable followed by strange images that flashed through her mind.

Greco had not been in the room at that time, he was cleaning up the mess that she had made when her body lost every muscle control of life, including the emptying of the bladder and bowels. That did not bother him, as he knew that was the process of death before rebirth.

When he entered the room he found Tessa naked on the floor curled up in the fetal positional. He quickly rushed to her, realized what kind of pain she was having at that moment. Since her body had already died, it had to be her hunger. For the first time in her vampire life, she was in desperate need for blood.

The agony of the hunger was much more than Tessa could handle, especially since she did not know it was hunger she felt. All she knew was that she had excruciating surges throughout her body, and deathly images flashed through her mind.

Greco pulled her up onto the bed and laid her back down. There was only one thing that he could do, and that was to feed her with his blood once again. He slit his wrist and watched as she suckled at the lifeblood that flowed out of his veins. She looked as though she were a newborn puppy pulling milk from its mother's nipple. He knew that he needed to feed her a few more times until she was ready to be amongst the undead.

It wasn't until the third day that Tessa fully awoke. She had most control over her body, and she felt very refreshed. As soon as she opened her eyes, a rush of vivid color and aura's appeared before her. She had to blink a few times before she could fully adjust to the world in high definition. She could hear the sound of a faucet dripping in the kitchen, which annoyed her slightly. She noticed an intoxicating scent pulling her to the man beside her. It was Greco's scent. It was very sweet and empowering, almost hypnotic.

"Hello, love. How are you feeling?"

"Much better."

"I think you have gone through the worst of it."

"I do hope so." She sat up. "It was completely unbearable." Tears flooded her eyes. "I know you told me how much it would hurt, but I really didn't understand what you mean until now."

Greco stroked the hair out of her eyes. "Until you experience it yourself, there really is no way for anybody to be prepared." He felt that he should explain to her what had happened. "Unfortunately, when you are turning into a vampire, you do not get the luxury of death, only its most terrible of problems. Your body is empty of active blood so it starts to die. The first thing that happens is your body reacts quite viciously, since it cannot stop any illnesses from attacking. My blood, which now courses through your veins, confused it enough that it attempted to keep working. Eventually your organs started shutting down one by one. That is where is started getting painful, and somewhat embarrassing, since every muscle in your body ceases to work." He continued on. "When that is successful, your body then takes a cue from the new blood running through your veins and realizes it will need to replenish that to keep functioning. That is what your other pain was; your dire need for blood, which I fed you with my own, following the rules of turning a human into a vampire."

"Am I through? Will I have to go through with anything else?"

Greco stood up from the bed. He held out his hand for her to take it. He handed her a robe and they walked into the bathroom where a young woman was lying in the bathtub with a big cut on her neck, barely breathing. Tessa gasped and turned her face into his chest.

"This is all a part of being a vampire Tessa. You knew this."

"I knew it, but I still am shocked. I thought that I would be drinking blood from bottles, like you do."

"Yes, that is true. I do drink my blood mostly from bottles, like fine wine. But I also know how to hunt, how to survive. You too need to know how to do that. Hunting and feeding is in your nature. It is something that should be done, although it is best for only occasions due to the fact that authorities would notice a terrible rise in human deaths."

She shook her head. "I can't do it. Not now. I just

can't." At that moment the hunger pains started coming back. She doubled over in severe distress.

"See. You need to feed. You have no choice."

"I can feed off of you." Tessa moved closer to Greco.

"No!" He pulled away from her. "You are no longer to feed off of me. You *must* take her blood before she dies or you will truly hurt and there is nothing I will do for you."

"You will let me die?"

"It would not be my choice. You are the one to choose whether to survive or not. And the only thing standing in your way is that body in the tub."

Tessa looked the girl over a few more times. Not certain as of how to go about it, she went over to the body, and looked up at Greco.

"I will walk you through this. I will be able to teach you how to be a vampire. I will make you proud of what you have become." He smiled. "But for now, I want you to start sucking her blood through the open wounds on her neck."

She did exactly as she was told, and it did not take long for her to get the hang of things. She had finally done it. She had become a vampire. From that point on she could be with Greco for all eternity, if they so chose to do so. The Tessa of old, the Emma that disappeared before that, was completely dead. What stood there before her in the mirror was a blood hungry predator that was more miraculous than any other creature on earth. Her time was coming.

PART III

CHAPTER EIGHT

"My Queen, the soldiers have returned from the out lands." A scraggly pale man scampered into the main hall of Tessa's modern 'castle'; one that happened to be the center of the Levé Empire.

"Well, what are you waiting for? Send them in!" Tessa waved to the fearful gent. It had been three years since Greco's assassination. She had ruled over her new land alone for the entire time. The four that stood in front of her were her strongest soldiers, ones that she felt she could completely trust to carry out her orders without question, and give her complete loyalty.

Tessa looked around at all the people in the room. "You are excused." She looked specifically at the man who announced the arrival, "and shut the door behind you. We do not want to be disturbed."

Once the doors were shut, Tessa looked at the four. 'Get up already!" They all stood on their feet. "You know that I dislike all this formality."

"But you are the queen of the Levé's." Spoke Bade, the most loyal of them all.

"And you are my kinsmen. Greco may have been okay with all this King and Queen stuff, but I would be completely satisfied if we could all just work together towards our main goal. I don't rule you, I guide you." She shook her head and sighed. "I wish you would all understand that."

Tessa looked to Drake, the most mysterious one of the bunch. He was tall, lean, and smoldering. His hair and eyes were as dark as possible, with a face completely chiseled; a person would have thought he had been carved out of stone. He was the most cunning of the four. “What news do you have for me?” She decided to get down to business.

“We have succeeded in neutralizing another city.” said Drake.

“Wonderful.” She said with a smile. “And the humans?”

“Unfortunately most of them fought with quite a bit of resistance. We only brought in a couple of hundred.” Vala spoke up. She was always one to not hold back what she thought, sometimes to a fault. She was the swiftest of them all. Her entire body moved like the winds of night; her long dark hair enshrouded her body like a veil of camouflage.

Tessa sighed once again. “That will have to do, I suppose.” She began to pace. “You know, I wonder why they fight so hard. All we have ever wanted to do was to have them understand us. The violence in the beginning was, by all means, a necessary evil. But you would think they would have stopped fighting by now and start listening so that we can continue towards the goal of equality.”

Andreas walked up to Tessa. Being the strongest of them all did not mean that he didn’t have a kind heart. He always was one to sympathize with Tessa’s plight. “Those words don’t sound like your own. It sounds more like The Nation’s ideas.” He gazed deep into Tessa’s eyes to catch her attention. “I know that your compassion for the humans is something very strong.”

Tessa’s response was to turn around and shake her head. “You give me too much credit. I know what I am here for, and I know what my duties are. I am only trying to fulfill Greco’s dream.”

Bade decided to speak up; “I agree with Tessa. She

knew what we were doing from the beginning, and the future outlook is what is important. All this bloodshed, these wars are for the greater good of both vampire and human species." He had always been the most quiet and reserved. He was a breed of special circumstances. He grew up in the Dark Ages into a family of pagan priests that called themselves Mystics. They practiced all sorts of magic and worked synonymously with nature itself. Bade became a vampire to unite the two orders together. His descendants still continued their practices throughout Romania. He was one of the most respected vampires due to the fact that he spoke with and listened to nature, and seemed almost able to control the elements. With his pale hair and kind eyes, nobody would even think for one second that he was a blood brother.

"Thank you Bade. I appreciate your backing; although I respect and understand each and every one of your concerns," she looked at the other three. "Is there anything else that I need to know?"

Andreas looked at Vala, then spoke, "There is one more piece of news."

"Well, go on." Said Tessa.

"We have caught wind of the whereabouts of one of the strongholds regarding the Independent Freedom Fighters." Vala spoke up.

"Have you now? And what piece of news do you bring me?" Tessa raised her eyebrow in interest.

Andreas nodded. "There is a small town at the southern tip of Illinois. It was one of the cities that we took control over a year ago."

"I thought we took care of most of the people there."

"As did we; but there seems to be a new leader of these fighters. The only name that we could gather was Melinda Baldwin."

Tessa had a look of horror upon her face. *Melinda Baldwin.* She hadn't heard that name in such a long time. She was certain it was the sister that she had been looking for all this time. She lost touch with Melinda after their meeting in the hospital. She knew that her sister was going to marry a man named Michael Baldwin, so *of course it had to be her.* She had been looking for her for a while, trying to make amends, never finding her.

"Have we subdued her yet?" Tessa asked.

"Not yet." Said Vala. "We have forces in there taking care of this as we speak. We are planning on leaving after our meeting with you to help take care of the situation."

"Then I plan on going with you." Tessa walked towards the group.

"Are you out of your mind?" Andreas asked. "You would be targeted before we even left the confines of our region. It would be too dangerous for you."

"I think that you worry too much." She dismissed the concern.

"You just have never gone out with us regarding these matters. I thought that is what you entrusted us to do?" Bade was slightly confused.

"Well, let's say that I have a personal issue with this particular matter."

"Do you know this Melinda?" Vala asked.

"We go way back." Tessa thought back to their childhood and happy times. Of course the bad memories took over the good ones with the betrayal and finally the parting of their ways. "Anyway, let's get on the road."

The five of them traveled as far as they could before it got to be sunlight and decided to rest until dusk. They found a safe haven not too far north of Benton, their destination.

As soon as the sun started going down, they prepared for the final part of their journey. Tessa covered herself up in a velvet cloak. It wasn't in her best interest to let everyone know that the Queen was venturing out into the outlands. A simple vampire was something of the norm and they were feared. If someone caught wind that she was outside of her haven, the opportunity of assassination would be too important to not attempt it.

Once at the destination they got out of their car, the four soldiers carrying their protective arms. Two seconds after Tessa got out of the vehicle, a band of rebels began to attack from behind them. Andreas instructed Tessa to run to safety while they began to fight them off. Tessa ran into a small home, one that looked abandoned. When she got into the building to hide she heard the faint sound of breathing. She followed the sound into the kitchen. In the kitchen she looked behind the table fallen against the wall and noticed a frightened little girl, eyes as blue as day and hair that could only be assumed to be brown since it was covered in dirt.

"What is your name?" Tessa asked in a soft tone. It had been a while since she had seen a human child, especially one so young.

Only silence came from the girl. She noticed the child's eyes darted around looking for the quickest escape route.

"I'm not going to hurt you." Tessa tried unsuccessfully to sound comforting. "I have no reason to hurt any of you children." She held out her hand. "Come with me. I will protect you."

The little girl shook her head in fear and cried out. "No!"

Just at that moment a man came running into the kitchen with two soldiers behind him. "Leave her alone!

She's just a baby." The two soldiers subdued him and Tessa noticed the look upon his face. It was fear, but not the fear of dying. Instead it was the fear of something happening to that child. He had a connection to her.

Tessa circled the man, who was pushed down and positioned on his knees. "Yes, I noticed that she is a child. So that makes me put into a quandary as of why you would even think of attacking us with such young babes in harms way."

"I believe it was your kind that started the attack. I am just trying to keep this innocent little five year old from dying, or worse, become a slave to you and your mindless bloodsucking band."

Tessa became outraged and pulled a dagger from her bosom; it was custom made per her orders. She had begun to carry the blade more often since her responsibilities grew daily and the idea of an attack left her with no option. She held it to his neck as the soldiers held him tight from behind.

"So you would rather her watch me slit your throat, drink every last drop from your body all while you struggle helplessly to your death?"

"Emma!" Just then there was a blood-curdling scream from the back door; Tessa stopped in mid motion of pressing the blade further into the man's throat.

"Shut up human." One of the vampire guards pushed the newly captured woman to the ground.

"Melinda, she's okay, I promise." The man said and looked into the Queen's eyes.

Tessa studied him quickly and withdrew the dagger, and turned her back to the woman. "Let the child and her mother go to the town center together, until we gather everyone to take back home with us."

The little girl got up quickly then ran to her mother, held her tight before they were taken away. One of the vampires grabbed hold of the man tighter the moment they were gone.

Tessa walked up to him. "Who are they to you?"

He looked at her defiantly and didn't speak a word. She nodded to one of the henchmen. On cue he twisted the man's arm around and let him scream for a moment, then relaxed enough for Tessa to ask the question again.

He looked up at Tessa with both hate and fear in his eyes. "My brother's wife and her daughter."

Tessa still looked at him. A bit of moonlight touched her face. He had a questioning look on his face, almost as if he had a sense of recognition.

"Do I, or did I know you?" He asked.

Tessa quickly covered her face with the hood of her cloak. "Doubtful." She turned around to look out the window. "You said he was, as in past tense."

"My brother was killed last year when your kind invaded. This left me to try to take care of Melinda and her two children, since you had the decency to leave them fatherless." He said angrily.

"So you have stepped up to the plate and have taken the place of their father. Interesting." She turned back around. "Have you been taking care of the widow?"

"That is what I said." He cocked his head at her, his blue eyes full of sadness and were completely void of that spark of life humanity was known for. "Is there a reason you are asking me these stupid questions?"

"Just curiosity. I was feeling out your sense of loyalty." She looked at the two vampire soldiers. "Find the other child then take them along with his family back to Chicago. I have plans for them all." She stepped up to the man. "Especially you," she paused, "I didn't get your name."

"Isaac."

"Well Isaac, I have special plans for you." She

motioned for them to take him away. Once they all left she stood in the empty kitchen with only her thoughts. She realized that she finally found her sister after all the years of searching. With her and her family back in her life there was no way she was going to let them get away again. She was going to keep them safe like a babe pressed against its mother's bosom. The hard part was how she was to proceed with letting Melinda know who she was. Her main fear, and probable outcome, was that Melinda would be appalled at what Tessa had become. So she had to tread very lightly on that journey into the next chapter of her life.

* * * * *

A week went by and Tessa had found herself caught up in the daily troubles of the multiple wars that had been waged right outside her very walls. On one side there were the Krones. Ever since Greco was murdered and Desdemona was given a guilty sentence, the two clans had become sworn enemies. Desdemona had loyal followers and underlings that were not going to let their new found power diminish anytime soon. They knew that their loyalty to their fallen queen was unquestionable and she would have wanted them to fight for her. There was always some sort of attack. It was all about territory and control, and that was something that The Vampire Nation could not keep hold of between the two clans, their efforts dwindled as it became obvious things would not die down. It was a major blood feud and winner was to take all. They decided that although they needed to deal with them regarding trade, and to continue their quest for domination, that they were going to stay out of the conflict as much as possible.

Then there were the rebels; self-dubbed the

Independent Freedom Fighters. They were the strong-willed humans willing to fight and sacrifice themselves for the greater good of their species. Although their numbers were small, they were a thorn in the side of Tessa's big plan. They made it more difficult in taking down cities and bringing them into her rule. She more often than not succeeded in her ultimate goal, but they made it quite difficult. As soon as she brought one down, another would pop up, almost as if they had become a virus spreading amongst the little people.

Her world had become so complicated in the last three years. If she had known what she was getting into, she probably would have opted out of becoming a vampire altogether. A lot of nights she spent staring out her window out into the vast city. But instead of seeing the bustling of thousands of people, it was desolate. All the humans were tucked away in their buildings being reconditioned to live their new lives. Lives with hope, promise, and understanding. Actually it was more of an understanding that they would forever be under the rule of the vampires.

Many thoughts circled in her mind. *What have I gotten myself into? I know I'm not fit to rule. Maybe Isabel was right all along. I had no right being by Greco's side. It was supposed to be her honor. Would things be different if that had happened? Would the rule not be full of doubt?* Those were the questions she always asked herself.

That night was just like all the others. All she wanted to do was to stay locked up in her home, but all the duties preceded anything that she wanted. She had people waiting in the main hall to speak with her regarding what everyone seemed to consider to be important of business matters. Her warriors awaited the next order of where to go and what to do. But until then, she was going to spend the next few minutes all to herself.

The minutes alone were very few. Bryon opened the door to the penthouse. He brought behind him Isaac who was tied up with a new kind of binding and was still wearing his tattered clothes from when they picked him up in the desolate city. Bryon pushed him on his knees. "Bow before your Queen."

"She is not my Queen; she is just an infestation, nothing more." Venomous words spouted from his lips.

"Curb your tongue." Bryon raised his voice and gave him a hard blow to the face.

"Enough, Bryon. You can leave now." Tessa said, somewhat appalled at her assistant's actions. It was as though he was already a turned vampire. The years had been harsh for him after the culling happened. His duties tripled and his fear for his family's safety made him even more determined to make sure things went as smoothly as they could. He easily had no feeling toward the humans anymore. His loyalty very much lied with her.

Bryon walked out of the penthouse and shut the double doors behind him.

Tessa held onto Isaac's arm. "You can get up now. Bryon tends to be overly formal sometimes."

Isaac felt the place on his jaw that Bryon hit. "Honestly I feel as though I am in medieval times. Queens, slaves, all things of that sort; never did I have a clue that I would actually be living in a time like this."

"It is just the process of the things for right now." She looked at him. "Did you know that King Victor was once a true king in Russia?" Tessa went around lighting candles. Fire, wooden stakes, garlic, crosses, and anything else one could imagine. None of that was completely true. Fire just happened to be just another one of those myths about what vampires feared. It was true that they did burn but it was just silly to be afraid of a little flame. Sunlight and silver were the best methods of course."

"And what about you? Were you ever a great Queen?"

She laughed softly.

"No, not me. I was only turned ten years ago. My maker and my King..." She paused; all those wonderful memories of him came flooding back. "Greco; he was over two thousand years old. He was a very wise man."

"Sounds like you really loved him." At that moment Tessa saw a true human being in front of her. Every time she forgot about compassion, it crept up on her. That time it was in the form of a human at his most humbling moment.

"Yes, I did." Tessa turned to looked at Isaac, who was studying her once more. "But enough of that, I want to hear more about you. Your organization."

"My organization? Up until the invasion started I was working in a small town clinic, I wasn't as big of a doctor as Michael but I was getting there. I moved back home to be close to my family. I did what I could to tend to all the sick and injured. People all around me kept dying, were captured, or turned. When my brother died I vowed to take care of Melinda and her two children."

"How..." Tessa paused. "Human of you." She stroked her chin in a quandary. "So you are not really a part of this rebellion. Not at all a part of those Freedom Fighters that wish to have your human existence be thoroughly erased for the sake of being free from enslavement."

No, I am not." He shook his head. "You said that you were turned just ten years ago." He took the conversation in a different direction.

"That's right."

"Have you forgotten human compassion? Why do you keep killing so many innocent people?"

She walked behind him. "It is not my wish to become a murderer."

"Then why do it?"

"It is a terrible misfortune when it comes to being the top species. Those that are dying are the ones fighting us, unwilling to cooperate with the new ways. So they die to make room for followers, or at least instill enough fear to get cooperation."

"You will never have true compassion will you?"

She stopped pacing. "I spared your life, is that not a sign of some compassion?"

Isaac thought for a moment. "Why was that? Your kind is ruthless, thoughtless, yet you did not kill me." He had a quick thought. "You weren't doing it for me were you? Something changed your mind."

"You overanalyze. I just simply felt like saving your slaughter for a time that better suited me."

"No I think it was something else."

"You try my patience," she said as she began to get aggravated.

"Then why is it that you have brought me here?"

Tessa could not ask the questions she had wanted; not then, he would surely know why she was asking them. She had a stern look on her face, "I wanted to tell you that you have become my servant and that all your loyalties will belong to me from this day forth."

"And if I refuse?"

Her eyed glowed and she came face to face with Isaac, "Then I will suck every last drop of your blood from your veins until your heart beats no more."

Isaac exposed his neck and puffed out his chest in defiance. "So do it, what's stopping you?"

"Be wary young fool. I don't take kindly to bluffs." She leaned in closer and whispered in his ear, "What would your brother think of you for leaving his family on their own, all so that you could justify your foolish pride?"

"You bitch!" He raged as he attempted to hit her with his bound hands. She backed up just out of reach.

She laughed a wicked laugh and called to Bryon. He picked up Isaac, and Isaac screamed to her, "You leave them alone. They have done nothing to you!"

"Goodbye." Tessa waved an enthusiastic farewell while the evil grin stayed on her lips.

As Bryon led Isaac out of the room, his niece and nephew were brought in. Isaac gave a mortified look in Tessa's direction, which almost telepathically told her that she dare not harm one hair on their heads. Of course she glanced away making it obvious his threats meant nothing.

"Please, have a seat." Tessa smiled as she studied the children. She immediately thought about how she would have loved seeing them grow up and a part of their lives. "Do you want some cookies?" She pointed toward the tray on the coffee table.

Emma reached out for them and her older brother pulled her hand back. He said, in a cold tone, "No thank you. Our mom has already told us that we are to have nothing to do with you, and that includes anything you offer."

"Well, that's too bad then isn't it? That's not very nice of her to say that about someone she doesn't even know." Tessa sat down in a chair directly across from the two, who were huddled together on the couch.

The boy pulled his sister close to him, but she pushed away. "Emma!" He yelled out.

"What?" She snapped back at him. "She isn't going

to hurt me." At that moment Tessa couldn't help but gaze at the child. There she was sitting in front of her, not realizing that Tessa was very woman she was named after; to honor her.

"You don't know that." He said with a bit of panic in the tone of his voice; he was attempting to look strong and protective of his sister, his fear held just below the surface.

Emma turned to Tessa, "Are you going to hurt me?"

Tessa shook her head. "On the contrary; I want to help you."

"Your kind doesn't help our kind; you just kill us." The boy, who was no older than ten, snapped.

"You are quite mistaken, young man. What's you're name?"

He didn't answer so Emma spoke up for him. "Jason." He punched her lightly on the arm.

"I wouldn't have brought you here if I didn't have a plan for you and Emma."

Jason listened, slightly curious. "And what is that?"

"Besides feeding, clothing you, and giving you adequate shelter, I want to send you to school. I truly want this next generation of children to trust and know the vampire, not to be afraid of us because we just happened to be something that is beyond your understanding."

"And what is it we have to do?" His guard lowered a small bit.

"Love me; listen to me. Spread my word amongst the young ones. Try to show them that this world is not much different that the one that was previously ruled by the humans. We are merely here to make our existence known amongst your people, and the only way for us to keep ourselves from being slaughtered was to take over. There were too many of our kind vanishing due to all the hunters out there, or people were too frightened of us before even understanding what we were. This time, we're at the top of the evolutionary charts. It's all about change."

"Why do you treat us all like slaves then?" Jason asked.

Tessa looked at him. *He looks just like his father.* "In all due time we will be back to being equals; this is the way that it all works. Read up on your vampire history." Tessa got an idea and went to the bookshelf in the corner. She pulled out a red leather bound book that looked a little worn for parts.

"What's this?" Jason asked as she put it on the coffee table. He was beginning to get interested in what she had to say.

"This is something that I want you to read. It is the history of the vampires, as we know it, including all the massacres of our people throughout history. This book belonged to my mate, Greco, but I will loan it to you until you get your own when you start school." Her sweet voice lowered the boy's guard even further.

"We start school soon?" Emma was very happy; she practically jumped up and down. "I've never been to school." She was around the age that she would have started kindergarten.

"Well this will be perfect for you." Tessa smiled and touched the brown locks of hair on Emma's head. She looked so much like her mother that it almost brought tears to her eyes and memories flooded back. "You start next Monday. And guess what?"

"What?" Emma eagerly awaited the response, as though she was about to get a great big surprise.

"Your mommy is going to be working at the school that you are going to. That way you can stay close to her and she can keep watch over the two of you."

"Yay!" Emma clapped.

"Now, it is getting late, so off to bed for the two of you." Bryon gathered the children.

Tessa watched as Jason grabbed the book off the table and held it close to him when they walked out the door. *There they go. The last shreds of my humanity.*

* * * * *

"Where are the kids?" Melinda glanced up from the sofa with a very worried looked on her face. Isaac had just been dropped off into their apartment, after his meeting with Tessa.

He shook his head and said, "They're in with Tessa."

"And you just let that happen?" She gave him a very wild look, almost accusatory.

"Like I had a choice; if you remember correctly I was bound and drug out of here like a piece of cattle." He walked over to her and sat down beside her, and draped his arm around her to comfort her.

She leaned into him, tears rolled down her face. "I just don't know what to do. I'm so scared. They're my babies."

"I don't think she'll do anything to the kids. She doesn't seem like that would be on her agenda. She didn't kill any of us back when they found us, now did they? I think that she has other plans, and those kids are probably the bulk of it."

"Like that is supposed to make me feel better." She moaned.

"Well, it is the best we can hold onto at the moment. It will bide our time until we can get a handle on our situation."

"And what is our situation? Are we guests, prisoners, donors, or snacks? Take your pick." She sounded full of panic and confusion.

"That's what we'll need to find out." Isaac pulled away from Melinda, enough to make her look him in the eye. "Besides, don't you think it would be great recon for you to send back to the rebels? What is better than an inside man?"

Her eyes twinkled with hope. "You are right. All I need to do is find someone with connections to the outside." She stood up. "And I'll be working at the school starting Monday. That will give me a chance to walk around and get a feel for who I can trust." She sounded more confident.

"See, now that's the Melinda I know. Always thinking about the cause and becoming pro-active." Isaac forced a smile on his face.

"That's me." She grinned. "And I suppose our cause includes you playing dress up." Melinda laughed and pointed to some clothes folded up on the lounge chair.

"What's that?" He walked over and started looking through them. One piece after another was black upon black.

"They said it was your new uniform." She laughed.

"Uniform?" He looked at the clothes. "I suppose it could have been worse. I had this strange fear that I was going to get stuck into some latex pants, chains, and a dog collar." He laughed. All their laughter was there to masque the worry that each of them had for the children, not knowing exactly what was going on with their visit with Tessa.

"Now that would be interesting to see." Melinda began to laugh, but before she could even get it out, her kids came through the door. She ran to them and hugged them tightly. "Are you guys okay? She didn't hurt you did she? Did she tell you what she wants with us?" She looked them over from head to toe to make sure they were completely unharmed.

Emma said, “She just wants us to go to school and learn about them.”

“Just like that, huh?” Melinda looked at Jason. “And what are your thoughts of her?”

Jason shrugged. “She wasn’t that scary. She seemed okay.”

“And that’s all she said to you. That you were going to school and learn?”

“Yes, mom.” Jason rolled his eyes and showed Melinda the old book. “She gave us this also. She said something about the whole vampire history. I don’t know why she gave it to me since she said we would be learning it in school.”

Melinda took the book from him “Let me see that.” She gazed at the cover of the book, the color of blood. It had a raised emblem on the cover, the same symbol that she had seen through the seized territories. Melinda traced her fingers across the binding and felt the age of the book. She turned back to her two children and said, “How about we not worry about this book? I would rather you not have to learn anything unnecessary.” She threw the book onto the coffee table and hugged her kids again. “Now let's get you off to bed. It is getting quite late.”

After the three of them were already down the hall, Isaac picked the book up off the table. It almost seemed as though it was calling out to him. He felt the history beneath the pages. Inside it was sure to note each triumph and each defeat. There was something about that very book and he knew that he was supposed to read it. Isaac took it back to his room and put it behind the headboard of his bed so that nobody would be able to find it there. He knew that the only way that he was to ever understand the vampires was to know all about them and to find out their weaknesses so they could successful escape the city.

* * * * *

A few years had gone by. Every day was more of the same for all. Emma and Jason were typical school children. The human school was a bit different than the one Tessa remembered going to when she was a kid, but she knew that they would get the education they needed to be able to function in the new word given to them. Melinda had become successfully a secret confidant to the outside world. It took her time to find someone of trust, but when she did she began a complete network inside the city limits and even inside the compound. She passed and received as much information that could possibly be used in their fight for freedom. She made it no secret of her distaste for the vampires, but she was harmless enough that she was left alone. Instructions from Tessa to treat her with the utmost respect didn't hurt either.

Isaac began to get quite close to Tessa. He had read the leather bound book from cover to cover, and although he was still with the human fight for freedom, he could sympathize with the vampire's plight a little more each day. He had not realized how hard it had been for them all the years they stayed in the shadows and kept secret from the world. He read it religiously as if it were his bible. It was almost saddening when he had to give it back to his Queen when she kept asking for it. He had relaxed more around her. He became her confidant in a way. Bryon spent less time watching over him meticulously which made it easier for Tessa to speak of all her troubles, fears, and frustrations. She had only had her journal for that and for some reason it wasn't enough for what she had to deal with. He realized that although her shell was of a vampire, her soul was sensitive, emotional and her fear of failure for her people was quite strong. All of those things had drawn him into Tessa's world, wanting to be much more than just a slave or confidant. He sat on every word that she spoke, taking in every breath.

Tessa began to notice Isaac's change. Although she was very cautious in showing him acknowledgment, deep down she began to have feelings for him. She was sure that nothing was ever going to be like the love she held for Greco. His memory would forever be etched into her heart and thoughts. He had loved her unconditionally and made her what she was. She was sure that what she felt was no more than a need for companionship. She felt isolated in her world no matter now many of her vampires attempted to keep her company. She was the Queen and that put a big flag up to stay away from any personalization with her. All her time spent with Isaac had been comforting and seemed to fill the void she felt since she had lost Greco. Isaac saw her for her thoughts, emotions, and as a person; not as a vampire, queen, or enemy. She desired someone to hold her and comfort her like nothing else mattered.

Isaac watched her every move. He wanted to fill the emptiness, almost sadness, that she had inside. He wanted to hold her, caress her, kiss her, and to make her know that no matter what was going on, everything would be okay as long as he held her in his arms. But all he had were confusing feelings. What stood in his way the most were his fears. He feared he would lose touch with his humanity, his sympathy and all that made him who he was. He feared of his family's rejection because he knew all too well how Melinda had felt for Tessa and the vampires. He also feared rejection, or ever worse, banishment or death. One thing that confused him about her was that she was very unpredictable. The woman who seemed so sad, lonely, and sometimes sympathetic, was also the same creature that was blood thirsty, full of hate and revenge, and cold-heartedly cruel to people that did not fit into her master plan. With those fears he kept tucked away to himself, the whole time pining away for something he knew he could never have.

One day he felt the need to strike up a conversation, since he felt comfortable enough talking to her. "I don't understand why Melinda is so important to you. Is it her children you are interested in? You have kept us all here in your compound for so long with no real master plan, or one that I have realized anyway." Isaac poured Tessa her blood wine as she sat on her chaise lounge, wearing only her robe. She kept to some of the same rituals her and her king had together, to give her a small piece inside of her the solace it needed to continue from day to day. This time she had decided that it was a day she did not feel the need to deal with anybody and felt Isaac's question a daunting task to take on. Instead she had retired to Greco's pride and joy, his roman bath. It always reminded him of his glory days and in return it reminded her of him.

"It is such a long story," Tessa sighed as she finally answering his question. "Melinda and I go way back." She lifted her cup and tasted the last bit of warm blood on her lips.

"Really? From where? She has yet to tell that to me." The only thing he had been hearing from Melinda were the hate filled words she had for a captor that has yet to reveal herself to her.

"That's because, even through all these years, she has yet to see my face. But when she does she will recognize me and things will change. I'm afraid of that change." She wiped the blood off her lips with the tip of her finger.

"She will still loath you for holding her captive you know." He was sure that Tessa wasn't oblivious of Melinda's hatred for him.

"She is allowed to roam free on the property and the job she has with the school. She should feel comfortable, I have provided for her more than most humans get." She proceeded towards the pool of water that Isaac has drawn, like many times before. Pink and red rose petals floated on top of the water that was illuminated by many candles placed around the Romanesque bath. Nothing could have been more beautiful than her at those moments.

"That is not freedom."

"You don't understand." Tessa sighed. She knew he was tired of hearing that from her.

"You won't let me understand." He walked up behind her and helped her disrobe. The touch of his warm soft fingers against her arms brought feelings to parts of her body that had not been awakened since even before Greco had died. She closed her eyes and savored the quick moment.

She turned to him and pressed her bare bosom against his already shirtless chest; her hot breath beckoned to him.

He tried to not take notice of the perfection that was in front of him, her curves, and her long hair that grazed her breasts. He pulled himself even closer than she had already come. He looked into her eyes, not able to break his gaze on her. He was searching for any sort of connection.

"I really don't want to talk about Melinda anymore." She muttered as she gracefully backed into the water, not for a single moment letting go the lock she had on his eyes. The connection was met.

Against all better judgment, Isaac dropped his black linen pants and followed after her into the water. "You never want to talk about it."

I have good reason." She said as he continued to move towards her.

"I have been your loyal servant for quite a while now. I do everything that you ask; even menial tasks such as this; bathing you. When are you going to trust me?" He came face to face with her. She was backed to the side of the bath.

"Never." Her words were harsh but her tone was subdued. She felt his heart beat nervously as he came within touching distance of her. "But don't let that stop you." A smirk positioned itself on the corner of her lip. She was going to see where everything was going, since she had imagined it for quite some time.

"Stop me from what?" It was obvious he knew what she was talking about, but his fear was not about to have him open his mouth to say something that he might regret.

You are attracted to me, yes?"

"I'm uncertain. Yes, you have this magical draw that has me wondering what it would be like to be with you." He then looked away. "But then I realize that it is something that you are doing to me, and not my own true feelings. It is your vampire way."

"Don't believe everything that you hear. It is true that I can use a heightened sense of psychic ability to a certain extent, but I have not used any of it on you." Her lips curved up a little more. "The only real power that I have is to stop a heart from beating." It was her attempt at humor that came off more unnerving than anything.

"Who's to say that isn't what you will do to me?"

"The only thing I want is for you to open your heart to the truth behind those feelings you are beginning to have for me." She had decided that it was time to put it all out on the table. The tension between the two had become so intense, even without a single word spoken about their feelings.

"I am still hesitant. All I know is that I feel as though I am connected to you somehow. My heart tells me to just go with it." Isaac started to back up nervously.

"Then why don't you?"

"I'm afraid."

"Afraid I might hurt you?"

"There is that and then I am also afraid that I will be lost in the depths of your dark soul." He stopped moving backward.

"It is not as dark as you think it is." Tessa grabbed his hand and pulled it to her chest. "Here."

"What? What is it?" He was afraid, yet felt warm inside from her touching him.

"Do you feel it?" The two paused. As gentle the feel of a soft raindrop he felt a double thump.

"What was that?" He said with startled confusion and pulled his hand back in reaction.

"That is my heart. It does beat like yours, just slower." She didn't want to tell him that small heartbeat was what was unique about her. Vampires shouldn't have one. She thought about the night Greco made her and why she shouldn't even have a single beat at all. She returned her mind to the present situation. She took his hand again and pressed his fingers to her lips.

"They're cold, but I feel your breath." He then took his finger and gently touched one of her protruding fangs. She let him do it with ease. Tessa felt his hands tremble and his heart began to beat at a faster pace.

"Don't be afraid, Isaac. I want you to be here. I

want you to know me."

He took his hand and rubbed her cheek. "I want to know you. I want to know everything about you."

At that moment Tessa leaned in and gently kissed him. "I won't hurt you." She whispered. "I want you to make love to me."

"I can't." He shook his head.

"Yes you can. Set your fears aside and embrace this moment before it passes. I want you to take over and make love to me like your thoughts have been suggesting to you, like your fantasies have shown you."

He had a massive buildup of emotion and kissed her deeply and passionately.

Tessa climbed out of the water with Isaac following her. He put his hand on her back and slowly lowered her down. He lay across her stomach and continued to kiss her, each one more amorous than the other. Their fingers intertwined as he pressed his flesh against hers. The two began to make love, on and off for the rest of the night.

Tessa felt like everything was falling into place. She felt needed, wanted, loved. Her feelings for Isaac were finally able to blossom. At that moment she didn't think about any of the consequences of breaking one of the main rules of being a head vampire, no human relationships. She was following Greco's lead once more by doing so.

* * * * *

"Where were you this morning?" Melinda asked accusingly, when she walked through the door of their dwelling.

"I was with Tessa." Isaac said as he put his finger on the page of the book he was reading, so as not to lose his place.

"Your shift ends at daybreak; I was expecting you for breakfast, to take the kids to school." Melinda slammed down the bag of perishables she had wrapped in her arms.

"They got there just fine, I suppose. That is what your bodyguards are for."

"That is not the point." She sighed and leaned against the counter.

"Then please, do get to the point."

"It's you. You've become so distant lately. We hardly ever see you anymore. You're always with the Queen." She said the last word with a snide tone.

"Haven't you ever wondered why she brought us here? Why we're here under her roof?" He set his book down and turned towards her.

"Every single day," she said. "What I really am curious about is why you're her right hand man, doing every little thing that she tells you to."

"That's my job. I am her servant." He brushed off her worry.

"You're her slave. You don't do this on your own free will. If it were up to you, you'd be out there helping those who fight for the cause of freedom."

Isaac raised his hands in the air. "What good will it do? Here we are protected, fed, clothed, and educated. I'm sorry if I feel that our actual lives are worth being truly alive for. Do you want to go out there and risk the lives of those two children for something that doesn't exist? For freedom?" He breathed heavy, his face red and upset. "Don't you think one dead parent is enough?"

Tears flooded Melinda's eyes. "She's gotten to you. All those days; those hours. She's brainwashed you." She turned to him and screamed. "It's because of you we are trapped here!" She moved back her arm and proceeded to slap him. He caught it in mid air and pulled her close to him.

"You are mistaken. You are the only reason we are here and you are the reason why we are still alive."

She pulled her arm away. "What are you talking about?" She rubbed where his tight grip has been.

"She says the two of you go way back." He spoke in a low voice.

"Sorry, I don't know any vampires on a personal level, only those that invaded our home and killed your brother along with thousands others!" She screamed, and then sat down to ponder.

"No, she said she had been turned not that many years ago. She seems like she might be around your age."

Melinda brushed what he said off then said, "Even so, I don't know anyone named Tessa. No one I would remember anyway. I have never seen The Queen's face either, though. Precautionary measures and so on."

"Think about it." He sat beside her. "She spares our lives and takes us in. She treats you and your family like royalty, like her own family. She definitely knows you."

"So why have I yet to see her? She only speaks with you and the children, which, by the way, that still makes me mad every time one of my children enters into her presence."

"She must be afraid. Afraid of what you'll think of her." He thought back to the discussion in the bath.

"Right now I despise her."

"You despise the thing that she's become, not her." He tried to explain to her the best he could. "I think she had come to Benton just to find you."

"So who is she?" Melinda asked quietly, just above a whisper.

"I don't know, but that is what I am going to try to find out."

* * * * *

Isaac walked into Tessa's penthouse. In just a short while she would awaken. The only difference between that evening and the previous one was that he looked at her in a different light. He sat on the side of the bed and gazed at her sleeping. She looked like such a sweet innocent child. He stroked her cheek and spoke softly. "Rise and shine."

Her eyes took a bit to wake up. When she did, she looked at Isaac and smiled. "Hi there."

"Bryon has a long list of things for you to do today." He informed her.

"He always does. Just let me wake up first." She sat up and touched his arm. "I was so afraid it was only a dream."

"Do vampires dream?" Isaac asked, half teasing and half curious to know if they did or not.

"You have no idea." Tessa joked and got out of the bed. Isaac couldn't help but gaze at her perfect body. Without even realizing it, a big grin appeared on his face.

Tessa smiled and walked towards the closet. "I am pleased to see you no longer hide your smile."

"What? Hide? I don't know what you are talking about." He lied quite poorly.

"Play innocent all you like," she turned to him. "But your duties still remain the same. Help me get dressed."

"Yes my lady." He lowered his eyes and began to help her into her dress. His heart started to falter thoughts of rejection.

Tessa turned to him and cupped his chin. "I am not being cruel to you." She lowered her hand and grabbed for his. “I know last night is something you are thinking heavily on. I, too, am indulging in the memories that we made for ourselves when we made love,” she tried to sound reassuring. “But this is something we need to keep between the two of us. We need to function as before so that everyone else, especially the vampires, do not suspect a thing.”

“I wasn’t expecting to announce anything to anyone. I have as much to lose if Melinda were to find out.”

Tessa paused before she said, “Isaac, you don’t even have a clue do you?”

“What do you mean?”

She took him by the hand and led him to the couch. “What we did is more than just bad publicity. In our nation, I mean The Vampire Nation, it is punishable by death to actually mate with a human. Sure, we can seduce, we can do many things, but that one thing, the one thing that we did most of our time together last night, that is what isn't allowed.”

“Why is that?”

“Many things are left up to speculation, and some I don’t even know. But one thing I am certain of is that it brings the vampire down and compromises our advantage. Another reason is fear. They fear that we will lose sight of what we are and revert back to our human existence.”

“It all sounds so stupid like they are still controlling even you, The Queen of this very nation.”

"I am a turned Queen, not born by one of the more pure bloods. That makes a difference. Greco skirted the boundaries of the rules for me. He was very old and had much importance in their world with his wisdom. The only reason I am here today leading these people is because of his assassination.” She took a breath. “See, it is much more complex than you think. It is very imperative that you do your job so that I can do mine." She smiled and looked at his hollowed expression, and then she stood up and turned away.

He shook his head in sadness. "Is this a one-time thing? Was I just being used?"

She looked over her shoulder. "You must come to that conclusion on your own." She turned around. "If you feel as though you cannot continue on a daily basis as my servant to the highest capacity and cannot hide your feelings, then yes, all good things must come to an end." Tessa walked towards Isaac and got close to him. "But if you think that you can act as my loyal servant, never look me in the eye, and keep the fear you have for me alive inside of you then we can continue to get to know one another on a more personal basis."

Bryon quickly walked through the door and she switched over to her Queen mode. She began to yell at Isaac. "Do you understand me?"

Isaac bowed his head in compliance; he has spied Bryon also. "Yes my lady. It will be done."

Tessa looked up at Bryon. "What is it?"

"The car is waiting for you downstairs." Bryon looked at Isaac, who was kneeling at Tessa's feet. "Is there something that needs my attention with this particular servant?"

"No, Bryon. I have everything under control. I just found things in less than satisfactory condition when I awoke. I was reprimanding him as you were walking in."

Bryon looked at Isaac. "Get up." Isaac did as he was told, since Bryon was the head of all the servants. "Now, I want you to stay behind and make this place spotless."

Tessa looked at Isaac with no emotion at all on her face.

"But sir; isn't that what the maid is for?"

"Not tonight. And when you are done, you are to join us over at the Levé Council to attend to your Queen's needs."

"Yes sir." He bowed.

Bryon leaned over to him. "And next time you displease your Queen I will take away a day's rationing of food."

Isaac watched, a nervous pang in his stomach, as Tessa and Bryon both walked out of the penthouse.

* * * * *

"Will my services be needed any further for the evening my Queen?" Bryon asked as he sat at the kitchen counter, which was only used by the servants since Tessa had lost her appeal for any other food besides blood.

Tessa looked out her window, as she often did after a night of being with the council. "No, you may leave. Go home to your family. I have Isaac here if I need attending to."

Isaac was sitting on the couch reading over the newest revision of rules for the humans to abide by. He watched Bryon walk out and then quickly went over to Tessa. He touched her waist with both hands. "How did I do this evening?"

"You did well, although I do apologize about you having to clean up this place." Tessa leaned her head back onto his chest; the two of them stared out the window together. "Do you ever feel as if you are not offering enough of yourself to people, no matter how hard you try?"

"Well, I learned back when I was working in the clinic that you could never fully do that because eventually it will take every piece of your soul until it leaves only the outer shell."

"Do you know that when Greco was alive, he would watch me stand at this window, knowing I was having conflicting thoughts and not join me, even once?" As much love as she had for Greco that was the one thing that she wished had been different. It had been so long since he had been a human there was a sort of disconnect on those feelings.

"That is the difference between him and me, neither one necessarily wrong." Isaac couldn't have said any better words to her as far as she was concerned.

"I did love him. I will always love him and miss him. His death will be justified by the war against the Krones." She turned to Isaac. "But as you hold me right here and now all those thoughts that run through my mind I want to share with you. All my feelings; all my strife and hardships. With you, somehow I know I am not alone."

Isaac looked into her eyes and saw such life in them for someone who defeated the very thing called life.

"I want to share something with you," Tessa said, breaking the tone.

"What is it?"

"Something I should have shown you a long time ago." She turned around to face him.

"So why now?"

"Shh I want you to close your eyes and clear all from your mind." He took a deep breath and closed his eyes. Tessa placed her palms at his temples. She had not connected to a human psychically but with one other, Bryon. That was only to test it out, to see how well she could do with a human.

Quickly images began to splash through his mind swirling like a wave of information. It was of two young children, little girls. It showed them together, growing up until the last and final image. It was of Tessa and Melinda together posing for a picture, they had to be teenagers but there was no doubt it was both of them in that picture.

Isaac was so shocked by the images that he saw, he pulled away like his energy had been drawn completely from him. “Melinda. She’s your sister?” He gasped.

Tessa nodded shamefully. “I would understand if you thought less of me.”

“No, I don’t. I now understand why it is so hard for you to come face to face with her. If she sees you and still rejects you...that could be devastating." He wrapped his arms around her. "But you will have to tell her sometime. The longer you wait the worse it is on the both of you.”

“I know.” She looked into his eyes. “There is just so much I have to tell her, I don’t want to leave anything out. I want her to understand everything I have done and why I chose the path I did.”

CHAPTER NINE

Tessa decided to hold a nice dinner and meeting with Melinda and her family. It was for her to finally "come out" to Melinda. She knew it wouldn't be good no matter the outcome, but she felt that Melinda had a right to know. There were only three other people that knew about their relationship. She was one and the other two were Bryon and Isaac.

In the formal part of the compound Melinda, Isaac, Jason, and Emma had a nice big meal, the table dressed neatly. They had been given fresh fancy clothes specifically for the special occasion. Emma seemed the most pleased; she could not stop dancing around, twirling in her crisp pink dress. They were given musical entertainment, games, and anything else imaginable to enjoy the evening.

When they were done eating, they retired to a room similar to a parlor where the kids played checkers while Melinda and Isaac sat there waiting anxiously. Melinda began to complain on how tired she was of waiting for the hostess that had yet to show up. At that moment, as if she had conjured him up herself, Bryon ushered out quickly what little help was left in the room. That was when Tessa entered.

Isaac gave her a nod of support and encouragement. Melinda, who had been facing away from the door, turned around and stopped dead in her tracks. In front of her stood what looked like her older sister. She looked exactly like she did the last time she had seen her, that day in the hospital room. She thought something had happened to her. She used a lot of resources to find her after the oppression. She was pretty much told that her sister was dead and had to give up the search. So the woman, still the young lady she used to know, standing in front of her was the fearless Queen.

"It's been a long time." Tessa said quietly.

"Apparently too long." Melinda didn't know how she felt. Would she be pleased that her sister was safe or upset that she went this long without letting her know who she really was?

"I couldn't tell you, not back in the beginning." Tessa began to explain.

"But I'm your sister." Melinda blurted out with a sadness that filled the room.

The kids looked at each other. Isaac motioned for Bryon to take the children back to their room. He kept watch over the ladies to gauge if he should step in at any moment.

"The day I walked out of that hospital room was the day you gave up being my sister." Tessa said, coldly.

"So I didn't think about what had happened to you the same way you thought I should have. It didn't give you any right to walk out of my life." Melinda attempted to make lighter of the situation than Tessa felt it was.

"It gave me every right!" Tessa yelled. "It set everything in motion as to who I am now." She walked closer to Melinda. Her frustration bubbled in Melinda's self-righteous face. "I was fucking pregnant by that bastard. The one you defended. I was walking around with my own uncle's child. How sick and twisted is that?"

Melinda avoided Tessa's glare. She had no words to say at that moment. She wouldn't even look in Isaac's direction. The subject was something that haunted her for a long time, and it took her many years to realize how much she did wrong by her sister. “I lived on the streets. I did what I had to do to get rid of the baby. I almost bled to death. If it weren’t for Greco, the one who made me, then I would have died that day.”

“Is that when he turned you?” Melinda asked softly.

“No. I didn’t even know he was the one who saved me.” Tessa sat down in an old empty armchair. “I didn’t embrace this life until well after I last saw you.”

“I thought you had died.” Melinda started shedding tears but then stopped crying. She turned towards Tessa with a colder glare. “But then you did die. You died and now walk this earth with your disgustingly rotten flesh.”

Tessa returned the look. “First of all my flesh is not rotting,” the childish part in her spoke up. Then she cleared her throat to say, “The day I was turned was the day I truly started living. Greco saved me from myself. I had nothing to live for. All the family that I knew were dead to me, I didn’t have a place in the human world that mattered and I loved Greco. I wanted to be with him for eternity.”

“That just turned you into a murderous monster.” Melinda justified her take on the vampire race as a whole.

“I hardly feed on any humans. There have always been donors.” She retorted.

“So what gave you the right to take over the world? Did you just feel a little frisky?”

Tessa took a breath before she explained, “We were being killed off. We were never understood and we had to let the world know that we were not a force to be reckoned with. It is a world of survival and we became the dominant race.”

Melinda walked up to Tessa. “There is one thing about the dominant race.” She started to pass Tessa when she stopped and turned her head over her shoulder. "There's always going to be someone there to try to knock you off." She headed towards the door.

"Mel," Tessa called to her sister with vulnerability. "I want to get past everything that has happened."

"I will *never* get past the murder of my husband. Especially now knowing that it was at the orders of my sister." Tears welled up in her eyes, filled with so much anger. "Don't think for even a second I am going to sit around this place and play happy family. You can forget about it. I'm not going to play your games. You better hope and pray that the next time you see me isn't when I'm taking your head off." Melinda opened the parlor door.

Isaac grabbed a hold of her arm. "Mel, she's trying. Hear her out."

"What the hell?" She was confused. "What do you care? This isn't your fight. Wait, actually it is. It is the human race against those creatures. Even if it didn't come down to it, it was Michael that died. All because of her!" Melinda pointed to Tessa. "What else do you want me to sit here and listen to?" She searched his eyes for an answer and then all of a sudden it was the light bulb that went off inside her head. "You knew about this! The two of you planned this." She pulled her arm away from Isaac.

"It's not like that." He said defensively.

"How long have you known? Were you the one that sent them to take us away?" Fear, anger, and panic filled Melinda to the top.

"No, Mel, I didn't. I just found out the other day." He shook his head. "I don't think you see the whole picture. I think that your thoughts are clouded."

"And yours are crystal clear?" Melinda looked at Tessa. "What has my sister done to you?"

"Nothing. She's done nothing but talk. And I think

you need to hear what she has to say." He attempted to be the only voice of reasoning amongst the family quarrel.

Melinda laughed. "I've heard all I care to hear. And Isaac," She looked at him with pity and warning. "You need to remember what side you are fighting on. You don't want to get caught in the crossfire."

He watched as Melinda left the room. He then turned to look at Tessa, who had practically fallen heartbroken into the closest chair. She only sat there for a minute before she yelled for Bryon. He quickly came into the room, like the little lap dog that he had become. "Don't let her out of the building. Use whatever means necessary to subdue her, but whatever you do, do not kill her." Bryon was about to walk out when Tessa interjected one more thing. "Keep her away from the children for now. We don't want her to taint them any more than she already has tonight." Bryon nodded and called security on his mobile. He shut the door behind him on the way out.

Isaac looked at Tessa. "Is all this necessary?"

She glared at him with stone cold eyes and said, "Very necessary. This was always a possibility."

"But she hasn't had any time to process this information. Give her time." Isaac placed one hand on her shoulder.

She stood up and pulled away, followed by a low growl. She turned to him, her eyes a bright almost iridescent red. "Her time is up. I have no more patience. I have wasted enough of my time digging into my old memories. I'm just a hideous malicious monster, and I will never be anything else. I will never forget that again." She proceeded to leave and Isaac stood in her way.

She stared him down and sensed his fear. She was

drawn to the pumping of his blood due to his rapid heartbeat. She became full vampire and moved into the inviting vein on his neck. His fear, mixed with her anger, was easily a dreadful combination. She got very close to his neck; he didn't stop her. She sensed his fear peak, stopped herself quickly, and pulled away. She saw the look of confusion, along with a broken heart, on his face. She sighed and ran out the door.

Tessa didn't stop until she was outside the compound. The only thing that she had been thinking of was how stupid she was to even think the reunion with her sister would have gone well. She thought to herself *how else would it have gone? What good did any of that do? All it did was give her a face to the furor. It did nobody any good. What was I thinking?*

She was uncertain of what she was going to do from that point forward. Was she going to keep Melinda under lock and key until she came to her senses? That would be a very immature thing to do. Should she let her leave the city? If that were to happen she would never see her sister again, along with Jason and Emma.

With all those thoughts racing through her mind she knew the only thing she would be able to do was to watch everything unfold. She would have to focus on the task at hand and what was best for her.

She ventured away from the compound, which was something that was advised for her never to do. She didn't care about that or that it was for her safety. All she thought about was her sadness, her doubt in herself, and her anger.

Everywhere she turned she saw her kindred enjoying the freedom of night. She felt happy that they had the chance to walk around like they could without restrictions. That was what her goal was, although slightly askew from her ultimate idea. She still had a long way to go to be able to see the world that she wanted to see. Nobody made it easy for her.

Tessa stopped when she looked at a shadowed pair pressed up against the stone wall of an old converted building. There was a tall and dark vampire. He was beginning to take in a feast from a cowering young lady. Tessa caught the focus of his eyes. He smiled as he bit the flesh of his peach perfect plaything. She moved in closer towards the two. As if the master sensed Tessa's desire he pulled away from his pet, blood dripped from his fangs to the bottom of his lip. Tessa leaned in towards him and licked the bloody lips, delving into a very lust-filled kiss. Her emotions brought her forward into being a full vampire, once again. When the blood kiss ended Tessa turned to the docile prey and began feeding. The two vampires took turns partaking in the very enticing meal. If Melinda said she was a monster, then she was going to prove her right. She feasted until she had taken most of the young ladies blood, leaving her for dead. She pulled away and let the human body collapse onto the ground. Tessa had not taken so much blood from a human since Greco was teaching her how to control her portions, even though she was in full vampire form.

Her feasting partner looked at Tessa with anger. "You've ruined her! She was my favorite and now she's useless. She won't recover from that!" He raised his hand and began to grab at her throat. Tessa stopped him by grabbing his wrist.

"Do you have any idea who I am?" She roared.

He searched her eyes, almost looking for the answer to the question. The realization hit him quickly that he was about to kill his leader. He pulled his hand away and bowed down before her.

'Forgive me Your Highness." He took a deep breath

almost in fear for his immortal soul. "I did not expect to see you out on these streets."

She tapped his shoulder signaling for him to get up. "It seems as though it has been too long since I've really come outside long enough to enjoy the night."

"It's not safe out here."

Tessa laughed and acted a little pompous for a moment. She waved her arms around, "What's so different between you and me? Who's going to get me, the Krone fighters? The rebels? Vampires like you?" She smiled, "Bring it on. I've been cooped up in that building long enough. I want to be out like you. I want to enjoy all that I have liberated our people for. I've been put upon a pedestal long enough."

"But you are our leader. That is what you do. You make important decisions for your people."

Tessa stroked his cheek and grinned. "Good to know there is such dedication. If only you had your true leader to look up to instead. It is such a hard job to do by myself."

"I think you're doing a wonderful job." As he spoke, Tessa wondered to herself if he really had been speaking the truth.

"No matter." She shrugged it off. "What's your name?"

"Vincent."

"Vincent, where do you reside?"

"Over on North Eleventh Street."

"Let me do this for you. I will send over a couple of fresh young things to take the place of this poor unfortunate child." Tessa poked at the lifeless body crumpled on the sidewalk.

Vincent smiled. "Thank you. Thank you very much."

She watched as he took off back down the dark

alley.

Tessa walked back to her sanctuary building. The moment that she arrived Bryon was there to assist her. She dismissed all his questions and concerns. “Do you have Melinda confined?”

“We’ve got three guards posted outside her door.” He nodded and answered.

“Good. But I want you to double security in the city and maybe even start sending more soldiers outside the city to take care of the rebels. Melinda’s threats and possible forewarnings concern me. I don’t want to take any chances with these humans. I may have compassion for their well-being but I will not stand to have my own people attacked and killed.”

“But Tessa, I don’t think we have enough fighters for that.” Bryon exclaimed.

Tessa stopped and thought for a moment. “What about our loyals? Do you think that they would fight for us and our cause?”

“They may help us defend the city from the Krones, but I am uncertain if they will help in our battle with the rebels.”

“Then put them on defensive and put our people on the offense. I think that we need to act before Melinda passes on information to the rebels.” She walked to the elevator as she dismissed Bryon.

When she entered her home the first thing she did was pour herself a glass of blood and stared out the picture window and into the darkness of night.

“I was worried about you.” Isaac’s soft voice spoke up. He came from the back room.

“There was no need.” She wanted to stay there, staring blankly, right in front of the window.

“I’m sorry things did not go well with your sister.”

“I expected it, although I would have thought I

would be more prepared."

"I've never seen you so vulnerable. Not like I did tonight." He tried his best to comfort her and to bring her to his level of understanding; to let her know that everything was all right.

"That is something that I will try to make sure never happens again. Not in the face of my enemy. I will be more prepared come next time." She took the last drink of her blood and set it down on a nearby table. "It is because I'm so young that the human emotions have yet to subside completely." She was talking more to herself than to Isaac.

"I thought you were empathetic to our needs? I thought that you were trying to integrate us with your kind so that we could live as one in this world." He seemed almost confused at her cold nature.

Tessa sighed. "You don't have a clue what I am up against; what I'm facing. All those ideas of equality are far into your future." She grew cold and withdrawn. "But for now I must rule with an iron first to do what is best for my kind." She turned back towards the window.

"Tessa, think about what it is that you are saying. Don't let one bad incident destroy all of your wonderful ideas. The dreams you shared with me."

"Enough." Those were the last words she spoke before Isaac gave up and walked away.

She seemed strong on the outside, but inside she felt her whole world crumbling around her; as if it were the Roman Empire destined for failure.

* * * * *

Melinda sat on her bed and looked at her surroundings. Cold and dark must have been the theme whenever they decided to decorate their wonderful holding cells. Everything around her was made out of glass, metal, and the occasional marble. She supposed that place was going to be her dwelling for a while, at least until she could figure a way out. They kept contact with her to a minimum. The only time she saw anybody was when they brought her food. Even then they hardly spoke to her. She wasn't even sure how long she had been there. Maybe a couple of months, but that was only an estimate. She had attempted to keep track of how long it was, but in the beginning things were such a blur. All she knew was that she had to get out of there. She had to get back to her children. She was left alone with her thoughts for more than she would like to be.

How could all of this have happened? She thought to herself. *Where did everything go wrong?* Had she really been the reason all this happened? Had her fear of the truth really been what condemned her sister to her dark path? She pondered quite a few things. *It couldn't have been that. There must have been something that added to all the mess.* Of course she felt terrible about her sister being raped. Even worse was when she found out what happened afterwards; but her sister had made all her own decisions in the end.

She tried to take in everything that had been placed before her. The sister she once thought was dead was now the queen of the most powerful vampire empires, and here she was the leader of the Independent Freedom Fighters; polar opposites so to speak. Was the Queen that had stood in front of her that night really and truly her sister, Emma? She looked like her and had her memories, but how could someone that used to be so loving turn into something so cold-hearted, ruthless, and merciless? That vile creature called Tessa was not her sister. She gave up that right the moment she condemned her first human to its death.

Somewhere amongst all those thoughts Melinda had fallen asleep. She hadn't even realized it until she heard the sound of her door being opened. She hadn't even stood up when she was approached.

"Melinda?" Asked the young stranger. She did not recognize her as one of the people who usually brought her food.

"Yes?" Melinda said with a sort of question to the answer.

"I need you to come with me, ma'am." The young woman gently grabbed a hold of her.

Melinda pulled away. "I'm not going anywhere. I have already said all that I am ever going to say to that Queen of yours."

"I'm not here for that." The woman looked around then turned back to Melinda. "I'm here for The Freedom Fighters. We are here to get you out."

Melinda nodded then quickly began to follow the woman. She looked around their path at all the involuntary slumbering people. Around the corner there were two other people that were there to help her escape.

They began to go over the escape plan with Melinda. She shook her head in frustration. "I'm not going anywhere without Emma and Jason."

They nodded in agreement. "We know. That is where we are going first before we get out of here." The middle aged man spoke. He then proceeded to lead the group in the direction of where the kids were.

When they approached the apartment, Melinda watched as her rescuers subdued the guards outside the door. She then followed them on signal. She was advised to quickly gather the kids and go. She first went into her son's room to wake him up.

"Mom?" Jason shook his head in confusion as he sat up.

"Shh," she whispered. "Don't ask too many questions. I need you to get dressed and come with me. We're getting out of here."

"I don't understand." He pulled up a pair of pants and started putting on his shoes.

"There is not much to understand. We're being rescued and that should be good enough."

"But I like it here. I get to go to school, I have friends." He told his mother.

"Now is not the time to argue with me, Jason. Just hurry up. I'm going to get your sister." Melinda said before going into her daughter's room.

Emma dutifully did what she was told, even though she practically was sleepwalking through it all. Melinda had both of them headed through the living room to meet their rescuers. They were almost out the door when she turned around. Isaac stood in the doorway. The two of them locked eyes. "Come with me," she pleaded.

Isaac watched as she headed towards the door. He stopped Melinda in the doorway where she was watching her children and their liberators go down the hall.

Melinda grabbed for Isaac's hand and repeated the words, "Come with me."

Before Isaac could utter a single word her heard screams from down the hall. "Stop them! They're trying to escape." At that moment all he could do was stand and watch what was about to be a train wreck of a situation. Melinda looked down one end of the hall where the new forces were coming from and started running the other direction towards her kids. Before she could get them, Emma, Jason and their two saviors were grabbed. Melinda stopped dead in her tracks.

The woman, who had been helping her, grabbed a hold of her arm a bit more firm. "We must go. We need to go now."

Melinda screamed out to her kids and they called back to her. She started to push away at the very person that risked her own life so that Melinda could be saved. The Levé forces closed in from the other side. "I can't leave them. No!" She screamed to her helper.

"If we don't leave now we will never be able to go."

Melinda didn't care about that. The only thing that she wanted was for her children to be safe, and at that moment they were in harms way.

Isaac realized Melinda's dilemma. He stepped into the hall and started pushing Melinda to the hatch where the rescuer tried unsuccessfully to persuade her into.

"No, Isaac. My babies." Tears welled up in her eyes and she pushed Isaac away.

"I will take care of them. You have to go." He said, trying to sound confident instead of scared. He knew that she had to get out of there or she would die sooner than later.

She looked at him as she was being pulled away into the hatch. "Promise me you will."

"I promise you. I will always take care of them." Isaac said and then watched her disappear into the vent. He took a deep breath and rushed the guards that came towards him. He fought just hard enough to give her time to successfully escape.

* * * * *

"What do you mean she escaped?" Tessa screamed at Bryon, who happened to be the bearer of bad news.

"I'm sorry. We tried everything that we could to catch her but they must have known the place inside and out." Bryon finally looked up into her eyes. "But she was the only one to escape. We stopped the children and their uncle before they could follow suit."

"Good." A disturbed gleam was in her eyes. "We're going to have to move them. It is evident that we are vulnerable here now." She went over to the map on the wall that was of their city. She placed her finger on their new destination. "We'll move to the Aurora building. There will be more room for us to stay there."

"Yes, ma'am." Bryon nodded and began to head out the door, but he stopped to ask a question. "I know the children are coming with us, but what should I do with the uncle and the two that attempted to make the rescue?"

"Bring Isaac with us for now. He could prove useful."

"And the others?"

She waved her hand in dismissal. "Drain them and get rid of their bodies."

When Tessa heard the door shut she walked over to the bookshelf and pulled the journal from its dusty caretaker. She glanced at it for a moment and then carried it with her out the door.

Hundreds of thoughts raced through her mind. She knew that everything she attempted with Melinda had failed. Her world was better off without her sister in it. She was uncertain as to why she thought that they could repair all the damage that had been done. They lived in two separate worlds; neither one truly helping what they had become. From that very moment Tessa knew they were always going to be at war with one another. Her only true hope in the future was to make sure each and every last Independent Freedom Fighter was eradicated. Her niece and nephew were the keys to a brighter future leading the next generation into a world where humans were submissively coexisting with the vampires. The world was going to change and she was going to ensure that it happened according to Greco's vision; no matter the cost.

* * * * *

Melinda crawled through the small opening that led her to freedom. Her room of salvation was in the cold and wet world under the compound. The door was about to be shut and sealed when Melinda rushed over to stop it.

"We have to seal it off before they realize our route." Her lady redeemer said.

"We can't!" Melinda panicked. "My babies are in there. We have to go get them."

"But ma'am, you saw that they were recaptured."

"We can still get to them. I can help."

"Calm down." An older gentleman grabbed a hold of her shoulder. "We'll send some people from the inside to go get them. Things will be okay." He looked into her eyes, which were still flooded with fear.

Melinda finally nodded. "Okay, but I won't rest until I am certain of my children's safety."

"I understand and we will do all that we can to try to make that happen." He breathed a sigh of relief when she loosened the stiffness from her body. "But for now, we need our leader back. We have been losing the fight against the vampires. We need you back in command to bring us forward to our dream of freedom."

"Then show me where to go so we can get back to business." Melinda put on a brave front. She was then led down a long and dark tunnel.

* * * * *

"So what was it that you were trying to accomplish?" Tessa stood behind the sofa in the living room of their new home. It had a totally different feel to it than her penthouse. The place had no sign that Greco ever was there. Everything was much too modern and minimalistic for his taste.

"I didn't do anything. I had already told this to Drake." Isaac defended himself.

"Well humor me and tell *me* what happened." She walked around to face him. He took his head out of his hands and sat back still uncomfortable with the situation before him. The woman in front of him was the Tessa that he feared the most. The Tessa that was filled with hate and vengeance.

"Like I told Drake, I heard a noise and went to see what it was. Melinda was standing in the doorway asking me to go with her. I saw Jason and Emma being grabbed and more people were coming from the other direction. I looked away, and then she was gone."

"See, now, I heard that you actually stopped my men from getting to Melinda." She said, unconvincing of his tale.

Isaac sighed. "What was I supposed to do? Melinda was miserable here from day one. She would have continued trying to escape. I'm sure your surprise revelation made it even harder on her to stay."

"But, Isaac, I trusted you." Her gentle voice toned down the hostility for just a moment. "I trusted you. I shared with you my thoughts, feelings, secrets, and even my body. I would have thought you would at least return the favor and stay loyal to me."

"What choice did I have? You put me in a terrible position. There was no way I could ever choose between you and Melinda. She was my brother's wife and the mother to his children. To turn my back on her would have been the same as doing it to Michael himself." He said with quite a bit of frustration.

She asked hesitantly, "Would you have gone with her?"

He took in a deep breath and then released. "Does it really even matter at this point? I'm here with you while she is on the outside."

Tessa looked at him questionably. "I'm just curious if the man before me is here as a prisoner or on his own free will."

Isaac fell silent. He refused to answer the question knowing he could not say what he did not know himself. He wasn't sure if his unfortunate hesitation meant that he was afraid to leave or afraid to stay. He probably would never know the answer.

* * * * *

Jason tucked Emma into her new bed and kissed her on the forehead.

"Jason, does Mommy not love us anymore?" Her innocent eyes filled with sadness.

"Of course she does, Emma." Jason said as he stroked her soft hair.

"Then why didn't she come back for us? Why did she just run away like that?"

"I'm sure she wanted to come back for us. She just couldn't at that moment. They were going to kill her if she didn't run away." Jason justified his mother's actions.

"So you think that she'll come back for us?" Emma asked.

"Of course she will. She's our mother." Jason said and smiled falsely. "I bet that right now, as we are about to go to sleep, she is devising this wonderful plan to get us out of here safely so we can be a family again."

Emma's expression brightened up at that idea. "I bet you're right! I'm sure she won't rest until we're rescued."

"That's right Emma." Jason walked to the doorway and shuts off the light. "Think happy thoughts."

Jason shut the door to Emma's room and leaned against the wall. He hated lying to his sister, but she was still so young. He didn't want to tell her that their mother probably didn't even look back once she left the compound. He knew she loved them; it was evident that she did. But he also knew that the most important thing in her life was to be an Independent Freedom Fighter. When their father was alive, she had a different objective. That objective was to protect her family at all costs; but things changed when he died. She became more obsessed with revenge and justice and she distanced herself from all that she had known. She never really even paid attention to how much she put her children into harms way. Jason resented her for that, although he could never hate her. He just thought that maybe, just maybe, he was where he was supposed to be. He felt safer with his aunt. He felt like he truly did have a stable life; not one that was constant running. He admitted to himself that he understood his aunt was a vampire. She was a ferocious killing machine. There really wasn't much that separated her from his mother. Both craved blood, just in different ways. The one big difference was that no matter how evil and nasty it got out in the real world, he always felt safe in Tessa's world. She showed how much she loved them in more of a way that he understood, and that is what mattered to him at that very moment. He just hoped his mother's separation from them gave light to a realization that they mean more to her than a stupid war.

CHAPTER TEN

Tessa felt around the wrist of her young lady donor. She couldn't be more than twenty years of age; her eyes already filled with emptiness and sorrow. She could tell that the girl had been a donor for quite some time, something she wasn't completely pleased with.

That did not, however, stop her from laying fangs into her wrist as she suckled the hot warm blood from her body. When she noticed the girl getting weak, she pulled away as blood trickled from the wound.

She looked at the girl's wrist and noticed Isaac in the background. She looked away from her donor. Instead she mentioned to Isaac, "Bandage her wound and send her home."

He did as instructed and Tessa went to clean up. As she dabbed the last bit of blood from the corner of her mouth, he appeared behind her.

"I just cannot get over watching you feed on helpless people like that." He sounded very disappointed.

She turned around, leaned up against the pedestal sink. "She was not helpless. She was a donor. That is what she does. It keeps us from having to hunt for our food unnecessarily."

Isaac shook his head in frustration. "It still doesn't make it right. It makes you out to be an animal."

She glared at him. "You knew what I was. Don't act all oblivious to your surroundings." She brushed past him and walked into the bedroom. "Besides, what does it matter to you? You are just a servant."

"Is that all that I am to you?" His voice breathed sadness.

"Maybe once you were more." She thought of their passion, and then grew cold again as she pushed it out of her mind. "But that went away the day you betrayed me."

"Is that what you are going to bring up? After four years you still believe I am a traitor?"

"You let Melinda get away. I call that betrayal."

"Yet I stayed."

"For what? You say it was for me and the children, but the trust just isn't there anymore."

"What do you suppose I have been doing these past few years? Sending your dirty secrets through the pipes? I have not left this compound the whole time." He wanted her to know of all the suffering he had to endure while staying there. He could not help his feelings for her, no matter how hard he tried to hate her.

"Even so, I still do not trust you." She shrugged him off.

"If that is true, then why, after all these years that you have sat and stewed in your 'supposed' betrayal that I handed to you, you have once again brought me back in as your servant?"

Tessa rolled her eyes. "The children begged for me to give you your old job back. They felt very sorry for you where you had been placed." The day Isaac was taken away, Bryon had ordered him to work in the clinic to make certain all the donors kept a clean bill of health. It was not an official place of healing. More like a security measure for the vampire's lifeblood.

"I doubt that was the only reason." He speculated. "You missed me."

"You flatter yourself." She laughed dryly. It was

true though. She did miss him, but she didn't want him to know that.

He walked up to her. "If I am lying, tell me so. But when you do that, do me a favor and send me back to the clinic because I don't want to be somewhere I am not needed or wanted."

She laughed dryly. "Like you have a choice. You forget the way things work around here. I am the leader of the Levé's. My word *is* the law. Even vampires take orders from me. You are just a low grade human. One word from me and you will be nothing but a sacrificial snack for my loyal brethren." Her tone was heavily pompous.

"I doubt that. It all goes back to what I was saying earlier." He got a little cocky, but was not really meaning to sound that way. He just wanted some closure to the matter. "You still haven't answered me."

Tessa turned away from him. It had been a lonely four years. She had kept herself busy so that she hadn't felt so alone. It just wasn't the same, but she wasn't so sure it had anything to do with Isaac. "I just miss companionship. Don't read any more into it than there is."

"I guess that is as good of an answer that I am going to get." He sighed.

"It will have to do. Now if you don't mind, I would like to be alone. Close the door and I will summon you when I need something."

"Fair enough." Isaac said as he turned away and left.

Tessa turned inward to her thoughts. She was unsure why she had held a grudge against Isaac for so long. There was no need. He obviously proved his loyalty, at least to the children which in itself, she was grateful for. They needed some kind of human raising if they are to be as she hoped for in the end.

*****

Isaac stood outside the door and took in a deep breath. He could not believe how bold and stupid he was. He replayed the conversation in his head and realized how needy he must have seemed to her. It was not that he did not have feelings for her. He most definitely did. But he still had to come to terms with what she was. Seeing her feed on that poor girl reminded him of that. He wasn't so sure that coexistence between humans and vampires was going to take place anytime soon. Tessa seemed to be veering off of her master plan for some reason. But maybe if he stuck around he could try his best to at least remind her of the future she had envisioned.

*****

"If you are going to go up against vampires and humans alike, you're going to have the think like both species." Andreas blocked a double kick from a young man, who happened to be in training.

The young man turned around quickly and ducked, trying to knock Andreas off of his feet. Instead he jumped and turned a flip behind the young man, grabbed him by the arm, twisted it behind his back, and placed a sharp blade at his throat. "I think that we still have a lot of work to do."

"And I think that Jason has had enough for now." Tessa stood in the doorway and watched the sparring match. "He has other duties to attend to."

Andreas backed away from Jason, who was shaking it all off. "Fair enough." He turned to Jason and they bowed to each other. “Until tomorrow.”

Jason walked over to his aunt. “I could have gone a little bit more.” He wiped beads of sweat from his brow.

Tessa shook her head. “You’ve got studies to do.”

“Why do I need to worry about them? I am already in training for battle.”

“So you think all it takes to be one of my elite soldiers is all brawn?” Tessa nodded towards Andreas. “He has much more to teach you. It takes a lot more than that to become one of my trusted advisors, something you are in training to be. You have to know everything; feel everything. You must know cause and effect. Without complete knowledge of the vampire way you will never know how to defend against our kindred enemies, the Krones. Without knowing the human’s history you will never be able to know their capabilities. You have to be aware of everything, predict the unpredictable; then and only then, will you be successful in our fight against both vampires and humans.”

“Yes ma’am.” He nodded in obedience and walked away. He trusted his aunt and took her word for what it was. She had not been the one to abandon him, not like his mother, who was the leader of his enemies.

Tessa walked over to Andreas. “I know you are training him well, but I believe we are going to need to enlist the help of the rest of our comrades.”

“I agree. He has a lot left to learn. He is careless and even though he is very strong, he thinks too much and is overconfident.”

“I am just torn. He still is just a boy.”

“Sixteen is a man’s age. You must let him be a man.”

Tessa sighed. “I know. I am just very protective.” Tessa drew in a deep breath. “Now onto business. Have we got everything prepared for my journey in a couple of days?"

"Very close but our Intel is still gathering information. The plane and security are all ready to be set in place."

"Good. I want this council meeting to go off without a hitch. No hiccups, no surprises."

She turned to walk out the door. "I trust that you will make all that happen."

As Tessa began to walk down the hall she stopped when she saw Bade. "Did Emma make it to her classes today?"

He nodded. "She put up a fight but we got her there." He looked at her. "That child is a real handful. She is very stubborn and headstrong."

"She'll have to come around at some point."

"And if she doesn't?" He asked.

"We'll come to that when it becomes necessary. But for now I think that as long as she is receptive to me, there is hope. I love her very much and would like to keep her happy." Tessa sighed. "She just hasn't stopped wondering about her mother. I don't blame her, but then I wish she would understand that she is better off here. The world out there is no place for her." She stopped for a moment and then pondered the situation. "Actually, why don't you bring Emma to my study? I want to have a talk with her."

"Yes ma'am." He turned and headed for Emma's room while Tessa went to her study.

When Emma had arrived, Tessa was sitting at the piano, playing a hauntingly familiar tune to the child.

She never stopped playing as she spoke to Emma. "Come here and sit next to me." Tessa scooted over as Emma plopped down beside her. "Do you know this song?" She had hoped she did.

"It seems as though I do, but I can't figure out what

it is."

"Well, when your mother and I were little girls we took piano lessons. I was very impatient with my lessons. It seemed like I thought I was too good to play such boring music. I wanted jazz, Broadway, maybe even some songs off of the radio. Your mother was very persistent, though. She loved playing all these classical tunes. She practiced constantly. Especially this song; it became her favorite. I am sure she had played it for you as a small child."

Emma's eyes filled with sadness. Tessa noticed it and stopped playing. She turned towards the blossoming girl and touched her face gently. Emma's first reaction was to pull away, but instead she took in the comforting.

"I'm sorry to have upset you. It wasn't my intention. I just thought that I would share with you a part of your mother you may not have known."

A tear trickled down Emma's face. "I just really miss her."

"I miss her too." Tessa stated. "I wish she had stayed. I wanted to be able to have my old relationship with my sister back, but it was evident that she did not want to have anything to do with that."

She came to her mother's defense. "She had a cause and she believed in it."

"That is true. Your mother always stayed with her convictions, but look where it has gotten her. She fights day in and day out and has gotten no further than when she started."

"She hasn't given up though." She said, still defensively.

"There is something she has given up." She began to work on Emma's fears. "She left you and Jason here."

"She didn't mean to. She will come back for us."

Emma started crying harder.

Tessa shook her head. “No, Emma, she’s not. She knew you two were better off here. At least with me you are guaranteed food, shelter, and education. She knew that I loved you like you were my own children.” Tessa knew it was a lie because she heard of Melinda’s plans for rescuing her children constantly. Every time she attempted, she was thwarted by one of Tessa’s troops.

She put her hands on Emma’s shoulders. “You do believe I love you and would never hurt you, don’t you?”

“Yes I do.” She nodded.

“I also want you to know that I will do anything for you.” She said and watched her stop crying for a moment. “And I will start with setting you up with piano lessons. I think that your mother would like that. Would you like it?”

Emma nodded. “Yes, I think I would like to learn.”

She gave her a big hug. “Your mother would be proud. You are turning into a beautiful young lady.” She pulled away to gaze into her eyes. “I’ve watched you grow up right before my eyes. It only seems like yesterday you were this very little frail girl. I love you very much.” She kissed her forehead then stood up. “Tomorrow will be your first lesson. I also think that we should start you onto a different learning path. I know how bored you are of your classes in school. I think that your learning needs to be more of a hands-on approach.” She motioned for her to get up. “Now, it is probably time to retire to your room. You will have a long day tomorrow.”

After Emma left the room, Bade walked in. She told him, “I want you to have someone keep an eye on her at all times. She is most definitely torn between me and her mother. I want to do everything possible to keep her loyal to me, but if she falls in the other direction I want to be ready for it. She will not be as easy to win over as her brother has been."

"I agree, and I assure you she will be looked after."

"That you; loyal friend." Tessa acknowledged.

* * * * *

Tessa stood just inside the doorway of the aged compound as she waited for the vehicle to show up to take her to her plane. She had not met with The Vampire Nation for quite some time, and actually felt sort of reluctant to go. Every time she stepped foot inside any room with the council, memories of Greco haunted her thoughts. Those thoughts kept reminding her of what she should be as The Queen of The Levé's; something she felt she hadn't succeeded as well as he had hoped.

The only reason she was going was because there were rumors that the new Queen of The Krones would be there. From what she understood, the Krones were trying to become part of The Nation once again. She could not let that happen. Not if the Queen was going to continue waging war on her clan.

"Are you sure I can't help in some way? It would be very good for my experience." Jason begged his aunt. He felt that he was ready to go out into the world with his skills.

"No, not yet." She shook her head. Her hand moved fast to his belt, grabbed his knife and held it to his side. "You still have much practice to do. I don't want to risk it on a possibility that something could go wrong."

Jason lowered his head in disappointment. "I just wanted to be able to protect you."

Vala stepped forward. "That is what we are here for." Right beside her was Drake, and Andreas.

"Bade will be staying here in my place until we return." Tessa nodded in his direction.

"Are you sure you have to go?" She could hear Emma coming down the hall. She was on the heels of her uncle Isaac.

He stopped and looked at her. "I've already explained this to you. It is my job. I go where she goes."

'But it's not fair." She whined.

"You will be okay. Jason will be here with you to keep you safe."

"I'm not worried about that. I'm more worried that you won't make it home."

Isaac looked at her. "Every day I get up to walk out that door there is a possibility that I won't come home. At least this way, I get to go on a plane ride." He tousled her hair in a playful manner, then stood next to Bryon who was preparing to usher Tessa to her car.

"My Queen, may I speak to you for a moment?" Bade motioned for Tessa.

She walked over to him, where he was practically hiding in the shadows. "Is something the matter?"

"I am not quite certain yet." Worry was written across his face. "The winds are speaking to me. They seem to be warning me of a sudden change of the balance coming soon."

"What does that mean?"

"It means be careful and never let your guard down." He laid his hand on her shoulder. His eyes closed for a minute then he gasped and pulled away.

"What is it?" She was concerned.

"There is something stirring inside of you."

"What do you mean?"

"It seems almost as if your body is trying to tell me something. It has this need for something. It feels almost primal of sorts."

"Maybe I'm a couple of pints short of a meal." She laughed nervously. "No matter. If you are not certain something bad is going to happen to me, I will take it as a friend's thoughts of concern." She dismissed Bade's warning kindly.

Bryon called out to Tessa, "Transport is a go!"

"Then let's get moving." She headed out the door with her entourage surrounding her.

About six hours into her flight, Tessa's patience grew fainter. She felt that her time could be better spent doing something else. She couldn't help but laugh at how she had the power to reign as a high authority, someone people looked up to for leadership, but there was nothing that she could do but wait on the plane to complete its journey. She had to travel just like an every day average human had to.

She looked around in her luxury liner. Vala had a series of blades laid out on a table alongside a couple of guns that held special bullets filled with UV light that triggered on impact. She picked up her knives one by one, inspected and sharpened them.

Drake and Andreas continued to talk war strategies, which obviously bored Bryon enough to get up and sit on the opposite side of the plane, along with the three human servants whose only job was to keep the vampires out of the light as much as possible. Time would be very short and if it wasn't done right, the transfer would equal fatalities, since they had no choice but to travel during the day.

The Covered City was actually more of a fortress than a city itself. It stood just outside of Prague, the capital of what used to be the Czech Republic. What was amazing about it was that the first Shade ever built, a veil of darkness, surrounded it. The biosphere enclosed over the fortress that was equipped with enough cutting edge technology of the time that it synthetically kept the sunlight out of it, essentially making it forever dark inside as if it were constantly night. It made things easy for The Nation to be able to convene whenever needed and for however long they wished. Tessa realized, as she looked at it, that Greco had come close when he redesigned The Shade, but nothing could compare to the beauty.

She looked across from her where Isaac was sleeping peacefully. There was something about him. She wasn't sure what it was. His perseverance was profound. For some reason he didn't seem to want to give up hope that she would keep to her main goal of uniting the vampires and the humans. That part of him is what gave Tessa hope, yet frustrated her at the same time. She hoped that he was right to stand by her and believe in her, even though she had all but abandoned hope of a peaceful unity as long as war continued to be waged from every angle. She then felt her frustration because deep down inside she was nothing but a vampire. She had to keep telling herself that. Her human side died with her and she knew she should have no ties to the human race. Yet there she held tight to her human family and her ideals of a perfect world. When she looked at him it made her think of old feelings that ran deep inside; feelings of being needed, being cherished for who she was, and that she was a better person than she took herself for. She knew that she cared for him for that. She also knew that her lust for him was great. She missed his touch, his lips, and his warmth. No matter how many times she fed or shared blood with someone, it just wasn't the same. When he held her she felt as though nothing else mattered in the world. Of course all that brought back memories of Greco and the love they shared. That love ran deep and the passion was profound. No matter what she felt for Isaac, it would never be the same as what she had felt for Greco. He was her true love and his memory always lived on in her.

She felt that there was too much going on in her mind and decided to get up for a little walk around the cabin. There wasn't time for her to delve into her feelings or deep thoughts. She had a gathering to prepare for. There was no telling what stunts might be pulled from the Krones. She had to be ready for anything that might come their way. With those thoughts she went over to her allegiants and called them to a meeting. It was how she felt that her time needed to be spent.

When the sun started coming up, the plane went on lock down. Every window that looked out into the world was sealed tight behind curtains of plush velvet for ambiance. They were just a part of the strategic methods used to make sure that the passengers were not burned from exposure to the sun. Once they had landed, they were ushered quickly and securely into their cars. From there they took a long drive towards the dome.

Tessa just stared silently as the vehicle traveled through beautiful Prague, with all its beautiful and historical architecture. Unlike most of the older vampires, she had never been to Europe before, let alone Prague. Every meeting that she had gone to had taken place in their territory or by video conference. She wondered how many times her advisors had been there through the centuries. She knew it was in her best interest to keep her awe to herself, though; for fear that it would make her look weak and naïve. Bryon must have noticed the twinkle in her eyes and leaned into her. "Master Greco lived her for some time. Maybe 300 years ago, I forgot the specifics."

"Did he?" She couldn't help but smile a bit.

"He lived here with The Vampire Nation. They wanted his help in designing what is now the beautiful fortress."

"He was good at that." She seemed almost content in her visit. She felt like a piece of Greco would be with her the whole time she would be here. It didn't keep her from her main objective, which was to watch out for herself, because she was almost certain she and her advisors would be targets for the Krones.

Once inside the dome, the atmosphere had changed. It seemed almost like she was in an old movie. Oddly enough, Dracula was the one that came to mind. The road was winding and narrow. The hill was steep and dead trees and rocks surrounded the path. Once at the front gate the convoy of cars came to a stop. After a very thorough examination of their passes, they were motioned on through the gate. Their final destination was a very grand building. It was the look of architectural genius. It was definitely old, but had quite a few modern tendencies to it. Never-the-less, the beauty of its grandeur was phenomenal.

Once inside the house servants greeted them, then ushered them to their quarters. They were given rooms in the east wing. The human servants carried the vampire troupe's bags to their rooms then were directed off to the servant's quarters. Bryon and Isaac were told to stay behind. Tessa had requested that they stay in the adjoining room so that they could attend to her needs.

Bryon opened the mahogany doors leading to her room. He waited until she went in then shut the door behind them. She couldn't help but stand still and looked at her surroundings. There was something about the room that gave her an eerie yet comforting feeling. Then she spotted the symbol. It was everywhere. It was carved into the bedposts, the mantle, and even the overhead of the door. She knew that symbol well. It was the same one carved into Greco's wooden box; the same one burned into her arm. It was the seal of the Levé's.

She covered her mouth in saddened shock, a light red tear trickled down her cheek. "Was this…"?

"Greco's room? I believe it was." Bryon finished her sentence for her. "They had asked me if it would be okay. Did I make a mistake in telling them it wouldn't be a problem?"

She shook her head. "No, Bryon. It is far from being a problem." Happiness and sadness both flooded into her heart as if a dam had broken. She wasn't sure if there would ever be a moment that she wouldn't miss Greco.

She walked over to the sitting area in front of the fireplace and sat down in a big velvet chair that looked more like it belonged on Masterpiece Theatre. She looked down at the coffee table and noticed a note sealed in an intricately designed envelope.

Inside the envelope was a notice on where and when they were to convene for the evening. Tessa looked at the porcelain clock on the mantle. She had a couple of hours until they were to meet in the great room. The note also stated that it was going to be a social gathering and she should dress accordingly.

"Bryon, you can leave for now. I would like some time alone before I have to go to the function. Come back in an hour with that servant girl so that I can get dressed properly." Tessa sighed. "It seems as though every high function in vampire society has to be so formal. I feel out of my element most of the time."

"Greco fit in with it wonderfully. All of the leaders do. You are of a rare breed. You are modern and young. That puts you at an advantage because you can be unpredictable and think outside the box. It is to your disadvantage too though, since you don't know fully what the leaders are capable of."

"Well, that was very helpful." She said dryly.

"Just be strong, confident, and social. Greco always told me that the elder vampires loved nothing more than to talk about themselves. You might learn a thing or two."

"Now that makes a little bit more sense." She laughed. "Now if you don't mind..." She waved Bryon out.

It had seemed only moments had passed when Bryon burst into the room with the servant girl in tow. She needed to get ready for the party. Time must have passed her by, as she did nothing but check out everything in the room. She found it so interesting the things she discovered and of obvious evidence that Greco had truly been there. The bed linens smelled like he had slept in them the night before. In the wardrobe she found a metal button that seemed to have fallen off of one of his elaborately decorated shirts.

Vala, Andreas, and Drake met her in the sitting room of the east wing. They thought that it would be best to all make an entrance together, like a true clan was supposed to.

"Are we all ready?" Tessa asked her compatriots. All of them were dressed as formal as her, although they seemed more awkward feeling dressed up than she did. They had been combatants for many centuries in one form or another. That is why they made the perfect advisors for her with their combination of intelligence, agility, and strength.

"I do hope that this evening doesn't last too long. I feel all too vulnerable in this dress." Vala tugged at the tightened frock.

Tessa laughed slightly. "Well, Vala, just think of this as gathering Intel." Her tone then became serious. "Seriously though, I need you all to have your eyes and ears open. I want to know as much about everyone that I can and their planned events. Don't let your guard down even for a single second. You are here to work. I want to know as much about this summons that I possibly can. If it is true that the Queen of The Krones and her henchmen are here, I want to know." Her advisors nodded in compliance. Then they began the walk towards the great room.

As she began her descent down the Grande staircase she took in the diversity of the room. Each head vampire hailed from different parts of the world. Each one had their own advisors, which seemed to have filled the room quickly. It felt as if every vampire of importance was in that room. It scared her a little when she thought of the possibility that they could be attacked. Their race would practically be wiped out. The idea made her just a little bit more aware of her surroundings.

She spent the next couple of hours painting a smile on her face with just enough seriousness to remind them that she was in fact a Queen. The entertainment was mildly amusing. There was, on one side of the room, a string quartet playing mostly melancholy music while beautiful vamps filled the plush seating surrounding them. On the other side of the room was a small section for gambling. It had poker, blackjack, craps, and roulette. One thing Tessa knew was that vampires loved their guilty pleasures.

She found Andreas speaking with a beautiful lady vamp. She had no qualms interrupting them because she knew that Andreas understood he wasn't there for fun. "Pardon me," Tessa nodded to the light brown skinned woman, naturally made for sunlight. "I will have to steal away my advisor for just a moment."

"You are Queen Tessa?"

"That I am." She nodded.

Andreas said quickly, "My Queen, this is Ashwayra of the Strega Klan. She is one of Queen Kali's advisors."

Ashwayra placed her hands together and bowed humbly. "It is an honor to be in your presence."

"Thank you." After she mirrors the bow she turned to Andreas. "Can I have a word with you?"

He excused himself as she pulled him aside. "Please tell me that you have some information for me. I do not want my utter boredom to be in vain."

"I have got some information, but I don't think that it really will help."

"Well, what is it?"

"It seems as though most of the other advisors I have spoken with are just as clueless as we are regarding the reason we are here. Some seem to think that a few key members of the council are implementing a new objective. Others think it could be a joining of smaller tribes amongst our council, which seems to have become something of a constant in the Africa and Asian continents. Then there are some, like you, who think that the Queen of the Krones is going to attempt to bring the Krones into the Nation once again."

"Have you found out who she is yet? Do you even know if she is here?" Tessa's nervousness was apparent.

"No, I haven't. Vala is trying to find out for you." He knew that would not be good enough for her.

Tessa said with frustration, "Well I hope she does find out. The future of the Levé's weigh heavily on any and all Intel on the Krones."

He nodded. "Yes, I understand."

The evening seemed to drag on and the stuffiness became too much for Tessa to deal with. She spoke to her advisors and told them she was going to retire early but she thought it would be in their best interest if they continue to gather as much information before the conference the next night.

As soon as she cleared the door she breathed a sigh of relief. She was quite happy to be out of there. Tessa knew that she was there for a reason but she couldn't help but think that she needed to blow off some steam. Tessa had never been to Prague and she wanted to enjoy the nightlife. She felt that since she was in a place that she would not be recognized as anyone important she should take advantage of it. It had been a long time since she got to do anything of the sort back home.

It did not take long for her to change, grab Isaac from his deep slumber, and head out into the dark European night.

CHAPTER ELEVEN

It may have been another country but the atmosphere was the same. "*Karmínově květ*". It meant crimson flower in the Czech language. The outside looked like an old stone gentleman's club dripping with ivy. Tessa had overheard many kindred speaking of it. She had been afraid that she was slightly overdressed since she had come from such an elite function, but then she saw the patrons entering as if they too were at a socialite party. They each had in tow a human servant, something she had also heard about. That is why she brought Isaac along. He protested of course, but she grew stern and told him he had no choice in the matter. His job was to take orders. She didn't want to have to explain to him the reasoning behind it, which boiled down to two factors. The first one eliminated the lower ranked servants simply due to wardrobe. They had nothing but standard fare; nothing worthy of a social evening. That brought Tessa to the second reason, since that left only Bryon and Isaac. To be honest, Bryon was getting a little old and her vanity demanded he be looked over as a choice; that left Isaac. Of course, she had a third choice, which was simply not to go, but she was determined to have a little fun more to her liking. It had been so long, maybe too long. That put her where she stood looking across the street to the club. She started to have second thoughts since it seemed slightly similar to the party that she had just left. But her determination won her over and convinced her that at The Crimson Flower she wasn't going to be looked upon as a Queen.

"Come, Isaac." She looked into his cold blue eyes. "I need you to do as I say."

"What is there for me to do?"

She shook her head. "I don't know. All I know is that for some reason a human *has* to be present with a vampire to enter."

He sarcastically said, "And this is what you think a good time involves? I think you should have found out a little more before you made your plans. Or at least found something more suitable to your tastes."

She turned to him and snapped, "Your job is not to do my thinking. This is what I want, end of story."

"This is the way to get me to do what you want. Continue yelling at me."

Tessa sharply turned around eyes glowing in anger. "I would advise for you to keep your mouth shut before I permanently do it for you." Her eyes burned deep into his. Tessa felt his fear, and then realized what she looked like to him. A vicious blood-thirsty killer. She turned away and mumbled. "And to think I actually cared for you."

"Is that supposed to make me feel better? Why are you telling me this? It doesn't matter now does it? I'm just your first-class slave, nothing more."

"That is not true." She responded quicker than she would have liked. It was too late to take it back.

"Oh really?" He raised his eyebrow in intrigue. "You still care about me?"

"You are the children's uncle. I love them deeply, so yes as their guardian I care what happens to you."

"That's not it." He knew better. He could sense it. As long as she was even a tiny bit interested, he knew there would be hope.

"No matter. Let's go so I can see what is so special about this place." She grabbed him and led him across the street. She waited her turn to enter into the building. Once there, the doorman asked her in the vampire tongue for her mark and name. She showed him the mark on her wrist then asked him, “Can I trust your secrecy?”

He responded. “Privacy is of our utmost concern. We do not tell the other patrons who you are,” He paused “But I cannot let you through without knowing who you are since this is a private club.”

“I am not a member. I am visiting from abroad.”

“No matter. Name please.”

Tessa leaned over in his ear and whispered her name. He looked into his handheld module for her identity. She knew he found her in the system as his eyes widened in realization of her importance. He slightly bowed his head to her. “I do apologize. It is my job to keep this place secure.”

“Protocol is important.” She smiled. “Am I secure?”

“You can be certain your identity is safe with me.”

“Thank you.” Tessa nodded then spoke over her shoulder to Isaac. “Come.”

The moment she walked through the doors she felt as if she had stepped into another place. Its walls ran deep with crimson hues accented only by black and gold.

“May I take your coat?” A tall human gentleman asked her. She handed it off to him as she stepped down the hall.

To her left, there was a billiard room filled with men and smoke. On the right was a room filled with laughter, mostly of women sitting on overstuffed couches and chairs.

The gentleman who took her coat yelled down the hall to her. “If you are looking for the discotec, it is at the end of the hall through the double doors.”

She wasn't sure what she was looking for, but it was always good to start where the music was. She felt at home, like she did before she was turned. One thing that she figured out quickly was that although it was filled with the socially elite, there was definitely something different from being amongst Kings and Queens. She felt more acceptable here. She was never really one to be so interested in the royalty thing. She did like being in control but something a little more modern would have been nice. Of course she had to play with the cards that were dealt to her.

She led Isaac through the double doors. As soon as they opened the silence was breached by loud pulsating rhythms. Lasers and lights filled the room as her nostrils soaked in the sweet aroma of blood.

"Stop." Said what looked to be a huge bouncer. "Your slave cannot follow you in there." He held out his hand and pointed to a crowded room to the side. "He must go in there."

Isaac looked at her questionably and she nodded. "Go on. I will retrieve you when I am done." The bouncer led him into the room as if he were taking a jacket to a coat room. It made no sense to her why she needed a human to be present at the entrance only to shove them aside in a room that made them look like sardines in a can. She pushed that thought aside and proceeded down the entrance, headed straight for the bar, and sat down. She ordered a brandy and savored the flavor. It was one of Greco's favorite human drinks. Most alcohols did nothing to the vampire in a drunken sense unless it was in the blood of a human. Blood was sweet nectar as it was, but to add a few tasty spirits into it was divinity. Pure enjoyment was the reason she sat there nursing her drink. She looked out around the club. It was filled to the rafters of beautiful vampires. They were not the same kind she had been spending the evening with or even the company she had kept for quite a few years. They were more free-spirited. They succumbed to their pleasures, gave themselves time to be what they wanted to be. Titles were left at the door, right along with people's expectations, their duties and obligations.

She decided that she was going to hit the dance floor, a place where she felt like the real Tessa; the one who wasn't a queen, let alone a vampire. The Tessa that worked hard for a living just to make it by and partied like a rock star to blow off some steam. As she moved her body to the music she closed her eyes and took it all in. She felt nothing but the energy of those around her and memories of a past that were slowly fading away. She moved as if she was walking on air for just a moment with no care in the world. Then she felt it; a familiarity, yet nothing like she had ever felt before. Her heart raced and her lust for flesh and blood alike awakened. She opened her eyes and looked around. She saw nothing but the crowd that surrounded her. She concentrated really hard on what was calling her. She closed her eyes one more time to see if that helped in bringing it back. Slowly the talking and the music faded into the distance.

"Come to me." She finally heard it. It was as if a tiny voice was speaking to her. She quickly opened her eyes, still fully concentrated on what was reaching out to her. Everything was hazy around her as she looked around. Things blurred into one another. Then she saw her. An aura of light surrounded her as if she were the mother of Jesus herself. Her lips pressed together mouthing those words, "Come to me." Her words beckoned to Tessa as if by force. Her mind kept recycling those words in her head as if it were a chant. She felt an uncontrollable desire to walk towards her and she didn't resist.

The dark haired woman sat at a corner booth. Her demeanor was cool and collective. "Why don't you have a seat?" She said.

Tessa looked around at all the enticing vamps that surrounded her. "Standing is fine."

"Nonsense." She looked at a beautiful dark woman sitting beside her. "Alanis will let you have hers."

The woman was surprised. "But..."

"No arguments. I would think you would have been hospitable enough to offer up your seat anyway."

Alanis pushed the young man beside her out of the booth as she followed behind him. When she stood up she glared at Tessa and showed her fangs.

"Enough!" The mystery woman said.

She slid in beside her. She felt as if she needed to be cautious of her surroundings.

"What brings you to this place?"

"I grew bored of being surrounded by stuffy aristocrats."

The woman laughed. "I completely understand." She motioned towards a waitress. When she arrived, Tessa was asked if she would like something to drink. She didn't argue when the woman ordered six shots of absinthe. She had never had absinthe. She was actually quite surprised she hadn't. It was the only alcohol that affected a vampire. It gave them great pleasure, almost like that of feasting. The best combination was when a human consumed the beverage and then shared its blood with a vampire.

"You called out to me. Why?" She tried to hide her awe at such a perfectly beautiful specimen for the vampire race. She looked Mediterranean with her olive skin, dark eyes and hair. She somehow was thinking she could easily be one of the Greek Goddesses.

"I just wanted your company, that's all. I'm Liana."

"They aren't enough for you?"

The woman just laughed.

"This was different though, how you did it. Only one other could call out to me like that."

"Greco, right?" The woman said, which threw Tessa off.

"Yes, but how did you...?"

"Let's just say we go way back."

"Is that so?" She raised an eyebrow.

Liana nodded, "Its amazing how much you look like her. I can see how he could be entranced by you."

"Excuse me?" Tessa asked, a little upset and unnerved along with a dash a frightfulness. *What was she talking about?*

"Let's not discuss this right now." The mystery woman dismissed the conversation and passed out the sugar laden drinks. "Drink up everyone." She lit the flame, burned the sugar, and they all took their drinks.

It did not take long for her to feel the effects of the drink. It was a warm sensation surging through her body. It was nothing like feeding. It was something in its own element.

"Waitress!" The woman snapped to get her attention. "Another round!" She kept the drinks flowing and with each one Tessa felt her inhibitions slip away. They laughed and talked for quite a while. It felt like she and this woman were the only two in the room once more.

The woman looked into her eyes. "You are very beautiful." She smiled and stroked her cheek. "So young and innocent to our world. Easily tucked away and coached by him. He did well with you." She cupped her face gently in her hands and leaned in towards her. "I can see how he fell in love with you." She leaned in even further and started to kiss her. Tessa fell into the moment and welcomed the warm embrace. She pulled away for just a moment and the woman asked, “What is your slave’s name?”

Confused, She answered, “Isaac, why?”

She shook her head as if she ignored the question. She called for the waitress one more time. “I want you to start Isaac on a little absinthe then send him upstairs in an hour.”

“What’s upstairs?”

The woman cocked her head and smiled mischievously. She looked around at her entourage and said, “She wants to know what is upstairs.” The group all burst into laughter as she felt like she had sunk into her seat from embarrassment. “Do you think we should show her now?” She asked with a unanimous vote to lead her into the unknown. “I agree that she is ready.” The flawless vixen had her group get up so that Tessa and she could slide out.

Once standing, Tessa felt quite unsettled, yet completely free as she wobbled a little from being inebriated.

“Whoa! Let me hold you up!” Thc woman offered as she grabbed Tessa’s waist. The group made their way to the elevator in the corner of the room. It was almost hidden in the walls.

Once out of the elevator, they made a long trek down the hall until they came to large double doors.

“I want you to come in and enjoy yourself with me. I want to share what is mine and we can make this about you and me.” She grabbed her hand and led her through the doors. In her current state, she really didn’t think about what she was getting herself into. She only thought about how wonderful it felt to be with someone again and not thinking about anything but pure hedonism.

Tessa stood in amazement and taken aback by what she saw. Vampire and humans alike lounging around the hot and steamy surroundings. Vampires were sharing themselves with other vampires. Biting, sharing blood, and fondling one another. They also took pleasure in feeding off their slaves, all in moments of passion. Some were laying there naked while others left their clothes on. Even a few of them were partaking in the taboo act of sexual behavior, out in the open for all to see. The whole scene brought the image of what Roman orgies were like.

"Will you share with me? With us?" The woman was obviously speaking of the group that came in and maybe their humans.

She he had heard of such things going on in the vampire world. Greco just attempted to keep her shielded from most of it. Once he had passed away, it left her with very little time out in the world to enjoy it fully. That is what led her to that precise moment.

Under normal conditions, Tessa would have probably assessed the situation more clearly, but she was far from normal. She was intoxicated and high, and felt all kinds of urges as they coursed through her body.

"Come with me." Those almost familiar words came out of the perfect Goddess's lips. She led Tessa and her friends to a pallet made up of satin sheets and pillows on the floor. It wasn't long before she felt as if she too had become part of the seductive crowd.

She began to get lost in all the pleasure. The woman seemed to focus all her attention on her. She reveled in the abundance of blood and sensuality laid out before her. All her senses were heightened, even for a vampire, with absinthe laced blood flowing freely to her lips.

As she held the naked body of her willing victim and drank profusely from the puncture wounds on her left breast, she sensed a presence in the room. It wasn't her mysterious lady since she lay beside her. It was something else. She closed her eyes and breathed in the aura of her visitor.

"Isaac." The words came out as if they were a breathy song. She laid the half conscious woman down and turned to face Isaac.

He tried to hide the bit of fear he was sure to be experiencing at that moment. He had never been around such bloody surfeit. He looked at Tessa who was completely naked. Her eyes glowed brightly and her fangs protruded prominently. Her mouth was completely covered in blood and more of it splattered around her body.

"I am glad you came. I was beginning to get bored with my current suitors." She motioned to the group of humans that surrounded her and her new found companion. "Come over here." She motioned with her finger.

Isaac stood there and did not move. He was almost too afraid to do so. He felt as if he had walked into a snake pit filled with slithering, deceptive, and dangerous vampires gorging themselves in the ecstasy of the bodies and blood of their drunken prey.

"Isaac, come to me." Tessa's voice filled with anger and uneasiness. She did not want to see her kind take note of such a weakness that her own servant did not obey her, no matter how much she truly respected him.

He couldn't help his fears; the green liquid had enhanced them, but also lowered his inhibitions, making it more difficult to respond. He just knew the woman, or creature, that stood before him was not the Tessa he knew. That Tessa made him afraid for his life.

Everything about her was different, as if she were under a spell.

Alanis slithered up next to him and began to catch his scent. "Looks like someone can't control their servant." She glared at her and then honed in on the pulse in Isaac's neck beating faster and faster. She ran her ebony fingernails on his chest. "Do you not respect your master?"

He refused to answer. He avoided looking in her eyes for fear of being drawn in by her hypnotizing nature. He kept his head down, but eyes glancing toward Tessa, who stood there silently.

"I think that I could have a lot of fun with this one." She licked beads of sweat that were on his cheek. "He tastes so yummy and sweet. I just want to gobble him up."

"Alanis!" The enigmatic immortal leader said to her. "Enough! You need to know your place."

She laughed wickedly. "I do not answer to her."

"But you do answer to me."

Alanis took her fingernail and scratched at Isaac's neck. "Just a little taste." She traced her tongue on his neck, and tasted the droplets of blood that dripped from it. The aroma of his sweet blood did nothing to help Tessa from the state she was in. She had never tasted his blood before. She couldn't help but wonder; which aroused her even more. She broke herself away from the fog, from the high she had experienced just enough to keep things from getting out of her hands.

She quickly moved towards Alanis and appeared in front of her. "You do not take things that don't belong to you. Unhand my servant or I will make sure that is the last drop of blood you ever taste." Tessa's eyes burned into hers.

The woman was not backing down. "Who are you

to make demands of me? He doesn't want to obey; I think he is fair game."

"That is not for you to decide now is it?" Her anger rose even more. She became aware of her nobility once again. "He is marked as the sole property of The House of Levé." She pointed to the back of his neck where the dark symbols revealed the truth.

"And that matters to me how? Who are you to make demands like this? What power do you have?"

She unraveled her leather binding around her wrist, the one with the mark of The House of Levé. Alanis took notice of the symbol quickly. There was no mistaking the Queen of the Levé's mark.

"Now can I have what is mine?" Tessa asked with a certain confidence.

Alanis let go of Isaac's arm and lowered her lead in shame before she left the room, devastated. She may not have been a member of her clan, but not respecting a Queen would be as damaging as if it were her own.

Tessa turned to her smoldering female paramour who had a smile of intrigue on her face. "I am glad we could amuse you this evening."

She ignored her bitterness. "I knew you would be able to handle yourself." She changed the subject. "Come back to me. Let us continue to tantalize our senses. You can bring your servant with you."

Tessa's eyes grew cold. "I do not intend to share him."

"Bring him anyway. I have plenty to choose from. But don't let my generosity be for naught. You don't want all this fresh blood to go to waste."

Tessa wasn't sure why she even entertained the idea, but then again she wasn't completely in control of her actions. Whatever her mysterious woman said seemed to embed in her senses and to ignore them felt somewhat unpleasant. For the time being she played along.

"Drinks for everyone!" The woman said happily as she motioned to one of her comrades, who prepared them quickly and passed them around.

"Drink this. It will make you feel better." Tessa said to Isaac. He looked apprehensive and uncertain what to do. She handed him a glass of absinthe topped traditionally with its faux silver spoon and sugar cube. As many drinks as she had already shot back she was becoming a pro at the method. She took the cold water, poured it over the sugar, and watched it dissolve into the liquor. He gave her a worried look but drank down one shot. She handed him another and grabbed one for herself. They repeated the ritual and indulged in the liquid ambrosia.

She leaned into his ear and whispered. "I will try not to hurt you."

"Why are you doing this?" He whispered back.

"Because I feel compelled to do so." Her words seemed to turn effervescent as she watched them pass from her lips into his ear. "It feels right."

She then turned her attention to his neck as she kissed gently towards the wound. She paused for just one moment, and then closed her eyes as her senses became heightened once again.

She opened her mouth and slowly ran her tongue against the wound. She had never tasted anything so heavenly before. Maybe it was the green goddess coursing through his veins or maybe it was the fact that all of it was taboo.

Whatever the reason, it kicked her instincts into overdrive. She bit into his neck surrounding the wound. The floodgate of sweet nectar filled her mouth. She felt Isaac struggling slightly but then calmed his body;

succumbing to her warm embrace. His confusion of the circumstances was understandably high but everything faded into a haze of bliss. That was standard fare for a vampire rendezvous. Seduction was key for getting the human aroused enough to submit to the culling.

She pulled away and wiped his blood from her lips with her tongue. She began to lead Isaac towards the back corner where a pallet of soft satin pillows filled the area behind a beautifully spun curtain. Before retiring behind the transparent drape, the mystical hostess came over and helped her undress him; she caressed both of them thoroughly in the process. After deeply kissing her new found mistress, Tessa sat him down on the pallet. She stopped her hostess from coming in after them, mentally stating the privacy she asked for. Tessa then slid in after Isaac, pulling the curtain closed. As she laid on top of him she looked into his clouded eyes with her glowing embers. Both were lost in seduction and their most natural instincts. She paired lovemaking with feeding; making certain she only took a small amount at a time. It lasted for hours until Isaac grew weak and needed to rest.

Tessa sensed dawn coming and heard the sound of a chiming bell, which was the universal sound for all vampires to return to dark safety. She peered outside the curtain and watched as servants rushed around sealing the room completely of sunlight. She also noticed the mystifying woman asleep amongst a group of humans, obviously passed out from the blood loss. She felt the heaviness of the sun coming up. She decided to retire behind the curtain and comfortably returned to Isaac's side as she drifted off to sleep.

* * * * *

Hours later, Isaac awoke dazed and confused. His head felt as if a hammer were banging down on it and his eyes had a hard time focusing. When he sat up he felt lightheaded. He didn't know where he was or even how he got there.

When his eyes began to focus again he turned to his right and saw Tessa sleeping beside him completely unclothed. He didn't even know how he ended up in bed with her. The last thing he remembered was going to a private club as her faux slave. Everything else was a blur.

He pushed aside the curtain of the small enclosure and grabbed his clothes on the way out. It wasn't until he was dressed that he noticed the devastation that surrounded him. It looked like he was in a creature's lair. Bare bodies lay on top of one another, each stained with blood. A vision flashed in his head. He saw the blood orgy for just a split second and then it disappeared. He was there. He saw it. The image of that female vampire that tried to feed on him and Tessa. Had she saved him, he wondered? The woman did go away so she must have. He then remembered her giving him something to drink. "*It will make you feel better.*" Those words echoed as Isaac remembered a naked Tessa handing him a few drinks. That must have been why he felt awkward when he woke up. He had too much to drink. But then a couple of words screamed heavily in his thoughts. "*I will try not to hurt you.*" He then gasped as he remembered Tessa baring her fangs and feeding on him. His heart was racing as he rushed around looking for a mirror. When he found one he looked at this neck and found what he was afraid of. Two perfectly rounded puncture wounds on his neck. She had fed on him. He felt betrayed and used. He never thought she would do that to him. *Was that all she did?*

Isaac went back to where she slumbered. He shook her fiercely. "What have you done?"

It took quite a bit of shaking to awaken her. When she finally came around, her natural instinct was to defend herself. Without much effort, she threw him off of her and onto the floor. She realized what she had done as she saw him on the ground looking up at her with both fear and hate.

"Why did you wake me?" Tessa protested.

"What did you do to me?" He screamed at her.

She tried to assess the situation, but her memories were also in a fog. She looked at him and noticed the marks on his neck. She remembered, at that point. She had fed on him.

Tessa bent down and examined his neck. She did remember that the night was intoxicating and filled with passion. All things pure and raw, which included sex and feeding. The woman who started it all was there and Tessa felt she was being tested at every move or decision that she made, almost like it was a secret rivalry. She knew she did what she did to Isaac because that was the only way to guarantee his safety. "I did what I did out of necessity."

He stood up, unhappy with her response. "You had plenty of her blood whores to fill your necessity. You did not have to feed on me."

She turned away and began to gather he clothes. "It wasn't my necessity, it was yours." She found what she was looking for and began to get dressed.

He growled in frustration and grabbed Tessa by the arm. "You make no sense to me. I want an explanation. I want to know if you did anything to me besides feed."

"Unhand me!" She pulled herself away from him. "And if you want to continue this conversation in a civilized manner I would advise you to lower your voice." She looked around at all things that might expose that she was not as ruthless and noble as previously established.

He apologized. "Did you attempt to turn me?" He finally asked the question he feared the most.

She shook her head. "No. That was the furthest thing from my mind." She looked at him slightly confused. "Why are you complaining? If I recall, you had been trying to bed me again for some time now. Is that not what you wanted? Why are you so upset?"

"You *bit* me! I never wanted that. What I wanted was for us to be together, but now that time has passed."

"It did not seem like you had any problem last night. You should just have just taken it for what it was. Pure, unadulterated, fantastical sex. We never connected as perfectly as we did last night."

He shook his head. "If it were that phenomenal, why do I not remember that much?"

"Probably because we were both intoxicated. But you will remember soon enough. My senses recover quicker than yours, but I am sure it won't be long until you realize how magical it was."

"This still does not explain why you did what you did."

She leaned into him. "It was the only way I could guarantee your safety. Just remember this one thing; no matter how terrible I may seem, there is always someone or something out there ten times worse." She moved her eyes around the room. She looked one more time at the temptress that started everything. She decided that she had talked enough and did not want to reveal anything else to him. "You woke me early, and for that I am unhappy. I think you should leave me to rest a little more and wake me after sundown."

"So now you are going to act like nothing happened?" He questioned her.

She looked at him with no expression. "That's the plan. I do not want you to ever forget that I am and will always be your master. Emotional attachments will only do you harm."

He felt like a knife ripped through his heart. He showed no emotion on his face though. He didn't want any more unsolicited advice. He turned and walked out of the room where more servants had gathered to wait on their masters to awaken.

Once back at the foreign estate, Tessa rushed to her room, Isaac was having a hard time keeping up. Her entourage on her heels informed her of the information gathered at the ball while she was away. Most of it was useless information but Vala seemed to have gotten the most vital parts of it.

"I know who the Krone Queen is."

Tessa stepped in front of the room to her door. "Tell me more as I dress for the summit."

"It took a lot of investigating, but I got it nonetheless." Vala said, practically patting herself on the back before getting serious again. "She is most definitely here at this summit."

"Go on."

"Her name is Liana."

Tessa stopped for a moment, hoping she had heard that wrong. "Liana?"

"Yes. I couldn't get a visual on her though."

Tessa sighed. "I believe I have."

"What? But how?"

"Long story short...Instead of retiring to my room last night I went out to a private club and that is where I met her. I had no idea, although looking back on it, I realize she was nothing but a corrupt seductress."

"What do you mean?"

She shook her head. "No real concern." She thought different to herself. She still was uncertain how she could have succumbed to being so fragile around a total stranger. The easy answer could have been absinthe and blood. But she knew better. There was something different about her. Liana heavily influenced her. No other vampire had done that to her, although Greco did say that he could have easily influenced her, but he refused to do so. She shook off her doubtful thoughts. "Let's go. I cut my time shorter than I would have liked." She said as she walked out the door.

CHAPTER TWELVE

Tessa stood outside the meeting hall. She took in a few deep breaths and fixed a stern cold look on her face. She knew that if any of the vampires sensed a weakness, whether physical, mental, or emotional, it could be the end of that particular vampire's reign. There are always those willing to rip you into shreds and eat you up from within, just to get ahead, no matter the damage. She knew from experience with Desdemona. She did not want to make the same mistake twice. It was the one thing that bothered her about her encounter with Liana. Did she appear weak to her nemesis, or strong?

Bryon and Isaac led the way into the cold, dark chamber. It was a perfect atmosphere for vampires. It kind of reminded her more of an arena of sorts. There were booths similar to opera boxes encircling an empty pit below. Above each booth, hung a flag, which Tessa recognized as the symbols for the ruling clans.

She took her seat, followed by her three trustees. She watched as others began to file in. She took note of each and every one of the lead vampires. She also noticed that there was still one empty booth left to fill. Above it flew the deep robust colors of the Krones. From that point She knew without a doubt that the Krone queen herself was going to make an appearance. It gave her a sickening feeling in the pit of her stomach.

At that point she felt like everyone in the room was watching and whispering about her; wondering what she was thinking with the possible new revelation. She realized it would not serve any purpose other than to show weakness if she looked afraid at that moment, although deep down her worry brewed heavily.

She turned to her advisors and discussed with them the strategies for every possible outcome regarding the Krone Queen. They did their best to assure her they would follow through on any order and protect her if needed.

At last the Krones started to fill their seats. The Queen was the last to enter, almost if she were determined to make the most dramatic entrance as possible. It definitely did just that. All eyes were on her. When they weren't they were watching to see if Tessa reacted in any way. The whole time she took slow and deep breaths. She couldn't help but notice how beautiful Liana was, even though she put on a cold persona. Tessa shook off those thoughts. She knew they were only planted there by Liana herself.

Once Liana took her seat, Braedon of the Falor stood up. The room grew silent, waiting for him to speak. "Welcome my kindred souls. It is a pleasure to be amongst you once again. We have come a long way since our domination of this world. Each one of us has strived towards our goal with some unfortunate losses." Braedon sighed and bowed his head in respect for the fallen, then broke his short silence. "But we also have been growing as our family has welcomed with open arms three tribes that were once thought to be long gone. Although they are the children of our ancestor's ancestors, we acknowledge them as a speaking voice in The Vampire Nation." Braedon looked around the room, nodded at three unrecognizable groups. "We have Cizin of the Thacotl who flourished amongst us, disappeared, and have now raised back The Mayans. Chisolo of the Berber tribe who hails from Africa and Tish-atal of the Zalianu tribe from the Hurrian Empire, one of our earliest times in the Middle East. Each was awakened after realizing it was safe to walk the earth once again. I want you to give them a big welcome for those of you who have not done so yet." Applause filled the stadium. Braedon took his seat as Victor stood up.

"Now for the reason we are here. We have summoned you, The Vampire Nation to make the decision on whether to accept the Krones back into our organization. We have the new Queen here today to give us her plea. This is an open meeting and each one of you will have a say in the outcome. I will now turn the floor over to Liana."

The air was silent as the Krone Queen stood up with such poise and grace. Her whole presence had Tessa realize she had been a part of the elite for quite a while, maybe even longer than Greco. She wondered why she didn't take note of that the previous night.

"My kindred souls. I humbly appreciate this audience before you, The Vampire Nation. I realize what it took for you all to gather here, and I wish that this hadn't been so secretive. Of course there was no easy way to be able to plead my case for acceptance into The Nation." She paused for only a moment. "As you know, certain circumstances brought us to this moment with the unfortunate demise of our beloved Renos and Greco along with the ostracizing of my predecessor, Desdemona. Although all of that was warranted and needed, I feel that the time has come where the Krones need to become once again a part of The Vampire Nation. We have grown and evolved; prospered and flourished. My people no longer harbor ill will towards our own kind. We just want to once again be one with our kindred, to share our knowledge, technology, and trade."

Layla spoke up. "Who is to say that you will not fall

into the same circumstances as Desdemona? We have no assurance that our safety is not at risk."

"She is right." Tyr said. "Those of us who know you, also know your closeness with Desdemona. You used to always share her ambition and determination."

"Yes, of course you have reason to be slightly apprehensive, but I assure you that I do not share in her dreams that had somehow become twisted and off the path to truly being an equal part of The Nation." Liana took a deep breath. "I may have been a daughter to Desdemona all those years she took me in and taught me all she knew. I had a few centuries to realize that I was not like her and that it was time I moved from under her wing to carve a path for myself. During that quest, I began to understand the true meaning of being a vampire."

Tessa tried to take all of it in. Liana's speech reminded her more of a politician than of true sincerity. She wondered more on Liana's relationship with Desdemona which opened up a Pandora's Box of questions, not to mention the question that weighed heavy on her mind; *how did she know Greco the way she spoke*?

Guayarokun said, "Why does it matter that you rejoin our ranks once again? What is the importance?"

"What was the importance of NATO? Of the Senates or Congress? It was to be able to flourish, ensure stability, and support. We need each other. To not be able to be a part of this organization, The Nation, would to not be a part of the decisions regarding our grand design. I have a vast kingdom that is growing more powerful every day, but will always be behind unless we can all co-exist. We are developing some wonderful technological advances that will benefit you all."

Kali interjected. “What about weapons? Have you been developing arms as your clan is well known for?”

Liana thought for a moment then answered. “Yes, we have come up with a few new weapons.” She followed her answer quickly to explain, “But just like all of your clans, I have come across some human resistance and want to be assured we are taking the correct course of action.”

Braedon asked. “What about weapons against the vampires?” They all waited for her reaction.

“No more than the rest of you. They are merely a means of protection.” She sidestepped.

Tessa had to interrupt at that point. She had sat there long enough and listened to the hollow words that came out of the vixen's mouth. She stood up. “I will have to disagree with your last statement.” She looked over at Braedon and Viktor. “May I have a moment to speak?”

Braedon nodded. “You may.”

Viktor added. “Being the circumstances as they are I think you have every right to speak.”

She took in a deep breath. “I know that they use vampire weapons for more than protection. Since Desdemona’s dethronement there has been a constant barrage of attacks coming from the Krones.”

Liana quickly responded. “I fear that that has been the work of independent supporters of Desdemona and are unhappy you took their Queen away from them. I have been giving it my all to keep this from happening. I am their Queen now and the Krones are quite accepting of that.”

“You know, I thought at first that may have been the case. No matter the circumstances we still have to protect ourselves from them. Their tactics were monotonous, almost like the rebellious humans. But then things began to change. The attacks became more elaborate and thought out. New weapons were being used. They even started murdering our humans, for what I am assuming is to take away our food supply and labor."

"What does that have to do with me?" Liana asked.

"It was around that time we began to hear rumors that a new queen had taken the throne. Everything was very secretive. Until now, we never knew who you were or what your purpose for continuing the attacks, no matter how much Intel we invested in."

"I am sure it is a big misunderstanding." She said.

Tessa got frustrated at her demeanor of just brushing the topic off. "How could it be just a misunderstanding? I have vampires and humans dying every day over these attacks. This is more than a simple 'misunderstanding'." Tessa shook her head. "I still don't know why we are being attacked."

"That, I do not know. I assure you, I will look into it." She seemed as though she was setting her even further aside.

Tessa turned towards Braedon and Viktor. "I am not going to agree on the Krones becoming part of The Nation again until I can have a guarantee the fighting will stop against my clan."

"Is that your vote then?" Braedon questioned her.

"Aye, it is. I cannot willingly sit on a council that will allow a feud to continue amongst its people."

"Would there be any way an agreement can be made?" Brynia, the quiet half of the Vordan asked Liana.

She shrugged. "I would have to look into the situation to see the intent of it, since I know little to nothing of the attacks."

Tessa spoke up. "I seriously doubt you are oblivious to what is going on."

Kali said, "I do think Tessa may be right, I know everything that goes on in my territory."

Layla added, "Even if you did not know anything you, as the Queen, should take responsibility of all actions of the Krones and handle them accordingly."

Viktor looked at Tessa and said, "Your vote cannot be swayed?"

She shook her head. "Not until there is peace once again." She lifted her chin as she added, "I am also prepared to withdraw from The Nation itself along with my researchers and engineers. I cannot willingly be alongside someone who has made themselves my enemy." Her words rang throughout the arena. People were astonished at her announcement. She was bluffing and hoped she wouldn't have to pull out of the only possibility of advancement in the vampire world. She knew it was important to look strong and courageous at that moment, to show no fear whatsoever.

Liana stood in her box, not seemingly shaken up. She looked down at her and everything she was saying like it didn't matter.

"Do you have anything else to add?" Braedon asked Liana.

"No. Not at the moment." She shook her head.

"Okay then, let us vote." Braedon looked at his peers.

"I vote Aye." Guauarokura said emotionless. Tessa really had no dealings with his clan so his priorities were simple.

"Aye." Said Tyr.

"Nay." Said Victor.

Kali said "Nay."

The votes kept going back and forth, leaving the last vote up to Braedon. He stood up. "It seems as though this vote has come to me for my final say. I would assume that a lot of you are just as torn about this situation as I am." He looked over at Liana. "It takes great strength to come here and humbly ask for a position your mother took lightly. There is not much room left in our Nation for wars amongst our own people. We were hoping, with Desdemona's demise, that it would unite us more as a Nation, which it did to an extent. Your reign as Queen seems to be that of enlightenment and with great advancements. We would like to be able to trade and share with you." The crowd gasped and started to mutter amongst themselves. Braedon turned to Tessa. "We also do not want to lose one our strongest contributors and allies." Braedon sighed. "So what are we to do?" He took a moment of silence and then spoke up. "I think that we need to take advantage of what the Krones have to offer, but...." He made sure they all heard his continuation. "The only way for things to work out in everyone's favor is to have diplomatic proceedings between the Levé's and Krones. They must come to an agreement. If The Nation is not satisfied, the request will be withdrawn and there will be no trade."

Tessa was outraged and stormed out of the summit, refusing to agree on it. She repeated that if the Krones were inducted she was pulling the Levé's and all trade out of the council.

"Are you mad?" Andreas asked as he tried to catch up with Tessa.

She was so furious with the events she practically ran for her room. "How dare they even suggest the Krones were suitable enough to join The Nation. She is Desdemona's daughter and I am sure she wants retribution."

Drake pointed out "She is not Desdemona and to the Nation she has done nothing wrong."

"She has done this to us. She continues to attack our territories."

"Which she says it is completely the independent fighters."

"She is deceitful. She got close to me when I was least expecting it." She thought of the previous night. "She has motives I am sure of it. She won't let her mother's demise go unpunished. She will continue to try to get to me."

"Aren't you just a little paranoid?" Vala asked.

Andreas stated, "If she does anything The Nation will banish her."

"It does not help me if I am dead. I cannot just wait around to see what is more important to her."

"What are you planning to do?"

She shook her head. "I am uncertain. I am going to have to think about this." She started to walk again, at least at a slower pace.

Vala, Andreas, and Drake stopped behind and discussed with each other. "I'm not sure she's thinking clearly." Drake said.

"Something has got her spooked. She's usually not this irrational." Andreas worried.

"She said she met Liana at a private club, but didn't know she was the Krone Queen until after I gave her my Intel. She said something about her being a corrupt seductress or something like that."

"What's that supposed to mean?" Drake asked.

Vala shrugged. "I guess she had the upper hand or things got complicated. But who knows. What matters is that Tessa came face to face with her and didn't get a very comfortable feeling. Maybe she is right to be paranoid."

"None of this will do the Levé's any good. We want what is best for our people. There cannot be personal feelings involved." Drake said sternly.

"I agree," said Vala. "But she is our queen and we will stand by her side no matter what."

Andreas sighed. "I just hope this doesn't put us in disfavor with The Nation." He shook his head and they all went back to their rooms.

* * * * *

Back in her room Tessa sat in the high-back chair just thinking about the situation. She couldn't help but wonder why Liana acted the way she did at the club. It was evident she had a plan, she just was uncertain of what it might be. She knew she couldn't be trusted, even then. Yet she still let her guard down somehow. She did more than just that. She entranced her. The Tessa, the easily manipulated young vampling, that was there last night was not the one she thought she was. She never would put herself in such a vulnerable situation. She became intimate with Liana. It had been a long time since she shared a feast with anyone, especially amongst a group of so many people. She immediately thought about Isaac. She put him in such a terrible position, and because of Liana, she had no choice to do what she did. She never thought she would have fed on him. No matter what had happened in the past, she had respect for him. She couldn't do that to the kids; she had breached that respect. She would have to face them and bring more doubt against her.

The phone rang and she snapped out of her thoughts.

"Queen Tessa, the council is summoning you to the arena." Bryon said on the other end of the line.

"Did they tell you why?"

"No, but they were very insistent."

"Thank you." She said and hung up the phone. If she were being led to her doom she figured it would be the time for it.

She made haste to her destination and was met with the group of the high council. "Tessa, we at The Nation do understand the reasoning behind your fears and concerns. Your past with the Krones is a heavy weight." Layla started off by saying.

"But," Viktor chimed in, "Your outburst and childish behavior is not acceptable. We expect a Queen to be more refined and reserved, not childish and irrational."

Brynia said, "Over the past few years you have done quite well and I am certain Greco would be proud of your progression."

Braedon added, "Greco would also want you to give this a chance; to at least make an effort towards diplomacy. You know I tell you the truth. He was that kind of man."

"Do you think he would if he knew he was agreeing to befriend his murderers?" Tessa points out.

"Liana had no part in that. Greco would have known that." Tyr said, seeming to know more about Greco's knowledge of Liana than any of them were saying.

Kali looked at Tessa, almost pleadingly. "We implore you to give this a try. It will benefit our whole race."

She sat down and thought for a minute. The moment they brought up what Greco would do, she had second thoughts on her actions. "Okay. I will make an attempt. But it will have to be on Levé soil."

The council looked at each other and discussed quietly. Braedon nodded. "Agreed." He looked at one of the guards at the door. "Send Liana in."

Liana stood next to her with her head held high. Tessa felt equally frightened and empowered.

"Queen Tessa has agreed to proceed to a diplomatic meeting. The only stipulation is that it is in her territory. Do you agree with these parameters?"

Liana took in a deep breath and looked at Tessa, then at the council, with frustration. "It is not something that I am very comfortable with. But I will go forth so that our people can try for unity once again." She smiled falsely and then looked at Tessa. The look sent proverbial chills down Tessa's spine.

It did not take long for them to decide it would be best to meet in New York City in a few weeks time. New York had great security measures and a quick means of escape without being in Tessa's backyard. Tessa and Liana both were eager to escape the confines of the company of The Nation.

She went back to her wing and ordered her entire party to prepare for the journey back home. She immediately flew home to prepare for the worst.

She hardly spoke to anybody the whole plane ride home. She was even afraid to speak with Isaac, let alone make eye contact with him. She felt that dealing with that situation demanded a well thought out dialogue and time completely alone.

A million thoughts raced through her mind. *Who was Liana really? Everything about her was a secret.* All she really knew was that she was being treated as Desdemona's Legacy. There had to be more to the story, she just didn't know what it was. She also wondered why the Krones, mainly Liana, were so determined to continue to wage a war that wasn't their own. There had not been any demands made and, until then, her identity remained a secret. *Could it be revenge for Desdemona? If it were, wouldn't that be at least an issue addressed even in private?*

Then the thoughts of what she did to Isaac crept back into her mind. Under normal circumstances it wouldn't even matter to her. She was The Queen of the Levé's. She had every right to feed and seduce any one of her subjects she desired without any apologies. But Isaac was different. He was a tie to her human existence. Maybe that is why she acted like a foolish human when it came to him, only to compensate with her even bitterer and cold vampire nature. If only she could explain to him; the full extent of those circumstances. Her credibility really wouldn't amount to anything being that she was inebriated at the time. She did what she felt she had to do. The truth of the matter, the passion was deep within her that night so she was just acting on those impulses and found it really hard to control.

Once back at the compound, she called for an immediate meeting of all high-ranking Levé's. They discussed precautions and strategies. She spent time with Emma, although their time together was hollow. Emma wasn't bitter, but it was evident her mind was in a different place. She knew that she would have to address those issues with Emma soon enough, just not until after the meeting had taken place. Jason's training was going well. Tessa was proud and he was happy of her admiration. It seemed as though he really looked up to her as a motherly figure and she wasn't about to change that. Those feelings were reciprocal.

She called Isaac into her study the eve of her departure to NYC. When he arrives she motioned for him to sit down. "How are you doing?"

"Things are satisfactory." He stood as a servant doing his job, not as someone who had been her lover.

"And the kids? Are you all getting along okay?"

"Very well thank you." He paused after all the

hollow rhetoric that passed as their conversation. "I'm sure you didn't call me here to talk about the family, so why *am* I here?"

"Actually this does pertain to our family." She then sighed and walked over to her desk. She picked up some papers and turned to Isaac once again. "As you may already know, I am departing for New York tomorrow to meet with the Queen of the Krones for diplomatic reasons. Although we are doing our best to take every precaution and protection, unknown things could happen as I know firsthand." She paused at the thought of Greco's murder, which was undoubtedly an unforeseeable incident. "Liana has taken the Krone throne and I fear she may be out for revenge for what happened to her predecessor."

"Liana? Isn't that the woman from the club in Prague?" His eyes widened.

She nodded. "Although I didn't know it then, I did sense the danger. That was why I claimed you for fear of what she might have done." She said it and it was out in the open.

Isaac sat back in a nearby chair and looked terribly confused.

She steered back on course and showed him the papers.

"What is this?" He asked her.

"These are your 'walking papers' should my demise happen while I am away."

"Do you really think you will be killed?"

"Anything is possible. I just want the children's future to be secure." She added, "But this is not just for one single incident. This is for any time I may perish from my enemy's hands. It must be in battle or at the very hands of an enemy vampire or human; not just anybody's hand. If you or anyone you have ordered decides to assassinate me, these papers get destroyed." She smirked. "Kind of an incentive to protect me isn't it?"

He looked at her blankly. "What exactly does it say? How do I know it will be legitimate?"

"Well, Isaac, it says that if I should demise in previous said ways, you and the children can be free from everything at your very wish. You will be given a hefty sum and living arrangements of your choice. You will be a free human, but always under the protection of my people. They can continue their education and training. No other vampire can own you or even touch you or they shall be severely punished. You will be untouchable. All in all you get to have the benefits of being part of my elite staff without the downside of servitude."

Isaac looked over the papers in confusion, and tried to make sense of it. Everything rushed around him so fast, he couldn't think. "How will I know it is legitimate, that this will be followed through?"

"Although I cannot give it a 100% guarantee, I will place this amongst my other documents for my advisors to carry out once I am gone. So all I need from you is your signature and I can put my seal on it." She handed Isaac a pen.

Once he was satisfied with the documents, he signed them and handed them off to Tessa, who sealed it with a prick of her blood with a stamp of the Levé symbol "Thank you Isaac." She said with a sincere smile. "That will be all." She dismissed him.

Before heading out the door, Isaac turned around. "For all it is worth, I don't wish for anything bad to happen to you while you are away, even for my freedom." He didn't wait for a response before he shut the door. If he had, he would have noticed a slight smile on Tessa's lips.

CHAPTER THIRTEEN

Tessa lay in her bed sleeping. She tossed and turned as her dreams had awakened her on the inside.

"Tessa." She heard her name faintly. She did not respond.

"Tessa." The voice was a little louder that time. It pulled her into her dream as she asked, "Who's there?" She looked around in the clouded room of her mind; her nightgown had an effervescent feel as the clouds themselves.

"Come to me Tessa. Come to me." She followed the voice down the long corridor, led by candles hanging from the walls. "Tessa come to me." The voice said again.

She came to the conclusion that it was coming from behind the door at the end of the corridor. She turned the knob and heard the squeak of the hinges on the door. She took three steps in and when she cleared the door it slammed shut behind her.

"Glad to see you came." A voice whispered in her ear but when she turned around, nobody was there. "I've been waiting for you." It then came from the right.

"Show yourself." She demanded.

As if on cue, two torches illuminated, revealing a woman lounging on a throne, a few yards from her.

"Liana." Tessa quickly looked around the room for an exit, but there were none. "What is it you want? Why are you here?"

"Is that any way to talk to your master and creator?"

She shook her head. "You are mad! Greco took that

pleasure. Nobody owns me now."

Liana leaned her head back and laughed so loud it echoed in the hall. "Who do you think created Greco?"

Those words rang through Tessa's mind. She had never really discussed how Greco had become a vampire. She never asked and he made no attempt to tell her. She shook the thought from her mind then said to Liana, "If that is true, it still does not make you my master."

"Of course it does my sweet young thing." She stood up from her throne and sachets towards Tessa. "I can enter your thoughts; I can read them; I can control them. My blood is now running through your veins and we are forever bound." She traced her blood red nails down Tessa's cheek and down to her neck.

Tessa said, "I don't think you have that much power over me. If you did, you would not be resorting to deception to gather information."

Liana turned quickly. "It is true I cannot gain full control of you, but my will is strong and your mind is weak. It is only a matter of time before you break."

"I don't see that happening any time soon." She said with empty confidence.

Liana closed her eyes and inhaled Tessa's true fear, then exhaled, "Soon enough my little darling. Soon enough." She walked slowly back to the throne and threw herself into it. "And when I do find out what I need to know, what is left of your human family will be eradicated right alongside you." Her eyes burned into Tessa's and everything grew dark. Just moments later she awoke in her bed, and knew that it was no dream. She had to do what it took to keep everyone safe from Liana, and she knew right where to begin.

As soon as she woke up from her surreal nightmare she jumped up out of bed and headed to the vampire prison. Tessa descended the cold dark staircase swallowed by narrow walls of stone. She continued through a labyrinth of twists and turns. She had reached her destination. Before her stood a large steel door guarded by six huge men. She got clearance and then proceeded through to the twelve inch thick glass inside the cell. She felt a cold breeze through the speaking holes. For a moment she hadn't thought anyone was there, but then she saw cold glowing eyes withdrawing from the shadows.

"What a lovely surprise." Desdemona hissed sarcastically. "What brings you to my humble abode?" Her sarcasm weighed thick.

She reached beside herself and pulled a chair closer. "Who is she?"

Desdemona looked confused. "You might want to clue me into the conversation. I have no idea who you are referring to."

"Don't you be coy with me. You knew that once you were gone she would claim your throne."

Desdemona was still confused. "I do not understand."

"Liana!" She yelled, and then watched Desdemona's face register the name. She actually looked a little more perplexed than before she heard the name. "Oh." She realized. "You didn't know, did you? You weren't expecting her?"

Desdemona sat down on her bed in bewilderment. "I wouldn't have even conceived the idea. I thought that she had dropped off the face of the earth after everything that happened with Greco."

"And what happened? She mentioned she knew Greco from a long time ago. She also said that I looked like *'her'* and that was why Greco was interested in me. But I don't know who this woman is."

Desdemona looked at Tessa sternly. "Why should I

tell you anything? You have done me no favors." She felt the scar on her forehead.

"Maybe to try to make amends for all your wrongdoings?"

Desdemona laughed. "That is not the way to approach it."

"Do you want me to get mean and nasty?" Tessa eyed her.

"Like you could." Desdemona crowed dryly.

"Is that a challenge?" She thought for a moment. "What about a little UV treatment? I hear that it really gets the blood flowing."

"You wouldn't." Desdemona said.

"Don't misjudge me. You do know I can be aggressive if I have to." Desdemona still didn't answer. "Okay then." She stood up and pushed an intercom button. "I need you to prepare the UV. We have an uncooperative prisoner."

"Yes ma'am." Said the voice at the other end of the speaker.

They could both hear a switch flip and the humming of the UV lights charging. She watched as panic grew on Desdemona's face. She had been through this before. "Okay! Okay! Turn it off. I'll talk." She screamed in fear.

She pushed the intercom again. "Cancel that." She sat back down just as she heard the lights powering down. "Now where were we?"

"You look like his wife." Desdemona said after a brief sigh of relief.

"Wife?"

"When he was human he had a wife. Portia I believe, but I could be mistaken. It has been quite some time and I never knew the woman myself."

"He never told me that." She shook her head. *He never told me anything personal about his life, only his accomplishments throughout history.*

"I'm sure there were a lot of things he did not mention. As you have already figured out, that when you become a vampire your human past tends to disconnect from you the further away you get from it. Once everyone you know is gone, it happens quicker as if it were a dream. Just imagine centuries passing by." She stated.

"So what does Liana have to do with you, Greco, and his wife?"

"To answer all that I better start from the beginning." Desdemona sat down and watched as Tessa listened intensely.

Desdemona began her story. "I found Liana one cold night back in what now would be called France, heading for Rome. She must have just been turned a few days before because she was wild and ravenous on the streets. In a small moment of weakness I took her in and took care of her as if she were my own. As the years passed, our relationship was quite close, although she began to get more and more independent. She would venture out for a long period of time. On one of those journeys, she met Greco. She immediately grew infatuated with him, following him around from the shadows. From what I understand, she became quite obsessed over him. After weeks of stalking, she finally made her move one evening at the tavern in the lower end of the isola he had grown up in before he moved to a different part of the city. Greco thwarted the advance quite easily. It did not stop Liana. She made a few more attempts, each time she felt as if she had gotten closer to him. Finally, after an ill attempt at a kiss, Greco pushed her away and told her that he was married. That infuriated her and she stormed off into the night. She thought nights on end what she would do to win his affection.

An epiphany came over her; at long last she knew what she had to do. The following night she watched quietly as Greco kissed Portia before heading off to grab a drink with a few mates. Liana's plan was in motion. She waited for a little while till the streets cleared up and then made her move. She grabbed a basket of fruit and proceeded to walk past Portia's house. At the precise moment Portia happened to be looking out her window, Liana tripped and fell, spilling the fruit everywhere. Portia came running out and asked if she was okay. Liana complained of a bad ankle. Portia helped her inside the house so she could attempt to fix her up. They made small talk while Liana was being bandaged up. She didn't linger long and hobbled to the door. Portia told her farewell and Liana said that it was a pity she had been so nice to her. Before she could be questioned, Liana slashed across her neck and body deeply with her nails then ran away leaving Portia on the ground not able to call out and bleeding to death.

From the darkness she waited for Greco to come home. When he did, she watched as he screamed out in agony, holding her bloody corpse close to him.

Liana was at the tavern each night as she watched him drown his sorrows. Over the next few weeks, he had begun to speak to her more often, although mostly what he spoke of was Portia. One night Greco had gotten piss drunk and she offered to help him home. The whole time he couldn't stop crying about his life being worthless and that he wished he had the nerve to kill himself so that he could be with Portia once again. She escorted him to his house and laid him down on his bed. She told him that she could make the pain go away. He doubted her and cried that the pain would never go away. She told him that there was a light at the end of his deep, dark, and dismal tunnel. She would make it where he can go on for eternity, feeling less and less pain. All he had needed to do was to submit to her. She wore him down until he finally agreed. That was all she needed. She turned him right there at that moment.

When he began to recover, he was confused and she explained what had happened. She told him that his recent transformation was what would make his life less bleak. He had many new things to explore and his talents were magnified, as his human life would grow into a blur. He detested it at first, but as his time with Liana continued things became clearer. His feelings towards his maker became stronger, tightening those bonds, although I am certain that he never forgot Portia.

It was a thousand and five hundred years until I saw Liana with her new companion when I decided to travel to Rome. I begged for her to come home, which she did not. She preferred her life there. She did agree to visit though.

I was in a high enough position that I was revered as near royalty in my land. I organized a grand celebration for what I was hoping would be a homecoming. I wanted to surprise her with a very savory offer.

When she arrived, she had Greco in tow. He was very humble at that time. The week long celebration took its toll on him. He did not care for the grandeur of it all. Liana was the exact opposite. She craved the decadent beauty of French elitism. Until she had come back, she had not realized how much she had missed it. She may have been from Italy, but in her heart she would always be French. I never conceived the idea we were Gaul or anything else. Always elite, always royalty. She would also always be my daughter and heir to my fortune.

Greco despised it so much he was determined to travel back to the beauty of the Mediterranean. He missed the life there; he did not like how we were. Liana was finally worn down that she agreed to go back with him. I made her a lucrative offer. For her to come back to me, I was to give her power, something she had not had before. At that point, I had been given a high position in the Krone clan, once I had gained the trust, and heart, of Renos. I wanted her to come to the new world with me, in what is now known of as Canada. She took me up on that offer, which I thought would have been the end of the relationship Liana and Greco had. He traveled back to Rome and she dutifully stayed with me. She pined for him terribly and it was if she wasn't even there anymore, her thoughts were always of him. She used one excuse after another to not be around. My heart was broken by my own daughter. I was distraught and was unsure of what to do. I turned closely to my lover Renos. It was during this time I became his Queen.

Even moving across an ocean could not keep Liana and Greco from one another for long. I thought that if I gave Greco a position in a more undeveloped part of the new world, she would be more loyal to me. That was the case for some time.

During all that, Greco had become some sort of leader in his own right and eventually all communication stopped. She quickly uprooted to go be with him. He had gotten together a massive amount of people and they were preparing for a rebellion. After not having any communication for a year I decided that I had enough and I prepared for a long journey. I brought a few hundred of my best men with me in preparation for the worst.

When I arrived, I was completely astonished at what things had become. The moment I saw Liana, I demanded for her to come back with me. Liana and Greco refused and stood their ground. They both told me they were no longer my servants.

There was a battle and it was hard and long. For a moment I thought that the rebels had won. That was quickly thwarted when my troops caught a second wind and forced them to retreat south into unclaimed wild lands.

Of course, I was completely upset that she had joined him and turned against me. I thought long and hard about what I was going to do about the situation. Renos wanted no part in it that time. I went, by myself, to their new settlement and pleaded with her. I was willing to offer her anything just to come home. She wanted nothing to do with me. Somehow she blamed me for ruining the one good thing she had going for her. At that moment, she told me to leave and never come back and that the next time she saw me would be the day she would rip out my heart.

At that point I was completely enraged. As soon as Liana went back inside her house, I ran over to Greco, and begged for him to give me a chance. Of course he refused, which I knew he would. It was at that precise moment, I knew what I had to do. That was when I told him what really happened with his wife. The look on his face was of sheer horror and agony; tears were running down his face. At first he didn't believe me, but then it sank in that I was telling the truth. I watched him struggle as I sunk into the shadows of the trees. It took everything he had to go inside that house. That was the last time I saw her. I believed her to have run off or be dead."

After finishing her tale, Desdemona had an evil grin about her. "Just a fair warning about Liana. Once she sets her mind to something it will not be easy to sway her. It seems to me that she finds you to be an opponent."

"I've done *nothing* to her." Tessa fumed.

"Oh but you have. You have stolen the heart of her beloved and that is enough to wage a war. History can tell you that."

"That makes no sense whatsoever. Greco is dead."

"That doesn't matter I am sure. It is the fact that you became his Queen. She should have been in your place."

"Oh God, not again!" Tessa felt like it was déjà vu. *First Isabel and now Liana.* "But she is a Queen too."

"You are over thinking things." Desdemona shook her head. "Liana is ruled by her heart and her desires. She loves three things: power, living lavishly, and Greco. She has the other two so now there is one thing left. She has to consume or destroy everything that was Greco; which means you and your clan."

"You're telling me that because Greco is dead, I must die too, by association?"

"Something like that. She probably blames you the most for being there when he died." A big grin grew on Desdemona's lips. "So enjoy your last days on earth because she is not going to stop until she gets everything she wants."

Tessa stood up and faced Desdemona through the glass. "I'm not sure what you are smiling about. You are enjoying the fact that I will perish, but how are you going to feel when she finds out you, Greco's killer, being alive and locked up?"

Desdemona gasped and a look of panic crossed her face. Tessa did not wait for a response before she left the prison. She now had more pressing matters to attend to.

* * * * *

Tessa paced nervously in her board room while she waited for her advisors to arrive. She had decided that it would have been very dangerous for her to go to New York City, realizing what Liana was capable of. She was almost scared of how irrational she could be, just from the fact that Liana entered her thoughts, and then from the history she had with Greco. The four of them rushed in quickly as if they had dropped everything they were doing, no matter how important, to meet with her.

"What is it?" Drake asked, full of worry.

"I've come into some information regarding Liana. It seems like we were correct in assuming she had an ulterior motive."

"And what is that?" He asked.

"The Levé Empire and ultimately my assassination."

"Are you certain?" Bade chimed in.

"Pretty certain. It seems that Liana had a very close relationship with Greco and is intimidated by my status in Greco's clan. Her claiming the Krone throne as rightful heir has given her every means possible to make sure I and all I have done become eradicated."

"How is that going to affect our standing with the council?" Andreas asked with worry.

"Considering the fact of my newfound information, and that I had ultimate decision on whether the Krones were to be a part of The Nation, I am certain things will be okay with them. If not, we will deal with it when the time comes."

"Okay, then what do you think we can do?" Vala spoke up.

"First and foremost, I need protection."

"You already have this compound protected completely." Andreas noted.

"What about the Underground?" Tessa was

referring to an underground compound that was the equivalent of a small city.

"Even though we've had the underground living quarters around for quite some time, they haven't completed your compound yet. The technological specifications are quite drastic. The safety protocols alone make it much more difficult." Drake said.

Tessa sighed in frustration. "How long until it is done?"

"They are saying eight months." Bade said.

Andreas chimed in, "But I think if we had them focus on a small portion, your quarters specifically, you might be able to get in as early as three months."

She nodded. "Let's do that then. I would like to be able to protect my family as best as possible."

"Not to mention you being out of harms way." Vala added.

"But for now, I suggest you stay inside this particular compound." Drake seemed to order her.

"Of course. I would not want to tempt fate." She agreed then thought about how her life had become her prison.

CHAPTER FOURTEEN

Tessa couldn't stand still as she walked around in her room, anxious for something to do. It had been a couple of weeks since her declaration of solitude and it was already getting to her. She knew it was for her own good, yet she also felt that she was missing out on things. She kept thinking about how it would be when she was underground and locked entirely away from the world. She shook those thoughts from her mind and decided that she was going to find something else to do. There had to be something that she could do without leaving the confinements of her own making.

She headed down the hall to the dining room, where her family was having their evening meal. It confused them when she showed up, knowing she never joined them. There really was no need other than socializing or heading to the back to grab some stored blood. Even if that were the case she usually sent someone to get it for her.

"What a nice surprise. "Bryon said cheerfully. He and his family were eating dinner.

"I felt that I should stretch my legs for a while. Ruling a nation can be so tedious some times. There is so much paperwork." She lied with a smile. She then looked over at Bryon's wife. "Vanessa, how lovely to see you. You are looking quite well."

"Oh yes, I feel wonderful. Thank you for your hospitality." Vanessa smiled happily.

Emma leaned over to her brother and muttered, "Does anybody not suck up to her?"

Before Jason had a chance to respond, Tessa turned quickly towards her. One thing that a vampire had was super hearing. If a person even whispered, she still would have heard them.

"Emma, do you have something to share with us?" The stern look on her face reminded Emma of one of her schoolteachers.

Emma gulped and shook her head no.

Tessa said, "I beg to differ. Why don't you tell Bryon and Vanessa your thoughts, since you seem so eager to talk about them."

"Uh, I..."

"Spit it out!" Tessa said with aggravation.

"It just seems as though everybody sucks up to The Queen, just because she is just that."

Vanessa swallowed her food and set her napkin down. "I'm not sure you get it. I have no need to 'suck up', as you call it, to her. She has been nothing but wonderful and loving towards my family and me. We enjoy her company and I, personally, feel as though she has become a part of that family."

Emma lowered her head in shame. "I do apologize."

Tessa chimed in, "And next time why don't you keep those kind of remarks to yourself since they will do you no favors." She then returned a smile to her face, as she looked at Bryon. "I have become bored of being alone in this secluded environment. I thought it would be wonderful to throw a party."

"A party?" Asked Bryon.

"Yes. I would like to have it by this weekend. Do you think that would be possible?"

"I thought you were under strict orders to stay away from the public for a while. For that matter I thought you hated those things."

"I'm tired of that. I'm bored and I need something

to do. So answer the question. Do you think it is possible?"

He nodded his head, “If I get enough help, I am sure that it can be possible.” Bryon pulled out his handheld planner, something he never went without. He started to enter in data. “What is the occasion?”

She laughed. “Why, the afterlife is celebration enough. But seriously, I just felt a little fun would be nice for a change. There has been non-stop doom and gloom for quite a long time. If I can’t go out and enjoy things, I will bring it here.”

“What shall the theme be?”

“I was thinking Renaissance.” She then thought for a moment. “Yes, that’s it. We will wear costumes and it will be marvelous.”

“Who shall we invite?”

“Standard fare, although I don’t think we need to invite The Northwest Sector. They have become so boring as of late.” She turned to Isaac who had been quietly watching her optimistic rant. “And you will be my date of course.” She smiled at him and he returned the smile, although not with as much enthusiasm as she had. She was overly chipper as if the weight of the world just dropped from her shoulders. She sensed his worry that she felt a little unsound.

“Do you think that I could come too?” Jason begged his aunt.

Isaac spoke up, “I’m not certain it would be in your best interest. Not the safest for sure.” He didn’t want Jason brought into her unstable antics.

She looked at Jason. “Of course you can come.” She then looked back at Emma. “I think that you would look gorgeous all dressed up.”

Emma stood up and shook her head no. “If you will excuse me, I think I am going to go to my room.”

"Her loss I suppose." Tessa shrugged it off. "I think I will go into the kitchen to have myself some dinner." She referred to the blood stock in the back of the kitchen. It was her own private reserve.

Once in the kitchen, she grabbed a few pouches of blood and warmed them up. Cold blood didn't suit vampires very well. It tasted better at 98 degrees or better, the temperature of a human body.

Isaac went in as she finished up a glass. "I'm a bit upset about being undermined in the dining hall, regarding Jason."

"Do you not feel it would be beneficial for Jason to come to the party?" She threw away the two bags and proceeded to grab a couple more out of the fridge to repeat the process all over again.

"Not at all. I needn't remind you he is still a kid."

"He is sixteen." She remembered what Andreas had told her. "He is a man in most cultures."

"Physically and emotionally are two different things." Isaac said, as he watched her warm up the blood. He was getting numb to it at that point. It was a lot different than watching her feed on a human. He preferred the current method much better.

"Jason has been training to be on my elite force; to be both a warrior and an advisor."

"I dislike that also. But of course I have no say in it." He sighed. He knew that his powers of raising the children were limited. She had the ultimate say in almost every matter. He was basically there as a human attachment to their old lives.

She poured the warm blood into her glass, constantly refilling it. "He is fine Isaac. He would be in the same situation if he were with his mother. Here he at least is more protected, and of course on the winning side." She smiled. "He is very special and is an intricate part of uniting our races. The fact that he is my legacy makes him untouchable by my vampire brethren, politically or by any other way a person could think of."

"What does that mean exactly?"

"It is a foot in the door. He will be the first human to hold such a high position since vampires started ruling the earth. Once he becomes an advisor, of course. Do you not think that is important?"

"I can't help but worry. Above all, he is my nephew."

"As he is mine. I'm not so cold-hearted that I do not see the dangers. But if I thought for one second he couldn't or shouldn't handle it, we wouldn't be having this conversation." Tessa said as she finished up her drink. There still was a deep calling from within her being. She had yet to be satisfied with the blood. She proceeded to go towards yet another round. "Now Emma; that is a whole different story. I am beginning to lose hope in that girl."

"She is young."

She shook her head. "That's not it." She placed the blood packs for warming, and then turned towards Isaac. "No matter what I do I cannot seem to be invited into her world. We can be in the same room, but only going through the motions. I extend my heart to her and I only get indifference in return. When she first came here she was so warm and loving towards me."

"She misses her mother. She is torn."

"Her mother made herself the enemy."

"Emma doesn't see it that way. She only sees you as the one thing keeping her from her mom."

"She can never go back to Melinda." She started to drink again. "It would be reckless on my part to do that. This is the safest place for her. At this point, even if I wanted to let her go, I couldn't. She knows too much about this place; probably even some of ours secrets. It would be damaging to the Levé's."

Isaac said, "I am only giving you insight to Emma's actions. Take it as you will." He watched her finish the bag of blood. "How much have you had?"

"Six, I think." Tessa said then thought to herself how odd it was after he pointed it out.

"I thought two kept you satisfied."

"It does, but I can't seem to feel quenched. It is like I can't get enough. Like I haven't even eaten."

"Are you alright?" He was obviously concerned. Her erratic behavior that evening was worrisome enough.

"I feel fine. Just hungry." She glared at him. "So if you don't mind, I would much rather dine alone." She dismissed him.

He walked out of the kitchen and over to Bryon, who was still trying to finish his meal. "I'm not sure if it is a concern, but while I was in there with Tessa, she downed six bags of blood in a matter of minutes. She keeps saying she is still hungry."

Bryon stood up, unsure of what to do. He knew that something was not right with the situation at hand. 'Thank you, Isaac. I will tend to her immediately." He wiped his mouth and set the napkin down, then ventured into the kitchen.

"Are you alright, mistress?" Bryon asked the distraught Tessa.

There were a few more empty bags of blood than Isaac had mentioned, which meant she was still feeding. She seemed almost confused at her hunger.

"I'm just so hungry." She said, nearly in tears. "It's as if none of it is even entering my body."

Bryon thought for a moment, since this situation has never come up before. Sure, vampires feed and sometimes would recklessly feast, but not really complaining of never being satiated. "Maybe you haven't really fed yet?"

"What do you mean?"

"When was the last time you took blood straight from the flesh?"

"The last time I did that was during the conference." She didn't want to mention that it was Isaac that was her last.

"That has been a while ago. Maybe your body is telling you that it is what you need."

"You may be right." She nodded. "Why don't you send up a couple of hosts to my room?" She mentioned as she left the kitchen. She walked confidentially past the dining guests, as she refused to show weakness.

Not long after the hosts were brought to her room she heard her name loudly. 'Tessa!" Bryon's screamed in her ear. "Stop right now. You're killing him!" He couldn't stand by and watch her drain the life of the man in her grasp. He knew she had gained more control than that.

Her bright eyes snapped up and looked at him first not in recognition, then another in shock. She pulled her fangs out of her victim who begged and screamed for her to stop.

Bryon rushed up and pulled the young man, probably twenty at the oldest, out of her grasp and said, "Go now." The man did not give it a second thought and ran out of the room.

"What is wrong with you?" Bryon asked, part concern and part distress. He had been with her for so long he seemed able to be freer with his words around her than most. At that moment, it was what saved that young man's life.

Tessa stared blankly into his eyes. "I'm just so

hungry."

"How can you be hungry? After everything you drank earlier, I sent up three slaves."

She shrugged her shoulders and sat there dazed. "I don't understand it either." After she said those words, an uncomfortable feeling came from what would be considered her stomach. Somehow she knew that feeling, but her memory didn't kick in until it was too late. She reached for Bryon's shoulder, but before she could, blood spewed from her mouth everywhere. She fell to the floor on all fours while she still vomited up blood.

Bryon didn't know what to do. Vampires just didn't get sick like that. He called for Andreas from his mobile, and then bent down to tend to her. She finally stopped purging and lay down on the floor surrounded by what resembled crimson water. It was definitely blood. What went in came right back out. She had gorged herself sick.

As she lay there moaning from half discomfort and half relief, Bryon grabbed a few towels. He picked her up and tried to wipe off as much blood as he could. "How do you feel now?"

"Well, I'm not hungry anymore." She joked in bad taste.

"What's going on?" Andreas stormed into the room like a bat out of hell. He took a looked at Tessa and rushed to her side. "Have you been attacked?" He looked all over her body for wounds. "Are you okay?"

"I just got a little sick, that's all." She shrugged his concern off.

"We vampires do not get sick. We are wounded for a short while or are dead. Nothing else."

"Well I guess this vampire became an exception to the rule." She looked at both of them and then said, "If you will excuse me, I believe a bath is in order." She slowly moved towards the bathroom.

Andreas turned to Bryon, who was wiping beads of sweat from his forehead. He got really scared when she grew sickly. "Okay, so what was that about?"

Bryon scratched his head. "My guess is that she gorged herself feeding."

"How did that happen?" Andreas had never heard of it before. He didn't know it was possible.

"She just kept saying she was hungry and could not be satisfied. She came really close to draining her third donor. She hadn't been this reckless since she was newly reborn."

"This makes no sense. What do we do about it?"

"Well, for now I am going to have someone clean up this mess. After that? I don't know."

"I will talk with the other advisors to see what they come up with to make sure this is an isolated incident." He informed Bryon and left him to take care of her unfortunate mess.

Tessa went fast asleep while the advisors gathered. They had decided that she needed to have one of the clinic workers take a look at her, one that was proficient in vampire health. While she lay asleep, unaware of what was going on around her, the doctor checked everything he could think of. He decided it was best to have one of the lab workers run more tests on her since he was at a standstill. It was not an answer the group wanted, but it was at least a step in the right direction.

* * * * *

"Aren't you a handsome one tonight!" Tessa straightened the ruffles on Jason's shirt. They were preparing to go to the party. She had recovered from her incident, which seemed to have been an isolated moment. None of the lab tests came up with any answer. "It is a shame your uncle became ill. But now I get to have the most handsome of escorts." She smiled at her nephew. Her adoration for him had grown greatly and she was very proud of him.

"I'm a little nervous." He tugged at his collar.

"You shouldn't be. It's a party, not a war zone. Just smile and keep your wits about you at all times."

"I think I would feel more comfortable in the war zone. I am not prepared for this." He breathed deeply and smiled. "Okay. I'm ready."

He stayed by her side, as instructed. He got to flow in and out of the crowd as if he were regal himself. There were so many interesting and unique characters he wished he had more time to speak to each and every one of them all. Of course, it was polite and cordial banter, but it didn't seem to matter to him.

"Are you enjoying yourself?" Tessa smiled at her nephew.

"Yes I am. Thank you for this opportunity."

She laughed lightly. "You will have to do this sooner or later as an advisor anyway. Not only can these parties be enjoyable, but they also can be heavily political."

"May I have a dance?" A finger tapped Tessa's shoulder. She turned around to see a tall, slender handsome gentleman in a blue powdered coat and tapered leggings.

"Hello there Mischa." Tessa said. "I was telling Jason here about how heavily political even the grandest of parties can be, and then you come before us at the most precise of moments." She looked at him with intrigue as she saw his reaction to her obvious jab. "How have you been?"

"Good, considering the circumstances." He shrugged then smiled.

She looked at Jason then said, "Oh I am sorry. Jason, this is Mischa. He is one of our Dukes from the east."

"Nice to meet you." Jason said with the utmost politeness. He extended his hand in courtesy.

Mischa looked at him for a moment, and then completely ignored him. He smiled at Tessa instead. "So how about that dance?"

Tessa saw the disappointed look on Jason's face as he lowered his head in embarrassment. She became infuriated from Mischa's ignorance. "When was it acceptable that you treated someone of equal class as a dog?"

Mischa was shocked. "But he is just a human. He *is* a dog. Nothing more than an annoying pet to house and feed; or cattle." He smirked as he glanced only for a moment at Jason.

"Do you notice any marking on him?" She pointed to the back of Jason's neck which was free of any markings. It was common for every vampire to quickly take a look for the possession of the human, especially one that was in the presence of royalty.

"No." Mischa shook his head.

"So that means he is neither dog nor cattle."

He scratched his head and said, "Okay, so why is he of equal class?"

"He is my advisor in training. As soon as he becomes one of my elite and all-powerful advisors, he will then be superior to you."

"How was I supposed to know anything about him? You have not made any announcement of such. Besides, a human is a human, never superior."

She was beyond mad at that point. "First and

foremost, I think you are speaking to your Queen more freely than you should. Second; as a Levé you know clearly that my mission is to work towards the common good between humans and vampires. Now I see why there has not been much success in incorporating such a goal in your territory, which bothers me deeply." She stopped for a moment and mulled over the current conversation for a moment, then added, "Actually I would like to see your progress. I think I will be sending one of my advisors to check up on your progress, or lack thereof."

Mischa stood there, jaw dropped in utter shock. There was nothing more he could say since it was his Queen that spoke to him.

She turned towards Jason, "Would you please accompany me to the dance floor?"

He nodded and headed toward the center of the room. The crowd watched as they proceeded to dance. All eyes were on the two. People whispered questions on who the human dancing with The Queen was. Of course, they would ask the question if it were Isaac also, but that would have been a much easier open and shut case. In actuality, she liked to shake it up amongst her melancholy associates and friends from time to time.

"Thank you for not letting me be humiliated," said Jason, in the comfort of his aunt's arms.

"Think nothing of it. I did not lie and I want to make sure each and every one of the Levé clan, no matter how big or small in power, know of your importance to all of us. You deserve the respect as an advisor. That is a very high ranking position of authority." She said in her politically reassuring voice. She looked at him, whose expression noted that those words might not have been what he was looking for.

Tessa thought for a moment, stopped dancing, and

met Jason's eyes with a smile. "Of course even if that were not true, you are my nephew and I will always stand up for you. I love you like my own son." That seemed to be what he was looking for.

She gave him a quick kiss on the cheek, mingled with her guests and introduced her nephew to all those of importance, and in having done so, made sure they knew exactly who he was.

When the party was over, Tessa decided she would walk Jason to his apartment. There were still four hours until it was time for him to be up, but she knew that he was still young and needed to get some rest. He had many things to do the next day.

As she was telling him how proud she was of him and hugged him goodnight, Isaac walked into the living room. Jason saw the look he gave her and quietly dismissed himself to his room.

"Did you have a good time tonight?" He asked, his arms were folded across his chest.

"It would have been better if you were there with me." She said, thinking to herself how she really meant the sentiment.

"I think you were better off with Jason by your side, than your human servant." Every time he called himself that, he cringed inside. He wasn't sure he would ever get used to being called that. He knew he wasn't like the other servants, but she had no problem reminding him of his place from time to time.

"Whoever happened to be at my side really did not matter."

"Let's just say that he is fascinated by your vampire world, so he was the better choice."

"What are your thoughts on my vampire world?"

"Complicated. Way too complicated. I try to only think about my family and the ones I love, even if they are intertwined with the vampire world." It was obvious Isaac wasn't only speaking of his brother's children but also of Tessa. His soft kind eyes looked over at her.

She smiled at him, comprehending his attentiveness to her. "I am not feeling the least bit tired. Would you walk me back to my place and keep me company for a while? It has been a little while since we really talked." She wasn't sure what she was doing, but she was overtaken by the sentimental moment that was shared between the two.

"I would like that." Isaac agreed under a moment of weakness before they took off for her abode.

Once inside, she breathed a huge sigh and turned to look at him. "How are we?" She just blurted out, not even sure where it came from and why it escaped her lips. Her thoughts came from deep within and were demanding a few moments of exposure.

He wasn't really sure how to answer that. He didn't really know himself. A lot had happened between them, and he was sure they were not through with the drama. 'We'll survive."

She smiled at him genuinely. "I hope so."

He walked closer to her and asked, "Which Tessa am I speaking with now? The Queen Vampire or the person?"

"Are they not one in the same?"

He shook his head. "No they're not. Sometimes they intertwine but most definitely they are not the same."

She leaned against the back of the couch. "It is really tough being me. A lot tougher than I ever thought imaginable. I always assumed I would be standing beside the ruling King, not as the lone Queen." She decided to let her guard down.

Isaac got beside her and lightly touched her hand.

"You don't have to go through this alone you know. You are just making it harder on yourself."

"You really wouldn't understand."

"I may not understand the whole vampire thing, but I do understand your emotions. You surround yourself with people and subjects and yet you are still lonely because you overlook the ones who really need to matter. You hide behind your title of Queen for fear that it would be found out that you really are just like everyone else."

He clasped her hand in his. "I'm here to give you full emotional support if you want it."

"After all that has gone on between us, you still offer up this?"

"I'm sure I'm crazy to do so." He laughed dryly. "We have been at this back and forth thing for quite some time. I probably should have thrown in the towel, but for some odd reason I haven't. I know hiding inside of you is the Tessa that I know. I just can't walk away from that, no matter how easy that might be sometimes."

"And what about what I did to you? Feeding off of you I mean."

The subject was bound to come up at one point and time. "That has been taking me a while to get over. There is so much complication in the matter. I really do see why it was necessary, but then again I can't help but feel used and betrayed."

"I am sorry for that, I really am."

"I know that and actually it is what is keeping me from hating you." He looked deeply into her eyes. "I did get something positive about the situation." He smiled.

'And what is that?" She asked.

"Phenomenal sex." He sported a huge grin and watched as the contagion reached Tessa's lips.

She bit the bottom of her lip with her a grin. "It was fantastic, wasn't it?" She couldn't help but giggle like a schoolgirl.

"I would like to say something though."

"What's that?"

"Maybe next time you will at least have the courtesy to ask me before you feed off of me?"

"I can make that attempt."

He leaned in to kiss her and she did not deny him. As a matter of fact she welcomed it. She sunk into the embrace, and released all the stressors of her being. When the kiss ended, she asked Isaac, "Will you keep my company tonight? I just don't want to be alone."

"I would be more than happy to." He said with an adoring smile.

*****

Various images floated in Tessa's dreams. In one she was wrapped in white cloth surrounded in a field of red flowers. Another was of animals being led to slaughter. Then there was the one that was of her drenched in blood from the mass of bodies that surrounded her. The images continued constantly adding other disturbing images; faster and faster they went. Her thoughts marched in rhythm one by one until she awoke with a gasp. She sat straight up, eyes glowing, fangs itching for a meal. Her strong desire to feed had fallen upon her once again.

Tessa looked over at Isaac who was swallowed up in the satin sheets. She knew she had to get away before she did something she would regret once again. She grabbed her robe and flew out in the hall in the direction of Andreas' room. He would know what she needed and had been taking care of her for the past week. Her advisors did not like what had happened to her and felt that maybe she needed a different method of getting blood into her system until they could figure out what was going on with her. After her last incident the only thing that the scientists could figure out what to do with her was to make a concentrated serum with synthetic blood that seemed to make a vampire's body feel as if it really had been fed. He had been working on it for some time but minor adjustments had to be made. He had set up what seemed like a workable treatment of high content of the synthetic blood and other possible nutrients that could be transfused directly into her veins.

No matter how hard she pounded on the door, the answer remained the same. He was not there. She went to the nearest soldier and confiscated his mobile. She attempted to ring Andreas, but was only met with silence. She then called Bryon who responded quickly. “Bryon, do you know where Andreas is? I am in terrible need for a treatment.”

“Andreas went to check on the construction of the underground. I will see if I can get a hold of him, or at least someone to set you up,” Bryon answered. In hindsight, he probably should have insisted harder to learn what needed to be done if she happened to relapse. “Just go back to your room and I will try to be there as soon as possible.”

Tessa agreed and slowly made it back to her room. As she stumbled in she heard Isaac’s voice. “What happened to you? I woke up and you were gone.” He appeared from the hallway.

Tessa felt sick again and tuned him out. Her body screamed out for blood. She felt her blood dry up as it sluggishly pumped harder through her body; her eyes flashed red with each pump. Dizziness set in and she did all she could to hold onto a chair in the living room. The need for blood went to the extreme as each muscle of her body started burning simultaneously.

Isaac rushed over to her as she cringed in pain. He attempted to hold her, to comfort her, but all she could see was an enticingly open neck. She awoke for a moment to realize who it was and forced those urges out of her mind long enough to scream out in full force, "Get away from me!"

Isaac was taken aback by her abrasiveness. She had become Queen Tessa, not Tessa the compassionate. "I can't leave you like this!"

She breathed in heavily as she pushed out the words, "I...need...blood...NOW!" As soon as the words came out, she buckled in pain, and then fell to the floor screaming as she pulled into the fetal position.

His eyes widened in both fear and shock, and then turned to head out the door and down the hall. He met Bryon, Andreas, and a team of nurses and frantically told them how serious of a condition she was in. By the time they had gotten back to the room, she had disappeared. Bryon quickly called Bade for help.

She found herself pushing towards the laboratory where her serum was produced. She needed it desperately if she wanted to relieve herself from her madness.

"Where is it?" She yelled at the man in the lab. Her eyes began to grow with equal parts panic and anger.

"I haven't synthesized any yet."

"What do you mean? Have you not kept any in stock?"

"You have been using so much of it we can't keep up with the demand." His fear screamed out in his voice.

Tessa moved in closer to him. "Are you telling me that it is my fault?"

"N..n.n..No ma'am. Not at all." He lowered his eyes in shame. "It is I who has not been keeping up with the demand. I should have been trying harder."

She felt her head throb terribly, but shook it off. “How long?”

“The cycle will be done in an hour's time.”

“An hour?” She shrieked. She looked around the room at all the workers in the lab. “You are telling me that you have all these workers in here and you haven’t been able to keep the serum on hand, then you tell me that I have to wait for something that should have been readily available at all times.” Her stomach cramped tightly. “Because of your lapse in judgment I now have to suffer.”

“It is not Eric’s fault. He has been trying so hard.” The voice of a pleading woman was behind her.

She turned quickly to see a waif-like middle-aged woman. “Who are you to address me as a simple human?” She picked her up by the throat with a single hand. “Are you one of the incompetent fools that cannot understand the severity of your mistake?”

The woman spoke through choking words. "We’re all just his assistants.”

“So you are not working on the formula?”

“She is only helping me.” Eric said in a worried tone for his colleague.

She locked eyes with the red-faced woman. “Then you are just a hindrance to this man.” With those words, she snapped her neck then dropped her to the ground. Gasps came from the room. “There is no place for useless people in my employment.” She walked over to a group of people that were huddled together with fear. “I think it is time to clean house.” She grabbed a young woman and drug her away from her counterparts. “I am starving so I will kill two birds with one stone.” She bared her fangs and proceeded to feed from her. The rush of blood entered into her body and she felt it scream for more after only a couple of minutes of draining her victim of every drop of blood she possessed. The lifeless body fell to the floor.

As she lunged towards the other two, she felt a hand touch her shoulder as if to pull her back. "Your highness, please stop." It was one of the vampire guards; he had come in quickly after the scientist pushed the panic button. She looked behind her then knocked him back with all of her force, sending him against the wall. She returned to her prey. She cornered one of them after his ill-fated attempt at escaping. His scream rang through her ears. She responded by yelling at him to shut up to no avail. She took her hand and in one quick swoop she scratched through his throat leaving blood to spew everywhere.

More guards came in, unsure of what to do since it was their queen, but ultimately it was their job to ensure the safety of the workers and they had to make that decision. One of them saw the last of the techs on the floor as she hugged her knees. He ran towards the scared human and pulled her from the ground.

Tessa looked over at them, blood splattered all over her body. "Leave her to me!"

"But ma'am..." He choked out.

"Know your role and mind my words unless you want to face the same fate as these pieces of human waste."

He backed out letting the woman's hand go. She felt a panicked rush through her system again. That time she felt like her limbs were in a volcano. She screamed loudly from the pain, then became even more enraged.

"Tessa!" Andreas' voice was faint in the background.

She barely heard him through all the loud pumping of rage in her head. "Andreas, go away!"

"I will *not*!" He screamed. He walked towards her

as she tried to shake off the loud commotion in her head.

"Do not cross me." She threatened.

"You know better than that. I am here to protect you."

"Do you think I need protecting?" She cocked her head at him.

"Right now it is from yourself."

A loud burst of agony rumbled through her chest and she screamed again. Andreas took that moment to send the guards after the soon-to-be victim. "What is going on?"

She pointed towards the scientist that had managed to get behind the safety of the guards.

"My serum. They piddled around in here and now I am burning with so much pain. They caused this pain."

Andreas looked towards Eric. 'Is this true?"

He nodded. "I have been working around the clock to try to get these ready, it just so happened we ran out. Every time we make one, two are used and we were having trouble keeping up with that demand. But we have some just about ready."

"How much longer?"

"Eric looked over at his bench. "Forty minutes sir."

"See!" She yelled and knocked over a table in the center of the room. "Their carelessness is the death of them."

Andreas took a few more steps towards her. "We will get it to you. Just try to calm yourself."

"Don't tell me to calm down." As soon as she said those words, a piercing pain ran through her body like thousands of needles pierced her all at once. Her agony was so great she dropped to her knees.

Andreas rushed over to her quickly. He tried to attend to her but she pushed him away. "Do not touch me." She said then buckled onto the ground wriggling with pain.

"Quick," he said to the guards. "Let's get her to her room." He then turned to the intercom system and called out, "Drake, Vala, Bade, meet me in Tessa's room. We have a major situation out of control." He turned towards Eric. "As soon as that treatment is finished you will bring it to her highness quarters, do you understand."

He nodded. "Yes sir."

With the help of the guards, Andreas grabbed Tessa and attempted to take her out in the hall. Even though she was in severe agony, she continued to kick and scream.

Her whole world dimmed as her body became that uncontrollable creature. It was if all her inhibitions went away and she turned into a feral creature. All she knew was anger and hunger; nothing else existed.

Once at her door, her three loyal subjects came to her aid. They took over the guards' positions as they firmly carried her into her home, listening to Andreas' explanation of what happened.

"What is going on?" The imagery of four of the strongest vampires he knew holding Tessa disturbed him completely. "What are you doing to her?"

Drake said. "We are trying to help her. You can do so by leaving us to take care of this."

Isaac shook his head. "I can't do that. I am supposed to help her in whatever she needs. I can't just leave while she may need me."

"We have this under control." Bade spoke softly as he guided Tessa to the couch.

"Just let me go! I'm hungry. If I can't have the treatment the least you can do is let me eat." Tessa cried out in pain.

Drake looked into her eyes. "You have drained too

many humans. You have had enough. Anything else and you will become sick like before."

She screamed out hideously in disgust of her captivity. Her mind then seemed to disappear into a fog, desensitizing her body from the pain that ravaged her system.

"What is happening to her?" Isaac cornered Bryon for some sort of answer.

Bryon shook his head. "All we know is that she is getting hungrier faster every day. She received a transfusion right before the party. She should not be like this, not yet at least."

"What does it mean?" He looked over at Tessa for a moment whose screams turned to whimpers in almost a catatonic state.

"I have no idea." Bryon sighed and shrugged.

"Well, I would suggest you find someone who would be able to figure it out." Isaac locked eyes with Bryon. "Whatever has been going on with her lately seems to be getting worse. I for one don't feel like sitting idly by and watch the train wreck happen. It also would be catastrophic to the Levé's if she could not do her job. So we owe it to Tessa and her people to get this situation taken care of." It was the first time Isaac talked with that much authority, which of course he really had none, especially over Bryon who had trained him how to be a servant his very first week in captivity.

Bryon remained calm as Isaac spoke to him. He did not get angry, which was well within his right, considering how Isaac was talking to him. Isaac was only saying it out of love and concern for Tessa. He had known a long time ago the situation between the two of them. Bryon turned to Isaac. "Be wary of your tongue servant." He then turned to Andreas. "Do you have the situation under control?"

Andreas nodded. "We have everything set for a few hours."

"Good, then I think we should let her rest in peace."

"She needs monitoring." He responded.

"I will have that taken care of. Bade, send for one of your priests that might be able to shed a light on the Queens condition. If anyone will know, the ancient tribe will."

"I will get right on it." He nodded then left with the medical crew. There was no way he could argue with Bryon when it came to her well being.

Bryon sighed with relief after he left the room. "You might want think twice about speaking down to me in front of a high ranking vampire. Your death could have been imminent."

"I'm sorry." Isaac said shamefully.

Bryon added, "You are going to have to wait until Tessa has decided it is safe to announce you as anything but her servant. *If* that time does come; until then you will have to deal with it and get your job done. I know you are concerned and we will figure it out. For the time being it wouldn't be a bad idea to stay with her for a while." Bryon saw Isaac nod in acknowledgment.

Vala approached him and looked into Isaac's fearful eyes. "You are going to have to trust that we are taking care of her. There is nothing more you can do except put yourself in harms way." He needed to be convinced. "Don't let your emotions get in front of your logic. Let us try to help her."

He was never sure on what her advisors thought about him. He wasn't even sure about what was going on between him and Tessa, no matter how messed up it was. It was apparent there was some acknowledgment, although he wasn't sure if that seemed to matter or not. "Okay, but I'm not going anywhere." He stated as if he had any ruling in the matter.

"Of course." She nodded. "Once she calms down and becomes a little more stable she may need your service."

He felt as if that was good enough, for the time being at least. He went outside of the apartment and found a chair not too far from the door. It wasn't long that he noticed someone from the lab running into Tessa's room. A few minutes after that, Drake walked out and glared at Isaac for only a moment before he walked down the hall with his phone to his ear.

Vala walked out about an hour afterwards and talked to him. "She is stable for now. At this moment she is resting. One of the Mystics is coming to look at her." She referred to the magical humans who worked hand in hand with the vampires; the same people Bade originated from. They were the closest things to real doctors for the vampires.

"Thank you for letting me know." He said and smiled.

"No need to thank me. Your sole purpose is to serve our Queen. I wouldn't want you to be disciplined if you were not there for her when she becomes better."

He sat for hours on end waiting for some news of her condition. He knew that stable never lasted, since he worked in the clinic before the culling of his people. The only problem was there was nothing he could do for her and maybe he was there over guilt of letting her get that sick.

An old woman was escorted past him. He was sure it was the Mystic Vala spoke of. He wasn't really convinced of her validity, since she looked like she had crawled out from an underpass. He chastised his thought and told himself that he was doing nothing but being judgmental, that she was the one they were all entrusting her life, or the closest thing to it, to this old woman.

The woman walked past all of the worried clan and straight into the bedroom. Tessa awoke with a start. She looked around and realized she was in her bed being looked down upon by a stranger. She quickly remembered the pain and agony, but that the pain was gone. She looked at her arm and noticed a needle in her hand connected to bags of blood at her bedside.

"How are you feeling?" The strange woman asked, while she approached the sickly queen. A shroud of mystery enveloped her with wisps of black. Her long midnight hair was streaked with silver threads that showed that she had been around for quite some time. She was human; that was easy to tell. Her face had too many wrinkles and her teeth were terribly stained.

"And who are you?" She asked the old hag, uncertain why she was there.

"Grüne." She responded quickly, as she began to open up what looked like the melding of a doctor's bag and a spirit medicine pouch. She knew she was one of Bade's people.

"I am assuming you are here to figure out what is wrong with me."

"Aye." She nodded then started to check Tessa's body from top to bottom like a regular doctor would have. It amused her since she knew The Mystics to be less like doctors and more similar to druids or witches, although that wouldn't be technically correct either, but it didn't matter to her. "You didn't answer my question."

"I am fine now, so it seems that your trip was for nothing." She dismissed in her mind what had happened not that many hours previous.

"Ah yes. You are fine, no problems. It will never happen again; blah, blah, blah." Grüne said with sarcasm, as her lips pursed together like a dried prune.

"You mock me." She said crossly. "It is not wise."

Grüne shrugged then went back to her bag to pull out what looked more like the things The Mystics would use. Talismans, vials of elements, runes, a bowl, and a silver dagger embellished with an oak carved handle tipped in gold. "I do not answer to you. If you do not want my help then dismiss me. But be warned that what is happening to you will only get worse." She held the dagger in her hands, which made Tessa apprehensive with the silver in front of her.

"By all means, let's get this over with so I can return to normal, whatever that might be."

"Good. Then hold out your hand." She did what the old lady asked and Grüne quickly sliced the blade of the knife across her palm. She felt the pain of the knife with every move it made. She then took her hand and had her squeeze her dark blood into the bowl. She yanked the bowl away and brought it to all of her equipment.

Her hand was not healing up quickly and blood began to drip on the floor, pooling up quickly. In frustration at the lack of bedside manner amongst other things, she yelled at the top of her lungs for Bade.

Bade came running in quickly. "Is everything okay, Mistress?"

Tessa rolled her eyes and sighed. "If you call being poked, prodded, mutilated, and disrespected, well then sure I am fine."

Bade sighed. "Grüne is one of the best healers my tribe has to offer, so be patient. She may seem a little eccentric but she will get you that help you so desperately need." He looked over at the witch chanting over the bowl.

"Well she has made a terrible mess by slicing me with silver, so now I've bled all over the place." She held out her drenched hand. "I need someone to clean this mess up immediately."

"Yes, my queen. I will have someone take care of this right now." He yelled out the door into the other room of Tessa's request then turned back to his queen. "If that is all you need, I will leave you in peace." Bade dismissed himself before he had to catch another earful of her misery.

She could hear her chant louder and louder, then suddenly stopped. Grüne looked at her with her coal black eyes, then back at the bowl of blood. She whispered something to herself, then set the bowl down. She then walked over to her bag and pulled out an electronic device that looked like a tape recorder with headphones.

"What is that for?" To Tessa it seemed somewhat dated and a bit foolish.

"To listen with." She stated what Tessa already knew, her sarcasm not well received by the queen. She pressed the end of it, the one that looked like a microphone, all along her chest and belly, paused occasionally to hear more intently. When she was done, she sighed heavily.

"What is that supposed to mean?" Tessa asked, overly curious.

Grüne ignored her and opened a very old leather bound book, and flipped through its pages.

"Okay, I am getting bored with all of this. Do you know what is wrong with me or not?"

Grüne looked up and nodded. "But it is more complicated than a simple answer."

"Well can you at least fix it?" She began to get worried.

"Possibly." Grüne said as she sat at the edge of the bed. "I will tell you that you are quite unique. So much so that only eight other vampires have been noted with this condition."

"Condition?" Tessa sat up quickly.

"Did you know that you were never fully turned?" Grüne blurted out with too much ease.

Tessa shook her head. "No, you must be mistaken. I am most definitely a vampire. The turn was successful." She continued, "If it weren't then I would either be dead or one of those zombie freaks, which I am clearly not."

"That is true, but it still is possible. All it takes is for one drop of human blood to remain in your system." Grüne said as if reading from a book. "Your maker was either careless or apprehensive." Grüne cocked her head and grinned. "He must have cared for you and became afraid at the end, not paying attention to even the slightest of detail."

Tessa shook her head. "So I've got human blood running through me?"

"Yes you do. But it is so miniscule that nobody would even be able to detect unless putting it through the tests that I just happened to have done."

"Is this what is wrong with me?"

Grüne shook her head. "No."

"Then why are you telling me this?"

"Because it is what made your condition possible."

"And that is..." Tessa was trying to pull the answer from her.

Grüne breathed in deeply then exhaled. "You are with child."

She stared at her blankly as if she were put into a trance. A nervous laugh escaped her lips. "That is impossible. I still am a vampire."

'That would be if you were 100% vampire, but you are not."

"So this very miniscule amount of humanity left in me makes me susceptible to those things?"

Grüne nodded. "And somehow you fell into the small parameters that resulted in the pregnancy."

"What are they?" She was completely confused and tried to grab a hold of every strand of the new revelation. She had more doubts than belief of what she was being told.

"Obviously your humanity and a much heightened encounter with high doses of hormones, pheromones, desires, and everything at its peak. At that point, the human in you took over inside the body. For all of those to be simultaneously at the peak is less than 1%," Grüne added. "There seems to be one more parameter."

"And what is that?"

"For you to have gotten pregnant, it most likely had to have been with a virile human. Have you taken any human lovers in the past few months?"

She knew exactly when this encounter happened. She did not have to be a genius to realize it. She nodded in response. "Only one." She said quietly. Tessa then asked, "So what now? Can this situation be taken care of? Will my hunger and sanity get worse?"

"It will come and go. It shouldn't be hard to come up with something to equal sustenance. Then again that is only if you keep it."

"What other option do I have?"

"Termination."

"That seems a little extreme doesn't it?"

"Being in such a high position politically there will be plenty of vampires discussing assassination."

"Why is that?" She had started to become quite scared.

"They fear the unknown. They fear a super race will start emerging and then the possibility of their extinction."

"It could also mean more peace for the future. It could be what unites the vampires and humans. That has always been my ultimate goal." Tessa attempted to justify the situation and gave it a more positive possibility. "Is there anything in your books that tell you about the child?"

Grüne shook her head. "That is where there seems to be a problem."

"What do you mean?"

"As I said there have only been eight noted pregnancies. Six of them were killed before even giving birth. This excludes your first ancestors of course."

"And the other two?"

"One mother survived but her child was murdered."

"And the last?"

"Died during child birth." Grüne lowered her head.

She fell into fear. "Okay, so the one that gave birth successfully, is there anything written about her?" Her mind began to crank with ideas.

Grüne nodded. "Quite extensive notes."

"Then I want all the information on her."

"I will see what I can do. I just want to caution you to please rethink this."

"I have made up my mind."

"You will be in terrible danger."

"Do not be worried about such things. There shouldn't be any attempts if nobody knows."

"How do you plan on keeping it from the public?"

She thought about the underground compound, her private quarters, that was being built. It would be the perfect place for her to be isolated. All of her meetings could take place underground, speaking only with those that were of any concern. "I've got an underground shelter. It will be ready for me quite soon. I should be safe until I have the child." She felt confident. "So if you could gather up everything you have on the subject I would most greatly appreciate it."

"I could do that, but I think there is a better way." She paused. "I am going to move into the shelter with you."

"What?"

"It would benefit both of us. I will be your caretaker helping you through this pregnancy and you will let me document everything."

"No way! I will not be the subject for any documentation."

"I will omit your name and title. You will only be known as patient X." Grüne tried to convince her. To her it would be the study of a lifetime.

After much thought, Tessa nodded. "Okay, you may stay. From this point on this is top secret with only a select few in the circle, do you understand?" She gained her regal stature back, if only for a moment. "Bade." She yelled once again.

He came through the door. "Yes, my Queen?"

"Find a place for Grüne to stay. She will be with us for a while until we get my condition cleared up."

"Yes ma'am." He turned to lead Grüne from the room before she called to him once again.

"I also want status on the Underground. I plan on moving in within the week."

"Isn't that a little premature?"

She looked at Grüne. "One can never be too cautious."

"I will get with Andreas to make sure this is going to be done in your time line."

Tessa nodded and watched as they closed the door behind them. She got up from her bed, pulled her steel tower that her serum hung from, and went to look out the window. The stars in the sky seemed to twinkle brighter than they ever had before. She knew it wasn't so, but it seemed like it all the same. Soon she would have to give up the stars and retreat to seclusion. She thought whether she had made the right decision. The child she was carrying was half-human, half-vampire. It would be hard to be accepted by either species. She also thought positively that it would be embraced and begin the peace between the two races.

CHAPTER FIFTEEN

"I don't understand why I can't go with you." Isaac tried to hold back tears as Tessa informed him of her short leave to the underground.

"It won't be safe for you. The witch is going to do everything to help me control my insatiable appetite and maybe give me some clarity. I do not want to put you in harms way."

"If I go voluntarily then that would mean I was willing to take that risk."

She shook her head. "Stop thinking selfishly for a minute and realize that you are more needed here; somebody has to look out for Emma."

"You mean Emma and Jason." He attempted to correct her.

"No, I mean Emma. Jason has his own path now. His role is of utmost importance."

"What? He is just a boy."

Tessa sighed. "I thought we got past this. He is well enough of age to fulfill his duties as an advisor-in-training."

"Don't you have enough of those?" Isaac was obviously upset.

She shook her head. "His role is slightly different. Probably the most important out of all of them."

"And he is going down to your secret little bomb shelter?" His sarcasm was bitter and dry.

She nodded. "Yes. He begins his journey into his new position."

He sighed. "I just don't understand you, Tessa. No

matter how hard I try I can never get past your secret motives and harsh façade."

She touched him on his arm lightly. "Why try to understand me? Our worlds are different and we go by different rules. Why not focus on what is important. That we have something special between us."

"Why do you think it is I want to be with you? I thought we had finally come to a place that we were able to be together?"

She smiled at him sadly. "Not yet. Maybe soon, but there are other things that are of more importance."

"That seems to be what our story is all about."

"I completely understand where you are coming from. I have been there before and it is not pleasant. But if you can wait six months more we can work things out."

"One of these days I will give up waiting."

"Just not yet. Please?" She looked deep into his bright blue eyes. She wanted so desperately to tell him she was carrying his child. She knew that he would never let her out of his sight and she was not willing to endanger him. There were also the other possibilities Grüne had warned her of. All in all she felt that she was saving him from heartache.

He nodded. "Just six months right?"

"Of course." She touched his cheek and kissed him tenderly on the lips before disappearing down the hallway. She hoped it would be six months, she would hate to have to wait a moment longer.

Tessa had called a meeting of all her advisors. She was about to enlighten them on the large task they were about to take on. Each of them sat there anxious to hear why she felt it was important for them to all be there.

"Tomorrow will be a very important day. Although it may seem as simple as moving into a new home, I assure you it is not such a light matter." She looked over at Andreas. "Do we have security at the highest level for the underground?"

"Yes ma'am."

"I want to be certain in that it will be impenetrable."

"I have my top ranked guards already placed. I also have doubled the security throughout the entire compound."

"I want it made clear that only me, you, Vala, Drake, Bade, Jason, and Grüne be allowed entrance. Nobody whatsoever for whatever reason shall enter. Understood?"

He nodded. "Yes, my Queen."

She acknowledged him and turned to Drake. "You need to step up your game in the fight against the resistance. It seemed as though the human's confidence is up enough that they feel as though they are winning. I want it clear that those who oppose me shall suffer greatly. I need you to implement your plan on rehabilitation camps. The rebels seem to be hiding amongst my loyal subjects and stirring things up from within."

"Yes, ma'am." He nodded in acceptance.

"Vala," Tessa said then looked at her. "I think that we need to delve deeper into the Krone territory. I am not getting good enough detailed information. I don't care how it is done, but I know for certain Liana is planning on a means of attack. First our humans, then us."

"I understand, but everyone is being silent. If there is a plan then nobody is speaking about it."

"Like I said, try harder."

She smiled over at Bade. "Have you set up the telecommunications system in The Underground? I want to have everything flawless."

"Everything is up and running."

"I hope so. I need my meetings to take place without a hitch."

"You should have no problem with it."

"And the telecommunications in the living quarters up here?"

"They are working also."

"Just because I will be away from the outside world does not mean my duties will falter. I just need to rely on all of you a little bit harder to get us through this. Is this acceptable for all?"

They all answered in agreement. Then Jason stood up. "What is my duty?"

She looked at him and smiled. "You have the most important duty of all." She saw the look of anticipation on his face; his first assignment. "You are to stay with me down in The Underground for the next few months."

His smile turned into disappointment. "I'm sorry to question your orders, but is that not something anybody else could do? I think my skill could be put to use doing something of importance."

She shook her head. "No. I am going to need your constant protection. Nothing must happen to me during this time. When your duty is over with me you will take on your new, permanent assignment."

"What will that be?" He asked.

She was quiet for a moment as she looked around the room at her most trusted and loyal. "To protect my child."

The room became completely silent as her advisors glared in disbelief.

"You're having a baby?" Jason seemed the least shocked about the situation; of course he didn't realize how much of a miracle it was. All he knew was that his aunt was having a baby.

Tessa nodded. The others tried to assess the

situation.

"But how?" Vala finally spoke up.

"Evidently Greco spared me just enough of my human blood to not fully turn me. That mixed with my pairing with a human caused me to be one of the few to become pregnant."

"With a human child?"

"Half-human." She corrected her. "This is why it is so important my child and I be completely protected. Vampire society in general won't take kindly for this child to be born, as history seems to have shown. They will consider it an abomination that will need to be eradicated. I see it as an opportunity to unite the vampires and the human race."

Andreas stepped forward. "I will do everything in my power to keep the both of you safe at all costs."

Vala nodded in agreement. "Same here."

"It will be an honor." Bade hit his fist against his chest, a military honoring salute of sorts.

Drake was the last to speak up. "I will do as you ask, my Queen." He spoke as if he had reservations.

She said, "Nobody should know about this, even closest confidants. It will be business as usual for everything. I find this to be a perfect opportunity to get the upper hand. I need this to be kept a complete secret."

Jason spoke up. "What about my family?"

She moved closer to him and shook her head. "As much as I love Emma, she cannot be trusted. It wouldn't take much for her to cross lines and join the rebels. Who knows what they would do with this information."

"And Uncle Isaac?"

"Especially him. This is not the time to get his thoughts cloudy and not be able to see past the true reality."

"And what is that?"

"After the child is born, Grüne will take it to be with The Mystics for a while to keep it out of harms way. You will go with them."

Jason realized what she was saying, that Isaac would not let the baby leave. "Is Isaac the father?"

She said nothing, but nodded in acknowledgment. "Now do you understand why he mustn't find out?"

"Yes, but are you going to tell him?"

"Eventually, when the timing is right."

"He may never forgive you."

"I have to take that chance. For the safety of the child." She ended the conversation. She wrapped up the meeting. "Let's implement this immediately. We have no time to waste.

The group said their salutations and left Tessa alone with her thoughts. She touched her belly as she thought about Isaac. She really was torn on what to do. Logically she knew what to do, but emotionally she felt he should be there with her and their baby. She pushed the thought out of her mind when she convinced herself that she would have plenty of time to contemplate the situation.

* * * * *

The halls echoed with silence and everything around Tessa was desolate. She knew it would be like that, but until she experienced it herself she really did not grasp the concept. It was just her and her thoughts as she paced through the empty chambers, the weight of the world barred down on her. The time that she was there felt like centuries. There was only so much that she could do while there and it seemed the hardest not having Isaac around just to talk to.

Things really didn't change in the outside world.

The months had gone on as status quo. One good thing was that the rebels had slowed their attacks down. Of course, she knew that it was just to regroup and try another tactic. She had not heard about Melinda for quite some time. That worried her a bit.

Drake's image appeared on a monitor at the end of the hallway. "The council meeting is about to take place. I would suggest heading to the conference room."

"On my way." She acknowledged, then hurried through the labyrinth to get situated before the meeting started. Once in the room, she took a deep breath and felt her expanding womb, then sat down. She knew that she had a lot to discuss with them about The Underground Compound. It was much different than the ones that were already in place. It meant they could peacefully live underground as well as they could above ground, anywhere in the world, no need for the shield technology to cover every inch of the planet.

"Salutations." Braeden spoke from his high back brown leather chair on one of the monitors.

Each ruler gave their greeting before they started business. After an hour of updates Victor asked Tessa, "I have not seen any progress from you as of late, the deadline for the self-sustaining underground compound is coming near. How are things going?"

"Actually everything is just about in place. I have been testing things constantly. I will have it completed in seven months time, then you will be able to see for yourselves."

"We are eagerly awaiting the results. I'm sure you realize the importance of this project." Kali said.

She nodded. "Completely and I won't let you down." The completion of the project was important because it meant that they would be safe underground, away from the rebels.

"I hope not." Viktor said sternly.

Tyr spoke up, "I think this wraps thing up. Until next time." He was the first to sign off.

Tessa sighed when the conference ended. It was probably the quickest one that she had with them up till that point. It wasn't hard to say that they could last hours. She looked over at Drake, who signaled the communication was out. She stood up and stretched. "I'm starving." She said, which was a constant at that time. The child's appetite kept getting more voracious.

"Let's get you to the sitting room." He escorted her out of the room.

Tessa sat down in a comfortable chair in front of a computer. Grüne came in with a stand holding two blood packs. She pushed the needle into her flesh and watched as the liquid flowed into her body. Grüne didn't say a single word, which wasn't unusual. She spent most of her time collecting specimens from Tessa, or writing down every move that was made. She seemed to prefer to study Tessa from afar if anything could be helped and constantly kept her notes secret. It didn't bother Tessa that much, as long as no information regarding her was put in the notebooks.

As quickly as she came in, Grüne left. Tessa shook off the creepy vibe she always got from her. Grüne was very mysterious. She was obviously old, for a human. Her role as the healer was something rare for The Mystics, where mostly the males dominated the higher positions. She happened to be a legacy and the only one of her generation. She had to be strong, stern, and powerful to keep the healer title so that she could pass it down to her son.

Tessa opened up her laptop and began to peruse the vampire archives, which thanks to her, had become digital. Her goal was to find anything that she could about the few vampire pregnancies there were. Although she had read a lot of the texts, she had not quite gotten to all of them. She knew it would be very hard to find it in the first place, since it was a taboo subject. The information Grüne had given her led her in the right path so it narrowed it down even further.

It had already been a few months since she had withdrawn underground and it had made her restless. There were only so many things that she could do. Her advisors came down constantly for one thing or another. Andreas worked with her to keep her fighting skills fresh, although he was very cautious. He did not want to do anything that would harm her or her child. Jason spent a lot of time with her. He was never far away. He promised that. Even if he was around just to keep her company, he did it without disdain.

Her hunger came and went. Most days it was easy to control with simple treatment. The few times it wasn't, drastic measure had to be taken. Humans were brought down from the prison camps, the ones that were already in the justice system that had committed heinous crimes, and brought to a special room. As ashamed as she was for what she was doing, she fed on them viciously to satisfy the child growing inside. She kept that part of her hidden from Jason, so as not to taint his image of her.

Grüne came back when Tessa's treatment was through. "How are you feeling?" She asked as she pulled the needle out of her arm.

"Well enough." Was all she said.

"Very good. Then I will see you tomorrow." She said as she wheeled the device out of the room.

Tessa went back to her reading. In her determination to find any pregnancies, she had come across quite a few interesting pieces. Something most modern humans would be surprised about, but would easily believe was the God system in early history. Of course not all of the early god's were vampires; some were. Some vampires started off as God's in the human's eyes, like a few of the war god's in many cultures. Ares was a strong one in history. There were many references to him. One benefit the vampire world had was that they had their own recollection of the events written down. He was very vain, although most vampires were. He adored his followers very much. When there were sacrifices made, he showered his people with lavish things. When he got bored he had no problem in instigating battles, even wars. It showed him how much faith his people had in him. It also made for a great gluttonous feast. Tyr was in there too. He was labeled as a Norse god. He was another interesting character. He was supposedly the original god of war in his land and sometimes stood with his people in battles and made their conquests successful. That was until he frequented them less and he grew out of favor with his followers, who then replaced his with a fictitious god, Odin, which fit in better with their belief system. Little did they know how silently he watched from the shadows, devising a scheme to take over the world.

There was one possible record of a pregnancy in the books, but she had to look through human texts. She read aloud to the child within her like she was reading from a storybook. As time went further along, she seemed to connect more with the child. There weren't words shared between the two in their minds, more like images. Sometimes the images were of loving, thoughtful things, and sometimes they were quite displeasing and made Tessa almost nauseas. She began the story.

It was of a young Goddess. She was one that

enjoyed all the pleasures the world had to offer. Unlike most of the Gods, she preferred to spend a lot of time with humans. She threw lavish parties, making sure she was the center of attention. She didn't really care for being worshiped but she did love to have all eyes on her. So much so, she always had the best clothes, housing, servants, banquets, and parties. There were many suitors that came to her door, most turned away; others went home with hardly a recollection of what happened. For the more unfortunate, some didn't even make it home.

One man had a different plan. He was determined to have her, even if for one night. He had been turned down many times before, which bruised his ego. He was one to always get his way. He was a soldier; a strapping, handsome man. He spoke to an alchemist one day for something that would win him her heart. He was given a small vial of what was said to be, "The Blood of a God." If he drank the blood, he would appear to be God-like and more enticing. He had to keep his identity secret, though, or she would find out that he was not a God when she looked at him.

The alchemist warned strongly that the effects were temporary, maybe lasting only a day. When he would drink the blood he felt strong, almost invincible. All his senses would be heightened, maybe too extreme for him to handle. Once the effects were to wear off he would possibly lose all favor with her. It was only going to be a temporary fix for him to achieve his goal, to bed The Goddess.

The following evening she was throwing a costume party, which was a perfect opportunity for him. Before he left his home, he took a deep breath and downed the dark liquid. Moments later he felt a surge of heat run through his body, then a pain in his belly. He buckled to the ground and began to shake uncontrollably. His whole body felt like it was on fire. Soon afterward he passed out from the intense pain. When he came to be conscious he stood up, relieved the pain was gone. Soon enough he realized that something was different. He was hearing a buzzing sound. He focused on it and the buzzing became louder. He looked around the room and noticed a fly flittering about. He watched its movements and grabbed it quickly. He successfully captured the fly. He felt he was confident enough for his next endeavor.

As soon as he had arrived at her domicile, he placed a mask over his face and blended with the crowd. He partook in the festivities; the food, the drinking, and the entertainment. For some reason, women flocked to him more than usual. He enjoyed it thoroughly until he saw her; his Goddess. She was straight ahead of him, lounging on exotic furs on top of a golden platform. She was surrounded by beautiful maidens attending to her every desire. A select few of the party guests were allowed through her heavily armed guards to enjoy her company. The man approached the platform, stopped by the guards. He was told by them that she had more than enough visitors. He argued that he was not like the other guests. As soon as she saw him, he explained, she would welcome him. The Goddess watched the whole encounter intently. He knew she sensed him, since he felt her presence strongly. Their eyes met and she waved him through, offering him a seat amongst the other privileged ones.

"Do I know you?" She questioned.

Playing aloof he said, "I don't believe so."

"I don't see many of our kind around. What brings you here?"

He sat down near her and leaned in. "I came here for you. I heard you were the fairest of all those around and I had to meet you myself."

"You intrigue me." She smiled at him.

The man felt their bond quickly become strong as though the two were being drawn into each other's gaze. The human drowned out all noise around him and focused only on her. He expected to hear her heart beat like he did the others around him, but nothing was there. He then realized his made no sound either. Desire overtook him as he leaned in towards her and approached with a kiss, that she did not deny. The kiss was long and heavy. Some of the other guests flocked towards them to join in with the festivities, which was happening all around them with the other guests. The moment the other women's hands touched him, the Goddess looked at them, eyes glowing frightfully bright, and hissed. "Be gone!" They stood up quickly out of fear and rejection and dispersed. She then motioned for her guards to close the curtains that surrounded them. She wanted the pseudo-god for herself.

She reached for his mask, to see his identity, but he grabbed her wrist strongly and told her no. He wanted to keep the mystery strong. Surprisingly their intensity grew stronger and she succumbed to his every advance as if she were powerless to stop him. His head filled with superiority and he began to take her. He grew into the moment and realized how much like a god he truly was and that his goddess was right there with him, connected as if forever. Her moans and wails struck his ego marvelously. At such a heightened moment she screamed in pleasure, as she revealed to him what she truly was as her eyes glowed bright and her fangs appeared. He was turned on and afraid at the same time. His movements became more intense and his groans matched hers in sync. After hours of unadulterated sin, they fell asleep in each others arms.

It seemed that they slept through most of the day, when the false god awoke. He thought it was all a dream until he looked at the beautiful creature as she slowly stirred beside him. She looked completely angelic with perfection.

"May I know my lovers face now?" She asked, as she sat up.

He quickly got up and shook his head no.

"How will I know you if you come calling again?"

"I am not sure I will be back. You would not accept me as who I am."

"You cannot be certain." She stood up and followed him from behind the curtains.

"Yes I am."

"Then take this." She took off the only thing on her naked body; a pendant. It was a serpent wrapped around a red stone. She placed it around his neck.

He accepted the gift cautiously. "I must now leave."

She watched him walk out the door and into the darkness.

He hurried home and only then he removed his mask. It was at that moment he knew he had to be with her again. He went back to the alchemist who reluctantly supplied him once again with a vial, at a much steeper cost. He added another warning about the blood. The more he used, the less human he would become. He ignored the warning and continued to see her each week for a month. Each time his face was hidden behind the mask. As the fifth week approached he returned to the alchemist who refused to sell him the blood, and said it was for his own good. The man grew irate and drew his short sword and pressed it up against his throat. The alchemist proved his point that the addiction had turned him into something not quite man, but not a god. He was stuck in the middle.

Distraught, the man left and made the decision to see his love, without the mask. At dusk, he appeared through her window as he had done many times before. He crept through to her bed and slid in beside his goddess, kissed her shoulder and up her neck.

She slowly stirred and indulged in the greeting. When she fully awoke she turned around and looked at the stranger before her. She screamed in anger and jumped quickly from her bed.

"Get out human!" She ordered in a fit of fury.

"Do you not know me? Do you not know your lover's touch or the sound of your lover's words?" He questioned her.

"You sound like him, your soft touch is like that of his, but you are no God! You are nothing but a weak mortal."

He showed her the pendant as she had told him to do to prove his identity. "I am your lover, you see that. You told me to show this to you for proof." He tried to fix the unfortunate situation he had put himself in. His lack of forethought proved to lead to a disastrous circumstance.

She looked at the pendant and up at him. Her confusion set in. "I do not take kindly to lies." She trusted him and he let her down. Her heart had been broken.

The man bowed his head. "Yes, I have deceived you."

"That is evident." She started to get annoyed.

"I just wanted to have a chance with you. As soon as I laid eyes upon you, I knew I wanted to be with you forever."

"How did you do it? I thought you were my kindred. That was the bond we shared. Your blood tasted like that of a god."

He lowered his head in shame as he revealed, "I was given the blood of a god, which temporarily made me like you."

She thought for a moment. "I suppose it would have." She looked at him, her eyes cold again. She yelled loudly in her native tongue, but never losing eye contact.

The man felt helpless in her gaze and was shocked when a group of soldiers rushed in the room. She continued in her foreign language, which became clear to the man they were there for him. Two of them grabbed him tightly; he did not struggle much.

As if in humiliation, she spoke to him, "Your punishment is solitude until I decide your fate. I do not like being played, and for that the price is high."

"Why not kill me?" He had asked.

She leaned in and whispered. "You have made a soft spot in my heart and killing you would not satisfy my taste for justice. Your life will be your punishment." She spoke again to her soldiers and they carried him away.

The man slaved hard and long. He labored hard in front of the very people who revered him as a strong and brave warrior. The man they saw in front of them was nothing but a frail, malnourished shadow of his former self covered with sores from being beaten constantly.

The Goddess found herself watching her former lover slave away with the other condemned souls. She felt joy and sadness for the sentence she bestowed upon him. Her thoughts of him became more pronounced as her belly swelled with the child he had gifted her. She was unsure whether it was a blessing or a curse. She had no answers as to how it happened in the first place. She was not herself, just one extreme or another.

One early evening, she woke to a loud noise coming from the main house below. "Where is she?" A deep voice boomed. She recognized it immediately and grew frightened. “I know she has been here, I sense it.” It was her master and creator. He was on a hunt for her and her child. She heard him barreling through each room slowly making his way to her room. She donned her scarlet cloak as she escaped out the window that had once been visited by her lover. She knew what her master was there for, that was for certain. It was an abomination to bear a human’s child. The bond with her master was forever linked. She had masked her condition as long as she could, but it was only a matter of time before he could sense her again.

She continued down the dark, dirty alleyways to put as much distance between her and her angry creator. She still could mask her whereabouts to an extent. It would only have him two days behind her, so as long as she continued to run.

“You cannot get far from me. I will find you, so you might as well give in to me.” His voice drew near. He was closer than she thought. She burst through the first forcible door and slammed it shut behind her, backing away into the shadows. As his voice grew louder she continued falling backwards into a bed of straw. She looked down at what tripped her and it was a lifeless body with flies circling it.

She leaned up against the wall while she listened to her master draw near, with more vain comments of superiority.

“Look what we have here.” An elderly man, crawling with day old dirt, said as he slinked towards her. She realized where she was, the slave stables.

The goddess pressed her finger to her lips to signal silence. The man ignored her and eased towards her. She had no patience with him. “I advise you to keep your mouth shut or I will permanently shut it for you.”

He touched her leg in defiance. "Beautiful woman is delivered to me as an answer to my prayers of The Gods. You belong to me."

Enraged, the woman's eyes glowed and she bared her teeth. She wanted to drain him of blood but knew the smell would only draw her master near instead. She grabbed the man's neck and snapped it in two. A group of huddled men backed away from her and towards the front of the stable. She heard whispers as they figured out the man screaming in the streets was looking for her. Some said she might fetch a hefty ransom that would buy their freedom. They said that in the state she was in she would not fight them. In agreement, they decided to call the master. "Sir." One of the men spoke up. A young man stood up and told him to be quiet. He refused and yelled once again. The young man looked towards the Goddess. She knew him. He was the man she sent to that very stable. His eyes looked longingly into hers. He grabbed the speaking man and held a knife to his throat. "Go! Through the back. I'm sure you can get past that door!"

She spoke his name as she looked at him. As if on cue the baby kicked inside of her which caused her to rub it. The man looked at the belly and back into her eyes. He teared up as she nodded in acknowledgment. She watched as an attempt from the man caused her lover to barrel at him. "Thank you." She mouthed as she broke down the door in the back and fled into the night.

The Goddess wandered night after night, not staying in one place for too long. A fortnight had passed and she found a den of enchanted ones without their master. She felt safe enough to relax. She hadn't been there that long when she felt the labors of childbirth upon her.

Her belly had to be opened to free the child from

the womb. It was just before sunrise when a familiar voice bellowed outside the door. It busted open and he ran in, the master fit with rage.

He looked at his underling and the child in her arms. “Do you realize what you have done?” He did have a soft spot for her, he loved her once. When he turned her, he felt the two of them had been meant to be together for all of eternity. All of those feelings made his orders much harder to follow through with.

“You don't have to do this.” She shook her head in fear. “They will never have to know.” She was speaking of their overlords, The Supreme Ones. “You could let us disappear and we will never show ourselves again.”

“It was our Supreme Mother that gave the order. You defied one of our most sacred laws.” He shook his head in sadness then turned full beast and grabbed the goddess. Just moments before, she handed the child to one of the humans that helped her give birth, and told her to run. The Goddess unsuccessfully fought him off. He threw her onto her knees in front of the moonlit window. He tied her feet and arms behind her back with a chord. He turned his attention towards going after the nurse and child.

It wasn't long before he carried the child back to the goddess. He killed the child in front of her eyes leaving her weeping as the sun began to rise. Being a descendant of The First Goddess of the Dark, sunlight was fatal. The master watched her burst into flames and turn into ash. There was no more of the story after that.

“Aunt, how are you feeling today?” Jason asked from the doorway.

Tessa looked up from the tale she had been reading. It helped her none except to realize how hard it would be to keep the child a secret. “As well as to be expected.”

“Uncle Isaac has been asking about you. He is

worried since he has not heard from you in a while."

In frustration she leaned back in her seat with a sigh. "And what am I supposed to tell him? Every day the baby grows and I haven't even been able to find out a timeline when it will be born, never mind the questions surrounding how I'm going to give birth." Her frustration was easily shown.

"You could tell him the truth." Jason suggested.

She shook her head. "I don't want him to be involved in a possible melee of events."

"You haven't given him the option."

"I don't want to argue with you. I will tell him when the time comes."

"And when will that be?"

"I will know when the time comes." She repeated.

"So I am to lie to him until you feel ready to reveal his child to him?"

"You have sworn your allegiance to me and your future charge."

He nodded. "I do understand that. I just feel that I am stuck in the middle."

"Jason, I know your feelings. But the less he knows the better for now. It may save his life."

"Will you consider at least talking to him? You seem to have no problem hiding your pregnancy from the council, how much harder can it be for Isaac?"

Tessa nodded. "I will think it over. Now if you don't mind, I feel tired. I am going to return to my room."

Jason nodded and left the doorway. She stood up, stretched, and walked back to her room. As she sat down on her bed, she glanced over at the videophone next to her bed. She laid on her side and thought long and hard about what Jason had been talking about. He had a valid point. Just speaking to Isaac might have made him more at ease with her absence, she thought. But then again, she felt like any contact whatsoever could lead to a compromising situation. Either which way it tore her up inside since neither answer would be the right one. She touched the screen and began to dial his room, but then turned it off again, letting her hand slip from the screen. She lamented for a moment then shut her eyes to the world.

*****

"It hurts!" Tessa screamed at Grüne who was rushing around grabbing things. Vala walked through the make-shift delivery room. Grüne had called her for assistance, although she was uncertain how well she could help since she had never had any dealings with childbirth before.

"Well, I'm sure it does. The baby seems to be ready to come out whether you like it or not." Grüne said as she sat Tessa onto the bed.

"I'm thinking most of them aren't trying to claw their way through the flesh though." Tessa said dryly through her teeth as pain shot through her body.

Grüne ignored her remarks. She knew what it was like to give birth and she was certain Tessa's was going to be a lot harder than hers was. She pushed the shirt up above the Queen's abdomen and observed the child in action. There was no doubt its activity was elevated. "Let me have a look and see what we have here."

"It's a baby and it wants out. What else do you need to know?" She screamed. "Just get it out of me. *Now!*"

Grüne put a cold gel on Tessa's belly and began an ultrasound. It showed what Tessa could have told her. The child was full grown and ready to emerge. She then ordered her to lie back onto the bed and lift her legs, she needed to see how things were going down there. "Hmmm." She said, as she muttered to herself.

"What does that mean, hmmm?" Vala asked, as she sounded helpless amongst the chaos.

"That means that it seems as though the baby's not coming out that way. I feared as much." Grüne looked at Vala then over at Tessa to explain. "It is obvious you are a being of a different nature and although you seem to have gotten miraculously pregnant, your body doesn't seem to want to finish the job. The only way we're getting that child is if we cut you open." No emotion slipped past her lips. She waited for Tessa and Vala to say something.

"Whatever it takes, get her out of there. She's angry and scared."

"Her?" Vala asked. "How do you know that? Have you checked?"

She shook her head. "I just know. I can feel her thoughts sometimes. It's complicated and not up for discussion at this very moment."

"Alright, Vala, I'm going to need your assistance. This is going to be tough and you're going to have to hold her down." Grüne ordered.

"Why does she have to do that?" Tessa looked with panic.

"There isn't quite the anesthesia available to numb a vampire's pain, and even if there were I wouldn't want to risk it to the baby."

"Fine." She groaned.

Vala positioned herself to hold Tessa down as Grüne used a special surgical knife to cut her belly open. There was a time limit, since she would heal up quickly enough.

As Grüne tugged and pulled inside her body, Tessa felt every bit of the pain involved. Vala had a hard time holding her down, and was certain that she could have been overthrown if it came down to it. Grüne finally pulled out the child and looked it over. Once the cries started, Grüne looked at Tessa and smiled for the first time in a long time. “It's a girl.” She confirmed.

There was something about the precise moment Tessa held her child in her arms. Everything else in the world seemed to disappear around them. She locked eyes with the youngling and held her gaze. Immediately, she knew of the child’s love for her. It was if she understood all of Tessa's thoughts and feelings. For such a short fleeting moment the child emulated understanding of her importance.

She finally broke gaze with her daughter and looked to her nephew, who stood awkwardly in the doorway. “Jason, come here.” She motioned to him. When he got by her side, she smiled at him. “Meet Ariana; your cousin, your ward, and our future.”

His eyes got glassy with joy and overwhelming fear at the same time. As he looked at the innocent child he asked his aunt. “Are you sure you want to give me such a huge responsibility?”

She touched his cheek. “I wouldn't trust anybody else.”

“I don’t think I’m ready. I still have much training to do. I don't feel like I can protect her like you want me to.”

She shook her head. “You will have plenty of time to continue practicing. Every day is a new lesson, and you will learn plenty through the years.” Tessa sat up and put the child in Jason’s arms. “Protect her as if she were your own. Do not stray too far from her.”

Jason’s heart melted, as he held the baby in his arms. She was so tiny and looked quite fragile. It wasn't until he saw the glow of her eyes that he remembered she wasn't a typical human child. The blood coursing through her veins were strong ties to Jason through both his parents; but they would never be the same. Ariana was special. She was born with a purpose in life and Jason hoped that purpose would be to unite the two races. He looked down upon her and quietly said. "We will have much to do, you and I." Almost on cue she grasped at his finger with her tiny hand as if she knew everything that he was speaking of. For that moment he felt that the world would truly be a better place.

After a few hours, Tessa had already healed completely from the wound she sustained to bring Ariana into the world. As soon as she could walk, she began packing. When dusk fell, she would be headed for the Mystic lands. Grüne and Jason were awaiting her as she traipsed through the doors to the outside world with the child in her arms, off to hopefully a more protected place.

CHAPTER SIXTEEN

"Why, after all this time, have you summoned me here?" Isaac said the moment he saw Tessa in the map room of her home on The Mystic Isle, one of the most sacred and secret places of where the Mystics lived. Its location changed constantly and had its own veil, although only a few knew the secret to that and they refused to share with the vampires. Bade could always find the open portal that could transport them there. She hardly looked up from what she was doing.

"I thought it was due time I saw you again." Tessa said with little emotion. She began to wonder if being away from him for so long had started to harden her heart once again.

He laughed sarcastically. "I'm so glad that you were thinking of me." He slowly approached her, as he took each step cautiously. "In all honestly I wasn't certain when or if you were thinking of me. You take Jason and disappear for eight months, not six like you promised, without a single word. I had to rely on the quick conversations with my own nephew to even know you were still alive." Concern was spread across his face, also anger and frustration.

She stopped what she was doing and looked at him. "As I told you before I left, it was for the greater good. Jason has had an extensive roll to play which may make him less accessible, but this was something you already knew." She smiled ever so slightly from the corner of her mouth. "I do want you to know there hasn't been a single day I have not thought about you."

"I can never be certain." He shook his head.

She looked at him for a moment then looked over to the guard at the door. "Can you go tell Jason that his uncle is here?" When the man left, she smiled at Isaac. "I'm sure after this long of a time you have reason to be uncertain of my intention, which is warranted. But you are going to have to trust me."

It seemed like only a minute had passed, the door opened slowly and Jason came through, holding Ariana in his arms. He passed the child to Tessa who gave the baby an endearing smile, before looking up at a very confused Isaac. "I would like to introduce you to Ariana, our miracle child."

Nothing but silence fell as the words echoed in his mind. He looked at the little girl and at Tessa, whose eyes were pleading for acceptance. "Excuse me?" He said after a few minutes of contemplation. "You're saying this baby is mine? More importantly are you saying she is yours?"

"That's exactly what I'm saying."

He let out nervous laughter. "Oh I get it. It's a joke. Something to break the ice." A little more laughter. "Because everyone knows your kind can't have babies." He looked over at Jason who seemed to have felt the uneasiness in the room. "You're in on it too. Marvelous. This is a great joke. I feel much better now."

She shook her head. "It's not a joke. If only it were that simple." The baby made a cute bubbling sound, then smiled at Isaac as if she were showing ownership.

He glanced over at Jason, who had his head down and avoided all eye contact. "But how?" He asked those around him. "I mean aside from the apparent."

"I would say a miracle would be something blunt. I could be mystical and tell you about how the stars, planets, moon were all in alignment, but I would think that just the right amount of circumstances brought us to this very point. The only thing that matters is that she is here now." Tessa tried to figure out Isaac's thoughts as she searched his eyes. When he looked at her slightly less frightened she said to him, "Would you like to hold your daughter?"

"Hold her?" He stuttered. "I...I..." He paused then smiled. "I would like that very much."

She lifted a very alert Ariana and spoke to her softly. "You're going to your daddy." The little girl smiled and cooed as she was passed off.

He locked eyes with the baby as he securely brought her into his arms. She smiled and grabbed his finger. He spent the next few minutes talking to her and felt the softness of her face and hands. He lost himself in her. He re-awoke to reality when he made Ariana laugh and smile and her eyes twinkled much brighter than any star that he had ever seen, similar to Tessa's when they glowed like embers when she filled with emotion. "She's a vampire, I guess." He said as more of a question than a statement.

Tessa got closer and smiled at the little girl, then looked up at the father. "She is not quite vampire and not quite human. She is of you and me. The uncertainty of yet nothing in comparison. Her true being is that nothing like this has a record, nothing past a birth. What she will grow up to be is something we are going to have to mold."

"I don't understand. How can we raise her if we don't know her capabilities?"

"As any parent would. She is our child and it is our responsibility." Ariana began to get fussy so Tessa had Jason take her away to be fed a special formula specifically for her needs, something very similar to the serum Tessa had pumped through her system many times of the day that she was with child. She looked back up at Isaac and her sincere expression warranted his attention. "But we do have to be very aware of everything she does and says. Right now she shows no vampire weakness. Her exposure to sunlight seems to put only a minor frustration on her. She has every body function that a human does, although we have to supplement her with a synthetic formula occasionally, which seems to satisfy her. She is growing as every human child does."

"So why keep her hidden away like a dirty little secret?" He looked at her slightly more upset. "You kept all of this from me. I could have been by your side through everything."

She shook her head. "It would have been too risky."

"How so?"

"I was in a rare circumstance. My blood desires and rage were lethal. I didn't want you hurt in case things got worse."

"That was my choice. One that I never got a chance to make."

"You might have gotten too attached. If something were to happen to me or the baby, before or after the birth, it would have devastated you."

He breathed deep with frustration. "So why is it you are out here, hidden away from the world?"

"This is for her safety. If the other vampires, especially our enemies, found out about her, they would kill her for certain. At her age, she wouldn't stand a chance out in the real world."

"Why would she even matter to them?"

Tessa became passionate about her words. "Can you imagine something greater being born? Human and Vampire strengths alike, hardly any weaknesses. The threat to the vampire species on a grand scale. No longer would we be at the top of the evolutionary list." She grabbed Isaac's hand and said. "Just imagine it. My hope for unity may be answered."

He pulled his hand away. "You may say you want to unite the humans and vampires, but I know what you really want."

"What is that?" She asked, slightly annoyed.

"You want to be able to rule over both races."

"War will cease." She ignored his response.

"It never will. You are delusional. War will never stop happening. There may be shifted purpose but that is all. You will still have your enemies, but with a slightly different agenda. Their fears of you obliterating everything will overtake them. All things unknown will bring fear into everything and for that reason progression will be lost and eradication will be the only answer that makes sense to them." He took a deep breath after his long monologue. "If you think the one child, your child, can change the world then you are deeply jaded. The only thing that will change is your power as a Queen; Overlord of everything."

She gasped then slapped him hard. "You are out of line." She raged.

He touched his pulsating cheek. He had forgotten how strong a vampire was. "You just proved what I was saying. Your grip on power is immense, your hunger for dominion is strong, and using your child to justify those means is only bitter, cold, and completely wrong."

She reached out and grabbed his throat, choking him slightly. "I warned you to hold your tongue. How dare you speak to me like this." She said, ignoring his struggles for breathe. "This child will be our salvation, but it won't happen overnight." She loosened her grip slightly. "We are going to have to make them understand, and that will mean forcing them to change.

That is one small change for the greater good." She let go of him and turned towards the moonlit window.

Isaac gasped for air and rubbed his throat. "I don't even recognize the Tessa before me. The one I knew had a true dream, not one of delusion and grandeur. I fear what compassion you once had is completely gone."

She turned around. "Do you really think of me as that unjust?"

"I didn't used to."

"I don't think that I have changed my ideals. All I know is that I will sacrifice everything for my child to survive. I believe she will be someone of importance."

"Why don't you just treat her like a child first?"

"What do you mean?"

"Raise her as a child, not an Empress."

"But she is special. We should nourish that."

"All children are special. What makes her so should matter more to you; that she is a very miraculous creation you and I have made that has defied all rules of logic. Don't you think that being a mother is more important?"

"You misinterpret my intentions." She said with sadness on how Isaac viewed her. "I want us to be a family first. I don't plan on locking her away and training her to be an oppressor of all things. I am quite disappointed that you feel like that, or that I am so power hungry that I would sacrifice the only good thing to happen to me, and this world, for my own benefit." She took a seat on the bench next to the window. "That is why I have brought you here. She needs to be raised with a vampire and a human."

"It seems that you have that covered, being here amongst these people. What about Jason?"

Tessa shook her head. "She needs more than that. She needs her mother and her father." She watched him smile just a little. "Together we can raise her with compassion, empathy, courage, ethics, humility, and of course love." She smiled back at him. "But I will tell you now that I will encourage and nourish each one of her abilities as they arise. She will know who she is."

Isaac nodded. "But we will get to that when the time comes."

"Agreed." She added and sent the proverbial elephant that was in the room right out the door.

Over the course of a few hours. Tessa gave him a tour of the private hideaway, all the while they caught up on past events. He told Tessa about Emma being withdrawn yet seemed peaceful at the same time. He knew the road would be tough up ahead with her. Tessa told him about what she had been attempting to deal with regarding the war effort while being tucked away in never-never land. Admittedly, it was very sluggish, but things were going to change. She also went into more depth of the pregnancy history that she had learned through the human texts.

The one thing she failed to mention was the psychic link her and Ariana shared. Every day the bond got stronger, and even though she was a baby, her thoughts and emotions were quite sound. There were a few times she felt as if she were looking out, through the child's eyes. Once, she saw herself through the eyes of one of the Mystics, in depth of a conversation she had no knowledge of. She didn't feel the need to burden Isaac with any information that would distance himself from his daughter even further.

Tessa stopped in front of the door to her quarters. "It's almost daybreak. I think we need to take a break and pick things back up when I wake." She suggested to the much calmer Isaac.

He shook his head no.

"Why not?"

"I've waited for too long to just watch as you slip off into your room. I'm not ready to let you go yet." He reached over and kissed her with certainty. Nothing else went through his mind except how much he missed being with Tessa.

She gave in quite easily. Tessa lowered her guard because deep down she had longed for Isaac's companionship. She pulled away for a bit only to pull Isaac into her quarters, to not emerge again until twilight.

The moment Isaac woke, he looked over at his beloved slowly stirring from the depths of slumber. He slipped into his clothes and sat at the edge of the bed.

"Hello lover." She said with a smile as she sat up. It seemed for only a moment the weight of the world was off her shoulders.

"Good evening Tessa." He said looking at her with intensity.

'What is it?" She asked, getting out of bed putting on a white silken robe.

"I thought I had been dreaming. That none of this was real."

She smiled. "Do you realize you are most definitely awake?"

He nodded. "I also realize that my role has changed immensely."

"Yes it has. Your role is very important." She paused for a moment. "I relinquish you as a servant." His eyes brightened in acknowledgment. "But I do want you near, for Ariana's sake."

He realized her words then stood up. "I would like to see her."

"Of course." She nodded. "You are free to walk around." She advised, as they walked down the hall into

Ariana's room. The both of them looked at her in her crib and couldn't stop smiling at the beaming face below them. She grabbed her toes and smiled a toothless grin. Tessa encouraged Isaac to pick her up. She was pleased to see him reach for their baby with no fear, or even thought, about what she was. She quietly watched the two interact lovingly and playfully. Slowly she turned away and snuck out of the room, leaving father and daughter to spend much needed time together.

The moment she shut the door she stopped before bumping into the absent minded Jason. “In a hurry?”

He snapped back to reality and awkwardly glanced at Tessa. “Uh, yeah. I was on my way to get Ariana. I thought that maybe I would take her with me to the feast they have prepared for Isaac.”

“How very thoughtful of you.” Tessa nodded. “But that won't be necessary. He is in there right now with her and I am pretty sure he is going to want to take her.”

“So is it nothing like we feared? Is he happy?”

“I believe so. But my fears were warranted and we still need to be cautious, at least for now. If you don't mind, could you check the perimeter once more? We can never be too careful.”

Jason nodded and left the way that he had come. After she spoke with her nephew, she realized how late it was and went to get child and father to prepare them for the celebration.

* * * * *

“Why are we doing this again?” Isaac asked Tessa as they slowly walked towards the bonfire in the center of the village; Ariana in his arms.

“These people hold much respect for visitors, especially allies of the Levé people. We have such a long history together."

"So, this is for me?" He asked almost embarrassed.

Tessa nodded. She knew that they wished to welcome and honor him. "It isn't what you have done yet, it is your future that will be important."

"My future?"

Tessa tried to shrug it off. "We will discuss it later, but I will tell you that being my companion and the father to Ariana is what they see as an honorable position, worthy of a grand feast."

"I won't argue with you now," he agreed. "But I think we will need to discuss this further."

The night was filled with extravagant festivities. The particular group of Mystics enjoyed their parties. Lavish drink and abundant food; music and dancing around the bonfire. Tessa sat at the head of a large table facing the party-goers. On one side sat Jason, who happened to be interacting with a very excitable Ariana. On her other sat a more relaxed Isaac.

The music died down as a group of young tribesmen walked up to Isaac and bowed. "We want to officially welcome you to your new home. We will treat you as we do the Levé Queen."

He smiled at the natives and glared at Tessa. "Thank you very much." He nodded with hollow emotions. "But if you excuse me, I think the night has worn me down." He stood up and excused himself.

She watched, embarrassed, as he walked away. Every bone in her body wanted to go after him, but she knew better. There was no way she could show weakness. Not even in front of allies. Especially in front of allies. So she drudged on as if it were the best celebration that she ever had.

Once the timing was right, she whisked away to her domicile. Thinking she would have to hunt Isaac down, she was quite surprised to see him leaning out of the balcony of her island sanctuary.

"Hi." She said quietly as she joined him on the balcony.

"Hey." He mumbled back.

"What happened back there..." She paused. "Wasn't the way things were supposed to go."

He turned to her. "Oh really? So how was it supposed to be? Are you telling me you aren't leaving me stranded in this place?"

She lowered her head. "It's not like that."

"So you are leaving."

She nodded in confirmation. "But not for long, I hope."

"Was this your plan all along? Bring me here so I could play babysitter?"

"No Isaac. That wasn't my big motivator. There are plenty of people that could watch Ariana and on top of that Jason is here to protect her."

"Then why me? Why string me around like a puppet?"

"First and foremost, like I said before, I didn't want to hide this from you any longer; that you needed to see your little girl. Second, you are probably the only person who could take my place here."

"And how is that? I'm not the leader of a vast people. I'm just a simple human."

"The human I have shared my thoughts, feelings, and wishes with. Who better than the person that truly knows me?"

He laughed dryly. "I know nothing about you and let's not pretend that I do." He sighed. "Look, if it will put you at ease I will try to help as best as I can from here. But don't give me a faux title with false responsibilities."

"That is not what I was doing." She defended herself, although deep inside she knew what he was saying was true. She wanted to give him a reason to stay.

"I'll stay here because you asked me to; and for Ariana. It will give me time to bond with her."

She smiled at him, truly happy. "Thank you Isaac. I owe you quite a bit for this."

He grinned. "Yes you do." He raised an eyebrow. "And as soon as you get back, maybe you can work on repayment."

Tessa laughed. "We'll see about that. I think I can put a down payment for it right now." She grabbed his shirt and pulled herself into a heated kiss.

*****

Tessa awoke to darkness; she had been lying on a stone floor. She felt the heat and smelled staleness in the air. Lights flickered for just a moment and then back off again, making it impossible for her eyes to adjust to the dark.

She stood up, began walking, and felt the cold floor under her bare feet. The flickering lights stopped momentarily. Just as she took a few more steps the lights danced like a disco ball. She forced her way around, as she relied on her other senses to get to a door that was in the far corner.

Once at the door, she rushed and slammed it shut. Her body felt the coolness of the room. Ice reflected everywhere. As she walked, her steps made a slight clicking sound. Tessa passed one block of ice after another. She looked deeper into one and realized there was a human inside, frozen with a looked of anguish upon his face. His arms attempted to shield him from his catastrophic fate.

As Tessa glanced around the room, she realized she was in a cavern of frozen blocks of ice. Humans forever stuck in the final fright of their lives.

"Poor, poor people." A feminine voice echoed through the cavern. "Destined to be nothing but cattle. What other use do they have?" Tessa realized the voice was that of Liana's.

"Their uses are plentiful." Tessa spoke to the air around her, no object to focus on.

"Ah yes, lovely enslavement." She heard Liana's voice much closer.

"You know it's not just that."

Liana appeared beside one of the ill-fated humans and ran her fingers across it as she moved towards Tessa. "Oh that's right, you sympathize with them. You wish for them to be free."

Tessa shook her head. "It's not like that." She didn't know why Liana was even discussing it. "I just think we can live together more peacefully. Their accomplishments become ours and we no longer have to worry about eradication."

Liana laughed. "You amuse me with all your rainbows and unicorns."

She stood face to face with Tessa, who held back her uneasiness as best she could. "Why are you here? In my dream."

Liana laughed. "Because I can. I told you before that I am your master and I always will be. No matter how many treaties we sign, I will always rule over you. Why did you not sign the last treaty anyway?"

"I knew it would come down to this, you attempting to assassinate me anyway. What was the point? As soon as you would go back on your word The Nation would ostracize you."

"That's only if they know it is me. I can easily take

you down from the confines of my own palace."

"What do you plan to do?"

Liana laughed. "Wouldn't you like to know?" She then lowered her voice to a whisper. "I will give you one tiny little hint." She put her fingers up, then snapped. At that precise moment all of the ice shattered into millions of pieces.

Tessa's eyes were in disbelief. With a simple snap of the fingers she understood that Liana was going to go after her human subjects. The symbolism was not subtle. Cutting off the food source was a great strategic move. She wasn't sure how Liana planned to do it, though. The Levé Kingdom was large, vast, and heavily populated.

When Tessa glanced down for just a moment, she realized her foe was gone. Just a second after that, the ground she was standing on began cracking and it opened up to begin her fall.

After a very long drop, she landed on her feet. As soon as she touched ground, she couldn't help but notice the sweltering heat. From what she could gather, she had landed in some huge pit, although she couldn't tell where the heat was coming from.

"Are you a little hot under the collar?" Liana's voice boomed from the void above.

Tessa screamed out, "Not in the least." She was not going to give Liana the satisfaction of her misery as long as she could help it.

"Oh my; then let me turn it up a little." The pit began to widen as the heat grew in intensity. An entrance to another room opened up, a wall along the ledge guided Tessa in.

She was in what looked like an old dungeon. Pits of fire burned strategically around the stone prison.

"Help me!" A weak male voice called from a dark

corner.

"Who's there?" She called out to him.

"It's me; Bade." She heard his voice become deeper as she edged towards the corner.

"*Oh!*" She gasped when she saw him shackled in silver chains, hanging from the wall. He looked worn out and sickly. "What are you doing here?"

"It's the Krones! They gave us a surprise attack. We fought as hard as we could but it was of no use. They were just too strong for us."

On the opposite wall, shackled, were Andreas and Vala. They too looked like death was at their door.

"Liana is strong. She captured me herself." Andreas forced out, his mouth ever so parched.

"We should have surrendered when she gave us the chance, now she is going to let the fire consume us." Vala cried.

"Or worse..." Bade cried out, "Starve us to death like they did with Drake." His eyes looked above Tessa with fear.

She looked up and gasped at the sight of Drake hanging upside down, shackled and lifeless. She gathered her composure and stood strong. "I'm going to get you out of here," she said. "As soon as I find you a way out of those chains."

"Do you think it will be this easy for you? Just to come in and rescue your people?" Liana's words echoed from the air again.

"I am much stronger and smarter than you may think." She yelled at the vapors that surrounded her.

"That sounds like a challenge."

As soon as she finished those words, she felt a burning sensation around her wrists. She looked down and saw she, too, had silver shackles on. She tugged at them, began to struggle, her chains started to pull her back towards the wall.

“How strong do you feel now?” Liana appeared before Tessa.

“My will does not falter.” She struggled harder as she looked for a way out.

“First I exterminate your precious humans, then I demolish your loyal subjects.” She pointed towards Tessa's advisors and she watched in horror as they lit up in flames, screaming in agony.

“No!” Tessa screamed. She tried everything she could to break free, the whole time crying inside for her people's pure endless pain.

By some force, she was pushed onto her knees and could not find her way up. Liana bent down face to face with Tessa, her cold eyes as venomous as their host. “You cannot defeat me.” She said in a straight tone. “I will always win.”

Tessa gave her an evilly smug look and said, “Desdemona said the same thing, and see how well that turned out.”

Liana didn't flinch like Tessa would have thought. She stood up and laughed. “I have something of more importance that she never had.”

“And that is?”

“Control over you!”

“You don't control me.”

“Ah but I do. I am your master and it is very hard for you to resist me. That is your downfall.”

“You underestimate my determination.”

She moved her hands in a downward motion and Tessa was thrust to the ground. Tessa felt as if a boulder were sitting on top of her.

“In your dreams I have total control. See, it's the perfect murder, nobody could ever prove my guilt. So I get to continue to be a part of The Nation and I will once again have my precious Levé's back." Liana motioned her hands towards the ground below and it began to crack. Flames reached up from the bowels of hell, searching for Tessa.

"You will *not* control me!" Tessa screamed out. She repeated herself over and over again as Liana laughed wickedly and the flames grew to surrounding Tessa. All she could do was close her eyes and keep screaming.

All of a sudden, the ground and the heat were gone. She opened her eyes and saw the comfort of her suite. She got up out of bed and got dressed. There was a matter that needed to be urgently addressed.

.

* * * * *

"I leave the moment dusk appears." Tessa said as she sat in front of her vanity, brushing her hair.

"So soon?" Isaac asked, as he propped his head up on the pillow.

She turned to him after she set the brush down. "It seems like now is the best time to strike at Liana. Her guard is down and she is vulnerable."

"What are you going to do?"

"I have quite a few teams ready to go, including my top knights, aside from Jason of course, since he will be here with you. As soon as I find her location, we will strike."

"You don't know where she is?" He sat up.

"Not yet, but soon." She stood up then grabbed her silken robe. "I'm going to go say goodbye to Ariana."

"Do you want me to come with you?" He asked.

She quickly headed him off and said, "No need. I will bring her to you." She didn't want him to worry about what she was going to do. She knew that he would not understand.

He seemed to accept that response so she traipsed out the door and down the hall. She slid into the room and looked into the crib. Staring back at her was a very happy child, cooing and smiling at her. “Hello precious. Are you happy Mommy's here?” She reached in and picked her up, the child giggled with glee. Holding her and talking to her just made the child radiate with joy. “Can you show Mommy Liana?” Tessa asked as pleasant as she could. Ariana could be quite fickle. Although she tried a few times before, to connect through someone else’s mind, she had never attempted such a strong pairing. Most of the time it was the child itself, even in utero, that chose who and when she connected with. If Ariana didn't want to do it, she had been known to take Tessa down a deep dark place full of despair, making it hard to disconnect. Tessa's goal was to join their natural sensory ability to make the connection to their lineage stronger.

The moments were never as strong as when she was pregnant, but they worked quite well. The good thing about doing it outside the womb is there is slightly more control and it seemed like a natural cloak, making it harder to be located.

Tessa held Ariana in her arms and looked down at her innocent face. She cleared her mind and delved into her eyes and on through to the mind, frozen in place. As if waking from a dream, she was successful in the dive.

As though she were standing in the room, she appeared in a ceremonial hall. She looked around at all the patrons and realized that she was indeed in the Queen's court. She looked further around the room and caught glimpse of Liana, sitting on an actual throne, embellished in gold and jewels. She sat there with her hand under her chin like she was struck from boredom. “Jean Luc!” She bellowed at the top of her lungs. A scrawny man came running from behind Tessa and knelt in front of Liana.

"Yes your majesty?"

"Please dear God, tell me that you have found that wretched Queen Tessa."

He shook his head no. "My Queen, we have not."

She sat forward, "Any idea where her armies may be hiding?"

He shook his head again saying no.

"Is there anything that you *have* found out, or have you been sitting on your bums twiddling your fingers?" She stood up and pulled the man from the floor.

He avoided her eyes, but they burned straight into his skull. "We have been working around the clock. Their troops only show themselves on the defensive, then disappear again."

She let the man go and spoke to herself. "What are you planning, Tessa?"

Tessa edged forward, technically it was her host body that made the movement. There were times when she would manifest inside a weak human, instead of being a phantom in the room.

Liana snapped a look in her direction. "You!" She pointed to Tessa's host. "Come here." Her voice was rigid and demanding. The Liana that she was seeing was nothing like the cunning, calm, and seductive Liana that had gotten the upper hand over her constantly.

"Yes your highness." She faked fear, for if her enemy sensed anything else her innocent host could be destroyed.

"What is so important that you have to traipse through my chambers like it was a train station?"

"Nothing." Was all she responded with.

"Nothing? Is that all you can say to your Queen? The one who saved you from being part of the human massacre?" She said as if she were truly benevolent.

"I just...I just wanted to give you a message."

"A message?" She was intrigued.

She swallowed hard and walked up to Liana. "Yes it is about the Levé Queen."

"Yes, yes, do go on." At that point she looked for any answer that would explain her incognito ways and strategies.

She moved the body closer, she sensed its portly heaviness as she walked. "Tessa, would like to give you a message."

"She, herself, sent you?"

The body nodded.

"Do go on." Liana was amused.

Tessa used all her strength, the strength Ariana willed her to have, to exit the body and become an apparition. She floated next to Liana and whispered in her ear. "I'm back and I'm coming for you."

Liana turned as pale as a vampire that hadn't fed in a long time. She quickly turned in all directions, looking for the figure the voice had come from. "Who said that?" She stood up and asked in a panic.

"Said what Madame?" A fledgling guard asked boldly.

"You do jest. You seriously are going to tell me that I am hearing things?" She questioned the naive guard.

"I just don't think we could hear it, that was all." He quivered.

"Enough!" She pointed at the two elder guards. "Take him away."

"Why?" He screamed as he was being drug away.

"For speaking to me, your Queen, out of turn and without anything significant to show for it."

Tessa leaned in closer, enjoying her ethereal state. "You know who this is, don't be stupid."

"What?" She looked around again, that time in frustration. She then looked at all who were in the grand hall. "Leave me at once!" She ordered. Everyone quickly dashed out of the room.

"Tessa! Show yourself." She demanded on the spot.

"There is nothing to show." She said slyly.

"Such childish games you play."

"I learn from the best." Tessa giggled childlike.

"I do not fear you. I pity you."

"Oh really?" Tessa asked, then used as much psychic power as she could, and turned her effervescent figure into something closer to a projection. She stood in front of Liana.

"Nice parlor trick." Liana clapped dryly. "So what now? Are you going to throws sheets on the furniture and cause them to levitate as your ghostly army?" She laughed deeply. "I'm terribly frightened."

"Actually what should frighten you is the legions of Levé's locked in on your location as we speak."

"You're a fool. They are no match for my loyal Krones. I'm not worried."

"You were quite worried a moment ago when it seemed like we had all but vanished from your radar. Stealth is something that can only be accomplished with discipline. My people have done quite well with that."

"So why are you telling me this? Send them after me." She bluffed.

"Be careful what you wish for, because I have one more thing to say," Tessa stared at her deeply with intensity. "I'm coming for you."

CHAPTER SEVENTEEN

As Tessa hugged her back to the wall, she held her gun to her chest. She waited for the right time to pass unnoticed through the obscene amount of guards that surrounded the overly golden doors to her 'Queen Nemesis' chambers. She knew she was there, she sensed it; thanks to her connection with Ariana.

She motioned to two of her soldiers to draw attention away from her approach. They acknowledged and began to make small noises, like that of whispers, only ones that were questionable to even a vampire.

"What's that?" said one of the guards in the direction of what might have been the sound.

It drew the attention of a few of the them and then Tessa's soldiers slowly wound through the halls. With three of the guards occupied, she headed towards two of her other soldiers. They quickly stepped out from the shadows across from Tessa and openly mocked an argument. Since those two had already infiltrated the fortress earlier, they were still in Krone uniform.

Tessa noticed two of the guards slowly advancing on the arguing bunch. She heard them involve the guard in the faux argument, asking for a settlement. She slipped past them unnoticed then hid in the shadows three feet away from one of the soldiers. One of the things that had been instilled in her was perfecting stealth. She had to be able to mask her presence from even that of the vampire, although it was quite tricky on ones with purer blood, but nonetheless was sometimes achieved. She holstered her gun, cinched her leather gloves, and with her free hand she grabbed a hold of her silver blade. Quicker than a human eye could blink, the throat of the guard was slit and he lay quietly on the ground. His partner's reaction was too slow as he attempted to approach her and was met by a silver stake through the heart. He immediately began to wriggle and turn to goo. He was a weak-blooded vampire, one whose blood was so diluted from pure blood, so he went quicker than most.

The hall was clear of any and all guards. They had successfully infiltrated the castle, so to speak. On the other side of the door was the one being that she despised the most. Her black blood began to boil with animosity and she closed her eyes. The images of the room on the other side of the door filled her mind as though she were standing in the middle of it. She sensed Liana on the other side. She crossed her fingers that her position wasn't given away.

She grabbed for the handle and pressed down very slowly so as not to arouse any suspicion from her intended target. As the door slowly opened, she crept in and surveyed the room that surrounded her. Still sensing her nearby, her blood pumped nervously which made it harder to focus and she seemed to not be able to find her. Had she been deceived by her own mind?

When she walked further into the room, she heard young sobbing and the sound of tears hitting the floor. Upon further investigation, she realized that it was coming from the couch in the far part of the room facing the shaded window. As she inched forward, she saw the back of Liana's head and beside her a young child, probably around the age of four. The thumb in her mouth was the only thing that kept her from bawling completely.

"Shh. Don't cry darling." Liana said as she brushed

away golden ringlets from the child's face. "Everything will be okay." The words seethed from her lips doing the best she could to not frighten the child. Children were much harder to convince to do a master's bidding. Their minds were much clearer and the innocence easily overcame anything the vampire could do. This innocence in mind, body, and soul made the drops of their blood seem like sweet ambrosia and was often thought of as a delicacy. The human race was not populating as they once were, making young blood even more savory.

She gently pulled the little darling to her bosom, still offering a false sense of security and comfort. As Tessa took one more step forward Liana's ears perked up, then looked down at the child. Without turning around for fear of frightening the little girl, Liana spoke in a calm voice. "I believe that I left orders to not be disturbed. Be gone before I alter your decision toward this intrusion."

Tessa took a few steps back and gripped from behind her the handle of the door then stopped as she watched Liana bare her fangs and sink them into the innocent one's neck. Hardly a scream or cry from her. There was nothing she could do for her at that moment except use it to her advantage.

Sneaking back up to her, Tessa drew her blade. She hovered over the feeding queen; blood stains seeped through the child's dress. Just as she was about to go for Liana's neck, she shot up quickly as if startled from a deep slumber. Liana threw the body to the ground and knocked the knife from Tessa's hand.

Their eyes met with equal parts fear and venom. She was certain Liana was trying to process how she had gotten so close to her without being sensed.

She grabbed for the gun, that she holstered

moments ago, and aimed it at Liana. The pulse had begun to charge waiting for the moment she decided to pull the trigger, blasts of condensed light would shoot from it.

Liana looked around for options and slowly edged towards Tessa.

"Don't move." Tessa boomed.

Liana lifted her chest with fabricated courage. "So this is it? This is what is has come down to?"

She smiled out of one corner of her mouth. "I suppose it is."

"How...anti-climactic." Liana slowly started stepping to the side.

She moved in closer. "Stop right now."

Liana laughed. "What are you going to do? It's obvious you're not really going to kill me."

"Oh really? And how do you know that?"

"You would have done it already." Two more steps to the side.

Tessa edged closer. "Don't think you know me, because you don't." Her voice rang like a teenager full of angst.

"Then do it. Put me out of my misery." Before she even finished her sentence Tessa pulled the trigger throwing pulses of light at Liana, who quickly dodged the fire and moved past her and on towards the door.

She spun around in time to see Liana step out the door. She darted behind her only to catch a glimpse of her streaking down the narrow corridor to the night.

She slipped past her for just a moment, stopped short, and knocked her to the ground. She climbed on top of her as she attempted to restrain her, but Liana rolled her around. "It's not so easy is it? I'm too cunning for you."

"You are delusional." Tessa laughed and rolled back

over to take the advantage. "I have gained an asset, one that you will never have." She pinned Liana's arms against the floor and looked at her, staring down at her prey.

"So what now?" Liana asked. "How, pray-tell, do you think that you can defeat me? Your arms are quite busy. You know the moment you reach for a weapon I will break free."

She was correct, although it didn't stop Tessa from trying. Once she broke free, Liana ran into a room, the same room Tessa foretold Liana's doom. There were statues, vases, and various artwork that adorned the hall.

Tessa crept from column to column, holding her weapon tightly, "You can't run forever, Liana. You're going to have to own up to your own fate."

Faint laughter heard from the shadows moved with each step she had taken. "Listen to you, sounding like a true Queen. If only Greco were here, he'd shed tears of joy." The voice moved further away, "But it is because of you that he is dead, so he will never enjoy this moment." Those words rang loudly through her ears.

"Is that what you think? This is all my fault? I beg to differ. My actions have nothing to do with his murder. Your mother's lust for power drove her to it." She glided once again between the columns. "And your misguided reason for revenge is going to be your undoing."

"Ah but my darling I believe it is you that is misguided." Her voice came behind Tessa like a whisper then vanished just as soon as it had appeared. She turned around as quick as she could, before hearing the voice fade once again. "I give into my true nature; you rely on the falsehood that humans will someday stand side by side with us."

She saw a glimpse of her in the corner of her eye and swooped in with a surprise attack, knocking her from her hiding place. "Maybe so." She said as she watched her challenger stagger before she kicked her in the stomach, followed by a right hook to the jawbone. "But vile creatures like yourself need to be eradicated before any vision of mine can be made possible." Tessa shoved her hard, falling onto her back. She hovered over her, engulfing Liana in her shadow. "And you, well I am going to thoroughly enjoy your extinction." Tessa aimed her UV gun at her head.

Liana's eyes were of pure fear. As Tessa pulled the trigger, by instinct, she covered her face with her left arm and screamed as it burned into a blaze, then to molten embers. She rolled over and ran out of the room, she held the arm that had begun to flake into ashes; she was screaming in agony.

"Shit!" Tessa groaned and ran off following her. It was easy that time. The smell of burning flesh filled the air. As she ran up the staircase a few more flights, the smell ended at a door at the top. At first, she hesitated, knowing that it led to the rooftop and she was uncertain if it had already become dusk. Her reasoning to continue came to the idea that if Liana had run up there, she had to of been certain the sun had begun to set; that is what brought her to charge through the door, as she watched it turn to nightfall. No rays of sun to burn her to oblivion. A very bold, and could have been easily stupid, move.

She looked around what seemed to be a barren rooftop. She stood amidst buildings of all shapes and sizes. It reminded her of home. She whispered to her inner mind. "Ariana, please help me find her."

Almost like an answer from a god came, her sight began to intensify her body and mind until she felt the presence of Liana once again. She followed that sense and ended up sneaking behind Liana, who was crouched behind an old shed like a human half afraid of its destiny to die.

She grabbed her from behind and put her arm around her neck. A struggle ensued for dominance. Tessa grabbed the almost non-existent arm and squeezed as hard as she could until Liana screamed in deathly agony and stopped her struggle. They staggered closer to the edge of the building. Tessa had a tight choke hold around her neck.

"You can kill me like you killed my mother, but know that someone will take my place as quickly as I did hers." Her eyes filled with tears of anger.

Tessa laughed. "Funny thing about Desdemona." She paused for a second. "She's not dead."

"What?" Liana gasped in horror. "But we heard you had killed her; executed her." She leaned forward amidst her shock.

"Just as I wanted everyone to believe, to cripple the Krone Empire into submission, that was until you came along."

"Why did you keep her alive? She killed Greco. You were supposed to exact revenge against her." Her words turned angrier and tears began to fall even more.

"Does it bother you? That your eternal love's murderer still lives to this day? Does it bother you that there is no way possible for you to find her, kill her, and watch all that disgusted you fade to nothingness?" Tessa continued. "I thought that by keeping her around I would be able to enjoy knowing that she had to bend to my will, her sworn enemy. Oh how I loved hearing all of her torturing. To be the face she looked at from time to time with her knowing that the 'Child Queen' reigned more powerful than her and the Levé's were dominant." Tessa's sounds of satisfied revelation infuriated Liana.

"Nothing will bother me." Liana confessed.

"Because now I have a new task at hand, and that is to hunt down my mother." She broke free for a moment. "After I take care of you." Liana's fangs drew sharply.

Tessa grabbed her free arm quickly and pulled her back towards her, bosom to bosom. "Unfortunately that won't be the case." Tessa took out the dagger that she had picked up off the floor earlier, and plunged it into Liana's heart. "I get to watch you die and fulfill my need for revenge."

Liana cried out. "No!" then fell backwards, screaming like a banshee in the night. She tipped over and fell off the rooftop. Tessa looked down as Liana fell onto the building below, screaming and bubbling under her skin. The silver burned her from the inside out. She jumped down and approached her. "I'm the master now." She boldly stated as she grabbed the dagger from the withering body and slashed the dreadfully disgusting neck, leaving a deep gash for black ooze to seep out. Liana's eyes widened in horror and Tessa tugged at her, twisting slightly until her head came clean off. She held it up to the world in triumph and bravery, much like Perseus did to the Kraken. The battle was over, she had won; her spoils strung through her fingers like dark threads on a loom. Her foe had been defeated.

CHAPTER EIGHTEEN

Tessa returned home from her triumph. She was welcomed with open arms by her lover and child, and a nephew glad for her safe return (although secretly relieved that his duty as protector of his ward was slightly loosened). Now she knew the time had come and she could not hold back the inevitable. Her defeat of the Krone Queen had brought upon a new age. With clans joined, the world would change. That time, though, she would not leave anything to chance. She would make haste back to Chicago and meet with her advisors and keep the wheels of progression moving forward.

The departure from their secluded safe-haven moved like a hush in the breeze. After a quick walk through a portal, they headed to nearby land. Ariana and Tessa were tucked away in a sealed car of the train. Isaac and Jason were within arms reach, being the only worthy company.

Tessa looked at the sleeping child lying in the bassinet beside her. If only it were as simple as the innocence before her. Sleeping in such peace with the world around her in perfect slumber, knowing not of the evil things roaming the earth willing to do whatever it took to eradicate her from existence.

Isaac sat down next to her and boldly grabbed her hand and looked over her shoulder at their beautiful daughter. “No matter what has gone on between us in the past and present, one thing I know for certain is that we have created the most beautiful child.”

She listened to his endearing words and lightly squeezed his hand in silent response. She could not argue with his sentiment. She turned to him with a slight smile and lovingly serious eyes. "As wonderful as she is, we are going to have to hide her from the world for a little longer."

He sighed and shook his head in quiet frustration; after a few moments he spoke softly. "As much as I would like to be such a doting father, I do understand the circumstances."

"This means we will have to keep her hidden away." She told him. "The Underground will work well as a nursery and she will have all the comforts of home, albeit a slightly secluded one." She stated then forced a smile. "She will have plenty of loved ones around her. But..." She leads.

"But what?"

"Emma cannot find out. Not just yet."

Isaac stood up and scratched his head in confusion. "Why the hell are we even going back to the city then? It seems as though we would have been better off with those nature witches, druids, mystics, whatever they were."

"I'm needed back in the city. I have been gone for too long and have to make plans. The rebellion has heated up once again and I cannot appear weak to the council. I have avoided them long enough and now that the war with the Krones has been won, I cannot use that as a cover for my absence."

"You could have left us behind." He muttered like a child that hadn't gotten its way.

She shook her head. "I'm selfish I suppose. I didn't want to feel like I was abandoning my child." Tessa said honestly. "And Emma really needs a parental figure in her life. You have been gone long enough."

"So how am I supposed to do this? I don't think I could bear to be away from Ariana for too long. Not now that I have met her."

"And you won't. You will just have to be quite careful." She looked at him seriously. "But for now you will only be allowed to see her while Emma is away. The rest of the time you must spend it as you had been in the past, not changing anything to draw suspicion. In your home you are her father figure."

He sarcastically laughed. "I have to give up being a father to be someone else's father."

"You must not even give her any doubt on your whereabouts and of Ariana. She is already sitting on the fence about her allegiance, we wouldn't want to give her any ammunition."

He nodded. "I suppose you're right." He paused then said, 'That girl is going to be tough enough as is. I'm not sure I'm going to be that much of an influence on her."

"All we can do is try." She said, then looked away into nothingness as she began thinking on all the matters she was going to have to address the moment she got back.

Upon arrival Tessa and her entourage slipped through quietly and hurried through her modern day fortress. Jason was up ahead, a bundled up Ariana flat against his chest, the best he could do to protect and camouflage her. He was advised to go ahead to the underground before anyone could catch a glimpse of the child.

Isaac unsuccessfully tried to keep up with the group. A human's pace compared to a vampire's was equal to that of a turtle to a cheetah.

"Uncle Isaac?" Emma's voice called out to him. He turned around and realized he was standing face to face with her. "When did you get back?"

He stammered nervously as he watched the group

fade into the distance, only seeing Tessa watch and wait for him. "Just now."

She looked at him expressionless and then at Tessa down the hall. "I hope you enjoyed your trip while I was here being slave-driven by the teachers and The Beastly Crew."

"I know better. You were left with the most trusting and capable of people."

"You should use the word 'people' sparingly." She said with haught.

He glared into her bitter eyes. "You should show some respect for the ones who took care of you while I was gone. They didn't have to but they did it as a favor."

"They wouldn't have had to if you hadn't decided to run off with that *thing*." She said loudly and points towards Tessa.

He grabbed her arm tightly and raised his voice. "What is your problem? She has never been harsh to you. She has put a roof over your head; given you food, clothes, and education. She is your aunt." He felt hot in the moment, he tried his hardest to calm down. He wasn't certain why he was so angered, but thought to himself that the conversation had been a long time coming.

Emma shook her head. "She stopped being my aunt the moment she gave up her life."

"You weren't even born then. Are you going to act as if she did this to you on purpose?"

"She is nothing to me. We have no ties. All she happens to be is the creature who took my father's life."

"You know it wasn't her."

"One does it, they all are guilty."

"Whether you like it or not you are her family, which means you will show her some respect."

"That is something she will never get from me and

she shouldn't be getting it from you either." She stared eye to eye and challenged his character. "Instead you decide that you are going to worship the ground she walks on. You have become nothing more than her slave and whore."

Before Isaac could stop himself, he felt his hand slap her cheek. She gasped and touched her burning face in utter disbelief. "You will not speak to me this way." He boomed with authority. "What I do is my business, and I couldn't care less whether you like it or not." He took in a deep breath calming down a little bit. "I'm tired of you parading around with a 'woe is me' attitude as though you are the only one that matters in this world. This stops now. You have no excuses for complaint."

"You don't understand me. You never did."

"I have done the best I could, given the circumstances."

"You should have let me go with Mom."

"Why? So you could end up a child casualty? You are much safer with me. Your mother has no regard for those surrounding her. At least with me you had a chance of a normal life."

"I'm not sure you know what normal is."

"It means you get to have all the good things in life and have a chance to become something important. You also get to be with kids your own age and do things you are supposed to do as a kid."

She scoffed at him. "Most of them are frightened of me thanks to Dear Auntie." She pointed at Tessa once again. "They think that they have to pussyfoot around for fear if I get upset I will sick my vampire army on them!"

"Is that what this is about? Friends? Fitting in?"

She rolled her eyes as most young teenagers did. "You just don't understand. I want a normal life, one with my mother, my friends, and no vampires."

"Well that's not going to happen."

She started to walk away. "Don't I know it." She decided the conversation was going nowhere.

"You better be going home." He ordered.

"I am. Don't worry. I've had enough for now."

Before he could scream back at her for disrespecting him, Tessa put her hand on his shoulder. "Just let her go. You are not going to convince her of anything at this point. We will take care of this at another time."

"We?"

"The vampires and I risk quite a bit if she leaves. We can't chance for her to end up on the rebel side. We will try to take care of this."

"She is your niece. You can't hurt her." He said in a pleading tone.

"No, that's not my intent. But she needs to be watched closely. See how important it is for you to be in her life? She needs a guided hand." She looked at him with a smile. "Now I want you to give Ariana a little time before you and Jason have a nice dinner together. I think he may be a neutral party in this family affair. The two of them used to be very close."

"Yeah, you're right. I think that will help, at least for tonight." He agreed.

*****

The advisors had finally met, each made plans in conquering the Krone kingdom once and for all, leaving nothing to chance. It was decided that Vala was to be in charge of the Krone territories, which gave her all but ultimate governing power. As one would imagine, she felt that she wasn't fit for the task at hand, but Tessa felt otherwise since Vala had always made wise decisions, especially as she looked at things as a whole. The Levé Empire had been fast expanding and Tessa felt the pressure mount, although she welcomed change with a new-found courage.

Later on the next evening Tessa sat quietly in her library and picked up the journal that had been hidden behind a bunch of untouched Bronte books. She brushed the dust off its jacket and reached for a pen.

I take pen to paper at least one more time. I feel alive once again. I feel as though I finally have begun the journey that I have been tasked with. With the death of Liana, I truly remain supreme and am revered by The Nation, putting to rest any doubt they had of me being a strong Queen. I am now a force to be reckoned with. With this new-found power and now the Krone troops bending to my will, I can eradicate the vermin that are the Independent Freedom Fighters once and for all.

I have looked into the eyes of innocence, my sweet Ariana; for she has foretold a sound future. Things will change and she will be at the center of it all, pushing forward to a new day; a new world.

She set the pen down and closed the journal. She looked up from her chair and out into the hallway.

"Oops! Sorry." It was Emma. She had bumped into a mouse of a girl. She bent down to pick up the books that had toppled to the ground.

"That's okay." The girl said with a nervous smile. She joined her with the cleanup.

Emma handed the young teenager back the last book and grinned with question. "I haven't seen you around before. Are you new?"

The girl nodded demurely. "My parents just recently got reassigned to the city, working for the Queen."

She rolled her eyes. “Like she doesn't have enough servants.” She muttered under her breath.

“What was that?” The girl couldn't hear what she had said, which may have been a good thing.

“Oh, nothing.” She shook her head and brushed the topic off. She then outstretched her hand. “I'm Emma. I live here in the compound.”

The girl let loose one of her hands from the books and shook her hand. “Harper.”

“Well, Harper, since you have just moved here I might as well show you around the place. It could use some livening up.” She said using dry humor to break the mood.

Harper laughed at her joke, then the two walked out of sight.

Tessa grinned at the moment. It seemed as though everything was going according to plan. Emma gained a friend, while she gained an informant; someone that in time would be able to bend the will of her niece the way she wanted it. Harper had been one of her trusted servants sworn to secrecy. There was nothing that she would not do for her Queen. Even if that meant befriending Emma so as to neutralize the threat.

Standing up from her chair she remembered there was one more thing that she needed to take care of, one thing that would be the most pleasurable of anything she had done up to that moment. She needed to give Desdemona a visit to brag of complete defeat.

Tessa slowly led the way down the cold stairs; a stalky vampire servant carried a heavy square box in his arms, although it probably wasn't as heavy to him as it would be to a human.

She went down the hall, through the checkpoints until she stopped in front of Desdemona's cage. Desdemona looked up in confusion at the visit. She silently watched as the guard faced her and demanded she step back. He had his hand on a flash stick, one similar to a cattle prod but slightly more geared towards vampires. It was quite painful as Desdemona had found out many times before.

Desdemona did just as he said as the man opened the door quickly and slid the package in and sealed the door quickly behind him.

"What is this?" She questioned, as she edged towards the box.

"A present for you." Tessa grinned.

"What is it?"

"Open it and find out." She urged.

Desdemona opened the box slowly, unsure of its contents. She covered her mouth in horror. "No!" She gasped. She picked up Liana's cold head from its encasement. "Why did you bring this to me?" She stammered and looked in Tessa's direction.

"I just wanted you to know that it was over. I have led the Levé's in defeat of your precious Krone's."

"So you have." She sighed and looked at the severed head.

"I have also come to a conclusion; something I have most recently acknowledged." Tessa added.

Desdemona looked back up at her after she gently put the head back in the box, like she was tucking a child to sleep. "And what is that?" She was full of questions, every bit of her being had turned into a helpless creature, and her frail face questioned with fear.

"I have grown bored of you." Not waiting for an answer Tessa pushed the speakerphone button, she quickly yelled into the box, "Proceed." She then turned back around as she looked at one extremely scared Desdemona. "I feel that I no longer have a use for you."

Just seconds later Desdemona heard the charging of

the UV weapon that surrounded the room. In panic, she pleaded. "You still need someone to help you with the knowledge of my kingdom and the secrets of The Nation. You are being brash in your judgment." The UV was almost at full power and began to lighten the room.

Tess turned around and followed the servant behind a protective barrier as the room filled brightly with ultraviolet light.

The sounds of screams and the sight of Desdemona's body as it burst into flames made her feel exhilarated and in control. The sound of her death was nowhere near the boring death of the Wicked Witch of the West as she melted into nothingness. Her death was like that of despair howling for a redemption that had come too late.

Once the lights turned off, she went into the room and looked at the pile of ash that scattered across the floor. She pulled out a small vial and scooped up what she could, sealed it back up and putting it in her pocket. She then proceeded towards the box, opened it, and faced Liana. She bent down and with her fingers she yanked out one of her fangs. As she clasped it in her hand she stood up once again, speaking aloud to herself. "This is only the beginning. The Levé's will hold true power and I dare anything to stand in my way!"

ABOUT THE AUTHOR

J.S. Riddle was born in Oxford, England but traveled most of her life. She has been in the southeast USA for quite a few years, although one can never make a traveler set down roots.

In her spare time she likes to read, watch movies that are the furthest from romance she can get, take quiet meditating walks for those days when the mind needs to be quiet, is an avid music listener, and enjoys playing a video game or two every now and then.

She loves to read and write most things of supernatural, paranormal, and fantasy of all kinds.

Made in the USA
San Bernardino, CA
01 May 2017